MATTHEW
REILLY

THE THREE SECRET CITIES

MATTHEW REILLY

THE THREE SECRET CITIES

ORION

First published in Great Britain in 2018 by Orion Books,
an imprint of The Orion Publishing Group Ltd
Carmelite House, 50 Victoria Embankment
London EC4Y 0DZ

An Hachette UK Company

3 5 7 9 10 8 6 4

A CIP catalogue record for this book is
available from the British Library.

ISBN (Hardback) 978 1 4091 6716 7
ISBN (Export Trade Paperback) 978 1 4091 6717 4

Printed and bound in Great Britain by Clays Ltd, Elcograf S.p.A.

www.orionbooks.co.uk

For Kate

Geopolitics, like nature, abhors a vacuum . . . Whenever a power vacuum emerges, someone will fill it.

THE FINANCIAL TIMES

THE MYSTERY OF THE WEAPONS

The first kills
The second blinds
The third rules

INSCRIPTION ON A TABLET BELIEVED TO BE IN EXCESS OF 5,000 YEARS OLD,
PRIVATE COLLECTION, NEW YORK CITY

THE TRIAL OF THE CITIES

No oceans.
No clouds.
No rivers.
No rain.
The world a wasteland
of misery and pain.

FROM *THE ZEUS PAPYRUS*,
PRIVATE COLLECTION, LONDON

THE AFTERMATH OF THE GAMES

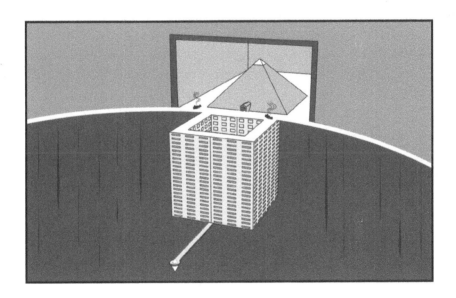

THE GREAT BEND

**THE GREAT BEND
THE UNDERWORLD, INDIA**

For three whole days after the Great Games, the Underworld lay silent.

The captive participant, Captain Jack West Jr—competing on behalf of Orlando, the King of Land—had prevailed.

Having overcome the same deadly challenges that the three previous champions of the Games—no lesser figures than Osiris, Gilgamesh and Hercules—had faced, to the surprise of many in the royal gallery, he had won.

But during the final ceremony to crown the winning king and impart to him the Mysteries that would see the Earth safely through the coming crisis, pandemonium had broken out.

Helicopters had assailed the mountaintop temple on which the ancient ceremony had been taking place. Lord Hades's own sons had tried to assassinate their father. And Hades's minotaur army—all four thousand of them, a lost population of Neanderthals who wore bull-shaped helmets—having discovered the plan of their master's sons to kill him, had risen up in revolt and stormed the mountain-palace. When the bodyguards of two of the fleeing kings had foolishly opened fire on the minotaurs, death and destruction had ensued.

Two of the four kings were torn limb from limb. All but a few of the royal elite who had gathered to watch the Games were also killed.

Only two kings had survived.

Hades, the King of the Underworld, who had fled with West and his loyal band of friends.

And Orlando, who had scurried away from the scene with his advisor, the Catholic cardinal and member of the Church's shadowy Omega Group, Cardinal Ricardo Mendoza, leaving the rest of his entourage and his fellow royals to die.

Never in all of history had the four legendary kingdoms been thrown into such disarray. For thousands of years, they had ruled the world from the shadows, installing governments as they saw fit and toppling them when they deemed it necessary, instigating wars and destroying empires.

Word travelled fast.

Elsewhere in the world, individuals with connections to the four kingdoms quickly learned what had happened.

Royalty demands certain things, the foremost of which is continuity. Heirs had to be found and crowned, but in the immediate aftermath of the Games, it was uncertain just which heirs had survived and which had not.

Another demand of royalty is penalty, retribution, blame.

Someone had to be held responsible for the outrageous end to the Games. And punished for it.

Most worrying of all, the Mysteries—the very reason for holding the Great Games in the first place—were *not* revealed, and the fate of the world depended on them.

All of these matters, however, would be dealt with by others, the King of the Minotaurs thought as he surveyed the now-empty Underworld, battered and broken after the chaos.

The Grand Staircase was horribly blasted-open in its middle. That had been West's doing.

The elevator giving access to the holy temple at the summit of the mountain-palace had been rent from its mountings.

Bodies lay everywhere. Many had fallen from the temple all the way down the mountain. It wasn't pretty.

As Lord Hades had fled from the Underworld, he had bequeathed his kingdom to the Minotaur King, Minotus, and his Neanderthals, so that they could live out their days in peace and obscurity here in the remote northwestern desert of India.

Minotus had given his army of minotaurs a few days to rest after the whole affair and now it was time to commence the clean-up.

Bodies were gathered up and burned.

The smashed stone blocks of the Grand Staircase were taken away in preparation for rebuilding.

And thirty minotaurs were sent to the Great Bend, the farthest corner of the Underworld and the scene of the Fifth Challenge, a wild car race that had taken place on an edgeless roadway around the rim of a dark fathomless abyss out on the Bend.

These thirty minotaurs were tasked with hauling away the crashed vehicles and dead bodies that littered the precarious road.

A key part of their task was cleaning up the area around the two mysterious structures that stood at the farthest end of this farthest corner of the Underworld: an enormous pyramid positioned in a box-shaped shelf and a many-levelled building that hung off the edge of the great abyss.

Cut into the flanks of this building in regular rows were hundreds of rectangular recesses, each containing a glistening silver coffin.

Every single one of these hundreds of coffins was etched with a carving of a man with the head of a long-beaked bird.

No-one had been in here when, shortly after the Games, one of those coffins had slowly begun to open.

Now, as the minotaur cleaning crew arrived, they saw the open coffin.

It caused quite a stir.

The hanging tower, ancient and still for so many years, had loomed in mysterious silence for as long as any of them could remember.

The leader of the cleaning crew radioed the Minotaur King and

informed him of the development. Minotus said he would come with a team of lieutenants at once.

The cleaning crew, unable to restrain their curiosity, edged toward the open silver coffin and peered inside it.

A six-foot-tall man-shaped figure lay in it.

The figure lay in perfect repose, on its back, as if sleeping.

It looked like a statue made entirely of bronze, with mostly human features: head, shoulders, arms, legs.

Except for one key feature.

The figure had no face.

It had no eyes or mouth and instead of a nose it just had a sinister-looking downturned beak.

Its hands were folded across its chest. They were crafted from the same dull bronze alloy that the rest of the statue appeared to be made of. It was a peculiar bronze: lustrous yet dull. The minotaurs' flashlight-beams reflected off it in a muted, hazy way. There were no seams on the statue's body. It was as if it had been moulded out of a single perfect pouring of the bronze alloy.

The members of the minotaur cleaning crew gazed at each other in wonder as they contemplated the hundreds of other coffins embedded in the flanks of the hanging tower.

None of those coffins was open. Just this one.

And then suddenly the bronze statue sat up, and with its eerie faceless head, stared right at them.

A toneless voice came from deep within it:

'*Kushma alla?*'

Minotus and a cadre of his best lieutenants arrived on the scene twenty minutes later . . .

. . . to find the entire cleaning crew, all thirty of them, dead, cut to pieces and lying in grisly pools of blood.

The open coffin was empty.

Then the bronze figure emerged from *behind* Minotus and his entourage.

'*Kushma alla?*' the faceless thing said.

Minotus frowned. The language was unfamiliar to him.

'I don't understand,' he replied.

And then the bronzeman raised its metallic claws and attacked them without fear, hesitation or mercy.

PROLOGUE II

ARAGON CASTLE
ISCHIA ISLAND, AMALFI COAST, ITALY
FOUR DAYS AFTER THE GREAT GAMES

In a soaring cavern inside a towering island-castle off the west coast of Italy, there was an octagonal chamber.

Within that octagonal chamber was an octagonal table made of worn timber that had once been the Porta Scelerata, the cursed gate, one of the gates of ancient Rome.

Occasionally over the centuries the table had been described as round, but this was not technically true. It was eight-sided, with a place for each of the eight men who for the last 1,600 years had resided here and claimed ownership of the table, the castle and the entire island of Ischia.

To those who knew of their existence, they were known as the Knights of the Golden Eight.

Their octagonal chamber was decorated with trophies from previous missions, items they had taken from their victims: swords, shields, crowns.

Today, a lone man stood before the Eight, on a precarious ledge situated across a chasm from their table. The platform was known as the Petitioner's Ledge and it had been designed so that the petitioner was forced to look up at the Knights.

The man standing on the ledge wore a translucent plastic medical mask over the lower right quarter of his face.

His eyes blazed with fury. He was in excruciating pain but he did not give voice to it. His doctor had prescribed potent painkillers, but the man wouldn't take them.

Right now, his pain fuelled him, drove him, reminded him of the vengeance he sought.

Vengeance that the Golden Eight would provide.

After the man in the half-mask had presented his case and provided the required gargantuan down payment, the leader of the Golden Eight stood and in a solemn voice addressed his seven brothers-in-arms.

'The price has been paid, so the mark has been made. In accordance with our long and sacred custom, the Knights of the Golden Eight accept this assignment.'

The leader picked up the three photos that the man in the mask had provided in his brief.

'The task is straightforward,' he said. 'One assassination, two kidnappings: this man is to be liquidated while the younger man and the woman are to be captured alive and brought before our noble employer here, for him to deal with as he sees fit.'

The leader of the Golden Eight nodded deferentially to the man in the mask. 'Our price is high, but then, in over two thousand years, we have never failed on a mission.'

He held up the three photos. They were shots of:

Jack West Jr.

His daughter, Lily.

And her friend, Alby Calvin.

FIRST PURSUIT

THE DECAPITATION OF HADES

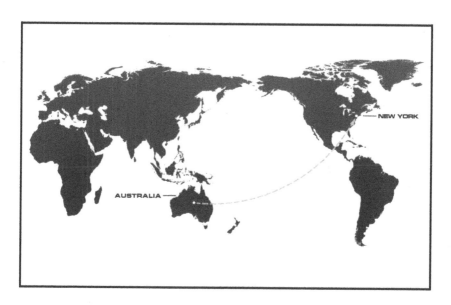

interregnum

n. (From Latin: 'between kingdoms')

The interval of time between the end of a sovereign's reign
and the accession of a successor; often a period of unrest,
strategic manoeuvring and war from which ultimately emerges
a new ruling order.

Jack West's plane shot across the sky faster than the speed of sound, rushing toward New York City.

Known as the *Sky Warrior*, the plane was a Tupolev Tu-144, a Russian-made clone of the Concorde. It was sleek in the extreme, clad in black radar-absorbent material, and like the famous Concorde before it, it was fast: really, really fast.

Jack had acquired the *Sky Warrior* from an old enemy after his previous plane, his beloved 747, the *Halicarnassus*, had been destroyed during a desperate mission at Easter Island.

Right now, flown by Jack's loyal pilot, Sky Monster, the dart-shaped plane was slicing through the air at Mach 1.5 at an altitude of 50,000 feet, far above commercial airliner routes.

As a man who often ventured to some of the more remote corners of the globe, the bustling metropolis of New York City was not one of Jack's regular destinations, but right now he was in a hurry to get there.

His haste was not just for his own reasons. It was also for the gentleman travelling with him: Mr Anthony Michael Dominic DeSaxe, known to the regular world as one of the richest men on Earth, a billionaire shipping and mining magnate, and the fourth member of his extremely old and aristocratic family to be appointed Marshal of France.

But that was the *regular* world.

In more shadowy circles, he was known as one of the four eternal kings who ruled the planet: Lord Hades, King of the Underworld.

Or at least he used to be.

Things had moved quickly for Jack and Hades after they had returned to Jack's home in the hours following the disastrous ending to the Great Games.

That Jack had won the Games was nothing short of historic, an achievement that would place him in an elite pantheon of heroes that included the mythic Greek warrior, Hercules.

Indeed, as Jack had discovered halfway through them, the Games and their many diabolical challenges and prizes were the source of the myth of the Twelve Labours of Hercules. It was that very discovery that had proved crucial to his ultimate victory.

Arriving back at his home in the vast Australian outback, all Jack had wanted to do was rest. He'd never chosen to go to the Games; he'd been drugged and kidnapped, then forced to fight non-stop for his life for two days and nights, all the while wearing a Homer Simpson t-shirt and jeans.

Honestly, now he just wanted to tend to his many wounds and sleep in his own bed for about a year.

But that was not to be.

First, his wife, Zoe—with her short blonde hair and bright blue eyes—had been waiting for him, freshly returned from her own investigative trip to the Mariana Trench, the deepest ocean trench on the planet.

Seeing the *Sky Warrior* making its final approach to the farm's landing strip, Zoe had hurried out onto the tarmac to meet it.

She couldn't wait to tell Jack of her experiences and she smiled broadly when she saw him, Lily and Alby emerge from the plane, followed by Pooh Bear and Stretch.

'Wait'll you hear what I saw—' she began.

Then she saw his shaved head.

And the many cuts and bruises on his face.

And the way he limped slightly and nursed his right arm. His left arm—made of titanium from the elbow down—was covered in dirt and scratches.

What had happened?

Then she noticed Lily: she wore a floral day dress that Zoe had never seen and she carried in her hands a pair of high heels. That was odd. Lily wasn't a high heels kind of girl.

Pooh Bear and Stretch looked okay, but Alby wore a bandage on his face covering a large cut of some kind.

Then Zoe saw Jack's mother, Mae, step out of the sleek black Tupolev.

Now Zoe felt completely on edge. If Jack's wounds weren't enough to whip up her anxiety, seeing Mae seized her full attention.

Dr Mabel 'Mae' Merriweather—all five foot two of her, with her short bob of hair and pixie face—was a formidable individual at the best of times. She didn't suffer fools and she guarded her seclusion fiercely. She lived in the distant coastal town of Broome and didn't emerge from her splendid isolation for anything but the most serious of reasons. (Birthdays and deaths were *not* serious enough, although thankfully Jack's wedding to Zoe had been.) Why Mae would be here with Jack now was a clear and present cause for concern.

And then the others had emerged from the plane.

First, Iolanthe.

Zoe did not like the British princess *at all*.

Aristocratic, poised, refined—and totally self-interested—Iolanthe was everything Zoe was not. The sister of Orlando Compton-Jones, the King of Land, officially her title was the Keeper of the Royal Records for that kingdom. On several occasions, their paths had crossed: Iolanthe had once tried to kill Zoe and Jack at Abu Simbel in Egypt; she had repeatedly tried to seduce Jack; but then, surprisingly, at an ancient underground site at Diego Garcia, she had saved Jack's life when she didn't have to. Zoe didn't know whether to trust Iolanthe or shoot her on sight.

And then came the two people Zoe didn't know: Hades—he was about sixty, tall and powerfully built—and a smaller, stocky fellow with unruly black hair, a fat nose, a thick monobrow and deep-set brown eyes. Jack later introduced him as E-147.

'Jesus, Mary and Joseph!' Zoe exclaimed. 'I go away for a week and look at you. What happened? You look like you've been to Hell and back.'

'That's a very interesting choice of words, honey. Let's go inside and sit down. I've got a lot to tell you.'

That was an understatement.

It took a while, but with the others' help, Jack told Zoe everything.

About his kidnapping at Pine Gap, the Great Games, the four legendary kingdoms, the help he had received during the Games from a fellow champion named Scarecrow—'and a fat but very gallant pilot who was a long way out of his comfort zone,' Sky Monster added, holding up his bandaged right forearm as proof—and of course the cataclysmic end to the whole thing, when the minotaur army had stormed the mountain-palace and everything had gone to shit.

Mae helped Jack explain the concept of the kingdoms to Zoe—the four ancient kingdoms of Land, Sea, Sky and Underworld—by showing her the special map of the world she had, one that showed the boundaries of the kingdoms superimposed over the usual national borders:

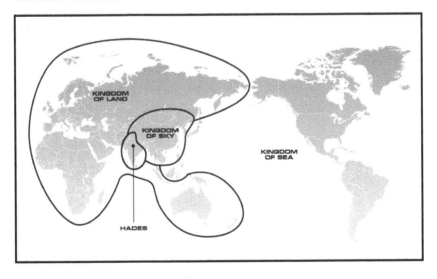

Zoe said, 'You're saying that nations, parliaments and govern-ments are just fronts for these four kingdoms? Tools for them to use?'

'Yes, exactly,' Mae said. 'They are the real power players of the world.'

Zoe shook her head. 'All right then, so what do they want?'

'What every ruler in history has ever wanted,' Mae said. 'To maintain their grip on power.'

'What about you?' Jack asked Zoe. 'What did you and Nobody find at the Mariana Trench?'

'Nobody' was the nickname of Professor David Black, their friend and one of the foremost deep-sea diving specialists in the world. A protégé of Robert Ballard—the famed shipwreck hunter who had found the *Titanic*—Nobody Black divided his time between hunting for lost Spanish galleons filled with treasure and studying the bizarre sea life found in the darkest depths of the world's oceans. He was part scientist, part seaman, all adventurer, and a good guy to boot.

It was he who had called Zoe away two days before Jack had been kidnapped for the Games—to come and see a discovery he'd made in the Challenger Deep, the deepest part of the Mariana Trench. That trip had put her completely out of contact for a week. It may also have saved her life by ensuring her absence when Jack had been snatched.

'What did we find?' Zoe said. 'Oh, nothing much . . . except for a sealed stone doorway *ten kilometres below the surface* of the Pacific Ocean with markings on it written in the Word of Thoth.

'The twins and I went down in a submersible with Nobody to investigate and do some tests. Ground-penetrating radar showed something *behind* the doorway: not a chamber or void of any kind but rather a colossal deposit of a type of volcanic stone called picrite basalt.'

'I'm thinking this isn't just any old deposit,' Alby said.

'No. This deposit is enormous and completely wrapped in a thin crust of sea-stone. It's also shaped like a perfect cube, seven kilometres to a side. *Seven kilometres.* With straight sides and edges. We also found more ornamental "doorways", a lot more, dozens of them located at regular intervals around the cube-shaped deposit. I took some photos of the original doorway.'

Zoe looked at Lily. 'I was hoping you might be able to translate the markings on it.'

'Sure,' Lily said.

Zoe handed her a photo of the submerged ornamental doorway illuminated by glaring floodlights. Square in shape and flanked by marble columns, it looked very out of place in the depths of the ocean.

Lily saw an inscription on its upper lintel and translated it: '*The world a wasteland of misery and pain.*'

She swapped a look with Jack as she said it.

Zoe shook her head. 'God help me. On any other day, mine would've been pretty amazing news, but after the time you've had . . . '

'Where's Nobody now?' Jack asked.

'He went back to his lab in San Francisco, to retest the geological samples and see if they've been found in any other locations around the world.'

'And Lachlan and Julius?'

Jack loved the twins: two red-haired chatterbox Scottish geniuses who adored astrophysics, history, video games and all things *Star Wars* in equal measure.

'They went back to London,' Zoe said. 'Despite his addiction to *League of Legends*, Lachie's a family man now. He has responsibilities.'

In the years since the twins had helped Jack find the Six Sacred Stones and unravel the mystery of the Five Greatest Warriors, they had shed a little of their Peter Pan natures and grown up.

While Julius was still determinedly single, Lachie had met and married a sweet Japanese-American astrophysicist on the Cambridge faculty named Dr Eriko Kinoshita. They had two cute-as-a-button four-year-old twins named Caleb and Willow.

Julius, ever the needler, took great joy in asking Lachie what kind of car he drove now.

Lachie would bow his head. 'A mom van.' It was a red Nissan Quest: the ultimate mom van.

On his birthday a few months back, Lachlan had awoken to find a racing number painted onto the bonnet and flanks of the red van: the number 55. A gift from Julius.

'I just wanted to make it a little sexier,' Julius had said with an impish grin.

For all that, the twins were still the twins: as thick as thieves, brothers forever. That, Jack thought, was a bond that would never be broken. Indeed, Julius lived in a detached flat in the backyard of Lachie's house just outside London.

As for Pooh Bear and Stretch, after all the reunions had taken place, they returned to Pooh's home in the United Arab Emirates.

They took Iolanthe with them.

They would take her as far as Dubai; from there she would return to the U.K. under her own steam.

'I have to get back to the Hall of Royal Records and pick up a few items before Orlando does,' she said to Jack as they stood on the dusty runway of his farm. 'Then I need to disappear for a while. I imagine my darling brother is quite upset with me.'

She scribbled quickly on a slip of paper: 'Here. This is the number for a disposable phone I have. If you need me, use a burner phone of your own and text it. And thank you, Jack. Well done at the Games.'

Then she kissed him on the cheek and left.

Standing nearby, Zoe scowled.

After the three of them were gone, Zoe and Lily sat down with Jack and set about stitching up his wounds.

'My God,' Zoe said at one point. 'You really got beat up.'

Jack winced. 'Trust me, I feel every single bruise.'

He wiped down his artificial left forearm—acquired after his own had been lost on the day of Lily's birth twenty years previously—with a cloth, warm water and dish soap.

Then he politely took his leave from everyone and, shadowed by his ever-loyal little poodle, Roxy, lay down for a hot bath in a corrugated iron tub out on the back deck.

There he closed his eyes and finally, completely *stopped*.

He breathed deeply, calming himself, letting the desert sun warm his eyelids, absorbing and enjoying the silence.

That was, after all, what he loved the most about his secret farm.

The silence. The calm. The total removal from the noisy outside world. He liked it here, away from everything.

And after that gloriously peaceful hot bath, Jack went to bed and slept for thirty-six hours straight.

Roxy remained by his side the whole time, lying on her back, paws skyward, equally exhausted.

Mae decided to stay at Jack's farm for a while, but for a specific reason.

She wanted to talk with Hades about the four legendary kingdoms, her life's work.

Indeed, for a woman who was known for her take-no-prisoners severity, she was positively giddy at the prospect of it: she was like a presidential historian who actually got to interview a president, or the conspiracy theorist who finally got to go to Area 51.

While Jack slept, she and Hades sat down together for lunch.

Lily and Alby joined them: Lily now dressed in a grey 'Han Shot First' t-shirt and blue jeans, and Alby in a maroon-and-yellow USC t-shirt and shorts.

'So,' Mae said. 'The four kingdoms rule the world from the shadows. There are a few things that I just have to know.'

'Okay,' Hades said.

'The Kennedy assassination. Was that the work of the kingdoms?'

'Yes.'

'Why?'

'We needed the Vietnam War to continue.'

'Abraham Lincoln?'

'Yes.'

'Why?'

'It was part of the deal we made with him.'

'Which was?'

'If he wanted immortality, he had to die.'

'Princess Diana?'

'No. That was just a drunk driver. A true shame.'

'The moon landing?' Mae's eyes narrowed. 'It *was* real, wasn't it?'

'Absolutely. And also very necessary,' Hades added enigmatically. 'The fourth landing was the important one.'

'Do you rig elections?'

'When we need to.'

'Such as?'

'Woodrow Wilson in 1912.'

'What about Trump?' Lily asked, interjecting for the first time.

'We didn't have to.'

'What do you mean?'

'It was going to happen anyway.'

'How do you know that?' Mae asked.

'Because democracy is inherently flawed,' Hades said. 'When the citizens of a democracy grow too wealthy, they begin to view politics as entertainment, and when voters do that, they elect those who will entertain them.'

Lily swapped an amazed look with Alby.

Mae sat back in her chair and stared in wonderment at Hades.

Hades gestured toward Alby's shirt. 'USC? Your name's Calvin, you say? Albert Calvin?'

'Yes, sir,' Alby said.

'I thought I recognised it. You're studying ancient history and mythology, are you not?'

'Yes.'

'But as I recall, you're also doing astrophysics at Caltech.'

'I am,' Alby said, surprised. 'How did you know that?'

'I know professors at both institutions. Call them scouts, if you will. Their job is to send me the work of talented students who they think show promise. I've received papers you've written from *both* of my scouts, on historical and astronomical subjects. You make an impression.'

'Well, I . . . thanks,' Alby said, a little chuffed.

Hades turned to Lily. 'As for you, young lady, you also make

an impression. Later, when things have quieted somewhat, I should very much like to speak with you about your singular heritage, your lineage.'

'Okay . . .' Lily said hesitantly. 'Sure.'

'Yes, *later*.' Mae swatted their conversation away with mock annoyance. 'Right now, Lord Hades is mine and I have more questions for him.'

Hades just gave Lily a quick nod and turned back to Mae.

And then, on the morning of his third day at home, Jack was shaken awake by Zoe.

'Jack,' she said urgently, 'your new buddy Hades says he needs to talk to you right away. He says his world just went to shit.'

'Captain,' Hades said, 'we have to go to New York. *Now*.'

'Why?' Jack asked, gripping a coffee mug.

With them were Zoe, Lily, Alby and Mae, all listening attentively.

'I just got this message on my emergency voicemail service from my butler in Manhattan.'

Hades clicked a button on his cell phone and a recorded message played on the speaker:

'*Sir*,' a very prim and proper voice said, '*it's Geoffrey. Your assets are being attacked. All your trust accounts and shareholdings are being liquidated as I speak. All of your passwords have been changed and all of our computers have been shut out. After what happened at the Games, the new kings held a conclave and ordered forced-abdication proceedings against you.*'

There was a long pause.

'*And, sir, the Slave King has been called upon to apprehend both you and Captain West.*'

Jack threw a look at Hades.

The prim voice went on. '*I have spirited away those heirlooms and works of art that I know you cherish. They are safe for now in your little hideaway in Rome, along with your emergency cash fund. The Slave King must be on his way here right now. If there is anything else in the apartment that you need or want, I suggest you come here immediately and get it. As you know better than most, the Slave King is not to be trifled with.*'

Click.

Jack looked hard at Hades. 'Forced-abdication proceedings? And who or what is a Slave King? Are there actually *five* kings?'

'No. Just four. "Slave King" is a name used by some in noble circles to describe a very dangerous royal official.' Hades stared off into space for a moment. 'I thought I would have more time. They moved fast. Two kings were killed during the chaos at the Games, but their royal families have clearly acted quickly and anointed their heirs as kings.'

He looked at the group gathered around him. 'And now the other three kings have turned against me. I am being decapitated. They are taking my crown from me. My title, my throne, my lands, my entire kingdom.'

'Why?'

'Formally, because the Games failed to produce a King of Kings,' Hades said. 'That was my sworn duty and I failed at it. Less formally, it's probably because I failed to stop *you* from disrupting the Supreme Ceremony that was supposed to install Orlando as the King of Kings. And then I fled with you.'

'And this Slave King, who is he?'

Hades shook his head. 'Every system must have a policeman, Jack. Someone who enforces the law. The four kingdoms are no different. When someone breaks the rules of the kingdoms—from assassination attempts to simple theft—they must be punished.

'In the shadow world of the four kingdoms, that individual is both chief policeman and chief jailer. He is officially known as the Governor of the Royal Prison at Erebus. Over the millennia, the various Governors have used slaves as guards at Erebus, so the holder of the position has become colloquially known as the Slave King.'

'And now he has orders to hunt down and arrest the two of us?' Jack said.

'Yes. And with the resources at his disposal, he is very well equipped for the task.'

Hades pressed his lips together tightly.

'Captain, we are entering a perilous new phase in the state of the world. The Omega Event is coming: the ultimate singularity, the instantaneous collapse of the universe as it reaches its expansion point. *The end of all things.*

'And with the failure of the Games to reveal the Mysteries to Orlando—and appoint him King of Kings—the royal world has been plunged into a very unstable interregnum.'

'I don't understand,' Zoe said.

'The Great Games had one paramount purpose,' Hades said, 'to select the "King of Kings", the emperor of the world, or as it is put in some texts, the Alpha.

'The winning king's prize for sponsoring the successful champion was twofold: first, to be installed as King of Kings; and, second, to *receive the Mysteries*, the sacred ultra-ancient knowledge that would guide us safely through the two trials that, when overcome, prevent the coming Omega Event.'

'Which is the collapse of the universe,' Zoe clarified.

'Yes,' Hades said.

'Kind of a big deal . . .' Alby said softly.

Hades said, 'What should have happened after the Games was this: after Jack won, his sponsor-king, Orlando, should have stepped inside the black obelisk in the temple atop the Underworld and received the Mysteries.

'Not wanting to see Orlando attain such power, Jack prevented this from happening, so Orlando did *not* receive the Mysteries and did *not* become the King of Kings. The title of King of Kings is now moot. To prevent the Omega Event, we must now find the Mysteries some other way.'

'And use them to overcome the two trials,' Alby said.

'Yes.'

'So what are the two trials?'

Hades said, 'The two trials are known as the Trial of the Cities and the Trial of the Mountains.'

'Wait,' Zoe said. 'The Mysteries. What exactly are they? Clues? Commands?'

'Information,' Mae answered. 'Instructions. Ancient information and instructions. Over the years during my research into the kingdoms, I've encountered only a handful of references to the Mysteries, fragments at best. There are, so far as I can tell, five or six Mysteries. They're a series of directives or instructions that guide one through the two trials and thus prevent the Omega Event.'

She looked at Hades, who nodded. 'This is correct.'

'Does *anyone* know what the Mysteries are?' Lily asked.

'Not in their entirety, no,' Hades said. 'That was to be the privilege of the king whose champion won the Games. Mind you, the Mysteries are ultimately information, and information can be unearthed in other ways.

'Over the centuries, many have tried to find out the nature of the Mysteries, including royal historians, disciples of the Catholic Church and even some noted members of the Invisible College. But after all that, as Mae says, all we have are fragments of the whole, fleeting mentions of the Mysteries by those who talked or wrote about them throughout the course of history.'

'Like who?' Alby asked.

'Well, like Zeus,' Hades said. 'He was the king who sponsored Hercules when he won the Games three thousand years ago. He was also a ruler of such charisma and power that three millennia of tales and legends have turned him into a god—the king of the gods, no less.'

Hades pulled out his cell phone and swiped to a password-protected photo album.

He pulled up a photo. It was a shot of a very old sheet of papyrus, encased in a glass frame:

Hades showed the image to the group. 'You will no doubt rec-ognise the language.'

'The Word of Thoth,' Jack said. The indecipherable ancient language that only the Oracle of Siwa—Lily and her twin, Alexander—could read.

'This papyrus belongs to the King of Land. It is held in a humidity-controlled vault in the Hall of Royal Records in England.

'I was privileged to see it during a dinner held there thirty years ago by a previous Land King and attended by the other three kings. This papyrus has been passed down from Land King to Land King for over three thousand years. It is known as the Zeus Papyrus since it was written at Zeus's personal command by the Oracle at the time of Hercules's famous victory.'

'Do you want Lily to translate it?' Zoe asked.

'I don't need her to,' Hades said, flicking to the next photo. 'Lily's grandfather, a previous Oracle, already did that.'

This next photo showed a sheet of paper with handwritten text on it in English:

When mighty Hercules won the Games for me, my prize was an army, an indomitable force of men of bronze, to guard me on my sacred mission to the Three Secret Cities.

I also received the Mysteries: wondrous visions seared into my mind as I stood inside the obelisk, including two odes regarding the two trials to be overcome.

THE TRIAL OF THE CITIES

No oceans.
No clouds.
No rivers.
No rain.
The world a wasteland
of misery and pain.

THE TRIAL OF THE MOUNTAINS

Five iron mountains. Five bladed keys. Five doors, forever locked.
But mark you, only those who survive the Fall,
May enter the supreme labyrinth
And look upon the face of the Omega.

The Mysteries guided me through the first trial. That trial required me to take the Three Immortal Weapons to the Three Secret Cities, empower the weapons at them, and, thus empowered, perform the sacred ritual with the weapons at the Altar of the Cosmos before the next rising of Sagittarius over the Sun.

Let all who follow in my footsteps know: the journey to the Three Secret Cities begins at the end.

The second trial only begins once the first is completed—

'That's where the papyrus is torn, cut off,' Hades said.

'Take the Three Immortal Weapons . . .' Lily said.

'. . . to the Three Secret Cities . . .' Zoe said.

'. . . before the next rising of Sagittarius over the Sun . . .' Alby said thoughtfully. He spun and started typing on his computer.

'The journey begins at the end . . .' Jack said.

'I know a little about the Three Immortal Weapons,' Hades said. 'But not so much about the cities and nothing about the celestial event mentioned in the papyrus.'

Jack turned. 'Alby? The celestial event?'

Alby looked up from his computer. 'I have a couple of ideas. Let me do some searching.'

Jack said to the others, 'I heard about the Three Secret Cities during the Games. Orlando's chief advisor from the Church, Cardinal Mendoza, mentioned them to me: Thule, Atlas and Ra.'

'The *fabled* cities of Thule, Atlas and Ra,' Hades said. 'Their locations are three of antiquity's greatest secrets.'

'But Mendoza didn't say anything about three weapons, let alone immortal ones,' Jack said. 'What are they?'

'They are, quite simply, the three most famous weapons in history,' Hades said. 'The Sword of the Rock, the Trident of the Sealord and the Helmet of Hades.

'They were sometimes called the Three Weapons of the Kings, since they have always been owned by three of the four legendary kings. The fourth kingdom, the Kingdom of Sky, being more spiritual than its brother realms, takes pride in *not* being hostile, so its military item is a shield. I don't know the locations of the first two weapons, but given that I was until recently the King of the Underworld, I do know where the Helmet of Hades resides.'

'Where?'

'In a vault in my apartment in New York,' Hades said. 'It is *my* helmet, after all. I also keep one artefact related to the Mysteries in that same vault, a stone tablet believed to be part of the altar mentioned in the Zeus Papyrus: the Altar of the Cosmos.

'But Geoffrey cannot access these two items: that vault is bio-metrically sealed. Only I can open it. If you want to save the world, Captain, you have to come with me to New York and open that vault *right now*.'

Jack stared at Hades for a long moment.

Then, despite his exhaustion and his wounds, he stood. 'Well, what are we waiting for? Everybody, grab your stuff. We're wheels-up in thirty minutes.'

Things had moved quickly from there.

Lily and Alby grabbed some clothes and computers and dashed into the *Sky Warrior*.

Sky Monster fuelled up the plane.

Zoe threw some rugged clothes and weapons into a suitcase: guns, ammo and a hockey helmet.

She said to Jack, 'I'm not gonna be on the other side of the world when everything goes down this time.'

Mae shoved past Jack and Hades and started grabbing books from Jack's office bookshelf: textbooks, scrolls, parchments.

'I gather you're coming along, too, Mum,' Jack said.

'Bet your ass I'm coming,' Mae Merriweather said. She jerked her chin at Hades. 'I've been studying these kingdoms my whole life. Not only do I want to see his artefacts, I want to keep learning everything I can about the four kingdoms from one of their kings.'

Twenty minutes later, everyone was ready and on board the *Sky Warrior*.

Only one member of the group remained behind: E-147. He needed to rest the foot he had broken during the Games. He would remain at the farm to mind the dogs.

'And remember,' Jack said to him, 'no eating the dogs.'

E-147 had nodded obediently as he'd patted Roxy.

★ ★ ★

The *Sky Warrior* lifted off.

After a short time, Sky Monster switched it over to autopilot and joined the others in the main cabin.

He sat down as Hades checked his voicemail service again, to see if his butler in New York had left him any further updates or, more importantly, warnings.

There were three messages on the system this time.

Hades played them on speaker so Jack could hear.

The first was from his butler, Geoffrey: '*Sir, all is well in the apartment, for now.*'

'Can you trust him?' Jack said.

Hades nodded. 'With my life.'

He keyed the second message . . .

. . . and out of the speaker came a voice that, by the look on his face, Hades clearly had not expected to hear, that of Minotus, the King of the Minotaurs at the Underworld in India.

He was shouting desperately.

'*My Lord! It is Minotus! After the Games ended, one of the silver coffins in the hanging tower opened!*'

A gunshot rang out behind him, loud and sharp.

'*A . . . a thing . . . emerged from it: a man made of armour, impenetrable bronze armour. He has killed fifty of my minotaurs so far and we are trying to contain him! Help us! Please!*'

The call cut off abruptly, crashing to static.

Hades grabbed another phone and tried calling Minotus immediately, but the line was dead. It didn't even ring.

Hades swallowed. 'Good Lord . . .'

Jack eyed him closely. 'Any idea what's in those coffins, Anthony?'

Hades nodded. 'Later.'

'Jesus, Jack,' Sky Monster breathed. 'There were hundreds of those coffins there.'

Of all the members of Jack's team, only Sky Monster had been with him through the entirety of the Great Games. It had been an illuminating and tough experience for him, especially given that he was a touch overweight and more used to waiting in the plane reading luxury jet and yacht magazines while Jack ran around in dangerous places.

Notably, Sky Monster had been at Jack's side during the dramatic car race of the Fifth Challenge, when they had seen the tower hanging above the abyss, the one containing countless coffins in rectangular recesses.

Jack said, 'I'll call Stretch and Pooh Bear. They're back in Dubai, so they're pretty close to the Underworld in India. I'll send them there while we go to New York.'

And then Hades played the third message.

A slow measured voice came from the speaker.

When it did, Hades visibly stiffened, his eyes widening with unconcealed fear.

'*Lord Hades*,' the deep voice said, '*this is Yago, the Governor of the Royal Prison. You have been charged with treason against the four thrones. A valid royal warrant has been issued for your arrest. Once apprehended, you are to be conveyed to the prison at Erebus and imprisoned there for the rest of your natural life.*'

There was a pregnant pause before the voice added: '*I'm coming for you, brother dearest.*'

'All right,' Jack said as they sat in a circle in the *Sky Warrior*'s main cabin almost twenty-one hours later.

They had flown almost halfway around the world and were now only an hour out of New York.

He looked at Hades. 'I want to know three things: first, everything you can tell me about the Three Immortal Weapons—in particular, this helmet in your New York apartment; second, what's going on at the Underworld; and third, why that prison-governor-Slave-King guy called you "brother dearest"?'

Hades bowed his head, nodding.

'The three weapons have wended their way through tales and folklore for centuries. The Greek myths say that they were forged by Cyclops—the master blacksmith and weapon maker—for the three greatest gods of his age, the brother-kings Zeus, Poseidon and Hades. But according to my history books, the three weapons pre-date those men.

'The first weapon is the Sword of the Rock, the blade of the Land King, an ancient sabre that has been wielded by many great Land Kings throughout the ages: from Zeus to the pharaoh Rameses II to Jesus the Nazarene to the British king known as Arthur. It has had many names over the centuries—Calibor, Caliburn, the Burning Blade, the Sword of the Rock, the Sword in the Stone, the Sabre of Fire—but the name that most know it by is Excalibur.'

'Oh, my . . .' Mae whispered.

'Is its location known?' Zoe asked.

'It is. The Sword resides in the same place it has lain for the last 1,200 years, the Tomb of Arthur in the crypt of the castle of Avalon,' Hades said. 'The ancestral home of the Land King.'

'And the second weapon?' Jack asked.

'The Trident of the Sealord,' Hades said, 'famously wielded by the man known to history as Poseidon. Strictly speaking, it is actually a triple-bladed *mace*, not a trident. Its location, however, is not known.'

'And the helmet?' Jack said.

'The Helmet of Hades,' Hades said, 'my unique crown. It is a wondrous thing, forged from a strange other-worldly alloy. Like bronze but not. As strong as steel, but lighter. It is fashioned in the style of a Corinthian helmet, with a sharply pointed nose-guard, cheekplates and a plume. In fact, there's a good picture of it—*and* the Sword, in fact—on the coat of arms of the US Military Academy at West Point.'

A quick Google search on Alby's computer brought up the West Point coat of arms:

Jack gazed at the helmet in the centre of the image and the sheathed sword behind it.

Hades went on. 'Like the Sword, over the aeons the Helmet of Hades has attained other names and mythical capabilities. It has been called the Helm of Darkness and the Helmet of Invisibility, but in my experience, it confers no such fantastical ability.'

'And it's in your vault in New York?' Zoe said.

'Yes.'

'Okay, then,' Jack said. 'What about the Underworld? What's going on there with the silver coffins?'

Hades said, 'Of course, as the King of the Underworld, I have long known about those coffins in the hanging tower. On my father's death, when I inherited his kingdom, my father left me a long note about the kingdom and, especially, that tower. Regarding the silver coffins, he wrote, *Do not even attempt to open them, for you will not be able to. They will unseal of their own accord when the time comes. And do not stand in the way of their occupants.*'

Hades looked away into the distance, remembering.

'I followed my father's advice and did not try to open those coffins. But I was curious. On a few occasions I tried to peer into them using modern techniques like X-ray and sonic resonance imaging.

'I saw man-shaped figures in them, lying on their backs, completely still. Scans showed that they were both inanimate and inorganic. Statues. Statues made of a dense metal of some kind. In all the years that I was King of the Underworld, they lay there silent and unmoving, so I eventually assumed they were simply votive or decorative. I never knew they could come alive.'

Jack nodded.

'And the governor of the royal jail, this Slave King, he's your brother?'

'My younger brother, yes. Yago DeSaxe. In age, we are only four years apart. When we were growing up, we were close. We did everything together. But we were competitive, competitive at all things.

'Jack, in the last week, a metaphorical curtain has been pulled aside for you, allowing you a glimpse of the true royal power system that runs the world. I have a feeling that as things progress, you're going to see more of that system. As you have seen already, it is based on a strict order of heredity. Well, let me tell you, in royal households *younger siblings can be deadly.*

'For it is the eldest son who inherits their father's title, castles and lands. Younger siblings get little or sometimes nothing at all.

To make matters worse, very often they find themselves having to obey without question someone who was once their childhood playmate.'

'Like Iolanthe and Orlando,' Lily said. 'During the Games, Iolanthe wasn't happy at all when he tried to sell her off into a strategic marriage.'

Hades nodded. 'It's exactly like that. Keep an eye on Iolanthe, though. She's a clever one. She is also the Keeper of the Royal Records for the Kingdom of Land, a modest position, to be sure, and one that many dismiss as a glorified librarian. But her twin libraries are very old and very comprehensive. I have a feeling that keepers of historic knowledge like Iolanthe will assume tremendous significance in the coming days.'

Hades sighed.

'Orlando and Iolanthe's relationship is positively sweet compared to mine and Yago's.

'When I inherited my father's throne in the Underworld, Yago stopped speaking to me, even though I gave him many properties and enormous amounts of money. After our competitive childhood, that wasn't enough. Yago saw me only through a lens of resentment, bitterness and envy.

'As our father aged and it became clear that I would inherit his crown and kingdom, Father arranged for Yago to be appointed Governor of the Royal Prison. The Prison at Erebus is remote, but Yago's is an important position and in certain circumstances, a very powerful one.'

'Like now,' Zoe said.

'Yes, like now,' Hades said sadly. 'For now my brother is the royal jailer who has orders to hunt me down. He will do it and he will do it with pleasure, because for many years Yago has believed himself to be not merely my equal but my superior, and with my kingdom stripped from me, now he is correct.'

A long silence followed.

Alby broke it.

'Jack,' he said. 'Lily and I have something to add.'

They had been busily working on Alby's computer for most of the flight.

'Shoot.'

'We've been looking up the celestial event mentioned in the papyrus: the "rising of Sagittarius over the Sun". As everyone knows, Sagittarius is a constellation of stars and a sign of the Zodiac. What fewer people know is that, when you look at it, Sagittarius is the closest constellation to the galactic centre, the supermassive black hole at the core of our galaxy, the Milky Way.'

'Astronomers call that supermassive black hole Sagittarius A* or Sagittarius A-star,' Lily said. 'As well as being the densest object in our galaxy, Sagittarius A-star is also a rich source of radio waves: a constant outflowing stream of them. Right now, owing to the time of year, Sagittarius A-star is hidden behind the sun.'

'Right,' Alby said, 'and according to our calculations, in exactly seven days—on 1 December, starting at 8:05 p.m. Greenwich Mean Time—for approximately twelve minutes, Sagittarius A-star will rise from behind the sun and bombard the Earth with its stream of radio waves. Then it will retreat back behind the sun.

'Don't worry about the radio waves; they won't hurt us. They'll just pass right through the planet and our bodies. But, do you remember that runaway galaxy that was charging toward Earth before the Great Games? The Hydra Galaxy?'

'Yes,' Jack said. It was hard to forget the image of the swastika-shaped spiral galaxy speeding toward Earth.

'Do you remember how it carved a perfectly straight swathe through other galaxies on its way toward us? Like an empty path through the stars?'

'I do,' Jack said. 'During the Games, Iolanthe even told me that the Hydra Galaxy was "clearing the way" for something, something connected to Isaac Newton's writings about some kind of "return call".'

'She was absolutely right,' Alby said. 'Get this: that perfectly straight path will be positioned right *behind* Earth when Sagittarius peeks over the sun. The result: its radio waves will pass *through* our planet and then out along that path of empty space right to the source of the Hydra Galaxy, way out in the centre of the universe. The Hydra Galaxy was literally paving the way for this event.'

'So the radio waves won't hurt us themselves,' Lily said. 'But when they pass through the Earth, they will somehow confirm that the Trial of the Cities has been fulfilled?'

'Correct. And if we fail to complete the trial,' Jack said, 'the world becomes "a wasteland of misery and pain".'

The cabin fell silent.

Jack looked at his watch. Today was 24 November. Crunch time was the twelve minutes beginning at 8:05 p.m. GMT on 1 December.

'So we have seven days to find the Mysteries and fulfil the first trial, the Trial of the Cities,' he said.

No-one spoke as the scope of their task set in: three fabled weapons, three lost cities and a sacred altar that all had to be found in one week.

'Fuck me . . .' said Mae.

'You can say that again,' Hades said.

'*Fuck me* . . .' Mae said.

'Okay,' Jack said. 'We know what we have to do. Everybody gear up and make sure you know your places when we get to Hades's apartment. Make no mistake, when we hit New York, we're going to hit the ground running.'

As Jack's jet shot up the eastern seaboard of the United States toward New York City, three other private planes were also heading there.

The first was coming from the south, from somewhere in Central America.

It was a privately-owned grey C-17 Globemaster III military transport plane, one that had been heavily modified.

On its outside, carefully blended into its flanks, was some state-of-the-art weaponry including AIM-120 AMRAAM missiles, M61 Vulcan rotary cannons and an AN/AAQ-24 directional infrared countermeasure system designed to protect it from heat-seeking missiles; on the inside, in its massive hold (which could store, among other things, an Abrams tank or a CH-53E Super Stallion helicopter) was its main feature and reason for being: a row of six reinforced steel cells.

The huge grey plane bore a special serial number on its tail that allowed it immediate and unquestioned landing privileges in any civilised country in the world. Indeed, it had just been granted priority landing status at Newark Airport, west of Manhattan, forcing every other aircraft on approach to hold back and wait.

This was because it was the personal aircraft—and flying jail—of the Governor of the Royal Prison at Erebus, Mr Yago DeSaxe.

The second aircraft speeding toward New York came from England. It also bore a special tail number—ostensibly registered to the

British royal family but in reality owned by the Land Kingdom—which also guaranteed it unfettered entry into any nation.

This plane was headed for JFK Airport, east of the city, and inside it was a very royal passenger.

The third and final plane racing Jack's to New York that day was the smallest but fastest of the three: a sleek Bombardier Global 8000, the most expensive private jet in the world.

In it were eight stony-faced men.

With them inside their luxurious jet was a small arsenal of machine guns, pistols, grenades—both incendiary and smoke—tactical helmets and Kevlar body armour.

Their plane had a cage in it as well, just a single one.

The Bombardier also possessed a special registration number that allowed it to bypass the usual entry requirements of the United States, no questions asked.

This plane had been cleared for landing at McGuire Air Force Base in New Jersey, to the south of New York City. It was coming from Aragon Castle in Italy and it carried inside it the Knights of the Golden Eight.

SECOND PURSUIT

THE NEW YORK TAKEDOWN

Let the mind be enlarged . . . to the grandeur
of the Mysteries.

FRANCIS BACON

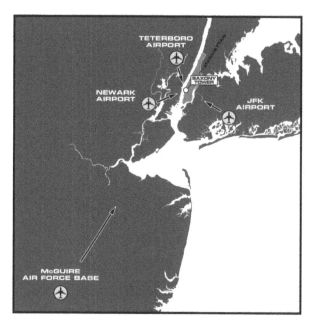

NEW YORK & NEW JERSEY

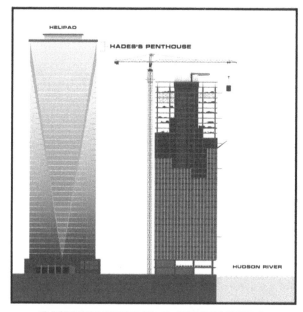

SAXONY TOWER & SURROUNDS

NEW YORK CITY
24 NOVEMBER, 0600 HOURS
U.S. EASTERN TIME

In the pre-dawn light, the *Sky Warrior* touched down at Teterboro Airport, a small private airport on the Jersey side of the Hudson, fifteen miles from New York City.

It taxied to a halt in front of Hades's personal hangar.

Two helicopters were waiting for it, their rotors already turning.

The bigger one was a huge AgustaWestland AW101, the same VIP model of chopper that, painted green and christened *Marine One*, flew the President of the United States.

The second chopper was smaller, a luxurious Eurocopter EC155, which in any other environment would have been a showstopper all by itself, but beside the AW101, it looked positively modest.

Jack, Lily, Mae and Hades strode straight off the *Sky Warrior* and into the big AW101. The helicopter's airstairs folded up behind them and it took off immediately.

Zoe and Alby boarded the smaller Eurocopter, heading for their positions.

No sooner were the two choppers in the air than Sky Monster taxied away in the *Sky Warrior*, soaring off into the sky to wait at Republic Airport, a little regional airstrip on Long Island.

The mighty AgustaWestland AW101 helicopter thundered through the sky, making a beeline for the southern end of Manhattan.

Speeding low and fast over the streets of Jersey City and then the broad expanse of the Hudson River, its journey—which in a car would've taken an hour—took exactly eleven minutes.

As they soared alongside the skyline of New York City, Jack gazed out at its many skyscrapers, including, right ahead of him, the enormous Freedom Tower at the World Trade Center.

As the chopper came to the Tribeca area, just north of Pier 26, Hades pointed at a glittering modern skyscraper featuring many balconies and reflective blue glass in its windows. It was at least sixty storeys tall.

'That's my building: Saxony Tower,' he said. 'My apartment occupies the top two floors.'

'*Saxony* Tower?' Jack asked. 'Is that connected to your surname in some way?'

Hades nodded. 'Saxony, Saxon, DeSaxe, Saxe-Coburg, they all derive from the same familial line. You're starting to understand the royal world.'

The tower, Jack noted, stood almost right on the bank of the Hudson, separated from it by a slightly smaller building that was under construction. Forty storeys tall, this second building had bare concrete levels, a gantry elevator running up its side and a crane mounted precariously on its roof. Jack had encountered the structure in his research on the way here.

Hades saw Jack looking at it.

'That tower under construction is called One Tribeca. Very trendy. They pre-sold every apartment off the plan. When completed it'll be filled with lots of nouveau-riche celebrities and rappers.'

As Jack had noted in his research, One Tribeca stood on the very edge of the Hudson River. It achieved this by incorporating an innovative tunnel at its base that spanned the riverside expressway.

Hades said, 'Its original plans had it slightly *taller* than Saxony Tower—seventy storeys—but strangely, despite the very wealthy and successful developers backing the project, the city planners killed those designs and the building was approved at forty storeys.'

'You intervened?' Jack asked flatly.

Hades shrugged. 'At the original height, it would have impeded the view from my apartment. So I made a call and their plans were amended.'

'Right . . .' Jack said. That *hadn't* been in his research. 'You live in quite a world, Tony. You just say the word and things happen.'

Hades bowed his head.

'I used to,' he said.

The big chopper landed on the roof of Saxony Tower, where a lone man in blue jeans, hiking boots and a tan 'Pine Valley' sweater was waiting for it.

He stood with perfect poise, despite the tornado of wind that the helicopter whipped up all around him.

Hades dashed out of the helicopter and clasped the man's hand with genuine affection.

'Geoffrey!' Hades yelled over the roar of the rotors. 'Meet Captain Jack West Jr, his daughter, Lily, and his mother, Mae. Everyone, meet Geoffrey Moles, my butler, executive manager and bodyguard.'

Jack assessed the man as they shook hands: he was in his early fifties, lean, bald and fit, with sharp, squinting eyes that assessed Jack from top to bottom in an instant. His grip was like iron.

'Captain West. The fifth of the warriors,' he said. 'And victor of the Great Games.'

'That's me,' Jack said.

Hades said, 'Geoffrey is a graduate of the Wharton School of Business and the South Philly school of street fighting, two vital prerequisites for his job as my adjutant. He's been my butler and friend for the last twenty-five years.'

Geoffrey ushered them quickly inside.

'Sir, if I may. The Slave King's forces just landed at Newark and are on their way by car with a police escort. We have maybe twenty minutes at best.'

They took a private elevator down to Hades's penthouse.

As they stepped out into it, Lily gasped. 'Whoa.'

To call Hades's double-levelled pied-à-terre opulent would have been the understatement of the century.

It featured floor-to-ceiling windows on every side, a sweeping marble staircase, *two* private elevators (one going up to the roof, the other down to the street), priceless paintings—including two Picassos and a Goya—sculptures, a Stradivarius violin and a Bösendorfer grand piano.

It had panoramic views of the city to the north and Upper New York Bay to the south, including an uninterrupted view of the Statue of Liberty.

A small six-person team of chefs, maids and a driver all stood to attention at the top of the curving staircase: Hades's New York staff.

Hades nodded to them all before pledging his apologies and hurrying down an inner hallway.

'The Slave King has a *police escort*?' Jack asked as he followed Hades.

'Remember, Captain, you have to view the world differently now,' Hades said as he walked. 'All the major nations of the world—countries like America, Russia, the U.K., France—all exist *to serve* the four kingdoms in some way or another. If someone with royal authority wants to, they can co-opt *any* agency of a country to use as they wish: the police, the army, the navy, tracking satellites, even nuclear weapons. All it takes is a phone call.'

'That's incredible . . .' Mae said.

'No, just real power,' Hades said. 'In this period of royal instability, the Slave King acts with the authority of three of the four kings. If he finds us, it will be very hard to escape his clutches.'

With Jack and the others racing to keep up with him, Hades turned abruptly into an office area, a vast corner suite the size of a suburban house.

It was the kind of private office Jack expected of one of the four wealthiest men in the world.

While the decorations in the larger apartment were more well known—Picasso, Goya, Stradivarius—in here they were more esoteric and ancient.

Partial stone tablets bearing strange carvings stood on pedestals.

Statues—some missing arms, some missing heads—stood on plinths.

An old wooden tree trunk depicted the Hydra Galaxy.

Hades marched right past them, hit a switch under his desk and a whole bookcase in the wall suddenly swung open on a hinge, revealing a massive silver vault door with a high-tech digital keypad and scanner on it.

Hades pressed his thumb to the keypad and his eyes to the scanner. A laser played over them and the screen beeped:

IDENTIFICATION CONFIRMED:
DESAXE, ANTHONY M.

FINGERPRINT ☑
RETINA   ☑
PULSE   ☑

OPEN VAULT.

'A pulse scan?' Jack said.

Hades said, 'So someone can't cut my eyeballs out of their sockets and sever my thumb and get in. If there's no pulse behind my eyes, this vault doesn't open.'

From deep within the thick steel door, unseen bolts unlocked and valves hissed, and then the vault door popped open an inch.

Hades pulled it wide. 'Come on in. This is where I keep the important stuff.'

Inside the vault, the windowless inner sanctum of Hades's sumptuous home, Jack beheld a shelf on which stood a handful of truly ancient wonders.

A small round shield made of shiny black metal.

A gold statue of a tall thin man with the head of a long-beaked bird.

Taking pride of place in the vault, however, were two items mounted on their own pedestals:

First, an ornate bronze helmet, encased in a clear glass dome.

It was a variant of the well-known Corinthian-style helmet: it had the distinctive noseguard and elongated cheekplates common to that design, but the brows above the Y-shaped aperture for the wearer to peer out through had been accentuated so it seemed harsher, angrier, more fearsome. The helmet's horsehair plume was long gone: its holder was just a curving metal spine.

And second, a triangular stone tablet.

Pale yellow in colour, it appeared to be made of weathered sandstone and it was absolutely striking. Covered in glyphs and symbols, it stood upright on its pedestal and was roughly the size of a TV, if TVs came in triangular shapes.

Jack noted the three weapons prominently displayed on it: a helmet, a sword and a triple-bladed mace or trident.

The Three Immortal Weapons.

He quickly snapped off some photos of it with his phone's camera.

As he did, he noticed that a section at the tablet's bottom-right corner had been broken off at some point in the past, disrupting its symmetry:

Lily went straight to it.

'That's the Word of Thoth,' she said, eyeing the many glyphs carved into its perimeter.

'Indeed it is,' Hades said. 'That tablet is over five thousand years old. It is one of my family's most prized secret possessions: my father, the previous Lord Hades, only told me about it as he lay on his deathbed and I was about to take his throne. He said it was a key piece of the Altar of the Cosmos.'

He turned to Lily: 'I tried to get your father—your *birth* father, the previous Oracle—to translate it, but he was an elusive and problematic man and he died before I was able to find him.'

Elusive and problematic, Jack thought. That was a nice way of putting it. The former Oracle of Siwa had been a spoilt and obnoxious drunk.

Hades said, 'Over the centuries, many of the four kings have employed linguists, codebreakers, geniuses and, in recent times, computer programs, to try to translate the Word of Thoth. The Catholic Church—the Cult of Amon-Ra with its obsession with ancient Egypt—has been at it for over four thousand years. I myself had a supercomputer purpose-built for the task of decoding the text on this tablet and after a week of rendering, it came up with nothing.'

Lily peered at the worn triangular stone . . .

. . . for all of ten seconds.

'I can read it,' she said. 'It looks like there were originally six messages on this tablet—two on each side—but because of the missing chunk at the bottom, there are now only five. Three of the messages refer to the weapons and two refer to the cities.

'The first set is about the Weapons. It says:

> *The first kills*
> *The second blinds*
> *The third rules.'*

She squinted. 'The second set is about the Cities:

> *First is Thule, plunging to fathomless depths.*
> *Second comes Ra, the great golden city.*

'I'm guessing there should be a line about the third city, but that part of the tablet has broken off.'

Hades just stared at Lily, slack-jawed.

'You just did in half a minute what I spent many years and millions of dollars unsuccessfully trying to do. Your ability is extraordinary.'

Lily, in her jeans and Han Solo t-shirt, just shrugged. 'Born with it.'

Jack was on edge. He didn't want to linger here, especially in a dead-end corner of the apartment.

'The missing chunk,' he said quickly to Hades. 'Do you know where it is?'

'No,' Hades said. 'No-one does. I was once told that an ancient tracing, or rubbing, of the entire tablet exists. It is supposedly held by a little-known order of Catholic monks in Venice known as the Fraternal Order of St Paul. They are a very peculiar brotherhood, ultra-conservative. They have something of a strained relationship with the Church in Rome, as they find it too *liberal* for their liking. It's entirely possible they have not even told the Church they have the full tracing. For a long time they have been avid collectors of relics and artefacts. Their monastery is part of the Gallerie dell'Accademia, the famous museum in Venice.'

'Who else knows about *this* tablet?' Jack asked.

'The other kings,' Hades said. 'Back in quieter times, it was common for us to have meetings at each other's homes. We would put our prized antiquities on display.'

Jack looked behind them, as if searching for a pursuer. 'Yeah, well, times have changed—'

Then suddenly, standing beside Hades, Geoffrey touched his radio-earpiece.

'Say again?' he said into his wrist-mike.

'What is it?' Hades asked, concerned.

'Someone just boarded your private elevator down in the lobby and overrode the scanners. Five men. They're coming up now—'

A burst of machine-gun fire echoed out from the atrium of the apartment, harsh and loud, followed by screams.

The screams of Hades's staff being gunned down.

Three more gunshots silenced them.

'Shit . . .' Jack whirled, looking for an escape.

But the vault was a dead-end. There was no way out of there except the way they had come.

They were trapped.

Hades, however, was already moving, back toward the entry to the vault where he crouched on his knees and peeled back a strip of carpet to reveal a handle embedded in the floor beneath it.

He turned the handle and a segment of the floor lifted on a hinge.

A secret compartment under the floor opened up before them. It was a panic room of some sort; about the size of a small closet.

'Everybody in! Now!' Hades whispered.

They all dived into the underfloor compartment.

Jack threw a glance at the helmet under its glass dome at the other end of the vault—weighing up whether he could get to it and back to the panic room before their enemies arrived—but Hades grabbed him by the arm.

'There's no time! Stay alive and fight another day.'

Jack leapt down into the secret compartment. Hades climbed down into it last of all, closing the hatch above them and using a hidden cable to pull the carpet back into place above it.

A black-and-white monitor in the panic room showed footage from various closed-circuit cameras in Hades's penthouse:

In the atrium, the dead bodies of Hades's staff lay strewn near the elevators in pools of blood.

On another monitor, five men wearing dark outfits and carrying machine guns ran into Hades's private office and straight into the open vault . . .

. . . where the first two men immediately opened fire, spraying the entire vault with gunfire.

The wave of bullets strafed every surface of the vault, pinging off the bulletproof-glass casings protecting the artefacts.

Jack's eyes went wide. Hades had been right to drag them into the panic room.

Everyone in the underfloor compartment held their breath.

Then the gunfire stopped and the leader of the group of intruders strode into the vault.

'There's nobody in here,' he said.

Jack didn't need to look at the monitor to know who it was.

He knew that voice. It was the voice of a man who hated Jack more than any other person in the world.

It was Orlando Compton-Jones, the King of Land.

Jack froze as he stared at the black-and-white monitor showing the vault room right above his head.

On it was the cruel king for whom he had competed in the Great Games.

Four men stood with Orlando. Two were obviously bodyguards: military men gripping Steyr machine guns.

Of the other two, Jack knew one: Cardinal Ricardo Mendoza. Compact, narrow-eyed and with a thin pencil moustache, Mendoza was a member of the Catholic Church's Omega Group. He was also Orlando's chief advisor. Jack had encountered him in the Underworld.

The last man in Orlando's entourage was everything Mendoza was not. He appeared to be of Indian or Pakistani extraction and was enormously fat, with a bushy grey moustache and many chins. His chubby neck was adorned with many garish gold chains.

'That's Sunny Malik,' Mae whispered to Jack. 'The black market antiquities expert from Karachi.'

Jack nodded silently. Mae had told him about her deadly run-in with Malik in Karachi with Stretch and Pooh Bear.

Jack gazed at Orlando on the monitor.

He hadn't seen the King of Land since the bedlam he, Jack, had created during the Supreme Ceremony atop Hades's palace at the Underworld five days previously. He'd heard that Orlando and Mendoza had got away from India but he didn't know where they had gone.

On the monitor, Orlando turned to his two advisors. 'Well?'

'The Helmet of Hades.' Mendoza pointed at the glorious bronze headpiece. 'Now you have the Sword *and* the Helmet. When you get the Trident, you will have all three of the weapons.'

Orlando casually upturned the glass dome covering the Helmet and took it. 'So where's the Trident?'

Mendoza turned to Sunny Malik.

Sunny said, 'According to several ancient Cretan texts, as the prized weapon of the Sea King, the Trident-Mace was buried with him. It resides in Poseidon's tomb.'

'And where is that?'

'The exact location is unknown, but by all accounts, it is somewhere near the City of Atlas.'

Orlando turned to Mendoza, who nodded.

'I concur,' the cardinal said. 'This matches our records in the Vatican libraries. It makes sense, too, since Atlas was the historic capital of the Sea Kingdom.'

'Atlas,' Orlando said sourly. 'That means consulting Sphinx. Fuck.'

Mendoza said, 'I have always found Lord Lancaster to be very pleasant company. He is well read and most refined: a man who honours the old ways. It is to your advantage that he is the watcher of Atlas. I imagine, as your blood relative, he would be thrilled to assist you in your noble quest.'

'Sphinx may be my cousin,' Orlando spat. 'But he is also a snake who knows every secret of every royal family in the world. How else do you think he got his nickname? He is also keenly aware when he has leverage. Mr Malik: while we speak to Sphinx, begin your own inquiries into the location of Poseidon's tomb and the Trident.'

'As you command,' Sunny Malik said.

While Orlando and Malik spoke, Mendoza stepped up to the triangular sandstone tablet and aimed a peculiar-looking device at it.

The device quickly scanned the tablet with a pair of green lasers.

Orlando said, 'My father told me about this tablet. He said Hades's father claimed it was part of the Altar of the Cosmos.'

Mendoza's device beeped . . .

. . . and the cardinal's face lit up as he read from its screen.

'*The Mystery of the Weapons: The first kills. The second blinds. The third rules.*

'And *The Mystery of the Cities: First is Thule, plunging to fathomless depths. Second comes Ra, the great golden city.*'

Mendoza looked like he'd seen God. He was ecstatic.

'This is incredible,' he said. 'These are two of the Mysteries: the *nature* of the Weapons and the *order* of the Cities. This is vital: without it we would not know where to start. We begin at Thule. We must also take this tablet to my lab at the Vatican to analyse it fully.'

In the darkened panic room below them, Hades turned to Jack and whispered, 'Like I said: translation programs.'

As the two thugs took the heavy stone tablet off its podium, Mendoza gazed at it in wonder. 'Lord in Heaven, it's magnificent.'

Orlando snorted. 'Whatever. Lord Hades has no claim to it any more. And no use for it, not where he's going. We, however, shall head for Thule right away—'

Suddenly, on the monitor, Orlando paused, listening intently to his earpiece.

'Copy that,' he said into his radio-mike. 'Gentlemen, we have to move. Others are on their way here and we do *not* want to be here when they arrive.'

Then as quickly as they had arrived, Orlando and his men were out of there, leaving the vault with the Helmet and the tablet in their possession, and rushing back to the elevators.

As soon as the elevator's door had closed, Hades pushed open the hatch.

'They took the Helmet *and* the tablet,' he said. 'Damn. At least we got a look at the inscriptions.'

'Who is that Sphinx guy they mentioned?' Mae asked as they all climbed out of the secret compartment.

'Have you heard about the Trismagi in your research?' Hades asked, reaching down to help her.

'Yes,' Mae said. 'They're the keepers of the three secret cities.'

Hades said, 'Sphinx—or more precisely, Lord Hardin Lancaster XII—is one of the Trismagi. He is the keeper of the greatest of the three cities, the City of Atlas.'

'Come on, folks, let's hustle,' Jack said urgently. 'We gotta get out of here, too.'

They hurried out of Hades's office, down the hallway and around the sweeping staircase, arriving at the elevators.

Hades stared sadly at the crumpled and bloody bodies of his staff. Geoffrey knelt down beside one of the corpses as—

Ping!

The arrival light on the right-hand elevator sprang to life.

Jack spun, exposed.

The elevator's doors opened . . .

. . . to reveal a huge, hulking man flanked by six heavily armed NYPD SWAT cops. But Jack could tell from their dead eyes that these were not real SWAT cops.

The hulking man saw the group before him—Jack, Hades, Lily, Mae and Geoffrey—and he smiled meanly.

'Why, hello there.' He stepped out of the elevator. 'Seems like I've caught you all in something of a hurry.'

He was taller than Hades, a solid six-three, and fit as hell. The likeness was unmistakable. His face looked just like Hades's—piercing maroon-tinged eyes, severe features and dark arched eyebrows—only younger.

'Brother,' he said, nodding with mock deference to Hades, 'so nice to see you. And this'—he turned to Jack—'I can only assume is the famous Captain West. I'm so very pleased to meet you. My name is Prince Yago DeSaxe, Governor of the Royal Prison, and I am here to arrest you both.'

They all stood there in a tense face-off.

'Yago,' Hades said carefully. 'Please. Let's talk.'

'There is nothing to say, brother. You committed treason against the four thrones and have thus been sentenced to life imprisonment at Erebus. You have been cast out.'

Jack heard his tone instantly.

Barely concealed contempt.

Yago, a proud prince consigned to the lesser rank of policeman and jailer, didn't care for Hades at all.

Hades wasn't giving up. 'Yago, please, we must find the Mysteries in order to stop the Omega Ev—'

'I *must* do nothing,' Yago spat. 'You have no power over me anymore, Anthony. Your role in worldly affairs is at an end. There is nothing left for you but pain and suffering at my hands and I will gladly carry out the sentence. As for Captain West here, he laid hands on a king—'

Abruptly, the building's emergency sirens rang out, shrill and piercing.

Yago whirled.

Jack did, too.

Then a deep throbbing sound could be heard . . .

. . . and a fearsome image rose into view outside the panoramic windows on the northern side of Hades's penthouse.

A gigantic hover-capable V-22 Osprey attack plane loomed outside the windows, its two upturned rotors blurring, its nose lowered menacingly, its cannons and missile pods levelled.

A second identical plane raced around behind the first one, banking fast, rotors thumping, moving in a wide circle around the high-rise tower.

Jack didn't know what was happening. From the surprised look on his face, neither did Yago.

A two-way stand-off had just become a three-way one.

Then the sirens fell silent and a man's voice came over the building's emergency public address system:

'*We bid you greetings, Prince Yago and King Hades—well, former King Hades. Such a pity to hear of your fall from grace.*'

The accent was European: part French, part German.

'*This is Jaeger Eins, and we are the Knights of the Golden Eight. We have been lawfully engaged to kill Captain West and capture his daughter and, if he is also there, her friend, young Mr Calvin. The price has been paid and so the mark has been made. They are our property now. Yago, I assume you are here for Hades and West. We will allow you to take Hades, but not West. He and the two youngsters are ours.*'

Jack's mind tried to keep up with everything he was hearing.

Were there actually *two* groups pursuing him?

Yago and these assholes—who it seemed were also after Lily and Alby.

And now these new arrivals were telling Yago—the official royal jailer—to essentially get out of their way.

The response from Yago surprised Jack.

Yago grabbed Hades roughly by the arm and hurled him to his SWAT guards, who cuffed Hades and shoved him into the elevator.

'Sir!' Geoffrey lunged after them, only to receive a sharp rifle-butt to the face from one of Yago's thugs.

He fell to the floor, bleeding.

Yago drew a pistol and calmly levelled it at Geoffrey's head.

'No!' Hades protested. 'Leave him be! He has done nothing but serve me well.'

'If he stays here, he is as good as dead, brother,' Yago said. 'You know how the Knights operate.'

'Please . . .' Hades said.

Yago holstered his pistol. 'So be it,' he said as he joined Hades and the SWAT team in the elevator.

As the doors began to slide shut, Hades's eyes found Lily's and he mouthed, *Run.*

For his part, Yago locked eyes with Jack.

'I leave you to the mercy of the Knights,' he said. 'You have my sympathies.'

The doors to the elevator closed over Yago's face and suddenly Jack, Lily, Mae and Geoffrey were left standing there in the magnificent penthouse, staring at the two military aircraft hovering outside its windows sixty storeys above downtown New York.

And then, spectacularly, the Knights launched their assault on Saxony Tower.

The rotary cannons on the first hovering Osprey blazed to life and an unimaginable torrent of fifty-calibre tracer rounds assailed Hades's penthouse.

Windows shattered.

Glass flew everywhere.

Bullet holes the size of softballs punctured the walls.

Priceless vases exploded.

Statues blew apart.

Books on shelves were eviscerated, their pages becoming confetti.

Couches were shredded, showering the apartment in a snow of goose down and feathers.

Jack reacted instantly. He crash-tackled Lily and Mae out of the line of fire and they went tumbling together down the curving marble staircase. Jack curled his body around Lily's as they rolled, protecting her from the bumps of the descent.

Geoffrey the butler wasn't so lucky.

He was *hammered* by the incoming gunfire.

The entire front of his body was turned to a bloody pulp as the wave of anti-aircraft fire hit him. He convulsed horribly as the fusillade of heavy-bore ammunition shot *right through* his body and ripped into the wall behind him, before, at last, the gunfire stopped and he collapsed to the floor, deader than dead.

At the base of the curving stairs, Jack scooped up Lily and Mae.

'Keep moving!' he urged.

Through the now-shattered panoramic windows, he could see the first hovering attack plane but not the other one—

—then, suddenly, black-clad commandos came swinging in through the shattered windows of the penthouse on ropes from the roof. The other V-22 must have landed up there.

There were six commandos and they all wore black goggles, black ceramic half-masks, and striking black body armour. As they fanned out into the penthouse with clinical precision, they all looked down the barrels of MP-9 machine pistols, military-style.

No wonder Yago got out of here, Jack thought.

'This way.' He hauled Lily and Mae through the hallways of the penthouse's lower level.

Outside, the hovering Osprey swooped swiftly and began firing at that level.

More windows shattered.

More walls blew apart.

'Zoe!' Jack yelled into his radio as they ran. 'We need you!'

'*I saw*,' Zoe's voice replied in his ear.

'Southwest corner!' Jack called.

'*On it.*'

They came to a bedroom in the southwestern quarter of the lower level: it was a corner room with windows on two sides and a breathtaking view of the Statue of Liberty and the distant Atlantic Ocean.

The Osprey appeared outside it like an angry hawk-god, its cannons levelled.

Jack drew his pistol and fired first, shattering the windows of the bedroom and hitting the cockpit of the Osprey, cracking its dome and striking one of its pilots in the chest.

The plane banked wildly.

Wind rushed into the corner bedroom.

Jack spun: and saw fast-moving shadows entering the hallway behind him.

They were close.

Then the European-accented voice came over the building's PA system again.

'*Captain West*,' it said. '*It is useless to run. No matter where you go, we will find you. It is what we do. It is what we have done without peer for two millennia. Trust me when I say it is better for you to surrender now. Our methods are as effective as they are notorious. You do not want to experience them. We need the girl and her friend alive; you, less so. That said, while we have been tasked with returning your daughter to our employer alive, we have not promised that she will be delivered in one piece.'*

Lily swapped a horrified look with Jack.

'Who are these guys?' she whispered.

The first two pursuers appeared in the hallway behind them, machine guns raised. Jack fired twice at them, forcing them back behind the corner.

The voice said, *'Captain. There is nowhere for you to run. We promise, if you surrender now, we will kill you quickly.'*

'Zoe?' Jack said urgently into his throat-mike.

'Go! West-side window. Now!' Zoe shouted.

Jack grabbed both Lily and Mae by the hand.

'Take a leap of faith with me?' he asked.

'Okay . . .' Mae said hesitantly.

'You bet,' Lily replied instantly.

And together they ran toward the wide-open western windows of the bedroom just as the Osprey that Jack had shot swooped back into position right outside it *and* as their pursuers launched their final assault on the room and charged in, guns up.

Jack, his mother and his daughter leapt clear out of the smashed window, sixty storeys above the world, right in front of the hovering V-22, out into the morning sky . . .

. . . Jack, Mae and Lily plummeted down the side of the tower—for exactly seven feet—before they landed with abrupt thumps in the steel basket of a crane: the crane they had seen mounted atop One Tribeca, the building under construction across the street from Saxony Tower.

Whereas before the crane had been resting horizontally across the roof of One Tribeca, now it was raised at a steep upward angle toward the upper floors of Saxony Tower, its basket perfectly placed just below the southwestern corner of Hades's penthouse.

In the cab of the crane sat Zoe, sent there earlier in the event a hasty escape was required.

Zoe swivelled the crane on its base, causing the basket hanging off its high arm to swing wildly around.

The two V-22s saw it and sprang instantly into action.

The nearer of the two Ospreys pivoted in mid-air, aiming its guns not at the basket but at Zoe in the crane's cab.

The Osprey opened fire, its fifty-calibre rotary guns making loud puncture-like *whump*s with every shot.

Zoe ducked.

The cab's steel flanks erupted in sparking bullet-impacts. All its windows shattered.

The wave of gunfire pummelled the crane, causing it to shudder and shake violently.

Jack, Mae and Lily were still in the basket, swinging around in a wide lateral arc, high above the streets. Their basket just managed to swoop in low over the roof of the construction tower at the exact moment that the Osprey's withering stream of tracer fire wrenched the crane's cabin from its mount and the whole crane came loose and—*bam!*—slammed down on top of the building.

Zoe dived out of the cabin, somersaulting onto the dusty concrete roof of One Tribeca as the crane's long metal arm bounced against the rooftop and the entire spindly thing tipped over the edge and dropped out of sight.

A short distance away from Zoe, Jack, Mae and Lily leapt clear of their basket and went sprawling onto the concrete . . .

. . . just as the basket was suddenly sucked off the roof.

Like some kind of giant long-armed insect, the crane sailed down the side of One Tribeca for a full forty storeys before it slammed in a tangled heap into the empty side street that lay between One Tribeca and Saxony Tower.

Up on the roof, Jack was already on his feet, scooping up Lily and Mae and joining Zoe in bolting for the nearest stairwell—while the two Ospreys banked around in the sky above them.

'Jesus, Jack,' Zoe yelled above the din, 'who are these guys?'

'Another part of the shadow world that wants to kill us,' Jack said grimly. 'Knights of some kind. They said they want Lily alive and me dead, and they've been paid to do it.'

The four of them raced down the dusty stairs.

As they did, through the open-air concrete levels of the construction tower, they saw the Ospreys circling the building, stalking them.

Jack keyed his throat-mike. 'Alby! Come in!'

'*I'm here, Jack,*' Alby replied immediately in his earpiece.

'Get into position! I was hoping we wouldn't have to use you, but I think we're gonna have to!'

'*I'll be there*,' Alby said.

Jack, Zoe, Mae and Lily were still quite high up on One Tribeca. They hurried over to the river-facing edge of the open-sided building.

The glittering waters of the Hudson River stretched out beneath them, running up against the base of the building. On the opposite shore of the wide river, the skyline of Jersey City glimmered in the morning light.

Jack eyed the waves thirty storeys below them.

'Three hundred feet, give or take,' he said. 'It's survivable. Just.'

And then their pursuers made their decision for them.

One of the Ospreys swung into a hover above the river about ten levels below them . . .

. . . and launched two missiles at the construction tower!

The two missiles streaked out of their pods, issuing dead-straight smoke trails behind them before they hit One Tribeca and detonated.

Two colossal explosions shook the building.

Jack and the three women struggled to hang on as the whole thing shuddered and swayed.

Girders squealed.

Concrete groaned.

And then the tower buckled—right in its middle—and folded, and like a slow-falling tree, the top half of One Tribeca began falling toward the Hudson River with Jack, Zoe, Mae and Lily in it.

It was an unbelievable sight.

It was as if a god-sized axeman had hacked at the midpoint of the forty-storey construction tower, causing it to fold and fall.

With a tremendous roar of cracking concrete and rending steel, the upper half of the building broke free of its lower half and fell toward the Hudson . . .

. . . where it crashed into the river with an absolutely gargantuan splash.

The great concrete structure—all 900,000 tons of it—slammed into the water, creating a massive wave.

The wave expanded in every direction, a surging wall of water. Most of it spread out harmlessly into the river, but the part of it that rushed back toward the island pounded against the seawall, hurling a mighty shower of water onto the riverside expressway.

For a brief moment, the enormous tower with its open-air concrete levels bobbed in the water—then those levels filled with water and the massive thing began to sink.

If one had been looking closely at the building as it fell toward the water—at its northwestern corner, to be precise—one would have seen four infinitesimally small figures leap off it at the very last moment, jumping clear of the structure and spearing feet-first into the river themselves.

As the colossal concrete structure disappeared below the surface in a roiling mass of whitewater, the two V-22 Ospreys prowled the air above it, searching for them.

★ ★ ★

In the first Osprey, the leader of the Knights of the Golden Eight, Jaeger Eins, stared at the sinking building in the river, searching for West and his daughter amid the wreckage and the waves.

But they didn't surface.

He waited a full ten minutes.

Nothing.

Then ambulances and police cars began to arrive at the shore. They weren't necessary; not a single bystander had been hurt by the building's spectacular collapse, but they could be inconvenient later. Likewise, early-morning joggers stopped and pulled out their earbuds to gawk at the sight and record it on their cell phones.

Jaeger Eins peered at the splash site closely.

Was it possible West and his daughter had drowned?

Yes.

But he didn't believe it.

West was too shrewd for that. He'd have had an escape plan.

'Let's pull out,' he said into his helmet microphone.

The two Ospreys boomed away to the south, away from New York City.

'Never mind, gentlemen,' Jaeger Eins added. 'We will simply have to bring them out into the open another way.'

As the two Ospreys peeled away to the south, a hundred metres to the north of the massive splash site, under the surface of the river, a pressure hatch was being opened in the roof of the Holland Tunnel.

When it opened in 1927, the Holland Tunnel was the world's first underwater road tunnel. Now it is one of two car tunnels that snake across the bed of the Hudson connecting Manhattan with New Jersey.

While most of the tunnel is cut out of the bedrock below the riverbed, at each end of it, where the road rises, short sections are exposed to the river proper.

In these sections are hatches—with internal pressure

chambers—that allow divers to access the tunnel in the event of an emergency.

Those hatches were Jack's escape plan. He'd figured, if the need arose, his team could leap into the river via the construction tower and, using small scuba breathers, make for the hatches in the tunnel.

Granted, he hadn't expected to plunge into the river on top of the *falling* construction tower, but the plan was essentially the same.

After Zoe, Mae, Lily and he had leapt clear of the falling building and speared into the water, they had bit into their breathers and swum for the tunnel.

Into one of the hatches, depressurising, and then emerging through an emergency door into the tunnel itself . . . where Alby pulled up in a little Toyota hatchback, collected them and sped off down the tunnel.

Jack sat in the back seat, sopping wet and thinking hard.

Hades had been taken by Yago to the royal prison, wherever that was.

The assassins in those Ospreys—the Knights of the Golden Eight, they called themselves; ruthless, well armed and not afraid to destroy entire buildings—were hunting Lily, Alby and him.

And Orlando now had a head start in the race to find the cities and avert the Omega Event.

Alby turned around in the driver's seat as they sped down the Holland Tunnel.

'Where to, Jack?'

'Republic Airport on Long Island. We gotta regroup with Sky Monster.'

THE UNDERWORLD
NORTHWESTERN INDIA
24 NOVEMBER, 1700 HOURS LOCAL TIME

While Jack was falling into the Hudson River inside a building, Pooh Bear and Stretch were arriving at the Underworld on the remote northwestern coast of India, where the Thar Desert meets the Arabian Sea.

The two of them landed in an amphibious plane on the placid waters of the Arabian Sea to the west of the Underworld and taxied to the shore.

The towering skeletons of derelict supertankers and container ships still loomed on the broad flat beach. A couple of them lay on their sides, thanks to an explosive chase involving Jack West Jr.

Looking past the ship graveyard, they saw a high concrete structure embedded in the sand-cliff: the western supply dock of the Underworld.

There were two minotaurs standing there waiting for them and they were waving frantically.

Within minutes, they were zooming in a jeep through the long tunnel that led to the Underworld.

After a few kilometres, they emerged from the tunnel in the high cavernous space of the minotaur city. Like a freeway flyover, their elevated concrete road passed over hundreds of rickety tenement-style structures on its way to the mountain-palace of Hades.

Stretch saw the palace looming in the distance . . .

. . . but they were not going to get to it.

'What on Earth is going on?' he said.

A gigantic crowd of minotaurs was gathered on the road in front of them—a couple of thousand of them—completely blocking the way.

Only they weren't *trying* to block the roadway.

Pooh Bear leaned forward. 'They're looking at something. Something down below.'

Their jeep pulled up to the edge of the crowd, where it was met by Minotus, the King of the Minotaurs.

'Mr Pooh, Mr Stretch, I'm so pleased you came,' he said breathlessly. 'It has been a terrible time here. It has killed over one hundred and fifty of my people already.'

Stretch blanched. 'One hundred and fifty of your—what has?'

Minotus guided them to the guardrail of the overpass and pointed downward.

'It was the only way we could contain it,' he said. 'We lured it into the alley and then brought down the building behind it. Four of my bravest minotaurs died in the act.'

Pooh Bear looked out over the rail and gasped.

'Oh my Lord,' he said.

Down among the tenements below them was a dead-end alley. Through the deft use of explosives, the minotaurs had indeed brought down a building at the open end of the alley, blocking it.

The result was a deep, sheer-walled chasm from which there was no escape.

And standing in that alley, pacing rapidly back and forth, looking this way and that, left and right, up and down, occasionally punching the thick stone walls of its prison, was a six-foot-tall man-shaped figure made entirely of bronze.

Stretch stared in shock at the thing. 'What . . . in the world . . . is that?'

Minotus said, 'It came out of one of the silver coffins at the end of the Great Bend. It killed a cleaning crew of thirty minotaurs before it made its way here and carved a bloody swathe through my people.

'To every individual it meets, it says the same thing: "*Kushma alla?*" If you do *not* answer it, it kills you and asks the next person. If you *do* answer, but answer incorrectly, it kills you and asks the next person. Since none of us knows the correct answer, all we could do was flee.'

Pooh Bear peered down into the makeshift pit.

The figure looked like a robot but somehow *not*: its movements were at the same time stilted yet smooth, awkward yet purposeful, robotic yet alive. It looked like a walking statue—a tall bronze-coloured automaton—but one that, caught in the dead-end created by the desperate minotaurs, could not carry out its simple programming.

The creepiest part about it, Pooh thought—apart from the murderous rampage it had gone on—was its face, or rather its absence of a face.

It had no discernible eyes or mouth.

It made it seem inhuman.

Emotionless. Pitiless.

Its only feature was a long bird-like snout or beak that seemed soldered to its face.

Minotus said, 'It is strong: it can hurl an entire car out of its way, punch through walls, and tear a man's head off with its bare hands. It is clever, too: it can open doors, climb ladders, solve problems.

'And its skin. Our bullets bounced off it. It was the same with our swords. Grenades did not leave a scratch. Flamethrowers did not slow it down. Its claws are like razors and it uses them to stab anyone who dares stand in its way. It is a walking metal demon. And it keeps asking that infernal question: *Kushma alla?*'

Stretch looked at Pooh. 'I don't know what it's saying, but I have an idea what language it's speaking.'

'You think it's *speaking* the Word of Thoth?'

'Exactly.'

Stretch pulled out his iPhone, opened the video-calling app and pressed Lily's number.

She answered on the first ring, her face appearing on the screen.

She appeared to be in a moving car—a fast-moving car—and it looked like she was soaking wet.

'Hey, Stretch,' Lily said. 'What's up?'

'You okay?' Stretch said, noting her appearance.

Jack's face appeared next to Lily's. 'Let's just say New York was rough. We lost Hades and the building we were in fell into the Hudson. What have you got?'

Stretch said, 'We've got a serious situation here. One hundred and fifty dead minotaurs thanks to this . . . *thing* . . . that emerged from one of those coffins you talked about.'

He reversed the phone's camera so that it showed the bronzeman trapped down in the alleyway.

'Hey!' Stretch called to the figure.

It looked up and saw him with its eyeless metal face and from deep within its body came an unearthly voice:

'*Kushma alla?*'

The deep voice reverberated around the cavern. At the sound of it, the assembled minotaurs fell completely, fearfully silent.

Pooh Bear said, 'We thought it might be the Word of Thoth, but in spoken form. What do you think, Lily?'

Lily was silent for a long moment.

'It's the Word of Thoth all right,' she said.

'What does it mean?' Pooh asked.

Lily said, 'It means: "*Are you my master?*"'

'It wants its master,' Pooh Bear said, gazing down at the bronze-man. 'But who is its master?'

'The King of Kings,' Jack said from the phone. 'One of the rewards for winning the Games was an army of men of bronze. Jesus Christ, what have I done?'

'Why do you say that?' Stretch said.

It was Minotus who answered him.

'Out on the hanging tower by the Great Bend, there are *hundreds* of coffins containing more of these things. This single bronzeman has killed a hundred and fifty of my minotaurs. Imagine what an army of them could do? If the others awake, there will be nothing we can do to stop them.'

'Stretch, Pooh,' Jack said. 'Events are starting to pick up speed. Kings are on the move, some bad dudes are hunting us, and we only have seven days to save the world.

'It's a good bet all those other coffins are going to open soon. Do whatever you can to help Minotus seal up the tunnels leading out of that Bend. If you have to block them up with fifty feet of concrete, do that. It'll slow them down when they wake up. Call me when you're done, because I need you out here in the field.'

A ROYAL HISTORY OF
THE WORLD

THE THREE SECRET CITIES

In Thule, there are perpetual days without nights.

SERVIUS, ROMAN WRITER
CIRCA 4TH CENTURY, A.D.

The *Sky Warrior* sped across the Atlantic, heading for Europe. After their spectacular fall into the Hudson, Jack, Mae, Alby and Lily had met Sky Monster out on Long Island and taken to the air immediately.

Jack gathered the group in the main cabin. Behind him, a small bank of TV sets played the four major news stations: CNN, MSNBC, BBC World and Al Jazeera. Right now, with the sound muted, all four showed different camera angles of the same thing: a crumpled New York City skyscraper lying toppled in the Hudson.

'All right, people,' Jack said, 'we've got our backs to the wall. We need to find the three weapons and the three cities. Our rivals have a big head start and we just lost our greatest expert on the royal world, Hades.'

Lily clapped Mae on the shoulder. 'We have our own expert.'

'Thanks for the vote of confidence,' Mae said. 'But Hades lived and breathed that world. I've only studied it in books and scrolls.'

'Where do we even start, Jack?' Alby asked.

Jack went over to his electronic whiteboard.

'I think Zeus told us. Remember what he wrote on that papyrus: *The journey to the Three Secret Cities begins at the end.* The end of this journey is the Altar of the Cosmos—that's where you have to go when you're done at the three cities—and we have a photo of a piece of that altar.'

Jack transferred a photo from his phone to the electronic white-board. It appeared on it in much larger size: the shot he had taken in Hades's vault of the triangular tablet.

'This tablet is our starting point,' he said. 'But it's incomplete. Part of it has broken off. Hades said there's a rubbing of the *full* tablet at the Gallerie dell'Accademia in Venice. In my experience, it's best to know everything you can about a task before you start out on it. Saves you from nasty surprises later. I want to see the full tablet, which is why we're going to Venice now, to the Gallerie dell'Accademia.

'On the way, we're all going to study up. I want to know every-thing we can about the Three Immortal Weapons, the Three Secret Cities and the Altar of the Cosmos.

'I also want to know about the royal prison they've taken Hades to, the place called Erebus, plus those Knights who are hunting us, the ones who scared off Hades's brother and *destroyed a building* in New York. That clear?'

Everyone nodded.

'All right. Hit the books.'

The team scattered around the plane and began tapping away on computers, reading books or perusing old notepads.

At one point, Jack took his mother aside.

'Mum, these guys who attacked us in New York, these Knights of the Golden Eight, who are they?'

Mae looked downward. 'I've read about them a few times. They're a very dangerous element of the royal world. In royal systems like the four kingdoms, there is always a hierarchy: kings and queens, princes and princesses, then earls and knights. Earls and knights pledge their allegiance to their kings and thus garner their patronage and support.

'The Knights of the Golden Eight, however, are different. They pledge their allegiance to no-one. They are the original *knights-errant*, guns for hire. The paid assassins of the royal courts.

'Over the centuries, they have acquired substantial land holdings and wealth which has afforded them a unique kind of independence from the four kingdoms. And as we saw very clearly this morning, they have no fear even of senior office-holders like the Governor of the Royal Prison.'

Jack swallowed.

'Their price is notoriously high,' Mae added, 'which means only the wealthiest royals can hire them. But then, according to the Knights' version of chivalry, they serve *only* their employer of the moment and they will not rest until they have accomplished their mission. They say: "When the price is paid, the mark is made." The death mark.'

'What's their price?' Jack asked ominously.

'The Knights don't work for money,' Mae said. 'They work for *land*. Regions. Sometimes whole countries. One thing is clear, whoever tasked them with killing you and grabbing Lily and Alby has the ability to pay them handsomely.'

Shortly after that conversation, while everyone else was working away, Jack slipped into his bedroom at the back of the plane, pulled out his phone and texted a new friend of his.

> Hey Scarecrow,
>
> Hope you're on the mend after your time in the U-world. Something came up and I'm back into it in a big way.
>
> Question: ever heard of some bounty hunters called the 'Knights of the Golden Eight'?

A few minutes later, he got a reply from Shane Schofield:

> Jack.
>
> I just showed your text to Mother. She says you're the fucking Energizer Bunny. (She also says hi.)
>
> I've still got a hole in my shoulder from a stab wound I got in the Underworld, so I'm not going anywhere for a month.
>
> Never heard of any 'Knights of the Golden Eight' but let me ask a friend of mine who might have.

A few hours later, after doing some research of his own, Jack gathered everyone together in the main cabin.

As the others joined him, he got Lily to add her translations of the Thoth markings on the tablet to the image of it on the electronic whiteboard:

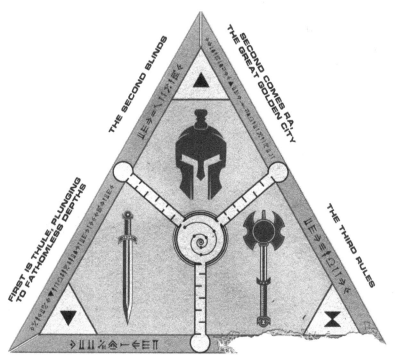

THE SECOND BLINDS

SECOND COMES RA: THE GREAT GOLDEN CITY

FIRST IS THULE, PLUNGING TO FATHOMLESS DEPTHS

THE THIRD RULES

THE FIRST KILLS

'Let's start with the three cities,' Jack said. He added the words *THULE*, *RA* and *ATLAS* to the whiteboard. 'Their histories, origins, special features and possible locations?'

Mae stood up. 'First of all, the names of the three secret, or hidden, cities—Thule, Ra and Atlas—are actually very widely known, as are the various legends about them. Having said that, all three cities remain stubbornly unfound despite centuries of searching for them.

'Thule is probably the least well known, so let's start with it. It's sometimes referred to as *Ultima* Thule and is mentioned by many Greek and Roman writers including Plato, Geminus and Virgil.

'Thule was said to be a fabulous city, built in a cold and icy land far to the north. The ancient writers claimed that during summer the sun never set there, and in winter it never rose. Thule was reputed to be four days' sail northwest of the British Isles.

'All this—especially the part about long days in summer and long nights in winter—has led modern scholars to speculate that Thule was actually a reference to Iceland, Svalbard or perhaps Greenland. But it remains speculation, because Thule has never been found.'

'Anything about fathomless depths?' Jack asked.

'Not that I've seen,' Mae said. 'I should also add that Thule was a topic of extreme interest to the Nazis.'

'The Nazis?' Lily said.

Mae said, 'As everyone knows, the Nazis believed in the Aryan race, a superior race of blond-haired, blue-eyed supermen and women. It was the Nazis' belief that the Aryan race began at Thule. Indeed, one of the key groups within the early Nazi Party, the one that looked into people's ancestry to ensure they had "pure" Aryan blood, was a very nasty group called the *Thule-Gesellschaft*, the Thule Society. Its symbol was a proto-swastika.'

'Charming,' Jack said. 'Okay, what about Ra? I can't say I've ever heard of a lost city of Ra.'

'Believe it or not, but I bet you have,' Mae said. 'The city of Ra is actually far more well known than Thule, only you probably know it by another name: the name given to it by Spanish explorers in the days of the conquest of South America.'

Mae turned to Lily. 'Lily helped me with this. Perhaps she can explain it better.'

Lily said, 'In Thoth, to say "the City of Ra", you say "*Do-Ra*". To say "the *Great* City of Ra", you would say "*Do-Ra-Do*".'

'Oh, no way . . .' Jack said, seeing it.

'That's right,' Lily said. 'One ancient Thoth carving we found stated that in honour of Ra, the streets of the great city dedicated to him were paved with gold, the metal most like the sun. Later, in their travels in the jungles of the new continent of South America, the Spanish conquistadors heard from the natives about a fabulous and ancient hidden city with streets of gold. To many, finding it would become an obsession and as rumours spread, this city dedicated to Ra the Sun-God—the Great City of Ra, Do-Ra-Do— soon became known by its crude Spanish equivalent: Dorado. El Dorado.'

'Is there any way to know where it might be?' Zoe asked.

'Given that word of the city only came to Europeans when they encountered the natives of Central and South America, it is presumed to be somewhere in the jungles there.' Mae held up her hands helplessly. 'For over five hundred years, many explorers— men like Hernán Cortés and Sir Francis Drake—have searched for El Dorado and not found it.'

'And Atlas?' Jack said.

'The name speaks for itself,' Mae said. 'It is the most famous lost city of them all. Plato was the first to write about it and countless others have pondered it ever since, from Francis Bacon to Jules Verne. Deep-sea divers have searched in vain for it while pseudo-historians have claimed that every advanced ancient civilisation, from the Egyptians to the Mayans, stemmed from it.

'It is the great cautionary tale that every schoolchild knows, the tale of a wondrous city that rose too high and was punished for its hubris when it was flooded under the waves of the Atlantic Ocean and lost forever. That's the City of Atlas, or as it is more commonly known, Atlantis.'

'Atlantis . . .' Jack said dubiously.

The others looked at him expectantly.

Then he shrugged. 'Hey, if you'd told me a week ago that I'd go to the Underworld and back, I'd have laughed in your face. A guy's got to keep an open mind in this business. And, clearly, they're not called *secret* cities for nothing. We've got our work cut out for us. Anything else about them?'

Lily raised her hand. 'One thing.' She pulled up a copy of Hades's snapshot of the Zeus Papyrus on her computer.

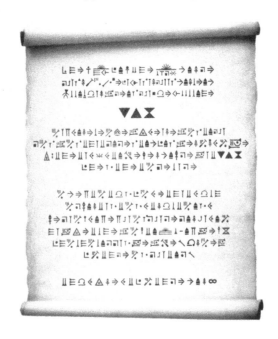

'The symbols for "the Three Secret Cities" in the Word of Thoth are in this note written by Zeus. You can see them on the fourth line:

'Now, if you look at the triangular tablet from the altar, you'll see those same three symbols carved into the *corners* of the triangle: the first upside-down triangle is Thule, the next one represents Ra, and the last symbol, two triangles forming an hourglass-like shape, is Atlas.'

Lily grabbed a whiteboard marker and drew three circles around the three segments of the tablet:

'This links each weapon with its city: Thule and the Sword; Ra and the Helmet; Atlas and the Mace.'

Jack nodded. 'Nice work, kiddo. Nice work.'

Lily smiled. She may have been a young woman of twenty now, educated and accomplished, but she still loved it when he called her that.

'I heard something about the Three Secret Cities during the Games,' Jack said. 'About their guardians.'

'The Trismagi,' Mae said.

'Yes. Cardinal Mendoza said that while the word translates as *three magicians*, I should think of them not as magicians but as the three most senior initiates of the civilisation that built the cities.'

Mae said, 'You do realise that *trismagi* is the name given to the "three wise men" who attended the birth of Christ by the light of an especially bright star.'

'Mendoza mentioned that, too,' Jack said. 'He said that very occasionally the three guardians venture forth from their cities to share their knowledge with each other. I assume they also emerge to attend major royal events. The birth of a royal scion like Jesus Christ—the merging of two great royal lines—was clearly one such event.'

'So who are they?' Alby said. 'Are they royalty? Maybe lower-ranked siblings like that Yago guy?'

'Hades mentioned that one of them is known as Sphinx,' Jack said. 'Beyond that, all I know is they're waiting at the cities and so will have to be taken into account.' He looked to his mother questioningly.

Mae shrugged and shook her head. 'This is where having an insider like Hades comes in handy. In all my studies of the kingdoms, I've only encountered two references to the Trismagi: the Christ visit, of course, and one reference where they were called the "three watchmen", because they watch over the cities. All I can say is that being the guardian of a secret city must be a tough job: lonely, isolated and a very long way from the luxuries of the royal world. Like being the Governor of the Royal Prison, I doubt being the watchman of a secret city is a sought-after position in royal circles.'

'Watchman . . .' Alby said thoughtfully, before standing up and grabbing his laptop. 'Funny you should use that word. Plato used a similar one: *watchtowers*.'

He brought up a scan of a tattered old scroll.

'Since Plato described two of the three cities—Thule and Atlas—I decided to look him up a little further. This is a scan of a scroll that Jack found at the Library at Alexandria, written by Plato himself.'

He started reading:

'To enter each city, you must first pass through its watchtower and navigate its sacred avenue. At its bridge you must overcome its silver guardians. Only then can you advance to its innermost vault and empower the weapon.

'But beware, the three cities are well defended. Woe betide he who awakens their silent bronze armies. For the armies will only allow one versed in the Mysteries to pass and keep his life. False claimants and intruders will suffer only death.'

'Silent bronze armies?' Lily said. 'Those bronze things.'

A silence fell over the group.

Jack gave voice to their fears.

'These cities,' he said, 'are starting to sound like very dangerous places.'

He stood up.

'This is a good start, people. Given that the tablet says Thule is the first city, let's focus on finding its location—'

At that moment, all at once, all four of the televisions behind Jack suddenly crashed to static, their signals seemingly lost.

Alby went over to them. 'Must be a glitch of some—'

And then the TVs came on again, all by themselves, and a face appeared on them: the same face *on all four televisions*.

It was the face of a man and he was wearing a black ceramic half facemask, black goggles, and a black helmet.

'*Hello, world,*' he said in a peculiar European accent.

Jack froze.

He knew that voice. It was the same one that had come over the PA system in Hades's penthouse earlier that day.

The voice of Jaeger Eins, the leader of the Knights of the Golden Eight.

Alby changed the channel on one of the televisions, only to find the same ominous masked figure on that channel . . . and the next one . . . and the next.

'He's on *every* channel,' Alby gasped. 'That's not possible. It would mean they've hacked every broadcast signal in the—'

'*People of the world,*' the masked figure said. '*You do not know me, but then, who I am is unimportant. Allow me, however, to introduce you to someone who is very, very important.*'

The screen changed . . .

. . . to a photo of Jack.

Jack stared in horror at the four TV screens.

On each of them was a still frame of him taken that morning from a security camera in New York. It showed him in mid-stride, looking desperately behind himself as he ran across the roof of One Tribeca.

Jack's mind reeled.

Right now, at this very moment, his face was on every television in the world.

The voice of Jaeger Eins spoke over his image. '*Good people, you do not know this man, but you should. His name is Captain Jack West Jr. He is a hero, one of the greatest men you have never heard of.*'

He said the word 'hero' derisively.

'*Hello, Jack. You didn't think we would stop, did you? I gather by now you know who we are. The price has been paid so the mark has been made. We will not stop until the warrant on your head has been executed. You should be afraid, Jack, that we are coming for you. No-one has ever outrun the Knights. But do not fret too much. In time, you will come to us.*'

And then, just as quickly as they had been interrupted, all the televisions resumed their regular transmissions.

On a couple of the TVs, the cable news anchors were visibly perplexed and mentioned something about the signal being lost.

If the others hadn't been there with him and seen it happen, Jack would have sworn it had been a dream.

'What just happened?' he said.

Alby said, 'They must have the master codes to *all* the TV satellites in orbit. They then utilised every country's Emergency Broadcast Network and took over the signal. Man, that's power.'

'Jack,' Mae said seriously. 'We're out of our depth. The cities, the weapons, the watchmen, the Knights. We can't figure all this out on our own. We need an insider, someone with specific real knowledge of the royal world, like someone who was, say, the Keeper of the Royal Records for one of the kingdoms.'

Jack knew who she was suggesting.

He threw a look at Zoe. She wouldn't like this at all.

Zoe just nodded. 'Mae's right. Do it.'

Jack pulled out his burner phone and the slip of paper Iolanthe had given him back on the runway at his farm.

He texted:

Need your help on a few royal matters. Are you free to meet? Maybe in England somewhere?

Moments later, his phone pinged with a reply.

Just saw you on TV. Thought I might be hearing from
you. I can meet: I'm in England, researching historical
battles from Marathon to Waterloo.

Zoe cocked her head to the side. 'What does that mean?'

Jack said. 'She's not revealing her location in writing, just in case
someone intercepts this. But I get it. I know where she is.'

He typed:

Done. See you there.

Then he smashed the phone under his boot.

'All right,' he said to the group. 'We split up. Alby and Lily, you
come with me to Venice: I might need some fast Thoth-translating
and an astrophysical mind. Zoe and Mum, you go meet Iolanthe in
England and find out whatever you can about the cities.'

'But where is she?' Mae said.

Jack pulled out a map and showed her.

'Oh,' Mae said.

Minutes later, Alby came over to Jack.

'Jack, given its value, that rubbing of the triangular tablet is
going to be hidden deep inside the Gallerie dell'Accademia. And
that museum is on the Grand Canal in Venice, one of the busiest
tourist districts in the world. How are we going to get in and out
without being spotted?'

Jack showed him a picture from one of Sky Monster's luxury jet
and yacht magazines. 'I thought we'd steal this and use one of its
special features to get inside the museum.'

Alby looked at the picture in the magazine and his mouth fell
open.

'Oh,' he said.

SOMEWHERE IN ENGLAND

Jack's message lingered on the screen of Iolanthe's phone:

Done. See you there.

Iolanthe quickly put the phone down, smashed it and tossed it in a trashcan.

Then she hurried back to her wheeled ladder: it was leaning against some high wooden shelves in a stone-walled medieval library.

She needed to grab as many documents related to the trials as she could find.

She found a parchment from Seville written by King Alfonso X— Alfonso the Wise—that she knew mentioned the Altar of the Cosmos, although here it was called the Altar for the *Rebirth* of the Cosmos.

She also grabbed an original copy of the Book of Genesis. It was the notorious copy that the writers of the King James Bible had rewritten because of its perceived blasphemies and shocking tales.

It contained the original Chapter 22 about the Binding of Isaac— the version in which Abraham actually slaughtered his son, Isaac, at the request of a very vindictive God. For the King James version, the rewriters cleansed the story and sent an angel to stop Abraham at the last second.

Iolanthe stuffed the priceless copy into her bag.

She didn't have much time. She had to be out of here before her brother Orlando got back—

Bang!

She heard one of the outer doors slam open. Damn. She had about ten seconds.

Iolanthe quickly stuffed her recent finds behind some thick books on the shelves and grabbed two random folios as—

Bang!

The heavy studded door to the ancient library was kicked in from the outside, and a squad of armed troops rushed in, followed by . . .

Orlando.

Iolanthe froze on her high ladder, caught in the act, gripping the two folios in her arms.

'Hello, sister,' Orlando said evenly.

'Orlando, I—'

'There is no need for an explanation,' Orlando said. 'You had your chance to stand by my side in the Underworld, and you did not. And now, here, I have seen all I need to see.'

Two of the troopers grabbed Iolanthe roughly by the arms.

Orlando stepped in front of her and stroked her porcelain-smooth cheek.

'So pretty, you are, my darling sister,' he said slowly. 'So very, very pretty.'

Then he slapped her across the face.

'Not for much longer.'

THIRD PURSUIT

THE WATER CITY AND
THE HALL OF RECORDS

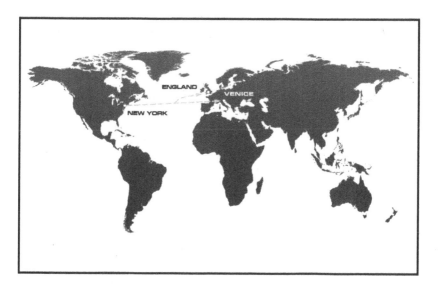

I am the Alpha and the Omega, the First and the Last,
the Beginning and the End.

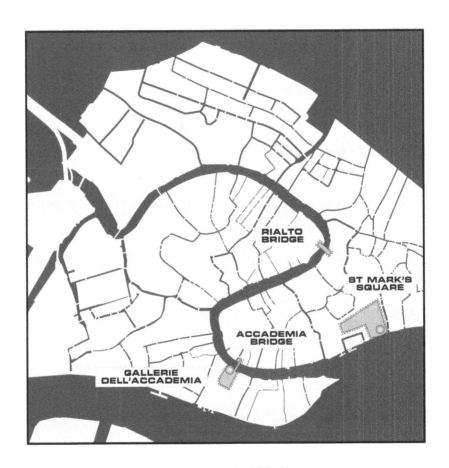

**THE GRAND CANAL
VENICE**

VENICE, ITALY
25 NOVEMBER, 0445 HOURS

The great waterborne city of Venice lay silent in the night.

The waters of the Grand Canal were calm.

The tourist hordes that would descend on the city in a few hours were still fast asleep in their hotels.

Gondolas and water-buses were tied up to their docks. A few delivery boats puttered away, but, forbidden from travelling along the iconic Grand Canal, they made their way through the city via its labyrinthine network of smaller back-canals.

Geographically, Venice sits in a sheltered bay at the top of the Adriatic Sea. The Grand Canal winds its way through the city in a sweeping reverse S-shape and is essentially the spine of the city, from which all the lesser canals spread.

At the northern end of the city, the canal meets Venice's only link to the mainland: a superlong and dead-straight road-bridge that provides train and car access to the island.

At its southern end, beside the soaring red-brick bell tower of St Mark's Basilica, the canal widens dramatically to almost a hundred metres, allowing for larger boat access and innumerable vacation photos.

Historically, Venice is a treasure trove beyond value. From landmarks like St Mark's Square and the Rialto Bridge, to famous citizens like Marco Polo, to the Republic of Venice's storied history as a seagoing superpower and its incredible mastery of living over water, it is a city that is unique in all the world.

And on top of all that, there is Venice's most famous resident, a gentleman known as *Vitruvian Man*.

It is the famous sketch drawn by Leonardo da Vinci showing the human form's dimensions within a square and a circle. It resides in the Gallerie dell'Accademia, deep inside the grand old museum, inside a sunless climate-controlled vault. It is rarely seen. Given its stature and delicacy, the priceless sketch is only brought out for public display approximately once a decade.

But it is not the only document kept deep within the Accademia. For the little-known order of monks who maintain the museum have been avid collectors of many arcane and mysterious objects over the centuries.

That night, if one were looking closely, one would have spotted a majestic 120-foot-long luxury motor yacht anchored just beyond the southern mouth of the Grand Canal.

It was a modern behemoth, sleek in the extreme, painted in metallic maroon and gold and containing every conceivable luxury, including a floatplane mounted on its stern (painted in the exact same colours as the yacht) and a personal submarine in its belly, also painted in gaudy maroon and gold.

Named *Belarus*, the superyacht was the trophy toy of a Russian oligarch who had not yet discovered that it had been stolen from its mooring at his summer home in the Adriatic.

And if one had been looking *extremely* closely that dark night, one would have seen a V-shaped stream of ripples stretching out from the superyacht, heading into the Grand Canal: the telltale sign of a submarine.

The fighter jet–shaped submarine cruised in almost perfect silence though the pitch-black waters of the Grand Canal.

Built by a company called Deep Flight, it was a 'Super Falcon' personal submarine. It seated two people—their heads poking up into individual acrylic domes—and was about the size of two motorcycles attached end to end. It had a long pointed nose and two stub wings that gave it a sleek aerodynamic look.

In the world of super-rich yacht owners, helicopters, floatplanes and speedboats had become passé. The latest thing to own was a personal submarine that launched out of the submerged hull of your yacht.

An inveterate reader of luxury magazines (they were often found in the pilot break-rooms at the exclusive regional airfields that he regularly visited), Sky Monster had told Jack about the *Belarus*, which was how he had known it was moored not far from Venice . . . with its own compact submarine.

His face illuminated by the dim blue glow of the Super Falcon's instruments, Jack guided the little submarine up the Grand Canal. Lily sat in the rear seat behind him, looking out through her own dome.

The Grand Canal was pretty deep near its southern mouth, maybe ten metres or so. But it shallowed as they ventured further into it, to about six metres.

Fortunately, the Gallerie dell'Accademia lay only a few hundred metres into the canal and they reached it quickly.

As they came to the venerable old museum, Jack hit the sub's exterior floodlights and the underwater world of Venice came alive.

'Whoa . . .' Lily breathed. 'You don't see this on the regular gondola tours.'

If, above the surface, Venice is a crazy hodgepodge of buildings that have been built and rebuilt all over each other for almost a thousand years, under the surface it's even crazier.

For while the city sits atop 120 small islands, many of its structures are *not* built directly atop those islands, but rather on pilings and stilts driven into the lagoon floor.

The underwater world of Venice, then, is a hazy maze of stone pillars, crumbling foundations and teetering brick pilings. Steel reinforcement beams have been crudely affixed to the foundations of many of the older buildings to keep them upright. Generally speaking, newer buildings sit flush on the floor of the lagoon, while most of the older ones stand on pilings above it.

'In its earliest days, the citizens of Venice would toss their excrement out their windows into the canals,' Jack said as he guided their little submarine under the museum.

The sleek sub cruised through the murk, banking between barnacle-encrusted pilings, its floodlights sabering through the gloom.

'How hygienic,' Lily said drily.

'Richer folk, however, got rid of their waste in a more discreet way. Their buildings were often fitted with a crude form of toilet— quite literally a *water closet*—a room that had a wide hole in its floor which opened directly onto the water beneath the building. Urine and excrement would be tossed down into it, to be washed away by the tidal flow.'

'Hard to believe Venice was a hotbed for plague and disease,' Lily said.

'True,' Jack said.

He keyed his throat-mike. 'Alby, Sky Monster, how're things up there?'

★ ★ ★

Lingering outside the mouth of the Grand Canal, out by St Mark's Square, Alby and Sky Monster stood on the bridge of the super-yacht, *Belarus.*

It was still dark.

The city of Venice loomed in the night, silent as the grave.

There were no boats, no ferries, no movement.

Alby scanned the sky through a pair of binoculars.

Sky Monster also looked out fearfully. 'Did I ever tell you, Alby, that I hate being on the ground?'

'You've mentioned it, yes.'

He held up his bandaged right forearm, wounded during the Great Games. 'When I'm on the ground, shit like *this* happens to me. But at least you can run when you're on the ground. I think being on water is even worse—'

Jack's voice came in over their earpieces: '*Alby, Sky Monster, how're things up there?*'

'All quiet out here,' Alby replied into his mike.

Jack guided the sub between the Accademia's aged brick pillars.

'Importantly for us,' he said to Lily as he looked up at the dark underside of the museum, 'the Accademia is not only very old, it's also actually a *collection* of old monasteries and wealthy homes that were joined together to form a single museum. One of those monasteries belonged to the Order of St Paul and the monks stayed on as caretakers and cleaners—there!'

He pointed upward.

Lily followed his gaze.

A rectangle of rippling water could be seen above them: it looked like a door in the otherwise black underside of the museum.

'A water closet,' Jack said.

He brought the submarine upward.

★ ★ ★

Jack and Lily's submarine rose inside a tight brick-walled room, its floodlights illuminating the space in a brilliant blue glow.

Jack popped his dome and stepped out. Lily did the same.

The water closet was absolutely covered in dust and cobwebs. A single wooden door led out of it, resolutely closed.

'This room hasn't been opened in years,' Jack whispered.

He went to the door. It was locked from the other side.

But its rusty old hinges were on this side and he made short work of them and within seconds the door was open and Jack and Lily hurried into the darkness of the Gallerie dell'Accademia.

Guided by the beams of their flashlights, they dashed through the silent corridors of the museum's lower levels, passing offices and storerooms that were off limits to the public, until they came to the museum's main vault room.

Whereas everything they had seen till then was old—wooden doors, crumbling walls, worn floors—this was modern.

A glistening steel door with a digital lock guarded the vault room.

Jack used a digital scrambler to overcome the lock and with a deep groaning sound, its heavy door swung open.

The vault, of course, was pitch-black, but as Jack and Lily stepped into it, their flashlight beams landed on the space's central podium.

Jack had seen reproductions of the object lying on the podium hundreds of times, but seeing it in the flesh made him gasp:

Vitruvian Man.

By Leonardo da Vinci.

The famous male nude figure with the mane of shoulder-length hair, standing with his arms and legs spread wide in two positions, touching both a square and a circle. The faded brown parchment on which it had been sketched was almost as famous as the image itself.

Jack had only ever seen it once, during one of its rare public displays, but he had forgotten how small it was. Like most people, he had seen it numerous times as a poster, but the original was far from poster-sized. The great Leonardo had drawn it on a piece of parchment barely larger than a sheet of modern A4-sized paper.

It was, naturally, encased in a frame of bulletproof glass. That frame was thick and it *was* the size of a small poster.

'I'm guessing that glass is also ultraviolet-proof,' Lily said. 'To protect the image from fading.'

There were a few other artefacts in the vault room: an ancient Greek mechanical device that looked like a sextant, a Roman centurion's breastplate and, most striking of all, a grey life-sized stone statue of a man with his hands behind his back and his face pointed skyward in what looked like an agonised scream.

By the wall were three large steel cabinets with wide shallow pull-out drawers: the kind that museums kept sketches and parchments in.

Jack yanked open each drawer quickly, scanning the parchment inside each of them with his flashlight.

He saw sketches and drawings that would be the envy of any other museum: Arabian mathematical formulas, Sumerian engravings, even one star map on a papyrus sheet that was titled in Latin, MAGNUM VIAM PORTAE QVINQVE.

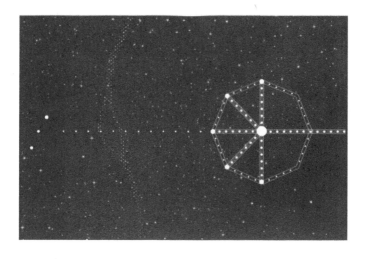

Jack translated: '"*The Five Gates to the Great Labyrinth*". Interesting.'

Lily went to the second cabinet and did the same. Upon opening its third drawer, she exclaimed in an excited whisper, 'Got it!'

Jack came over and gazed at the contents of the drawer.

It was a classic tracing or rubbing: a sheet of thin paper that had once been placed over the triangular tablet and then someone had vigorously rubbed a piece of charcoal across its surface, causing the inscriptions on the stone to be replicated on the paper in white on black.

Jack and Lily beheld the complete tablet:

Jack's eyes zoomed to the bottom-right corner of the triangular image, the part that was missing in real life. There were glyphs there written in the Word of Thoth.

'What does it say?' he asked. 'Is it about the third city?'

Lily scanned it. 'Yes, but . . . oh . . .'

'What?' Jack said, alarmed.

Lily said, 'It says:

The third, Atlas's mighty citadel, holds back the ocean.

*But beware. Begin not your quest until you have
companions at all three cities.*

*For when you open the first, you open the second and
the third.'*

She turned to face Jack. 'Orlando said he was going to the first city, Thule, *right away*. I don't know what's going to happen, but if he opens Thule, he triggers Ra and Atlas, too.'

'This is not good,' Jack said.

'No, it isn't,' a deep voice said from the darkness behind them. 'Not at all, fifth greatest warrior.'

Jack and Lily spun.

They hadn't even heard them enter the vault.

Five men dressed in hooded robes stood calmly behind them, blocking the exit.

Their robes were striking: off-white on the outside but blood-red on the insides of their hoods. The five men also wore ornate chains around their necks from which hung curious bronze-and-glass pendants.

But it was the glares of the five men that struck Jack.

They were piercing, deadly.

Their hands were drawn up into the folds of their sleeves. Whether they held weapons or not was an open question.

Jack's right hand hovered over his thigh-holster, but he didn't draw his gun. Yet.

The leader of the group of monks stepped forward. He was in his forties and he had pale flaky skin. His vivid blue eyes darted ever-so-briefly to Jack's hovering gun hand.

When he spoke, his voice echoed in the vault room.

'Captain Jack West Jr,' he said evenly, 'the fifth warrior, unexpected winner of the Great Games and singular disrupter of a royal system that has governed this planet for five thousand years.

'It is nice to finally meet you in the flesh. We have been hearing of your exploits for some time now: the finding of the capstone of the Great Pyramid, the decoding of the six Ramesean Stones. Correct me if I am wrong, but you were once known by the nickname Huntsman, after the variety of spider, were you not?'

'I was,' Jack said warily.

'Well, Captain, you have just entered the web of some infinitely more dangerous creatures.'

The leader smiled. It was a truly sinister grin.

Then the two monks nearest to him removed their hands from their sleeves to reveal fully automatic Glock 19 pistols with long 33-round high-capacity magazines jammed into their grips.

Jack's eyes locked onto the Glocks.

On full auto, those two pistols could tear him and Lily apart in about three seconds.

He was glad he hadn't drawn his pistol and he didn't dare reach for it now.

What he did do was twist his chin ever so slightly, triggering the throat-microphone he wore around his neck.

On the *Belarus*, Alby and Sky Monster heard the click of Jack's radio coming online.

'And this, I assume, is the Oracle . . .' a stranger's voice said. '. . . The one you raised as your own and named Lily.'

'Damn it. They're in trouble,' Alby said to Sky Monster.

He keyed the radio. 'Sit tight, Jack. We're on our way.' Then to Sky Monster: 'Let's move.'

The leader of the monks gazed at Lily.

'I am,' Lily replied.

The monk made a strange face, as if wincing.

'You may call me High Brother Ezekiel. I am, for want of a better title, the leader of our brotherhood.'

He began to pace slowly in front of Jack and Lily.

'Ours is a very old and very private order within the Catholic Church. We are not smug intellectuals like the Jesuits. Nor are we sanctimonious prudes like the Franciscans. Nor are we vocal. We live away from the world and keep our opinions and our code to ourselves, and so the greater Church leaves us alone.'

As he spoke, the leader fingered the bronze-and-glass pendant hanging around his neck.

Jack noticed that it was actually a very small hourglass and inside its lower glass bulb was a strange dark-grey powder.

The leader went on. 'To those who are aware of us, we are known as the Fraternal Order of St Paul, quiet and humble experts in holy art and antiquities, devotees of the doctrine of St Paul, and the non-speaking cleaners of this establishment.'

He stopped walking and his glare became severe.

'But to the more select audience of the royal world, we are known as the Order of the Omega. Studying the Omega Event, the end-times, is our calling, our focus, our reason for being. You have defiled our innermost sanctum. Can you explain yourself?'

Lily said, 'We were searching for—'

'*Do not speak!*' Ezekiel barked, almost squealing in his explosive anger.

Lily took a guarded step backwards.

Ezekiel regathered himself and whispered, '"*Do not permit a woman to speak or to have authority over a man; she must be silent.*"'

Jack recognised the quote instantly.

It was from the Bible, from the writings of St Paul, the notorious woman-hater, and suddenly the 'doctrine' of the Fraternal Order of St Paul became clear to him.

Ezekiel looked up again. 'The female voice is a foul and disgusting thing. It is offensive to our ears. Profane. God himself did not wish for women to speak, so why should we hear it?'

He looked hard at Lily. 'Woman was put on this Earth to bear children for Man or, if not, then to serve him with total and silent obedience. That is how the nuns function here. I was not addressing you, young lady. Further to that, if I am speaking, you can presume that I am *not* speaking to you.'

Lily's eyes went wide.

'I think someone's been living away from the world a little too long,' Jack muttered.

Brother Ezekiel glared at him. 'I said, can you explain yourself?'

Jack took a deep breath. 'We are trying to overcome the Trials and thus avert the Omega Event. To that end, we are searching for anything that mentions the Mysteries and thus informs us about what must be done at the three secret cities. We became aware of this rubbing and so we came to see it.'

'Why didn't you just ask us if you could examine it?'

'We were told that you were—' Jack hesitated. 'That you were . . . extremely possessive of your treasures.'

Ezekiel smiled thinly again.

'You were well advised,' he said. 'We have killed intruders for less.'

He nodded at the life-sized stone statue next to Jack: the one of a man with his hands behind his back and his face pointed skyward in a silent scream.

At first Jack didn't get it.

Then, looking more closely at the statue, he saw that the man-shaped statue hadn't been *carved* into that shape.

No, the black-grey stone looked like cement, cement that had been *poured*—poured over a man while his hands had been bound behind his back. Then the liquid stone had set and dried in that shape.

There was a man inside that stone statue.

The monks had entombed him in the stone. If he hadn't died during the pouring, he would have died an agonising death inside it, slowly suffocating or, worse, starving.

And suddenly Jack recognised the black-grey stone.

He had seen this material before: in the Underworld, during the Games. This same 'liquid stone' had been used to execute the hostages of the champions.

'Are you going to kill us?' he asked, swallowing.

'Normally, we would, and we would take great pleasure in it,' Ezekiel said. 'But not today. There are considerable prices on both of your heads. When they realised you were coming here, the Knights of the Golden Eight called us . . .'

Jack felt his blood run cold.

'. . . and asked that we hold you till they arrived.'

At that moment, Lily and Jack heard a monstrous roar from somewhere overhead and looked up.

It was the sound of an aeroplane—a large aeroplane—coming in low over the Gallerie dell'Accademia.

'That sounds like them now,' Brother Ezekiel said.

It was still before dawn in Venice, so only a handful of early risers saw it.

And, boy, was it a sight.

A big CL-130 Hercules military plane came thundering in low over Venice from the north, before sweeping around into a banking turn directly above the lower end of the Grand Canal . . .

. . . where it suddenly released three parachuted men from its open rear ramp.

A trio of directional parachutes blossomed above the canal and proceeded to speed down toward the city in fast diagonal flight-paths, heading right for the Gallerie dell'Accademia.

The Hercules itself kept going for a short distance before it banked again, this time performing a wide U-turn and beginning a descent designed for a water landing *right in the mouth* of the Grand Canal.

For this was no ordinary Hercules. The letters 'CL' designated it as the fabled amphibious version of the classic military plane: this Hercules had a curved underbelly and pontoons hanging from its wings, making it capable of water landings and take-offs.

One of the handful of people who witnessed the Hercules's extra-ordinary descent toward Venice was Alby, standing on the bridge of the now-speeding *Belarus*.

'Jesus Christ,' he breathed as he watched the three paratroopers glide swiftly in the direction of the Accademia.

As the paratroopers descended on the museum in front of him, and the Hercules swooped down toward the water's surface behind him, Alby's Russian-owned superyacht raced into the Grand Canal.

The *Belarus*'s powerful twin engines created a gigantic wash behind it as the enormous powerboat shot past the Basilica di Santa Maria della Salute at the mouth of the Grand Canal and raced toward the Accademia three hundred metres away.

'Jack!' Alby called into his radio-mike, 'you got three paratroopers inbound to your location. ETA: maybe three minutes.'

As Sky Monster drove the boat hard, Alby kept watch on the sky.

Ahead of them, the three paratroopers landed on the square in front of the Gallerie dell'Accademia.

Behind him, the dawning sky was filled by the shadow of the incoming amphibious Hercules.

'Drive faster, Sky Monster!' Alby yelled above the howling wind. 'Get there!'

The Hercules touched down on the Grand Canal right between St Mark's Tower and the Basilica di Santa Maria—and only a hundred metres behind the speeding superyacht driven by Sky Monster and Alby.

It then proceeded to roar *right up the Grand Canal itself*, its wingtips almost touching the multicoloured buildings on either side of the broad waterway.

Both vessels—the megayacht and the seaplane—produced surging bow waves that sloshed wildly against the foundations of the buildings flanking the canal. Such bow waves, had they been made by any other kind of boat, would have incurred hefty fines for the vessels' owners.

The *Belarus* sped up the Grand Canal, chased by the Hercules, perhaps the only seagoing vessel that could make the *Belarus* seem small.

The superyacht arrived at a small dock in front of the Accademia—metres short of the wooden footbridge that spanned the Grand Canal right in front of the museum. It practically skidded to a halt, kicking up a fierce side wave.

Alby and Sky Monster leapt out of it, not even bothering to tie it up or drop the anchor.

The front doors of the Accademia museum lay open.

Three empty parachutes lay on the small piazza in front of them.

Alby dashed for the museum. 'Figure out a way to get us out of here, Sky Monster! I'm going after Jack and Lily!'

Seconds later, the giant Hercules seaplane, its engines roaring, its colossal bulk almost filling the Grand Canal, just crunched *right over* the megayacht, hitting it perfectly amidships, the plane's reinforced nose smashing right through the yacht's flank like it was made of tissue paper.

As if cruising down the Grand Canal weren't brazen enough, now it had just bulldozed right over a $200-million superyacht.

The *Belarus* crumpled under the weight of the massive seaplane.

It folded in its middle, causing its bow and stern to be hoisted high into the air. Then, parked alongside the Venetian dock, right up against the wooden footbridge, with a Hercules seaplane sitting across its crushed waist, the luxury motor yacht began to sink.

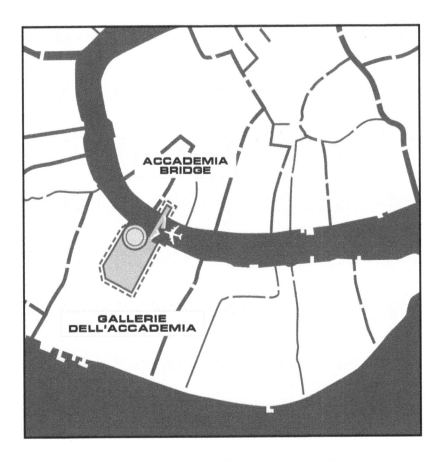

ACCADEMIA
BRIDGE

GALLERIE
DELL'ACCADEMIA

**THE MUSEUM, THE GRAND CANAL
AND THE HERCULES**

Inside the vault room deep within the bowels of the Gallerie dell'Accademia, Jack and Lily were still surrounded by the five monks of the Order of the Omega.

Jack had heard Alby's warnings through his earpiece: three paratroopers, most likely members of the Golden Eight, were close. And he and Lily were stuck here.

He looked around himself for something, anything, he could use.

And he saw it.

Maybe . . .

'Lily,' he whispered. 'When I do what I'm gonna do, get behind me, okay.'

'Do *what*?' she hissed.

'This.'

Then, like a Wild West gunslinger, Jack drew his pistol from his thigh-holster and fired it into the chest of one of the two monks armed with the 33-round automatic Glocks.

That monk dropped like a sack of shit.

Shocked by Jack's lightning-fast move, the second one turned and opened fire with his modified Glock, right at Jack.

The pistol unleashed a withering burst of automatic gunfire, echoing loudly in the tight space of the vault room, expelling its thirty-three rounds in a brutal second-and-a-half.

There was no way Jack could get out of the way.

But then that hadn't been his plan.

★ ★ ★

As soon as he'd killed the first monk, Jack had reached out to his right and snatched up the most valuable masterpiece in the room—

—Da Vinci's *Vitruvian Man*—

—and held it up in front of himself like a shield!

Lily, as instructed, dived behind him.

The second monk's spray of gunfire *slammed* into the sketch's bulletproof-glass frame and bounced off it in what seemed like a million sparks. Two of the shots hit Jack's gloved hand gripping the glass shield: but it was his left hand, which like the forearm above it, was made of titanium.

And then the monk's clip was empty and Jack levelled his pistol over the top of *Vitruvian Man*, and with two booming shots, dropped him.

The three other monks, including the leader Ezekiel, scattered, and suddenly Jack and Lily were racing out of the vault room.

'Shut the door!' Jack called as they hurried out.

Lily hit a switch and the heavy vault door *whoosh*ed shut behind them, locking the remaining monks inside.

Through the museum they ran.

Sirens began to blare.

Yellow emergency lights spun.

Up a stairwell, then down two hallways lined with priceless works of art. Around another corner and—

—the three-hundred-year-old painting on the wall beside them was shredded with machine-gun fire.

Two black-clad, ceramic-masked paratroopers were charging down the corridor toward them: it was definitely the Knights of the Golden Eight again.

'Jack! Lily!' someone called from their right and they saw Alby down another corridor, standing at an open window, waving at them. 'This way!'

Jack pushed Lily toward Alby—

—just as a thick-barred security grille came rushing down from the ceiling, landing with a clang against the floor *right between* Jack and Lily.

They were separated.

'No,' Lily gasped from the outer side of the grille, Alby's side.

'Go,' Jack said. 'Please. I'll catch up.'

The look in Lily's eyes showed that she didn't like this at all, but she knew she had no choice.

'I love you, Dad,' she said as she took off down the corridor.

With the two paratroopers advancing, Jack slipped into a nearby stairwell.

Alby and Lily leapt down from the open window, landing in a narrow cobblestoned alleyway that ran down the side of the Gallerie dell'Accademia. Dim streetlights lit the alley in a sickly yellow glow.

At one end of the alley lay the Grand Canal, at the other, a maze of smaller alleyways.

'Their plane is on the Grand Canal,' Alby said. 'We have to go into the alleys and disappear—'

'Hold it right there,' a dark figure said, emerging from a side alley filled with dumpsters, leading with his MP-9 submachine gun.

The third Golden Eight paratrooper.

'You two shits are lucky the price on your heads demands you be brought in alive,' the paratrooper said, his accent French. 'Hands where I can see them.'

Defeated, Alby and Lily placed their hands on their heads.

'Who are you working for?' Lily demanded.

'We work for a royal gentleman. One who harbours a burning rage against you and your father; although we can bring your father in dead.' The paratrooper jerked his gun in the direction of the Grand Canal. 'Move. This way—'

Whack. The paratrooper was struck from behind—with a pipe—by someone else in the dark side alley.

Sky Monster stepped out of the shadows.

'This is why I hate being on the ground,' he said. He keyed his radio. 'Jack, I have the kids. We're on the south side of the Accademia. How the hell do we get out of here?'

Jack's voice came over his earpiece. '*On the Russian dude's floatplane.*'

'The one on the stern of the *Belarus*? Last I saw, it was on the boat when the bad guys rammed right over it.'

'*I'm on the roof of the museum and I have a visual on it. It's still in the game, which means so are we.*'

Huddled behind the front corner of the museum, Sky Monster, Alby and Lily peered across the small piazza in front of the Gallerie dell'Accademia.

In the dim early-morning light, they saw the Hercules seaplane parked near the dock there, on top of the wreck of the Russian superyacht, the *Belarus*.

The superyacht had been cut cleanly in half by the colossal weight of the Hercules, broken into two pieces.

Those two pieces had now settled on the bottom of the Grand Canal, but given that the canal was only six metres deep here and the *Belarus*'s main deck usually rose about six metres above the waterline, its floatplane now sat perfectly level with the surface, still tied down to the stern of the yacht.

Despite the horrible wreckage all around it, the plane was entirely undamaged, fresh as a daisy, its maroon-and-gold flanks still as shiny as the day they had been painted.

'Huh,' Sky Monster said, seeing it. 'How about that?'

Police sirens cut through the silence.

Four blue patrol boats with 'POLIZIA' on their hulls and flashing lights on their roofs were rushing down the canal—two from each end—converging on the bizarre sight of the Hercules on top of the demolished superyacht.

The Knights of the Golden Eight were nowhere to be seen.

'Jack, I see the floatplane!' Sky Monster said into his radio.

'*Go now. I'll cover you,*' Jack's voice said.

Sky Monster, Alby and Lily broke cover and dashed across the piazza.

As they did so, a Knight appeared in the cockpit windows of the Hercules—the pilot, no doubt, who'd stayed with his plane while the other Knights had gone inside—and extended a pistol at them . . . just as the fuselage of the plane all around him erupted in bullet-sparks, from shots fired by Jack on the roof of the Accademia.

The pilot took cover inside his plane while Sky Monster, Lily and Alby hustled safely past him, hopscotching off the dock onto the wreckage of the *Belarus*.

They quickly unlatched the straps tying down the floatplane on the superyacht's stern and climbed inside it.

Sky Monster silently marvelled at the controls of the little plane. It was a single-engined Piper PA-18 150 Super Cub—a classic lightweight plane mounted on two long pontoons—only this one came with all the options and it appeared to be brand new. The controls were spotless. It even had a new-car smell.

Within seconds, he had the nose propeller of the Piper sputtering to life before—*voom!*—it began blurring with speed.

Then he guided the floatplane away from the wreck of the superyacht, edging it between the Hercules and the footbridge in front of the Accademia.

But the pilot of the Hercules wasn't going to just let this happen.

For, right then, the gigantic Hercules powered up and—completely ignoring the incoming police boats and the bleary-eyed people opening their windows on the shore—it began to move.

Engines rumbling, it jerked backwards, reversing its awesome bulk off the wreckage of the *Belarus* with a series of loud crunching sounds.

Then, slowly, it began to rotate laterally on the surface of the Grand Canal, turning to the right, its nose following the movement of the little Piper.

'Jack! Where are you!' Sky Monster yelled into his radio.

He had to keep the floatplane moving—or else the Hercules was going to box them in by slamming its nose into the walls on the opposite shore.

'*Don't wait for me!*' Jack's voice replied. '*Either I'll catch up now or I'll catch up later. You have to get Lily and Alby away.*'

'There he is!' Lily pointed.

Like a bullet out of a gun, Jack came sprinting out of an alley on the northern side of the museum, running for all he was worth . . .

. . . at the same time as two Knights of the Golden Eight appeared in the front doors of the Accademia and opened fire, their bullets chasing Jack, strafing the ground at his feet, peppering the wooden rails of the footbridge as he raced up it.

By this time the Hercules, still rotating, was right beside the high wooden footbridge.

It was almost perfectly side-on to the direction of the Grand Canal now, its nose only metres away from the northern shore. If it touched that shore, it would block the floatplane from escaping.

But Sky Monster pushed forward on his thrusters and the little maroon-and-gold Piper squeezed in front of the Hercules's nose, its left wingtip scraping the wall of a building on the northern shore, and suddenly the floatplane was out in the open with a clear view of the mouth of the canal ahead of it.

'Jack?' he called. 'Last chance!'

'*Coming!*'

While Sky Monster had been squeezing past the nose of the turning Hercules, Jack had been racing up onto the footbridge.

He dashed around a small Italian Tourism Bureau information kiosk on the bridge just as the kiosk was pummelled by gunfire.

Jack then danced up onto the railing at the same moment that the turning Hercules's left wing came within a few feet of the footbridge . . .

. . . and without missing a step, he leapt off the railing, diving onto the wing of the moving Hercules.

Jack landed with a graceless *thump* on the wing of the military plane and quickly scrambled to his feet. Then he ran forward, along the roof of the massive plane—just as Sky Monster brought

the Piper past the Hercules's nose—and took three bounding steps over the Hercules's cockpit and dived full-length off its nose . . .

. . . down onto the roof of the floatplane!

He had run completely over the Hercules.

'Holy shit . . .' Sky Monster gasped, looking up.

'*Punch it!*' Jack called, lying flat on the roof of the floatplane.

Sky Monster jammed the thrusters forward.

While Jack had been running over the top of the Hercules, the two Knights of the Golden Eight who had fired at him from the entrance to the museum took off after him.

One leapt *into* the Hercules via its rear loading ramp while the second Knight was stopped by a Venetian police boat.

'*Tu! Fermare!*' two Italian cops on the boat yelled.

The Knight gunned them down.

Then he stepped into their police boat, tossed their bodies overboard and took off after the Hercules and the Piper.

The Piper shot away down the Grand Canal with the Hercules surging along the surface behind it in hot pursuit.

It was a race now between two wildly different aircraft: the little Piper was nimble, with rapid acceleration but less overall speed; the Hercules was big and bulky, and thus slower to speed up, but once it attained planing speed, it would easily run down the smaller floatplane.

The Piper picked up speed as it careened down the Grand Canal with Jack West Jr on top of its right shoulder, the colourful buildings of Venice rushing by on either side of it.

It was heading for the end of the Grand Canal and the few hundred metres of clear water it needed to take off.

The Hercules roared along behind it—outrageously huge, and gaining.

Behind the Hercules, their lights flashing and sirens wailing, were the Venetian police boats, trying to keep up.

As the Piper skimmed along the surface, the tiny figure of Jack could be seen on top of it—lying on his belly, the wind buffeting him, hanging on for dear life.

Then the floatplane's pontoons began to skim faster on the surface, lifting ever so slightly.

'We just hit planing speed!' Sky Monster called, grinning. 'We're gonna make it!'

It was right then that two Italian Army AW129 Mangusta attack helicopters—the Italian equivalent of the Apache—swooped into position in front of the fleeing floatplane, hovering menacingly above the exit to the Grand Canal.

More Knights.

'Oh, *shit* . . .' Jack gasped, seeing them.

The two choppers opened fire with their cannons.

Superhot tracer fire strafed the water all around the speeding Piper. Bullets sliced past Jack's head, missing him by inches.

Beside him, the Piper's right wing was shredded. Its tip was blasted apart and suddenly the wing was a metre shorter than it was supposed to be.

The floatplane immediately lost all lift, and with its right wing cactus, it swung wildly to the left.

Sky Monster grappled with the controls.

'Damn it!' he yelled. 'We can't take off anymore—'

At that moment, an absolutely shocking salvo of tracer fire from one of the attack choppers came roaring in through the little floatplane's forward windscreen.

The whole windscreen exploded with cracks, instantly *annihilated* by the sizzling gunfire.

Glass rained into the cockpit.

Alby and Lily ducked as the tracer fire shredded their seat backs.

Sky Monster dropped, too, but not by choice: he was thrown backwards when a high-velocity tracer round slammed into his left shoulder and went right through it. His blood exploded all over the inside of the cockpit.

Now pilotless, the Piper wheeled unchecked to the left.

Alby yanked Sky Monster from his seat, took the controls and gunned the engines.

'Jack!' he yelled into his radio. 'Sky Monster's hit! What do we do!'

'*Go back!*' Jack's voice said in his earpiece. '*Back into the city! Our only chance is to lose them in the canals!*'

The scene on the Grand Canal was now one of pure mayhem.

The Piper—trying to outrun the Hercules and the police boats, and with the two Mangusta attack choppers in front of it—turned in a fast banking arc to the left, skimming on its pontoons and kicking up spray.

As it did so, the Hercules turned, too, again trying to block the way with its nose.

But the Piper was too quick and it shot past the Hercules's bow and zoomed back up the Grand Canal, now heading *toward* the footbridge in front of the Gallerie dell'Accademia . . . with Jack on its roof, blood all over the insides of its windows, and the two Mangustas in pursuit.

The Hercules finished its turn and powered up angrily.

The big seaplane gained speed quickly and soon it was thundering along behind the wounded Piper, its massive nose edging closer and closer to the little plane's tail.

The Hercules had a wingspan of about forty metres and the Grand Canal at this point narrowed to a width of about fifty, so the great plane almost filled it entirely as it roared up its length, chasing the fleeing floatplane.

On the roof of the Piper, Jack turned and saw the Hercules, impossibly huge, its engines roaring, *right behind them*, barely ten feet away.

It was going to run them down.

Jack drew his pistol and fired it back at the cockpit of the Hercules.

His bullets pinged uselessly off the big plane's metal hide. One round cracked the windshield but that was all.

Alby called, 'Jack! Hang on! This is gonna be close!'

Jack snapped to look forward in time to see the wooden footbridge in front of the Accademia rushing at him.

Whoosh!

The Piper shot under the soaring wooden bridge, whipping beneath it.

A half-second later, the Hercules *smashed right through* the footbridge!

The eighty-year-old wooden bridge was blasted into a million splinters as the mighty plane burst through it and kept on coming after the Piper.

'Are you kidding me?' Jack's eyes boggled.

The two amphibious planes banked to the right, following the sweeping curve of the Grand Canal as it headed deeper into Venice, the roars of their engines tearing through the pre-dawn silence.

Then they rounded the long sweeping bend fully and burst out onto a straighter section of the canal and Jack beheld the iconic Rialto Bridge up ahead: the gorgeous 400-year-old single-span white stone bridge with its famous multi-arched portico. There was no way the Hercules could blast through that—it would be way too strong—but at their current speed, they weren't going to make it there anyway.

'Alby! We gotta get off this main road! Cut left into that side canal!'

In the blood-smeared cockpit below Jack, Alby drove while Lily yanked open a first-aid kit and got to work on Sky Monster. The big-bearded pilot's shoulder was a mess of blood and torn fabric and his face was going seriously pale.

Alby looked left and saw several narrow side canals branching off the larger Grand Canal.

One seemed a little wider than the others, maybe twenty feet across. But the Piper's wingspan was—

'Jack! We're not gonna fit!'

On the roof of the Piper, Jack was peering fearfully back at the Hercules, rising up behind them, outrageously close.

'It's the only way we'll get clear! Do it!'

'You asked for it!'

With a grim shake of his head, Alby yanked the little Piper hard to the left, a millisecond before it was going to be hit by the bow of the Hercules, and the Piper skipped across the surface of the Grand Canal and, with its thirty-five-foot wingspan, rocketed into the twenty-foot-wide side canal.

The tips of both wings of the speeding Piper were shorn off in an instant as the little floatplane shot into the side canal at blistering speed.

One second they were there, the next they were not.

Sparks flew, fibreglass shattered and suddenly the plane had two stub-wings instead of real ones.

Jack ducked his head as the Piper zoomed into the deeper darkness of the side canal, still travelling at phenomenal speed, kicking up a churning wake in the narrow confines of the canal.

Behind them, the big Hercules overshot the side canal and rumbled to a halt—

—but the open-topped police boat immediately behind it—the one containing the Knight—didn't.

It rushed into the tight canal, the Knight at its helm resting his MP-9 on its windshield and blazing away.

Alby steered gamely with the Piper's rudder, banking and weaving past parked boats and gondolas. This canal had all manner of things jutting out into it: terracotta windowsills with flowers in them, wrought-iron signs and lampposts. Trying to put space between them and their pursuer, he blasted right through one windowsill, smashing it to smithereens.

But it was no use. The police boat was built for exactly this sort of thing: it was both faster and more agile than the half-wrecked Piper, and it stuck to them like glue.

★ ★ ★

Out on the Grand Canal, entirely unbothered by the lights in the homes and hotels that were coming on all around it, the Hercules rotated once again on the surface of the urban river.

It had gone as far as it could.

But the Mangusta attack choppers hadn't.

They roared over the Hercules, thundering over the winding maze of side canals into which the Piper had fled, their searchlights blazing.

In the tight confines of the side canal, the police boat zoomed right up behind the Piper's tailfin.

On the roof of the Piper, with the walls of the canal rushing by on either side of him, Jack took in the situation.

'Alby, Lily!' he called into his radio-mike. 'We need to get out of Venice or disappear *into* it before the sun fully rises and patch up Sky Monster. Which means getting away from this asshole or at least—'

He cut himself off.

'*At least what, Dad?*' Lily said.

Jack heard the deafening *whump-whump-whump* of helicopter rotors overhead and glimpsed the shadows of the two Mangusta choppers prowling above the rooftops, peering down into the canals with their searchlights.

It made his decision for him.

'Or at least taking his boat,' he said.

And so he did.

Without any further thought, Jack rose into a crouch, took four quick steps down the roof of the Piper and then launched himself off its tail, hurling himself at the police boat rushing down the narrow canal right behind it.

Jack hung in the air for a brief moment before he came smashing down against the windshield of the police boat, leading with his back.

The glass was safety glass, so instead of shattering, it broke out into a spiderweb of cracks, acting like a net, and it caught Jack perfectly.

The Knight driving the police boat couldn't have been more shocked.

Jack dived over the windshield and crash-tackled him to the floor, parrying his gun away.

The police boat kept on going—its thrusters still pushed forward—shooting down the tight canal, caroming off its concrete walls.

The Knight was a tough bastard and he unleashed a couple of high kicks at Jack, but Jack ducked under them, grabbed him by the lapels and pushed him upward—

—at the exact moment the open-topped boat rushed under a bridge spanning the canal and the Knight struck it and was swept out of sight.

And suddenly the boat was Jack's.

'Alby!' he called into his radio. 'Slow up! I'll come alongside. Let's get everyone onto this boat.'

'*Copy that, Jack.*'

Moments later, still hidden from the choppers by the high walls of the canal, Jack pulled his boat alongside the beaten-up Piper.

The two watercraft kept moving, drifting side-by-side up the canal.

Lily kicked open the side door of the floatplane and leapt nimbly across onto the police boat.

'Pass him over,' she said to Alby.

Moving awkwardly inside the little plane, Alby pushed the wounded Sky Monster out through its side door and into the waiting arms of Jack and Lily.

Sky Monster groaned.

'You okay, buddy?' Jack said as he took his friend's weight and saw the blood all over his left shoulder.

'Hate being . . . on the ground . . .' Sky Monster mumbled.

Jack and Lily gently lowered him into the rear seat of the police boat.

Then Jack turned to Alby, still in the floatplane, and reached out a helping hand. 'Okay, Alby, come on over—'

A beam of blinding light and a barrage of tracer rounds sliced between them.

It had come from behind them, the bullets carving a withering line up the length of the narrow canal—strafing the water, kicking up spray—a line that sheared right *between* the Piper and the police boat, almost chopping off Jack's outstretched hand.

Both Jack and Alby fell back into their respective watercraft. In the police boat, Lily dived on top of Sky Monster, covering him.

One of the enemy choppers had spotted them and had lowered itself into a small intersection a hundred metres behind them—the only space wide enough for it to fit.

It now hovered barely four feet above the water, its rotors roaring, its nose-mounted cannon blazing forth a terrible tongue of fire.

And then its razing gunfire hit the pontoons of the floatplane, blowing them clean off, and with a jerk, the Piper's cabin dropped into the water, landing with a splash on its belly.

Still inside the Piper, Alby was thrown sideways, and to his horror, the battered floatplane—now both wingless *and* pontoonless—began sinking into the canal while Jack's police boat kept drifting onward.

On the police boat, Jack and Lily both raised their heads to see the Piper dead in the water ten metres behind them.

Jack leapt into the driver's seat. 'We gotta get back to him—'

More gunfire peppered the water around his boat, strafing its hood.

The second chopper—no doubt called in by the first—had lowered itself into the next major intersection a hundred metres *ahead* of them.

They were sitting ducks, caught between the two choppers.

'*Jack!*' Alby's voice exploded in his earpiece. '*Get out of here! They said they have to take me alive, but they'll kill you if you stay! Go!*'

Jack swapped a look with Lily. He didn't want to do it, but he knew it was the right choice.

Lily nodded. 'We have to.'

Jack gunned the engines of the police boat and swung it into a tiny cross-canal, out of the line of fire.

'Hang in there, Alby,' he said. 'We'll find you.'

He ducked and weaved through several canals before arriving at a covered dock, where with Lily's help, he carried Sky Monster onto land, through some courtyards and a church, disappearing into the rabbit warren of Venice's alleyways until they came to an abandoned, derelict hotel that would suffice as a place to hide.

When they were safely inside the crumbling hotel, Jack fell to the floor, breathless.

'Fuck,' he said. 'Fuck, fuck, fuck.'

Back in the side canal, covered by the two choppers, Alby climbed on top of the now fully sunken, stationary Piper.

There was nowhere he could go: the walls on either side of him were sheer, the next bridge too far away.

A second Venetian police boat approached his immobile plane slowly.

In it were Jaeger Eins and two of his Knights, dressed in their black combat gear. There was fresh blood on their boat's gunwales.

At the sight of Alby stranded on the remains of the floatplane, Eins smiled.

'Hello, Albert,' he said. 'Have no fear, Captain West and his adopted daughter will be joining you soon. I have seen his weakness and I intend to exploit it. In the meantime, you will come with us. There is someone who would really like to talk with you.'

A short time later, as the first full rays of dawn hit the city of Venice, the Hercules took off from the southern end of the Grand Canal, soaring away into the sky, leaving all manner of death, wreckage and destruction in its wake and carrying Alby Calvin in its belly.

From the rooftop balcony of his abandoned hotel deep inside the dense western sector of the city, Jack watched it go.

Lily stood by his side, gazing anxiously at the plane taking Alby away.

Behind them, Sky Monster lay in a rusty old bed, his eyes closed, his left shoulder bandaged.

Jack stared intently at the departing plane.

'The Knights of the Golden Eight,' he said grimly. 'If we're going to save Alby, we need to find their base.'

'How are we going to do that?' Lily asked.

Jack turned to face her. 'My mother was right. We're outmatched information-wise. We need help. Someone who knows the royal world in detail. We need Iolanthe. Hopefully, Mum and Zoe have found her.'

**ST MICHAEL'S MOUNT
CORNWALL, ENGLAND**

MOUNT'S BAY
CORNWALL, ENGLAND
25 NOVEMBER, 0900 HOURS

After flying into the U.K. from New York, Zoe and Mae had taken the overnight train from London to get here.

Known as Land's End, Cornwall lies at the very bottom of England, at its remote southwestern corner. The region is home to several historic places, including St Ives, Penzance and, apparently, the Hall of Royal Records.

It was a cryptic reference in Iolanthe's text message that had brought them here.

> I'm in England, researching historical battles from Marathon to Waterloo.

Jack had figured it out. '"*I know the kings of England, and I quote the fights historical / From Marathon to Waterloo, in order categorical*",' he had said to Mae before they had parted. 'It's a line from the Gilbert and Sullivan musical, *The Pirates of Penzance*. Iolanthe is directing us to Penzance and the historic castle near there.'

'Oh,' Mae had said, realising. 'St Michael's Mount . . .' she'd added, a little bit of awe creeping into her voice.

St Michael's Mount is one of two striking islands dedicated to the archangel Michael that stand on opposite sides of the

English Channel: it sits on the coast of Cornwall while over in France one finds its twin, Mont Saint-Michel.

Both are large tidal islands whose causeways get flooded at high tide. And both bear on their peaks impressive medieval structures: the French island features a fabulous, towering, many-levelled and multi-spired cathedral that looks like something out of *The Lord of the Rings*.

St Michael's Mount, on the other hand, is far more English.

There are no fairytale spires to be found on it. No fabulous towers. Rather, it bears a stout, square and sturdy castle on its back, one that has stood for eight hundred years and which has been owned by the same aristocratic family, the St Aubyns, for most of that time. Its mighty walls are pale grey, almost white.

Old, enigmatic and owned by the bluest of blue-blood families, it was a perfect candidate to house Iolanthe's place of work, the Hall of Royal Records.

Zoe and Mae stood on the shore of Mount's Bay, gazing out at St Michael's Mount.

Its curving cobblestone causeway stretched away from them for several hundred metres before arriving at the island. The island had a pier and a little village at its base, then a pleasant forest climbing its steep slopes, before, standing proudly above it all, one found the castle.

'Pretty cool, huh?' said the young red-haired man standing beside them. 'Best place to run in the event of a zombie apocalypse, in my humble opinion. It's very well defended: vertical walls and cliff faces, and the causeway disappears under the incoming tide, although that assumes your zombies can't breathe underwater.'

'Thanks for that, Julius,' Zoe said. 'You always know the best way to reduce something to a zombie apocalypse.'

Julius Adamson smiled brightly at that.

He had met them when they landed at Gatwick the night before and taken the overnight train with them. Today he wore an R2-D2 hoodie over a t-shirt that read 'USCSS NOSTROMO' (Neither Zoe nor Mae got that movie reference.) His twin brother, Lachlan, had not been able to join them on this occasion: he had family commitments in London.

For their part, Zoe and Mae wore more regular British tourist attire: blue jeans and a West Ham soccer jersey for Zoe and a large straw hat, floral blouse and sandals for Mae.

Tagging along behind a gaggle of morning tourists, they set off across the low causeway.

Julius said, 'You know this island was Church property until the English crown seized it. There are creepy ruins of a monastery underneath it. The monastery was owned by the same monks who run Mont Saint-Michel over on the other side of the Channel. I wouldn't be surprised if both islands of St Michael have halls of royal records.'

'I knew we brought you along for a reason,' Zoe said.

Mae said, 'Are you aware that *before* the monks set up shop here, a pagan religion worshipped at a stone circle on the summit of the island? Druids who counted among their ranks an enigmatic priest known as Merlyn or Merlin.'

'No, I did not know that, Madam Merriweather,' Julius said. 'I don't suppose you'd like to join my team for trivia night at the pub this Thursday? We could use you.'

They arrived at the island.

It rose before them, soaring into the cloudless morning sky.

They paid the admission fee and ascended the winding path leading up to the castle.

They were halfway up it when, abruptly, they heard the sound of a helicopter starting up from their right.

They hurried to an escarpment branching off the path and, looking down on a grassy clearing, saw a British military chopper sitting beside the base of one of the castle's taller cliffs.

A World War II pillbox had been dug into the base of the cliff and to their surprise four figures strode out of it and marched directly to the chopper: three men and a woman.

The lead man was tall and blond and he wore aristocratic outdoor clothing: a tweed hunting jacket and riding trousers; the second man was shorter, with black hair, a thin black moustache and a black suit with a priest's collar; the third was a fat Pakistani wearing a Tommy Bahama shirt and several thick gold neck chains.

The woman was younger, in her mid-twenties and beautiful, with chestnut hair and pale skin. She also wore riding clothes: tweed jacket, form-fitting riding pants and knee-high boots. She walked with her nose held high. Zoe wondered who she was.

Zoe snapped off a couple of photos of them with her cell phone.

No sooner had the four figures stepped aboard the big chopper than it took off, banking away into the sky.

Zoe exchanged a look with Mae. 'Do you know them?'

'I know the three men,' Mae said. 'That was Orlando Compton-Jones, Cardinal Ricardo Mendoza and Sunny Malik. I don't know the woman. This is very troubling. They beat us here.'

Once the chopper was long gone, the three 'tourists' clambered down to the concrete pillbox at the base of the cliff and, after checking that no-one was looking, ducked inside it.

Inside, it was barren and musty, the walls coated with wind-tossed salt and graffiti.

'Nice touch,' Julius said, eyeing the graffiti. 'Really sells the abandoned look.'

An iron-barred cell stood at the back of the dark pillbox, held shut by a padlock.

Zoe picked the lock and it dropped away.

Stepping into the cell, they quickly discovered a hatch in its floor.

Zoe opened it . . . to reveal a set of old stone stairs disappearing into darkness.

She drew a pistol from the back of her jeans. It had a small flash-light attached to its barrel. She flicked it on.

'What do you say, boys and girls?'

Raising the gun, she led the way into the darkness.

The stairs opened onto a long horizontal tunnel that delved into the mountain under the castle.

The walls of the tunnel were solid stone and the passageway itself only one person wide. It stretched away into blackness in a dead-straight line, so far that Zoe's little flashlight couldn't find the end of it.

After two more iron gates—equipped with slightly more modern locks that took Zoe a little longer to pick—they came to some stairs that wound upward in a tight spiral.

Rising up the stairwell, the stairs ended at a doorway sealed by the largest iron-barred gate yet.

A pained scream from somewhere on the other side of the gate made them all jump.

Cautiously, they stepped up to the gate.

Zoe peered out through it.

'Lord in Heaven . . .' she gasped.

Julius and Mae joined her and beheld the grisly sight.

'Jesus Christ . . .' Julius said.

'Oh, that is *messed up*,' Mae said.

Through the bars of the gate, they saw a dungeon—a genuine medieval dungeon—all stone walls and cages, chains and bloody chopping blocks, racks and other torture devices; all of it lit not by flaming torches but by the harsh white glare of modern fluorescent light-tubes, which, if it were possible, actually made the chamber seem even more horrific.

And in the middle of it all, her hands and feet manacled to a hideous high-backed wooden chair, bloodied and battered, her head lolling to one side, was Iolanthe.

Zoe stared in horror through the bars of the gate at Iolanthe.

Despite their chequered history, what Zoe saw now sickened her to her very core.

Iolanthe—once beautiful and poised, a modern-day princess with perfect skin and shiny auburn hair—was now a wreck of a human being.

Her hair had been shaved off.

Her face was covered with cuts and bruises. One of her eyes was so inflamed it had swollen shut. Her lips were cracked. Dried blood covered her chin in a thick crust.

But that wasn't the worst of it.

It was her nose that was the worst.

Orlando had put a ring in it.

A thick brass nose-ring like the kind you put on a bull. It had pierced the septal cartilage that separated her nostrils.

With her shaven head and chunky nose-ring, the one-time elegant princess looked like a bizarre kind of Goth punk rocker. All she needed were some tattoos.

A rusty hinge squealed from somewhere and footsteps stomped into the dungeon, trudging heavily down a set of stairs directly above Zoe's closed gate.

A fat bald man in a blood-smeared leather apron entered Zoe's field of vision and stood over Iolanthe.

He held a gun-like device in one hand.

'Found it!' he said brightly to Iolanthe.

She didn't look up.

He smacked her hard across the face and her good eye shot open, bloodshot and defiant.

'Now, now, here, here,' the fat man in the apron said. 'I is just followin' orders, missy. Blame yer brother. He's the one who wanted you to suffer. I just enjoy doin' it, is all. Call it a fringe benefit. I love to hear the ladies scream.'

He held up the device again for Iolanthe to see.

'Like I said. I found it. Me tattoo gun. Haven't used this in a long time. Yer brother told me that he wants you to remember your betrayal every time you look in a mirror.'

He fired up the tattoo gun. It whirred menacingly.

Iolanthe—her face a mess, her hair shaved—leaned back in the wooden chair, hyperventilating. But there was nowhere for her to go.

The torturer leaned in close.

'Keep still now and it won't—'

'Freeze, asshole,' Zoe said from behind him.

Iolanthe's head snapped up at the voice.

Her tormenter also turned, holding the tattoo gun pointed upward, more surprised than shocked.

Neither of them had heard Zoe open the gate and enter the dungeon.

'And who might you be?' the torturer asked with an unctuous grin.

Blam!

Zoe shot him in the face.

The torturer dropped to the floor, squealing, gripping his bloody face.

Zoe stepped over him and put two more bullets in the back of his head and he went still.

'No conversations for you, shithead,' she said. 'You just die.'

Iolanthe stared up at Zoe. She seemed dazed, in shock, traumatised.

Mae and Julius hurried to Iolanthe's side and quickly released her hands and feet from their manacles.

'Can you stand?' Julius asked.

Iolanthe mumbled something in the affirmative.

She looked dazedly from the body of her torturer to Zoe, her bruised and cut face the picture of confusion. There was no other woman in the world whom she thought *less* likely to save her than Zoe Kissane.

Zoe leaned forward, peering closely at the thick nose-ring puncturing Iolanthe's nose, trying to figure out how it was attached.

She reached forward and Iolanthe flinched, jerking back from her with a frightened squeal.

Zoe and Mae swapped a look: what the hell had Orlando done to her?

'It's okay,' Zoe said gently. 'I'm not going to hurt you. No-one's going to hurt you any more. I just have to remove that nose-ring.'

She reached forward again, more slowly this time, gently unhooked the nose-ring and tossed it away.

Then Julius and Mae helped Iolanthe out of the horrible wooden chair, looping her arms over their shoulders.

'Jack sent us,' Zoe said. 'We need your help. Let's move, we have to get out of here before anyone comes back.'

Iolanthe blinked weakly, and then with great effort, nodded. 'I . . . I . . . records . . . upstairs.'

They hurried up many stairs and stairwells even though they were still far *below* the castle that stood atop St Michael's Mount.

Zoe led the way while Julius and Mae carried Iolanthe slung between them.

'After Zahir and Benjamin . . . dropped me off in Dubai, I . . . flew straight here,' Iolanthe rasped. Her voice was hoarse, parched.

'I thought I could . . . get in and out of the Hall of Royal Records before my brother got back, but he caught me as I was leaving and sent me down here, to the dungeon. To be tortured by Longworth, his personal psychopath and torturer.'

The four of them rounded a corner.

Mae said, 'During my studies, I've often wondered what the Hall of Royal Records looks like . . .'

Her voice trailed off as she saw the space in front of them.

A gorgeous high-ceilinged chamber the size of a basketball court opened before them, comprising hundreds of shelves filled with leather folios, pigeonholes packed with scrolls, stone tablets on pedestals, and six towering statues of grey stone.

'The Hall of Royal Records,' Iolanthe croaked. 'I managed to hide some documents before Orlando caught me. We must grab them and flee before anyone discovers something is amiss.'

Fifteen minutes later, four figures in tourist garb strode across the cobblestone causeway back to the mainland from St Michael's Mount.

No-one noticed that they had gone over to the Mount as a three-some or that the new person in their group could barely walk on her own.

Mae and Zoe held some ancient books and scrolls under their clothes while Julius helped Iolanthe. She staggered along the cause-way with her head bowed, the blue hood of an R2-D2 hoodie worn low, covering her hideously bruised and beaten face.

They rented a car in Penzance and began the long drive back to London.

No sooner was Iolanthe safely in the car than she fell into a deep sleep. She slept the whole way.

When they got to the safehouse that Jack kept in Vauxhall a short distance from the Thames, Mae tended to her facial wounds and gave her a sedative and she slept even more soundly.

A few hours later, Jack called from Venice.

'Have you got Iolanthe?' he asked.

'We have her,' Zoe said, 'but she's in bad shape, Jack. Orlando tortured her. She'll be out of it for a while. How did it go in Venice?'

'Not good. We saw the full triangular tablet at the Accademia. We think Orlando may be rushing too quickly to the first city. But then those Knights of the Golden Eight arrived and took Alby. We need Iolanthe to tell us a few things, including where their home base is so we can rescue him. Are you in London?'

'Yes.'

'Stay there. We'll come to you.'

A GIRL NAMED LILY

PART VI

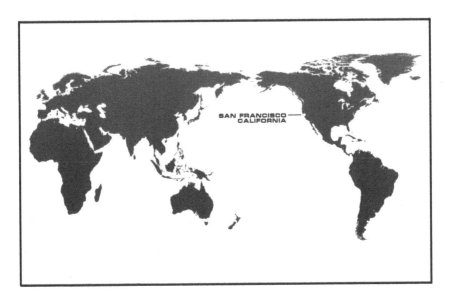

Childhood is the kingdom where nobody dies.

EDNA ST. VINCENT MILLAY

STANFORD UNIVERSITY
CALIFORNIA, U.S.A.
TWO MONTHS EARLIER

A couple of months before he was kidnapped and taken to compete in the Great Games, Jack travelled from his hideaway in the Australian desert to visit Lily at Stanford.

It was during that trip that he'd met Dion DeSaxe.

Dion.

At that time, Dion had been on a couple of dates with Lily. Of course, back then, Lily had been entirely unaware of the four kingdoms, let alone the fact that Dion was the son and heir of Hades, the King of the Underworld.

What a difference a few months would make.

In addition to almost marrying her—in the ultimate royal wedding—and threatening Lily with a sadistic life after that, Dion had held a red-hot poker inches away from Alby's nose and, later, during the mayhem that had occurred after the Great Games, had aimed a gun at the defenceless Jack.

As the furious Dion had been about to pull the trigger, Alby had appeared at the last moment and shot him through the back of the head and they'd got away.

But before all that, back when the world had made sense, Jack's trip to Stanford had been great.

Lily had loved showing him around the campus, introducing him to her friends and even taking him to a Giants baseball game in nearby San Francisco.

But most of all she had just enjoyed spending time with him.

One evening, as they'd eaten together at a pizza place in San Jose, Lily had said, 'Daddy, what do you think of Alby?'

'What do you mean?' Jack asked, intrigued and a little surprised. This was around the time Lily had introduced Jack to Dion and announced him as 'boyfriend material'.

'As . . . well . . . more than a friend?'

Jack smiled. He hadn't known Lily might have thought of Alby in that way and he kind of liked it. He also hadn't known that Dion had some competition and he *really* liked that.

'Kiddo, a lot of parents weigh in on who their kids date, but for me, who you choose is entirely up to you. The only thing I'll say is this: date a man, not a boy.'

'But what makes a boy into a man?' Lily asked.

'The loss of innocence,' Jack said simply and firmly. 'The moment you find out that the world isn't always your friend, that bad things happen to good people, that people die. I've known Alby since he was twelve years old. His own father wasn't supportive of him—thought he was a weakling, a nerd—and yet Alby pushed on with his studies anyway and now he's one of the smartest guys I know. The world wasn't his friend but he stuck at it. He's a fine young man.'

Jack also thought: *He's also as loyal as the day is long and would step in front of a bus for you, kiddo.* But he didn't say that. That was for her to figure out.

A few days later, Alby himself came up from L.A. to join Jack and Lily for a while. One night, the three of them dined at a funky Mexican place called Sixto's Cantina.

They discussed a wide range of things: Lily's language studies at Stanford, Alby's studies in history at USC and astrophysics at Caltech, their previous missions and the changing world.

Lily complained about one subject she was doing on indigenous South American linguistics. She hated it, but she had to do it, since once she finished the subject, she would have completed the requirements of her undergraduate degree.

Jack smiled kindly. 'Come on now. You know what I always say. *You didn't come this far just to come* this *far.* You gotta finish and finish strongly. The world doesn't care for half-finished undergrad degrees.'

They also chatted about a recent trip Alby had taken during summer break: a solo vacation to Europe.

It had been a classic rite-of-passage trip. Travelling alone with a backpack and a Eurail pass, Alby had visited all the classic museums of Europe—in Florence, Rome and Paris—plus a few more idiosyncratic venues that he just found intriguing: like Neuschwanstein Castle in Germany—the famous 'fairytale castle'—the Jungfrau mountain in Switzerland with its hollowed-out core and the mighty Rock of Gibraltar hanging off the southern tip of Spain.

During his many train rides, he'd also read a bunch of books, the kind every student reads, from Kerouac to Salinger, but also some more esoteric stuff about mythic heroes, like *Beowulf* and Joseph Campbell's *The Hero with a Thousand Faces.* It had got him thinking.

'Jack,' Alby asked, 'why do you do what you do?'

'What do you mean?'

'Step up. Be a hero. Save the world. The people of the world don't know who you are. They don't know what you've done for them, what you've sacrificed: friends and loved ones you've lost, like Wizard, for example.'

By then, they were pretty much the last people in the restaurant.

Jack looked at Alby and Lily and smiled sadly.

They were no longer the two boisterous kids scampering in the dust around his farm.

Lily was tall, beautiful and smart. And Alby—once small and bespectacled, with a Cochlear implant, thick glasses and slightly inflected speech—was now fit and lean, with contact lenses instead of glasses. His speech still had an ever-so-slight fuzz to it, which Jack thought gave him character.

They had grown so much.

It was time.

'Lily, Alby, there's something I need to get from both of you.'

That got their attention.

'It's something I've asked of every person who's joined me on my previous missions. You were too young to do it before, but now I think you're old enough.'

Lily and Alby said nothing.

Jack said, 'From Wizard to Zoe, Pooh Bear and Stretch, I've asked everyone who has joined my team to write an email and send it to me, a special email, one to be read upon their death, should it happen during a mission.'

Lily and Alby remained silent.

Jack said, 'Death is sudden. None of us knows when it will come. And when it occurs in the chaos of a mission, there's no opportunity to say goodbye. In our very first mission, when we went after the Seven Wonders of the Ancient World, we lost Doris and Noddy, two wonderful people. When that happened, I realised that we needed to be able to say goodbye. The emails do just that. I call them Messages from the Other Side.'

He bowed his head for a moment, biting his lip sadly.

'I keep copies of everyone's emails in a special file on my phone and as hard copies in a locked drawer in my desk back home. I don't read them when I receive them, so I don't know what they contain. I just file them away for opening when the time comes. Sometimes a member of the team comes to me and says they've written a new message or wants to update their old one and I replace it.

'In some cases, I've also given copies of messages to certain members of our group with special relationships: deep bonds of friendship that go beyond me. For instance, Julius and Lachlan have copies of each other's messages; Pooh Bear and Stretch; Zoe and me.'

He pulled out his phone, tapped it a few times and passed it to Lily and Alby. 'Here is an example of one.'

They both leaned close and read the email on the screen:

Dear Jack,

It was the honour of my life to accompany you on your travels around the world, discovering so many wondrous places and things.

When Doris was killed in Kenya, I was lost. Your friend-ship saved me: you hugged me, you listened to me, but most of all, you brought me back to the world by giving me purpose. Many will call you a hero for leaping onto speed-ing planes or running into danger, but I think you are a hero for carrying me through that time.

If you're reading this, then I am gone, gone to the undis-covered country from which no adventurer, however brave, returns. Know that I died content, content that my life meant something to the world, even if the world didn't know it.

And don't cry for me, because I'm with Doris now.

We will be watching over you, together, from above.

Your friend forever,

Max T. Epper

The Wizard

A tear trickled down Lily's cheek.

Alby swallowed.

Jack said, 'I don't know if there will be any other missions, but if there are and you're willing to join me on them, you both should write me an email, just in case. And given your special friendship, I'd suggest you also give each other your messages for safekeeping.

'To answer your question, Alby, a hero is someone who stands by their friends in their hour of need. That's it. That's all. And that's why I do it. I don't save the world for glory or power. I have neither and I don't care for them. In fact, I quite like it that the world *doesn't* know my name. I just do what I do for the people I love.'

Both Lily and Alby sent Jack emails of their own a few days later.

Without reading them, Jack filed them away.

★ ★ ★

On that same trip to San Francisco, while Lily had reluctantly gone to an evening lecture on South American linguistics, Jack had dined alone with Alby.

'Hey, Jack,' Alby said, shifting uncomfortably in his chair, 'can I ask you something?'

'Sure.'

'Do you think . . .' Alby hesitated. 'Do you think, if I asked her, Lily would ever, you know, go out on a date with me?'

Jack smiled inwardly again.

'To find that out, I think you have to ask her,' Jack said.

Alby bowed his head, uncertain.

'But for what it's worth,' Jack added, 'I think you'd have a better-than-average chance of her saying yes.'

There was another reason for Jack's trip to the west coast of the United States at that time.

He had wanted to catch up with his good friend, Professor David Black, the renowned oceanographer and wreck hunter. Black—known as Nobody—worked out of a marine lab not far from the Port of San Francisco.

One day, Jack, Lily and Alby went to Nobody's lab to check out his deep-sea submersibles.

It was a seriously cool place and, wearing his trademark flip-flops, torn shorts and ratty t-shirt, Nobody guided them around it.

One of the things he was working on was a modified submarine that could act as a mothership for four smaller submersibles. For that purpose, Nobody had bought an old submarine from the Norwegian Navy with his own money.

He also gave Jack a special black case for his iPhone. 'Here, I thought you'd like one of these. It's the latest Navy tech,' Nobody said. 'Lightweight carbon fibre shell. All but indestructible and waterproof down to four hundred feet. I love it. I can check file photos and other research while I'm diving round a wreck.'

Jack examined the sturdy phone casing, showed it to Lily. 'What do you think?'

She screwed up her nose. 'It's too chunky. It'd never fit in the back pocket of my skinny jeans.'

'Lucky I don't wear skinny jeans,' Jack said, inserting his iPhone into the casing. 'I think it's great. Thanks, Nobody.'

The two old friends grinned.

Lily just shook her head.

As they left Nobody's lab, Alby said, 'He bought a submarine *with his own money*? How?'

Jack said, 'You wouldn't know it to look at him, but Nobody's superwealthy thanks to all the treasures he's found in sunken galleons around the world. He started out as a submarine engineer in the U.S. Navy. Now he has homes and dive boats all around the world, including here, Sardinia and Barbados.'

Alby frowned. 'I have another question. Nobody is tanned, fit and good-looking; fifty-seven years old, humble, single and rich. He's smart, funny and women practically melt in front of him. He served in the Navy and now he's a world-class oceanographer. Given all those achievements, can you please tell me why his nickname is *Nobody*?'

Jack smiled knowingly. 'Because Nobody's perfect.'

Nobody had also been something of surrogate uncle for Lily while she'd been studying at Stanford.

In Jack's absence, Nobody was always happy to join Lily for a chat or to give her some advice.

On one occasion, he met up with her in a bar near Stanford. It was the weekend of a huge football game between Stanford and the University of Alabama, the reigning college champions, and the bar was packed with rowdy college kids wearing their teams' colours. A proud alum of Stanford, Nobody had come down from the city to join Lily and watch the game.

Lily saw it as an opportunity to ask for his opinion on something.

'I'm thinking of taking on a second major,' she said. 'My language studies are fun but they're kinda easy. I was thinking of doing pre-med over the summer. What do you think? Is it too much?'

'Pre-med?' Nobody smiled broadly. 'Hell, I think that's awesome. I think you'd make a wonderful doctor.'

Lily bowed her head bashfully. 'Yeah, but, honestly, do you

really think I can do it? There's a lot of physics and chemistry, and they're not really my thing.'

'Hey,' Nobody said, suddenly stern. 'Never say that. Anybody can learn anything; some of us just need more time than others do. Besides, you've got something beyond physics and chemistry that'll make you a super doctor.'

'What's that?'

'Your heart.'

'My heart?'

'Lily,' Nobody said, 'your dad loves you more than life itself. He's so proud of you. But do you know what he's most proud of?'

'What?'

'Sure, you've got this gift for reading that ancient language and that's all well and good. But that's not all there is to Lily West. Not by a long shot. Jack once told me that there's something inside you, something sweet and tender, that he never wants to see extinguished. I mean, look at you now: talking about becoming a doctor, helping other people. I reckon he'd be thrilled to hear this.'

Lily looked around at the students in the crowded bar, drinking and cheering and having a good time.

'He was the one who made me that way,' she said. 'When I was young, maybe seven, living in Kenya, a local girl named Kimmy was having a birthday party. She lived on one of the neighbouring farms. She invited me but I said to Dad that I didn't want to go because Kimmy had no friends. I didn't want to go to an unpopular kid's party.'

Nobody waited for Lily to go on.

Lily said, 'I'll never forget what Dad said. He said very firmly, "And that's exactly why you're going to go, young lady. How do you think Kimmy would feel if no-one came? Maybe this is her way of reaching out to become friends." So I went and when I saw Kimmy's face light up with a huge smile on my arrival, I understood. Dad made me care about how others feel.'

'He's a shrewd dude, your old man,' Nobody said. 'You know something? He's got a smile that's reserved only for you. You probably don't see it, but the rest of us do. It's that special smile that fathers have for their daughters—'

'Hey!' Someone smacked Nobody roughly on the back of the head, making him spill his drink.

Lily and Nobody turned, shocked.

An absolutely gigantic guy in an Alabama football jersey stood above them. He was a football player, for sure. Three hundred pounds, shaved head, cruel eyes.

He kicked Nobody's chair. 'Hey, old man. Leave the young chicks for us young dudes, huh?'

A gang of Alabama fans yucked and chuckled behind him.

'You tell him, Travis,' someone sniggered.

'Fuckin'-A,' another agreed.

Nobody stood up. Slowly.

'Son,' he said. 'Do you really want to play it this way?'

The player towered over him, a foot taller, thirty years younger and a hundred pounds heavier.

He jabbed Nobody in the chest with every word: 'Fuck. You. Old. Man.'

On the last jab, Nobody did something very fast and suddenly the massive footballer was on his knees, his head pressed down against the floor and his right arm twisted upward. Nobody was gripping his wrist with one firm hand. With his boot, Nobody pressed the kid's head against the beer-stained floor.

The kid howled. '*Owww! Fuck! Lemme go! Owww!*'

Nobody was unperturbed.

'Young man,' he said. 'You just interrupted a very pleasant dinner I was having with my good friend's daughter. Are you going to apologise?'

'I'm s-s-sorry . . .' the football player squeaked.

'I gave you a chance to walk away,' Nobody said. 'And you didn't.'

The football player grunted in pain.

'Big boy like you has got a lot of strength,' Nobody said. 'But with great strength comes a responsibility to use it wisely, not selfishly. Isn't that so?'

The player grunted in the affirmative.

'What's your name?'

'Travis. Travis Johnson.'

'Are you playing tomorrow, Travis?' Nobody asked.

The big football player nodded vigorously.

'No, you're not,' Nobody said, and gave the kid's wrist a sharp jerk, just enough to hyperextend the ligament. 'When I played football at college, we were taught to treat everyone with courtesy. Be a little more courteous in the future, Travis.'

Then, to the shock of Travis Johnson and his friends, Nobody calmly guided Lily out of the entirely silent bar.

FOURTH PURSUIT

THE LONDON SHOWDOWN

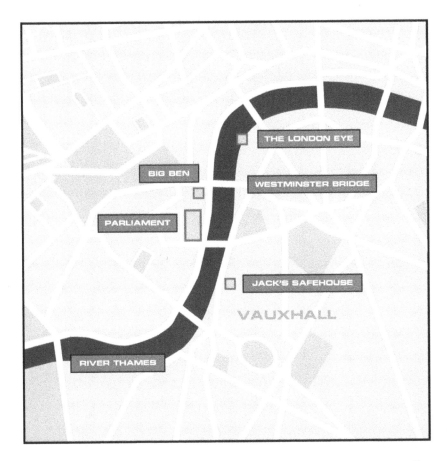

Everyone thinks they're a gangster, until a real gangster walks in the room.

QUOTE ATTRIBUTED TO JOHN GOTTI, GANGSTER

Twenty-five hours after their wild chase in Venice, Jack, Lily and Sky Monster rendezvoused with Zoe, Mae and Julius in London.

It had taken Jack a little longer than usual to make the trip: patching up Sky Monster's wounds had made getting out of Venice unseen much slower.

They met in the little flat in Vauxhall that Jack kept as a safe-house. It was entirely unremarkable, one of a thousand such flats on the south bank of the Thames about a mile from Big Ben and Parliament: the kind of place you went to disappear and regroup.

Like now.

When Jack arrived in the early hours of the morning, Iolanthe was fast asleep in the second bedroom, knocked out.

With the others standing behind him, Jack gazed at the British princess as she slept.

By any reckoning, with her flowing auburn hair and flawless skin, Iolanthe had been a beautiful woman. Now, with her head shaved, her faced battered and with a large hole in the central cartilage of her nose, she was practically unrecognisable.

'This is what her own brother does to her . . .' Jack said softly.

He gently shook her shoulder, rousing her. 'Iolanthe, wake up.'

Her eyes opened and she squinted weakly up at him. 'Jack . . . Jack West?'

'Sorry to wake you, but we need your help right away.'

★ ★ ★

Ten minutes later, Iolanthe was sitting gingerly in the living room of the flat, wrapped in a fluffy dressing gown, with a cup of warm tea held in both hands, surrounded by Jack and his team.

She glared hard at one of the photos Zoe had taken at St Michael's Mount: of the four people leaving the island by helicopter; Orlando, Cardinal Mendoza, Sunny Malik and the pretty young woman in tight riding clothes and with the proud nose.

'The woman is Chloe Carnarvon,' Iolanthe said. 'My assistant. Lily, you met her in the Underworld, during the Games. She helped with your clothes and make-up before the gala dinner.'

Lily nodded. 'I remember her.'

'Ambitious slut,' Iolanthe growled. 'I'll bet you a thousand pounds she's sleeping with my brother. If she's working for him, that's a problem.'

'Why?' Jack asked.

'Because for the last two years, Chloe has been more than just my assistant. She's been my shadow, my second brain. She's very clever and she knows everything I know: about the Omega Event, the three weapons and the three cities. If she's helping Orlando, he has a very competent guide. And don't discount Sunny Malik. He may not be classically educated, but he's street-smart and unusually adept at finding lost treasures.'

Jack quickly told Iolanthe about what had happened in New York and Venice, about Orlando's actions there and the appearance of two sets of hunters pursuing him: Yago, the royal jailer, and the Knights of the Golden Eight.

'Right now,' he said, 'I need to know a few things. The Knights of the Golden Eight have captured our friend, Alby Calvin. They also have contracts out on me and Lily: me dead, her alive. I want to know where their headquarters are.'

He handed Iolanthe an iPad with Google Maps on it.

She quickly brought up a spot on the Italian coast.

'The Knights of the Golden Eight reside here, in a castle near Naples known as Castille Aragonese: Aragon Castle. If they *captured* your friend, then they were contracted to take him alive, too.

Trust me, the Knights much prefer killing their targets. But if their commission was to capture him, then they will be keeping him at Aragon Castle for presentation to their employer.'

'And who would that be?' Jack asked. 'If we know who hired them, we might be able to get some leverage that way.'

Iolanthe said, 'For over two thousand years, the Knights of the Golden Eight—or as some call them, the Blood Knights of Ischia or the Knights of the Round Table—have been the hired assassins of the royal world, killers with no patron or master. Myth and legend has portrayed them as unwaveringly chivalrous and loyal, but myth and legend inadvertently reversed the details. The Knights are unwavering, sure, but only in the execution of a paid task.'

Jack said, 'For which they're paid in land?'

'Correct. Vast swathes of land. The Knights own the entire southwestern coast of Italy from Naples to Messina, large portions of Nigeria and Morocco, and all of Ethiopia. They prefer regions rich in minerals so they can exploit them.

'What all this means is that whoever hired the Knights is probably someone very senior, most likely a king or a wealthy lord. Someone with the authority to give the Knights a very sizeable plot of land. We're talking a region the size of a small country.'

'Why so large?' Lily asked.

'Because a contract to kill the fifth greatest warrior and capture his adopted daughter—you, the Oracle of Siwa—is momentous,' Iolanthe said. 'Forget your friend, Albert; he's just a minor bonus. You two are *very* big fish and a mission the Knights would relish.'

'Their employer. Could it be your brother, Orlando?' Jack asked.

'Possibly,' Iolanthe said. 'My brother has used the Knights before. But, then, if the Slave King is also after you, Orlando might just leave the task to him. Don't forget, you upset a lot of people at the Games, Jack, so it could be anyone.'

'It's hard enough finding and solving the Mysteries,' Jack said. 'Doing it with two sets of assholes hunting me makes it a lot harder. Can we take that castle? Storm it?'

Iolanthe gave him a look. 'Others have tried to take back loved ones captured by the Knights. None have succeeded.'

Jack bit his lip. 'Will they kill Alby?'

'The Knights won't,' Iolanthe said. 'Given that the commission was to capture him and Lily alive, I would imagine it is their *employer* who would like the opportunity to kill them both. If Albert isn't already dead, it can't be long till he is.'

Jack threw a worried glance at Lily.

He shifted gears. 'What about Hades? His brother Yago caught him and took him to that royal prison.'

'Erebus,' Iolanthe said softly, reverently. 'If Hades has been taken by the royal jailer, then he is even more lost than your friend being held by the Knights. The location of the prison at Erebus is one of the royal world's most closely guarded secrets. Once you go to Erebus, you do not leave. And no-one can rescue you because no-one knows where it is.'

'Do you have any ideas?' Jack asked.

Iolanthe shrugged elaborately. 'Rumours about the location of the royal prison have existed for centuries: some say it is buried underneath a fortress on Malta; others in Crete; some say it is the labyrinth at Knossos; others say that Troy was not a city at all but actually the prison and that Agamemnon's famed siege of it was an attempt to break out his brother's wife after she was imprisoned there. Most believe that Erebus is somewhere in the Mediterranean, but beyond that, its location is a mystery.'

She shook her head.

'You would do well to forget Hades. Once someone goes to Erebus, they are never seen again.'

'Okay, then,' Jack said, 'confirm a few other things for us. Like this papyrus, which I'm told was kept in your Hall of Royal Records for many years.'

Jack placed a photo on the table in front of Iolanthe. It was the shot of the Zeus Papyrus that he had taken in Hades's vault in New York. The papyrus read:

> *When mighty Hercules won the Games for me, my prize was an army, an indomitable force of men of bronze, to guard me on my sacred mission to the Three Secret Cities.*
>
> *I also received the Mysteries: wondrous visions seared into my mind as I stood inside the obelisk, including two odes regarding the two trials to be overcome.*

THE TRIAL OF THE CITIES

> *No oceans.*
> *No clouds.*
> *No rivers.*
> *No rain.*
> *The world a wasteland*
> *of misery and pain.*

THE TRIAL OF THE MOUNTAINS

Five iron mountains. Five bladed keys. Five doors, forever locked.
But mark you, only those who survive the Fall,
May enter the supreme labyrinth
And look upon the face of the Omega.

The Mysteries guided me through the first trial. That
trial required me to take the Three Immortal Weapons to
the Three Secret Cities, empower the weapons at them,
and, thus empowered, perform the sacred ritual with the
weapons at the Altar of the Cosmos before the next rising
of Sagittarius over the Sun.

Let all who follow in my footsteps know: the journey to the
Three Secret Cities begins at the end.

The second trial only begins once the first is completed —

'You know this papyrus?' Jack asked.

'Of course.'

'We calculated the "next rising of Sagittarius over the Sun": when radio waves from the supermassive black hole known as Sagittarius A-star will pass through the Earth and shoot down the path created by the Hydra Galaxy.'

'How long have we got?' Iolanthe asked simply.

'It happens on 1 December, at 8:05 p.m. GMT,' Jack said. 'Which means we *had* seven days, but that was two days ago. Now we have only five days to find the Three Immortal Weapons, empower them at the Secret Cities and then use them in some ritual at the Altar of the Cosmos. Do you know what *empowering* involves? And anything about the ritual and the Altar?'

Iolanthe said, 'Empowering involves placing a special kind of blue gemstone on each of the weapons. The blue gems are kept at each city, in their innermost chambers.

'As for the Altar of the Cosmos, it's a very ancient legend. It is mentioned in mythologies from all over the world, from Meso-American cultures like the Olmecs and Incans to Greek, Egyptian and Viking legends. It is said to be an altar the size of a mountain.'

'The size of a *mountain*?' Lily said.

'If it's that big, wouldn't it have been found already?' Zoe asked.

Iolanthe said, 'Some say it already has. Mount Kilimanjaro in Africa is a prime candidate: it has many hidden chambers within its volcanic core. Mount Olympus in Greece is another, for obvious reasons. Personally, I like Mont Blanc in France. Apparently, buried within it rocky core is a strange hollow structure that dates back over five thousand years. Once, when I politely asked to inspect it, the then King of Land—my own father—would not let me.'

'Do the four kings know where it is?'

Iolanthe said, 'No, just the Land King, since it resides in his domain. On his accession to his throne, the new king is told the location of the Altar.'

Jack gave her a look. 'Come on, Iolanthe. I would imagine the Keeper of the Royal Records must come across slivers of information on topics like this from time to time.'

Iolanthe returned his look with interest.

She pulled a weathered file from the stack of documents and scrolls that she and the others had taken from the Hall of Records on their way out.

The file was stamped: *K.E.O.*

'What does "K.E.O." stand for?' Lily asked.

'"King's Eyes Only",' Iolanthe said. 'It's the only file of this kind I've ever seen. I discovered it in a bunch of boxes filled with secret cables that were hastily brought to St Michael's Mount during the dying days of World War II. Cables between royals and fleeing Nazis. In the rush, this K.E.O. report must have got caught among them. Of course, I couldn't resist looking at it.'

She opened the file. It was empty save for a single slip of worn paper. It was titled:

K.E.O. REPORT
CORPS OF ROYAL ENGINEERS
178th TUNNELLING COMPANY
12 May 1942

Your Majesty,
During our excavations of Arrow Street an unusual chamber was found. It appears to be the holy chamber of the Altar. Photographs are enclosed.
The men who found it were duly executed.
Brigadier James Conn Jr
Chief Royal Engineer

Iolanthe said, 'It's the only thing I've ever found referring to the Altar.'

'"*The men who found it were duly executed*",' Jack read. 'He reports it so casually.'

'Royal secrets are worth more than the lives of a few common soldiers,' Iolanthe said.

Lily took a photo of the document with her phone and uploaded it to their secure server in the Cloud.

'Any idea where this Arrow Street can be found?' she asked.

'None,' Iolanthe said. 'Chloe and I worked on it for a week. We found a number of Arrow Streets in cities around the world, but all our inquiries led to nothing. That said—'

She hesitated.

'Go on,' Jack said.

'There's one other thing about the Altar of the Cosmos. In some places, it is known as the Altar *for the Rebirth* of the Cosmos.'

'And?' Zoe asked.

Mae's eyes narrowed. 'The ritual. You're thinking of the Mayans and the Aztecs?'

'I am.' Iolanthe nodded. 'In historical matters, words have meaning. Specific meaning. The phrase "Rebirth of the Cosmos" occurs a lot in Meso-American cultures, in particular those of the Mayans and the Aztecs. To pay for the sun *to be reborn* every morning, both famously practised human sacrifice. Very gruesome human sacrifice.'

Julius said, 'You think the ritual to be performed at the Altar of the Cosmos requires some sort of human sacrifice?'

'I don't know for certain, but I'm thinking that's a possibility, yes,' Iolanthe said.

'Just what we need,' Jack scowled. 'That said, unless we find the cities, the Altar is moot, so let's move on. What about the poem? No oceans, no clouds, rivers and all that. Any idea what that means?'

'It is punishment,' Iolanthe said simply. 'Punishment for our failure to complete the first trial. If humankind proves to be unworthy, then the Earth must not only be extinguished, it must *suffer*.'

'Suffer?' Lily said.

Iolanthe nodded. 'There will be no sudden explosion or flash of light and everybody just drops dead. Oh, no. This is a warning. A warning of what will occur if we fail. I do not know *how* it will happen, but I interpret this poem as an image of the world turned dry, transformed into a desolate wasteland incapable of sustaining life.'

The group fell silent.

'Good God . . .' Mae said quietly.

Jack said, 'The three weapons. Hades told us that the first is a sword, the blade known as Caliburn or Excalibur, and that it has long been held by the Land Kingdom. Is this Orlando's focus? Has he gone to the first city with the Sword?'

'That's correct.' Iolanthe nodded. 'To enter each city, he must first go to its watchtower where he will meet its watchman. Now that he knows Thule is the first city, he will go there. According to several ancient sources, it's in Iceland.'

'Wait,' Mae said, 'you *know* the locations of the three cities?'

'Just Thule,' Iolanthe said. 'The legend of the city of Ultima Thule is a very Anglo-Saxon one, so there's a lot of information about it in British, Norse and Roman records, alongside tales of Merlin, King Arthur and the druids.'

Lily said, 'But Orlando hasn't seen the *full* triangular tablet. He doesn't know that by going to Thule, he will set in motion mechanisms at the other two cities, Ra and Atlas. In his haste, he could kill us all.'

Jack's eyes narrowed. 'Tell us about the watchman of Atlas, the magi in charge of it. The one called Sphinx.'

Iolanthe looked hard at Jack. 'Sphinx is indeed the guardian of the City of Atlas, although not by choice. Sphinx is my cousin: our fathers were brothers. In recent years, I have seen him irregularly, mainly at royal weddings in Europe. He is rich beyond measure, but his role as the watchman of Atlas is a solitary one. And his relationship with my brother is complicated.'

Jack said, 'The weapon that must be taken to Atlas is the Mace of Poseidon, which rests in Poseidon's tomb. As far as we know, that's never been found. Correct?'

'Correct,' Iolanthe said.

'And the last city, El Dorado. Any idea of its location?'

'I fear I do not know where Ra is. Somewhere in South America.'

'How else can we find the cities then?' Jack asked. 'Are there any records or maps?'

Iolanthe said, 'I know of one ancient map—of a sort—that shows the locations of the cities. It is held by the Cult of Amon-Ra.'

'The Catholic Church,' Lily said.

'Yes. The map once sat atop their holiest shrine, the obelisk in St Peter's Square, out in front of the Vatican in Rome.'

'On *top* of the obelisk?' Mae said.

'The obelisk in St Peter's Square is the oldest and most sacred one to have been taken from Egypt,' Iolanthe said. 'It is rumoured to be over four thousand years old but no-one knows for sure. It is also the only obelisk in the world to have been surmounted by a small metal sphere.'

This was true, Jack knew. Many had wondered about the little sphere on top of the mighty obelisk.

'That mysterious sphere already sat atop the obelisk when it was brought to Rome from Egypt by Caligula in 37 A.D.,' Iolanthe explained. 'But it was removed in 1585 by Pope Sixtus V and replaced with a brass forgery. The original sits safely inside an air-sealed vault deep within the Vatican—alongside other historical treasures—and if you look closely at it, you will see that it shows an image of the Earth as seen from space.'

'But that's impossible,' Zoe said. 'How could the Egyptians build such a thing?'

'They didn't,' Iolanthe said. '*Others* did. I have seen it, although it was only a fleeting glimpse. In addition to continents and oceans, clearly marked and labelled on that metal globe are the locations of the three cities and the five iron peaks.'

Jack grimaced. 'Which means Cardinal Mendoza knows the locations of all of them.'

'Yes,' Iolanthe said, seeing Jack's face fall. 'But having said that, I know of someone else who claimed to have found the three cities.'

'Who?' Jack sat upright. 'Can we meet him?'

'You can't meet him, because he's been dead for five hundred years.'

'Who are you talking about?'

'Why, the greatest seafarer in British history,' Iolanthe said. 'Sir Francis Drake.'

'Francis Drake?' Jack repeated.

Drake was, quite simply, a legend: the great British sailor who circumnavigated the world in the late 1570s and whose fleet famously defeated the Spanish Armada in 1588, but not before he'd finished his game of lawn bowls. To the British of the time, he was an unqualified hero. To the Spanish—whom Drake hated with a passion—he was a ruthless pirate.

Loyal to his queen, daring to a fault, and possessed of a famous sense of humour, he was arguably history's greatest swashbuckler.

'One of the perks of being Keeper of the Royal Records,' Iolanthe said, 'is that I get to read the correspondence between some of history's most remarkable figures. One such letter was sent from Sir Francis Drake to Queen Elizabeth I—the famous Virgin Queen—about a secret mission she had sent him on late in his life.'

Iolanthe grabbed one of the leather-bound volumes she had taken from the Hall of Records and pulled from it a sheet of weathered brown parchment.

On it was a handwritten message, written in a flowery script.

'Drake died in mysterious circumstances off the coast of Panama in 1596,' Iolanthe said. 'He was reputedly buried at sea in a lead coffin near Portobelo. That coffin, despite much searching, has never been found. This is the last letter that he sent back to Elizabeth before his disappearance.'

Jack read the five-hundred-year-old letter:

My Queen,

I have taken ill with the fever. I cannot get back. I doubt I will survive the next five days.

But know that I found them—all three of them—as you commanded. Their locations will be buried at sea with me in a lead coffin here in Portobelo.

As I approach my last sunrise, I remain forever,
Your loyal servant,
Drake

Jack looked at Iolanthe questioningly. 'Elizabeth sent Drake in search of the Three Secret Cities?'

'Yes.'

'And he found them.'

'So it would seem.'

Jack stood. 'Mum, take Iolanthe and find Drake's coffin. Call Nobody. He has a place in Barbados. He can help you out with a submersible, which you might need. I'm guessing that Drake's reference to Portobelo, Panama, is a code for some other place in or around that region, so it's a good place to start.'

'Where are you going?' Mae asked.

'Where else?' Jack said. 'I'm going to get Alby—'

The sound of police sirens cut him off.

Two police cars sped by outside.

Jack looked out the window. It was 7:00 a.m. and the sky was beginning to lighten. Despite the early hour, he saw people pointing and hurrying toward the Thames in large numbers.

In the distance, ominously, he heard the *thump-thump-thump* of a helicopter.

Worried, Jack flicked on the television.

The BBC came on. It showed live footage of London, specifically the River Thames in front of Big Ben.

A stocky Black Hawk military helicopter hovered above the river, with something dangling from it, from a cable of some sort.

'Is that a *car . . .?*' Lily said.

It was.

The TV news camera zoomed in on the car hanging from the helicopter and Jack saw that there were people inside it, four of them.

Jack stared in horror at the image.

The vehicle looked like a van of some kind, a red civilian mini-van. Oddly for a van, it had a number painted on its side like the number on a racing car.

The number 55.

'Holy shit,' Julius said from behind Jack, his face going pale. 'That's Lachie's car.'

Suddenly the television cut to hash and Jaeger Eins appeared on it, just like he had before.

The Knights had hacked the airwaves again.

'*Hello, world,*' Jaeger Eins said from the screen. '*And hello again, Jack. We warned you. We really did. I understand you are somewhere in London, so you cannot be far from this.*'

The image cut back to the TV news footage of the red van hanging from the helicopter in front of Big Ben.

The Black Hawk helicopter, Jack now saw, had grey-painted windows: the telltale sign of an unmanned drone-conversion being flown remotely.

Then the shot zoomed in again on the minivan to clearly show two adults in the front—Lachlan Adamson and his wife—and two children in the back, all duct-taped to their seats.

'*You must think we are monsters, Jack,*' Jaeger Eins's voice said. '*Yes, we are monsters.*'

Then, shockingly, the red van dangling from the drone chopper exploded.

Julius lunged at the television set.

'No!' he cried.

The minivan's windows blew out in gouts of fire, its doors flung open by the violent force of the blast.

And then the van dropped from the cable attaching it to the helicopter and plunged into the River Thames.

No-one could have survived it.

Jack stared, stunned, at the television. That these assholes had killed a friend of his was terrible enough, but his family, too: his wife and young children.

'No . . .' Jack breathed. He rushed to Julius's side and threw an arm around him. Lily did the same.

Zoe put a hand to her mouth.

Mae just stood there, frozen.

And then Jaeger Eins appeared on the television again.

'*I told you, in time you would come to us, Jack. Come out and face us now, on Westminster Bridge in front of Parliament and Big Ben. We can kill more of your friends if we have to. Or perhaps we will test their loyalty . . . and kill their loved ones. Like, for instance, the residents of 14 Honeyfield Street, Wellington, New Zealand.*'

At the mention of the address, Sky Monster looked up.

'Oh, God,' he said.

'What?' Jack asked.

'That's . . .' Sky Monster said. 'That's my parents' address.'

'*After we lost you in Venice, Jack, we sent one of our men there.*'

And suddenly the image on the television changed . . .

. . . to show a little weatherboard house on a quiet street in Wellington, New Zealand . . .

. . . with two figures *crucified* to its front walls.

It was a man and a woman, both with grey hair. Their arms were spread wide, *nailed* to the front wall of the house with their heads bent.

'Oh, Jesus Christ in Heaven,' Sky Monster said. 'That's my parents . . .'

Jack spun from the TV to Sky Monster, his face white with shock.

And then—*boom!*—on the television, the entire house exploded. Glass and rubble were thrown outward and the two crucified figures disappeared in a cloud of fire and smoke.

'*Come out, come out, wherever you are, Jack,*' Jaeger Eins taunted. '*Face us. Now. Westminster Bridge. And bring your daughter, too.*'

Jack spun to face Lily, his mind reeling.

This was happening too fast.

He looked at Julius and Sky Monster as his brain tried to make sense of it all.

By doing what he did, he assumed the risk of crossing unpleasant people and facing potential death. So did his team.

But not their families.

It had never occurred to him that someone would do this: attack the families of his friends and thus test their loyalty to him and the greater mission.

And suddenly all thoughts of secret cities and immortal weapons and even saving Alby flew from his mind.

He looked at Lily and Zoe, their eyes filled with tears.

'I don't have any choice. I have to go out there.'

'*We* have to go out there,' Lily said. 'He wants me, too. And as far as we know, they need me alive, so maybe if I stand in front of you, I can keep you alive a little longer.'

Jack pursed his lips. 'Like I'm going to convince you otherwise.'

He hurried into the other room and quickly grabbed some clothes.

Until then, he had been dressed in simple jeans and a white t-shirt. He put a shoulder holster on over his t-shirt and jammed a Desert Eagle into it. Then he threw on his canvas miner's jacket over that.

He looked at his fireman's helmet on his bed, thought for a moment . . .

. . . then grabbed it and put it on.

'*You're taking too long, Jack,*' Jaeger Eins said from the television in the other room. '*Perhaps we can motivate you and young Lily to hurry up a little.*'

Screams and shouts from outside made him spin.

It had come from the people on the streets: regular folk who had come out to watch the drone chopper that was still hovering above the spot where the exploded minivan had dropped into the river.

Jack ran to the flat's front window. Through it, you couldn't see Big Ben or Parliament but between two buildings across the street, you could glimpse Westminster Bridge.

And in a fleeting instant, Jack saw it.

A large olive-coloured vehicle. Rumbling across the bridge.

'What is that?' Lily said.

'That,' Jack said, 'is a tank.'

It had come out of a classified emergency bunker.

It was one of ten such vehicles kept in the bunker, a block away from Parliament, for use in the event of a terrorist emergency or an attack on the British centre of government.

With its wide tracks, armour plating and imposing turret-mounted 120-millimetre cannon, it was a 62-ton behemoth designed to intimidate and destroy anyone who dared oppose it.

It was a Challenger 2 main battle tank.

The massive tank rumbled out onto the middle of Westminster Bridge and abruptly stopped.

The drone Black Hawk helicopter still hovered over the river not far from the bridge.

After several terrorist incidents in recent years, London's finest were there in minutes. Police cars blocked off either end of the bridge. SWAT vans arrived soon after. Given the hour, there were few cars about to stop. Two police boats secured the river in either direction.

The TV news vans turned up next, their occupants leaping out and filming the scene.

The tank just stood there—ominously still—in the centre of the bridge.

And then it fired its cannon.

The first shot hit the London Eye, the colossal ferris wheel on the bank of the Thames just north of bridge.

One of the Eye's pods blasted out into a thousand fragments and fell off it, tumbling into the river.

Of course, the tourist attraction wasn't open yet, so the pod had been empty. Nevertheless, screams and gasps burst from the crowds on the riverside paths.

In the apartment, Jack spun at the booming sound of the shot.

'Jesus Christ,' he breathed.

Out on the bridge, the mighty tank's turret rotated and it fired again.

This second booming shot hit Big Ben.

Bricks and glass rained down onto the street below. The historic clocktower groaned . . . and swayed.

More screams.

But what could the police do? It was a fucking tank.

In the apartment in Vauxhall, with Lily beside him, Jack raced frantically for the door—only for Zoe to step in front of him, stopping him.

'Hold it,' she said. 'What are you going to do? Do you have any kind of plan?'

Jack's eyes were wild, darting this way and that.

'A plan? No. I just . . . I just have to stop this. I can't let'—his gaze drifted to Julius and Sky Monster—'I can't let any more innocent people die because of me.'

'Jack, please . . .' Zoe said.

'*Jack*,' another voice said softly but firmly.

He turned.

It was Sky Monster. Due to his recent wounds, he looked pale and drawn, but there was an evenness to his tone.

'Buddy, listen to me,' he said, his voice calm. 'We've been through a lot together, you and me. Flying into dangerous places under fire, running through challenges in that godforsaken Underworld. But now . . .'

He paused, bowing his head. There were tears in his eyes.

'Now, you have to *keep your head* and keep going. You can't let these assholes rattle you. Right now you're rattled, and I've never seen that before.'

His red eyes bored in Jack's. 'And please know this, because it's important: *you are not responsible for my parents' deaths.*'

Sky Monster's level stare brought Jack back, made him calm down a bit.

'I repeat: you're not responsible. I am. They're dead because I chose to go with you. It was my choice.'

'Sky Monster—'

Sky Monster held up his hand. 'Jack, you're a first-class, grade-A, gold-minted hero. I'm not. I'm just a dumb-ass pilot. But when I fly with you and get you out of tight spots and help you do great things, a small amount of your hero-stuff rubs off on me and makes me a hero, too. I made my choice to run with you, and it was *my* choice that got my parents killed. I have to live with that, but you don't.'

Jack was silent for a long moment.

Then he nodded. 'Thanks, Monster. Let me go and make this right.'

After taking a few seconds to gather his thoughts, Jack said, 'Okay, here's what we're gonna do. Zoe: find a perch overlooking that bridge. You're our sniper—'

The cocking of a gun made everyone turn.

It was Julius.

He was gripping a pistol. His eyes were like steel. 'Those bastards just killed my brother and his family. I'm going, too.'

Jack gazed at Julius, sorrow in his eyes. 'Julius, no.'

'I'm going.'

'You're not thinking straight.'

'They just killed my—'

'I know.' Jack glanced at Zoe. 'How about this: you go with Zoe. Be her spotter.'

Julius thought about that and acquiesced, nodding silently.

Zoe said, 'Jack, I don't have a sniper rifle. Just a few pistols.'

'You're the best marksman I know,' Jack said. 'You can make the shot if needed. Sky Monster, can you drive with that shoulder?'

'I can manage.'

'Then you're our ride.'

'Jack, wait,' Iolanthe said, observing all this from the side.

She reached into her bag and pulled out a laminated identification card.

A label on it read 'C-9'.

Jack had seen ID cards like this before: they were used by intelligence agencies like MI6 and the CIA. They designated their holder as a government agent who was not to be detained by the police under any circumstances. They were known in the trade as 'Get Out of Jail Free' cards. A C-7 card told the police to let you pass without question. A C-9, two levels above that, was the highest classification in the entire British government system.

'Take this,' she said. 'It'll get you past the police.'

Jack took it.

'And Lily, here.'

Iolanthe handed Lily an ornate little pistol with a pearl handle. 'Just in case.'

Lily jammed the gun into the back of her waistband.

'All right,' Jack said. 'Let's go out there.'

The tank was still standing on Westminster Bridge when Jack and Lily arrived at the police cordon at its eastern end.

Jack showed his C-9 ID card to the cops and said, 'I'm Jack West. The one they want. She's with me.'

The dumbstruck cops let them pass.

Jack and Lily strode out onto the wide bridge, approaching the massive tank.

It stood before them like some kind of huge metal beast, tensed and ready to attack.

To the north, the London Eye was a smouldering ruin, one of its pods gone. At the opposite end of the bridge, Big Ben gave off a plume of rising smoke, wounded in its middle.

And the drone Black Hawk helicopter just kept hovering above the river a short distance to the south of the bridge, robotically still.

Jack stopped ten metres from the stationary tank.

Suddenly, loudly, Jaeger Eins's voice blared from a loudspeaker on the tank.

'*People of the world! Meet Captain Jack West Jr. I told you once that he was a hero. Now let me call him something else. Dangerous. He is a danger to all of you.*'

Jack called out, 'We came! What do you want us to do now?'

'*Come and join us in the tank, Jack,*' Jaeger Eins's voice said over the loudspeaker. '*You and Lily.*'

Jack stood his ground, cautious.

'*I said, come and join us in the tank,*' Jaeger Eins said.

In his heart, Jack knew that to step inside that tank meant death.

'*People of the world. I told you.*'

And then Jack heard it.

The sound of another helicopter—louder than the first one, a deeper *thump-thump-thump*.

Jack turned.

A huge twin-rotored Chinook chopper thundered into view over the buildings to the south and zoomed up the river toward his bridge.

Like the first chopper, this one also had painted-over windows. It was another drone. Also like the first chopper, it had a vehicle hanging from cables beneath it.

'Fuck me . . .' Jack whispered when he saw what the vehicle was.

'You have got to be kidding . . .' Lily gasped.

It was the most quintessentially London thing.

A red double-decker bus. Hanging from the underside of the helicopter.

And it was filled with people.

The Chinook pulled into a hover right in front of Westminster Bridge, barely ten metres out from it.

The bus suspended from the helicopter was so close, Jack could see the frightened faces of the passengers inside it.

'*Give yourselves up now or we drop the bus into the river. Captain, your continued existence has been responsible for six innocent deaths so far. Do you really want to add the poor souls on that bus to that tally? As you have seen by now, we do not bluff.*'

Jack's mind reeled.

He didn't know what to do.

This was totally surreal.

Here he was, with Lily, in the middle of London . . . standing on a bridge . . . with a tank beside them . . . facing a chopper . . . that was holding a London bus hostage above the river.

And that wasn't even mentioning Big Ben and the London Eye—both smoking—and the cop cars, media and crowds gathered on the shoreline, watching it all play out.

Zoe observed the scene from a rooftop on the eastern shore of the Thames with Julius by her side.

'Why are they doing this?' she asked. 'What's their plan?'

Julius said nothing in reply. He just stared off into space.

Out on the bridge, Jack was thinking the same thing.

Why are they doing this? Why go to all this trouble?

Think.

First, Lachlan. Then the bus. Two choppers. Both drones.

Drones . . .

His eyes fell on the tank.

'There's nobody inside that tank . . .' he said, realising.

As if in response, Jaeger Eins's voice came over the loudspeaker again.

'*Too late*,' he said, and to Jack's disbelief, the Chinook released the bus . . .

. . . and, in horrifying slow motion, the big red double-decker bus fell through the air before, with a gigantic splash, it plunged into the waters of the Thames.

Chaos took over.

Onlookers screamed.

The police boats on the water immediately moved in toward the bus now bobbing on the surface—only to be driven back by ruthless bursts of machine-gun fire from the two drone choppers hovering above it.

'We have to save those people!' Lily yelled to Jack above the din. 'We're closer than anyone else!'

She was right.

The bus bobbed in the water fifty feet below their bridge, a short way out from it. It was too far from the shore for anyone else to swim to, even if they could get past the choppers with their guns.

Lily drew her pearl-handled pistol and yelled to Jack. 'I'll get those people out!'

'I'll take care of the choppers!' Jack yelled back.

And so they split up: Jack sprinting toward the tank, Lily dashing toward the railing of the bridge.

Jack raced for the tank, scrambled up onto it, sliding beneath its cannon and in through its forward driver's hatch.

He encountered no resistance, because the interior of the tank was empty.

The only movement: dozens of blinking lights. The tank was indeed a drone, like the choppers. The Knights weren't going to strand themselves in the middle of London.

Jack found and yanked off the radio transponder connecting the tank to the Knights and suddenly the tank was his.

He leapt into the gunner's chair.

Outside, Lily took a bounding stride up onto the railing of the bridge and launched herself off it, leaping high into the air above the river.

She fell in a high arc, feet first, before she plunged into the Thames a few metres from the stricken bus.

The bus was sinking, slowly but steadily.

Its lower level was filling rapidly and the twenty or so people in it had moved to the upper level.

Lily swam to its rear . . .

. . . and saw some kind of gluggy industrial glue—Araldite maybe—plastered all over the edges of the bus's rear emergency escape window, sealing it.

Lily hauled herself out of the water and onto the roof of the bus. She came to a hatch there.

The passengers on the bus were hammering on it from below, from the inside, but Lily could see why they couldn't open it.

A padlock.

Someone had padlocked the hatch from the outside.

Above her, the two drone choppers were still creating an almighty racket.

They were still firing their guns—but not at her. They were firing at the police boats, keeping them away from the bus.

And then—*BOOOOM!*—without warning, the bigger of the two choppers exploded, hit by . . .

. . . a shot from the tank on the bridge!

The great chopper rocked in the air and fell out of the sky, splashing down into the river a moment before a second shot from the tank hit the smaller one, the Black Hawk, and it too dropped from the sky.

And suddenly Lily had the bus to herself.

Two shots from her pistol took care of the padlock.

Lily yanked open the hatch and before anyone could emerge from it, she leapt down *into* the sinking bus.

Inside the bus, panic reigned.

The entire lower level was underwater and the waves of the Thames lapped against the windows of the upper level.

'Go!' Lily yelled to the passengers. 'Get out!'

But it quickly became apparent that they wouldn't all get out in time.

She needed to find another way out.

'Oh, to hell with it,' she said, and she opened fire on all the windows of the bus's upper level.

One after the other they shattered and water began to pour into the bus through them.

Her quick thinking had given the occupants many instant exits, and they all began diving out through the now open windows, leaping into the river outside as the bus sank lower and lower.

Up on the bridge, Jack emerged from the tank and raced for the railing.

He peered down at the river below him and saw the big red bus, now half-sunk, with only its upper level above the surface.

People were leaping out of it, emerging from the shattered windows on both sides of the bus.

'Good work, Lily,' he said softly. 'Good work.'

But he didn't see Lily—not on the sinking bus or among the crowd of people swimming away from it.

He hurled himself over the railing, falling for fifty feet before plunging into the river.

Zoe was watching all this helplessly from her position on the bank of the Thames.

She stood.

'Come on,' she said to Julius, 'we gotta go help—'

It was only then that she noticed that Julius was gone.

Inside the sinking bus, Lily now stood in waist-deep water, helping the last two passengers—an elderly couple—get to the smashed windows.

'Lily!' She heard Jack's voice from the hatch. 'You in there?'

'I'm here!' she called as she shoved the couple out through a window.

The water was up to her stomach now.

She took a final look around her. The bus was empty. The passengers were safe.

It was time to leave.

She turned toward the window just as something—someone—under the surface of the water gripped her firmly by the ankle and pulled her under.

Seconds later, Jack dropped down into the interior of the sinking bus, landing in the chest-deep water.

Only the whole bus was empty.

Lily was nowhere to be seen.

'What the hell—?' he gasped.

And then a strong hand gripped him by the ankle and yanked him underwater—

—and suddenly Jack found himself struggling with a man in a scuba-diving suit, inside the still-sinking bus!

Bubbles flew up all around them as they fought. The river water was a sickly green.

Then the flashing blade of a knife came rushing at Jack, but he parried it away.

At that moment, the entire bus went under and abruptly, beyond his attacker, through all the bubbles around them, he saw Lily being dragged out of the sinking bus by two more divers in scuba gear.

They had jammed a full-face breathing mask over her head and were taking her away on a propeller-driven underwater sled.

Jack screamed soundlessly through the water as Lily disappeared into the gloom.

And in that instant—as he struggled against his own assassin—Jack saw the Knights' plan.

They'd got him hook, line and sinker.

They'd known he and Lily would leap into the river to save the bus, and while their drones had been causing havoc up top, the Knights of the Golden Eight had been waiting here, underwater, in scuba gear, to take Lily and kill Jack.

Anger surged through Jack.

He rounded on the diver holding him, disarmed him and stabbed him through the throat.

Then, his lungs burning, desperate for air, Jack swam out of the sinking bus for the surface.

As he swam upward, his eyes searched the murky water for Lily. He saw the big red double-decker bus drifting down through the off-green haze, toward the riverbed.

But no Lily.

Then he broke the surface and sucked in air. Deep heaving gasps.

The two police boats were picking up the passengers from the water near him.

A third police boat swept in beside him and a SWAT officer reached over the gunwale and pulled Jack out of the water in one swift movement.

'Please!' Jack said, hurriedly finding his C-9 card in his pocket and holding it up for them. 'Please! You gotta listen to me, they've taken my daughter and I—'

'I have one of those cards, too, Captain,' a tall hulking figure said as he stepped out from behind the SWAT cop.

It was Yago.

Hades's brother and the royal jailer.

'It's a "Get Out of Jail Free" card. But trust me, it doesn't apply to the jail you're going to.'

'Wait!' Jack said quickly. 'Yago, wait! Listen! Orlando is going to the first city and if he—'

He never finished the sentence, for it was then that another SWAT officer hit Jack in the back of the head and he saw nothing but black.

ICELAND
THULEAN PLATEAU, NORTH ATLANTIC OCEAN
400 MILES NORTHWEST OF BRITAIN

At the same time as London was roiling in chaos, Orlando Compton-Jones, the King of Land, was arriving in Iceland with Cardinal Ricardo Mendoza, Ms Chloe Carnarvon and a squad of twenty crack members of the Swiss Guard, the traditional mercenary guards of the Vatican.

After leaving St Michael's Mount and dispatching Sunny Malik to find Poseidon's tomb and the Mace, Orlando and the others had come here.

With its black-sand beaches, active volcanoes and forbidding mountain peaks, Iceland is one of the most isolated, rugged and spectacular places on Earth. It is assaulted by some of the most inhospitable weather found on the planet: bitterly cold winds; slashing rains; and temperatures that hover just above freezing. For three thousand years, Icelanders have been known as hardy folk.

Its coasts are exceedingly difficult to access. Due to its violent seismic origins—Iceland sits not only at the junction of two tectonic plates but also atop a hotspot—Iceland's mountains and volcanoes often plunge directly into the ocean. Thousand-foot-high cliffs are common.

After spending a day in Reykjavik equipping themselves and their Swiss escorts—there was no knowing how long they might be inside the secret city of Thule, so they took food and water for three days—Orlando, Mendoza, Chloe and their troops helicoptered to the most distant corner of Iceland, its southeastern tip.

No roads came here. It was accessible only by chopper, and then only on fine days. Communication was also limited: electromagnetic interference from the constant subterranean volcanism made satellite phones and radios all but useless.

At length they came to a very remote and very high cliff gazing out over the raging waves of the Atlantic.

Chiselled into the deep grey stone of the cliff just below its summit—and cut in such a way that only those who looked for it would find it—was a stone structure with three windows in it that looked like the cupola of lighthouse.

If one looked closely at the entire cliff below this cupola, one could just discern the outline of a colossal lighthouse carved into the face of the cliff. The illusion was achieved because the stone of this lighthouse's walls looked as if it had been melted.

A lone man was waiting for them.

An old man.

The keeper of the City of Thule and this, its watchtower.

'Your Majesty,' he said as he bowed before Orlando. 'I am Sir Bjorn, the First of the Three Watchmen, the Trismagi. Welcome to the Watchtower of the City of Thule.'

Sir Bjorn guided Orlando, Mendoza and Chloe down a worn stone stairway inside the lighthouse.

It ran in a tight spiral. He lit the way with a flashlight.

Oddly, the further they descended, the fresher the air became. They felt it rushing against their faces.

At length, they came to a stone chamber that opened onto the sea, barely ten feet above the raging waves. It was a small room, square in shape, with walls of stone; a shelf cut into the cliff, designed to look out over the furious sea.

Waves crashed against the cliffs, sending spray into the chamber. Indeed, every surface of it was slick with wetness and stank of the ocean.

'The watchtower's entry sanctum is tidal,' Sir Bjorn said. 'It can

only be accessed at low tide. The rest of the time, this entry cave is underwater.'

At the back of the shelf-like room was a flight of broad stone stairs going up. Like the room, they were carved into the cliff.

The four of them ascended the stairs.

At the top of the short staircase—above the high-tide mark— they found themselves inside a small antechamber, in the centre of which stood a low altar made of a peculiar type of cloudy white stone. Delving into the rear wall of the chamber was a tunnel that stretched away into darkness.

'Is that a diamond?' Chloe gasped as she circled the altar.

It did look like an uncut diamond: a *waist-high* slab of diamond with a single slot cut into its top.

'You have the weapon?' Bjorn asked solemnly.

'I do,' Orlando answered.

He removed the fabled sword from its scabbard. Its silver blade glistened in the dull light.

It had been known by many names over the millennia: the Sword of Khufu, the Blade of Christ, Caliburn, Excalibur, the Sword of the Rock, the Sword in the Stone.

'Being the first of the three cities confers on Thule a singular role,' Sir Bjorn said. 'For the entry into Thule by one bearing the Sword marks the commencement of the First Trial. Please insert the weapon into the altar and the trial will be formally begun.'

Orlando's eyes gleamed as he stepped up to the white-diamond altar. Like the sword he held in his hand, the altar was beyond ancient.

This is historic, Orlando thought. *Historic on a level unheard of in any era of the world.*

He held the sword above the slot in the altar, noting that they matched in size.

Cardinal Mendoza stared intently at his king, holding his breath in anticipation.

Chloe gazed proudly at Orlando, her expression a mix of ambition, adoration and lust.

Orlando plunged the sword into the white-stone altar and for a brief moment the altar blazed with other-worldly silver light, illuminating all of their faces.

'Godspeed and good fortune to you all,' Sir Bjorn said. 'The Trial of the Cities has begun.'

THE TRIPLE-ARCHWAYS

Instantly, a second blast of silver light blazed out from the far end of the tunnel, the inner end, from perhaps a kilometre away.

It created a tiny dot of light at the end of the long tunnel.

But the light also revealed something *in* the tunnel: a short way down it, three archways spanned its width. They looked like three open doorways side-by-side.

Looking further down the tunnel, Orlando saw half-a-dozen more triple-archways marching down its length. One thing was clear: to reach the city, you had to pass through all of them.

'What is this?' Orlando asked.

'The Great Avenue of the City,' Sir Bjorn said. 'It is approximately one kilometre long. Each of the three cities has such an avenue and each avenue is defended by seven triple-archways. Only one who knows their secret can pass through the arches. Those who don't will die.'

Orlando scowled. He looked at the triple-archway directly in front of him. 'So one arch is safe, the other two are booby-trapped?'

'Yes.'

Orlando threw a look at Mendoza. 'Please tell me you know how to choose the correct arch.'

Mendoza nodded. 'But of course, Your Majesty. Let me show you.'

Mendoza pulled out a photo of the triangular tablet with the missing chunk and, using it in a certain way, he guided them safely through all seven triple-archways.

Thus they passed through the Great Avenue of the City of Thule, trailed by their force of twenty Swiss Guardsmen.

So absorbed were they all with getting past the archways, they never noticed that both the ceiling and the floor of the long tunnel were made of long grey rectangular paving stones, each about seven feet in length and a few feet across.

Finally, after stepping safely through the last triple-archway, they emerged in a wider underground space, where the silver light was brighter.

'Goodness,' Chloe said.

Mendoza's jaw dropped.

Orlando just smiled.

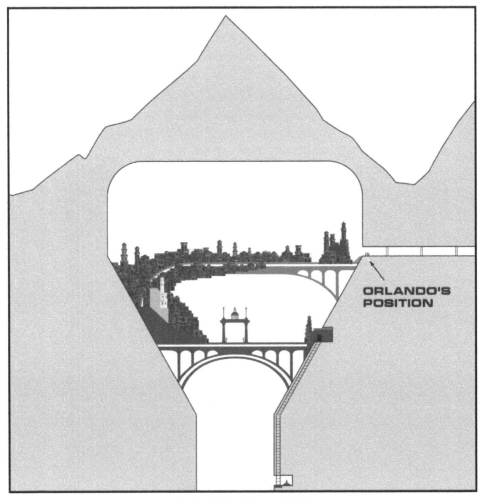

ORLANDO'S
POSITION

THE CITY OF THULE

They stood at the top of a gigantic funnel that delved into the Earth.

A descending circular path wound around the edge of the funnel in a colossal spiral, crossing it at one point via a spectacular bridge with an open-sided cupola in its middle.

Battlements and ramparts, temples and arches dotted the path until a many-levelled castle connected the curving road to the bridge.

The source of the shining silver light came from deep within the giant abyss, way down at the bottom of the funnel, where its sloping walls went vertical.

The ethereal glow came from within a stone door burrowed into the wall there, at the base of a vertical ladder. It was strong now but visibly dimming.

'The Vault of Thule,' Sir Bjorn said. 'That is where you must take the Sword. That is where you will empower it.'

Orlando spun, energised.

'Very good,' he said. 'Cardinal? Can you accomplish this task? With all the seismic interference, you won't be able to radio for assistance.'

'I have waited my whole life for this time, Your Majesty,' Mendoza said. 'We will succeed here for you.'

Orlando nodded. 'Excellent. Chloe, you will go to Ra with the Helmet. I shall see how Malik is progressing in his search for the Mace and once we have it, get it to Atlas.'

★ ★ ★

And so Cardinal Mendoza stayed, and with his cohort of twenty Swiss Guards, began planning their descent into the secret city of Thule.

Orlando and Chloe left, guided by Sir Bjorn.

They retraced their steps through the kilometre-long tunnel, passing through the safe archways, and back up the spiral staircase inside the cliff.

Sir Bjorn bid them farewell and soon they were in the air, heading back to Reykjavik.

They never saw what happened inside the Great Avenue minutes after they departed.

Never saw the polished rectangular paving stones in the floor and the ceiling fold open like doors or, rather, like the lids of the stone coffins that they really were: coffins exactly like the ones in the Underworld at the Great Bend.

Cardinal Ricardo Mendoza and his Swiss military escorts didn't see them open either.

They stood at the top of the great funnel-shaped city of Thule, assessing it, figuring out how they would tackle its sweeping, descending path.

And then they heard it.

A deep chilling intonation from inside the Great Avenue behind them. It sounded like the chant of an unholy choir.

Three hundred voices called as one, '*Kushma alla?*'

'What was that?' the soldier nearest to Mendoza said.

Mendoza's eyes went wide. 'The guardians of this place.'

The next thing they heard—again coming from the long tunnel—was the rhythmic stomping of three hundred pairs of heavy feet marching in time and getting louder.

'Go!' Mendoza yelled to his men. 'Go!'

At that same moment, in the other two cities at their secret locations elsewhere in the world, similar things happened.

For both of those cities also contained hundreds of ancient coffins.

And they too began to open.

For when you open the first, you open the second and the third.

THE SECRET ROYAL WORLD

THE PRISON AT EREBUS

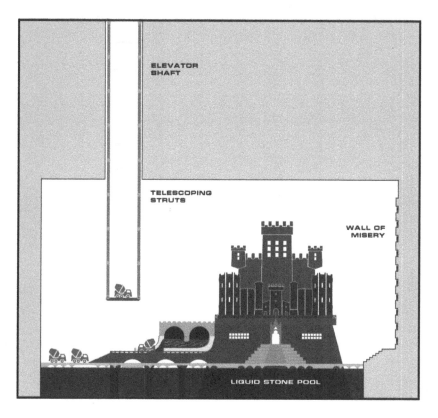

When they reached the mountain's summit, even Clancy took a pull,
It well might make the boldest hold their breath,
The wild hop scrub grew thickly, and the hidden ground was full
Of wombat holes, and any slip was death.
But the man from Snowy River let the pony have his head,
And he swung his stockwhip round and gave a cheer,
And he raced him down the mountain like a torrent down its bed,
While the others stood and watched in very fear.

A.B. 'BANJO' PATERSON, 'THE MAN FROM SNOWY RIVER'

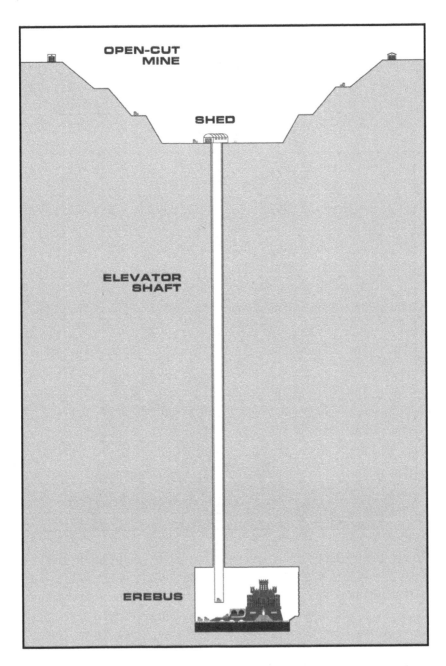

THE MINE & THE PRISON

THE ROYAL PRISON AT EREBUS
LOCATION: UNKNOWN
27 NOVEMBER, TIME: UNKNOWN

When he finally awoke, Jack found himself, oddly, standing upright.

Well, not quite upright. He was tilted backwards at an angle.

Then he realised that he was on a wheeled hand-truck, his arms and legs bound to its struts with thick buckled belts. His head was also tied back, fastened to the hand-truck by a leather strap that covered his mouth.

He was inside the hold of a military plane of some kind and it was in flight, engines whining.

Two guards in black uniforms saw him wake and they alerted Yago, sitting nearby, wearing a pair of noise-cancelling headphones.

Yago looked idly over at Jack and nodded to one of the guards.

The guard promptly smashed Jack in the face with the butt of his rifle and Jack's world plunged into blackness again.

Jack was jerked awake by sudden and intense bright light.

He was being rolled out of the rear ramp of the cargo plane into brilliant sunshine.

Searing heat engulfed him. Desert heat.

Jack squinted in the blazing sunlight.

He glimpsed a vast sea of sand dunes stretching away before him and the ocean behind him. He was on a tiny airstrip between them.

A gargantuan skeletal structure towered over him: a conveyor belt mounted on high iron pylons. It was the kind of industrial-sized conveyor belt one saw at iron ore mines. It stretched for a full five hundred metres from somewhere inland to a concrete dock beside the airstrip, where it poured grey ore into the hold of a cargo ship parked at the dock.

A desert on a coast, Jack thought.

North Africa, maybe?

Suddenly, Yago appeared in front of him.

'You are fifty miles from anywhere, Captain,' he said. 'There is only desert on three sides and on the fourth is the sea. And it is all my property. Even if you could escape, you wouldn't survive a day out there.'

Jack was wheeled up a ramp into the back of a canvas-covered truck.

After a short drive inland, the truck came to a colossal hole in the ground: an open-cut mine.

A single narrow road was cut into the perimeter of the deep circular crater. It spiralled downward from the crater's rim, sheer cliffs dropping away from its inner edge all the way down.

Tiny cement trucks worked their way up and down the gently-sloping road.

To Jack, they looked like toys.

It was only when his vehicle passed one of the cement trucks—it was going up while his was going down—that he realised the monumental scale of the place.

First, the spiralling cliff-side road wasn't narrow at all; it was wide enough for two trucks to pass one another side-by-side.

And second, the cement truck that had rumbled past him was *enormous*. Its tyres alone were twenty feet high: huge rubber things that turned slowly. The constantly-rotating cement mixer on its back was at least the size of a shipping container.

Jack also noticed another thing about the cement truck: it had no driver.

It was automated. This was common in mining nowadays and it was very easy to do: you just programmed the trucks to know the roadway's GPS coordinates and up and down they went, all day, every day, perfectly safely.

Jack's truck arrived at a huge shed at the base of the crater.

It was an old rusty structure, circular in shape, with flimsy corrugated-iron walls and a flat sheet-metal roof. In the already relentless desert sun, it looked like a heat-box.

Jack sighed. *Shit.*

Still bound to the hand-truck, he was wheeled into it.

Inside the shed, filling the entire space, was a huge round turntable, perhaps ninety feet in diameter.

A cement truck rolled off the turntable and headed outside while a waiting empty truck rolled forward onto the turntable.

With Yago walking beside him, Jack was wheeled onto the turntable beside the big cement-mixing truck . . .

. . . and suddenly with a mighty mechanical groan, the steel turntable began to go *down*.

It wasn't a turntable.

It was an elevator.

An open-sided roofless elevator.

The stone walls of the cylindrical shaft *whoosh*ed steadily upward as the huge industrial elevator descended into the Earth.

This elevator, Jack saw, had no cable.

Given the size and weight of the trucks it carried, it needed a more robust motor than that. To that end, the shaft had two huge ladder-like structures on either side of it made of sturdy iron. Jack guessed that on the underside of his platform was a pair of motorised cog-wheels that locked into the ladders, driving the elevator up and down the shaft.

The elevator descended steadily for a full five minutes.

Yago said, 'This elevator travels for exactly one mile, straight down. One thousand six hundred metres, all of it vertical.'

At length, the wide steel platform emerged in a large cavern deep within the bowels of the Earth and as it did, Jack felt his blood curdle.

The elevator platform had come out of a round hole in the ceiling of the cavern, three hundred feet above its floor.

To reach the floor of the cavern—to cover those last three hundred feet—the iron ladders set into the walls of the shaft extended downward like a pair of telescoping rails.

When the platform touched the ground, those extendable rails immediately withdrew back up into the ceiling, making escape impossible.

What Jack saw around him was like nothing he had ever seen: an incredible space that held a grey castle-like structure, a giant wall filled with what looked like rectangular bas-reliefs or frescoes, and a wide pool of bubbling grey-black liquid.

But it wasn't the sight that had made Jack recoil.

It was the sound and the smell.

Wails and screams: cries of desperate agony that echoed across the cavernous space.

And the stench of human urine.

'Captain West,' Yago said. 'Welcome to Erebus, the Royal Prison. It is a place of much pain and no pity, and it will be your home for the rest of your miserable life.'

Jack was rolled on his hand-truck across the gigantic subterranean cavern.

The short journey gave him a brief chance to take in the space.

To his left, looking out over the cavern was the castle. Made of black-grey stone, it appeared to be embedded in the northern wall, kind of like the carved buildings of Petra, Jordan.

Its design was magnificent.

It bore pointed towers, twisting pillars, curved balconies and a broad staircase at its front. The truly incredible thing was, *the whole structure appeared to be cut from a single piece of stone.*

There was not a single seam to be seen on the entire edifice.

Jack wondered how anyone could have carved such a complex structure out of stone.

The floor of the cavern also caught Jack's attention, because it was *not* solid.

It was composed almost entirely of a bubbling grey-black liquid that appeared to have the texture of quicksand. The shifting ooze gave off steam, warming the otherwise cool cavern.

A low cement bridge spanned the pool, crossing the cavern and passing in front of the castle. Smaller side-bridges branched off it, disappearing into tunnels from which a constant stream of cement trucks came and went, loaded with dark-grey dust of some sort.

Looking down at the bubbling grey-black pool, Jack suddenly realised that he had seen this curious substance before.

In the Underworld.

It was the same steaming conglomerate that had been dropped

on the hostages when their champion had died in a challenge, drowning them.

He had also seen it in Venice, in the lair of the Order of the Omega: where they had used it to turn a captured man into a statue.

Yago saw the realisation dawn on him.

'It is called liquid stone,' he said, 'and it is a most remarkable substance. It acts rather like cement and, in the hands of a master craftsman, it can be moulded into all manner of complex shapes: bridges, pillars, castles, towers, temples. When heated to the right temperature, it exists in semi-liquid/semi-solid form, enabling it to be shaped and moulded. When it cools, it becomes fully solid.'

Yago grinned. 'Which allows me to use it in one especially handy way.'

It was then that Jack came close enough to see the high wall at the end of the cavern, and now he saw that the rectangular bas-reliefs in it were not bas-reliefs or frescoes at all.

They were slabs of stone, and embedded in each slab was a person, with the back half of his or her body *set into* solidified liquid stone.

Jack counted six rows of the slabs rising up the high wall, five or six prisoners to each row.

This was the source of the screams and wails: for the people set into the stone slabs *were still alive*. They didn't all scream and wail. Some groaned in pain, others just hung their heads, while one poor fellow babbled incoherently, clearly insane.

They were also the source of the rank smell of the place. Since they couldn't move from their individual stone prisons, they were left to urinate on themselves.

'It is known as the Wall of Misery,' Yago said. 'An apt name.'

And then as his eyes roamed over the wall, Jack saw him, in the bottom row, his body encased in the liquid stone, his chest bare, his face twisted in pain.

Hades.

'It's so nice to reunite you with my dear brother,' Yago said, glancing at Hades. 'In the royal world, punishment is clear and severe. It is the only way to ensure respect for the existing order.'

He removed the leather strap that covered Jack's mouth.

Jack stared helplessly at Hades.

Yago said, 'I believe you once also met my dear friend, Vladimir Karnov, the former King of Land, known to some as Carnivore.'

Jack nodded.

'I heard you killed him,' Yago said. 'Is that true?'

'Yes.'

He didn't say that he'd shot Carnivore to death with a wave of heavy-bore anti-aircraft rounds from almost point-blank range.

'To be fair, you didn't know he was a king at the time,' Yago said. 'He was a fine man, Carnivore. Firm. Strong. A man of deep conviction. I miss him. You know, he used to keep those who wronged him in formaldehyde tanks. Few know it, but Carnivore was actually inspired to do that by a visit to this place. But formaldehyde, well, it doesn't act in the same way liquid stone does.'

Jack's hand-truck was stopped in front of a rectangular stone tray about the size of a large bathtub.

Inside it was water.

The two guards pulled Jack from the hand-truck, tore off his shirt and lay him horizontally on his back in the water inside the stone tub.

Jack lay face-up in the water, his arms still tied behind his back, the water rising to just below his ears.

Then Yago stepped up into his field of vision.

He held between two fingers a pinch of grey-black powder. It looked like gunpowder, only finer, much finer.

'This is what we mine here,' Yago said. 'It is an old and rare substance, found only in six places in the world, the core ingredient of liquid stone. In dry form, both visually and in chemical structure, it is easily mistaken for fine volcanic soils like picrite basalt and pitchstone, but it is capable of so much more than they are.

'It has been called stone dust, grey matter, greystone and, my favourite, Gorgon Stone. It is how the ancients built their colossal structures, from Hades's mountain-palace to my castle here to the six temple-shrines of the Great Machine that you rebuilt. Allow me to show you how it works.'

He sprinkled a few grains of the grey-black powder into the water of Jack's tub.

Jack felt the reaction instantly.

The water around his body began to press against his sides and somehow *thicken*.

It was a terrifying sensation and Jack began to breathe faster.

He turned his head slightly and saw that the clear water around his body had become an opaque black and as it changed colour, it also changed form: from liquid to solid.

It was becoming denser, heavier.

'I would advise you not to turn your head too far, Captain,' Yago said. 'Whatever position your head is in will, very shortly, be its final position. I'd hate for you to spend the rest of your life with a crick in your neck.'

Panting now, Jack quickly returned his face to an upward position and felt the grey-black ooze pinch around his head, legs and ribcage.

It was getting noticeably thicker, more gluggy.

'The reaction of the grey matter to water is quite remarkable,' Yago said. 'My scientists tell me that on a molecular level, it is forming what is called an *exponential lattice*. It is like a nuclear chain reaction. For every bond the grey matter makes with the water molecule, one hundred more are made, which is how such a small amount of powder can solidify the entire tub around you. It also has to do with the special properties of water, like its ability to form ice.'

Abruptly, Jack heard a series of ominous cracks and to his horror the inward press of the substance suddenly took on a different quality: the grey-black ooze around him had started to *harden*.

Jack clenched his teeth at the pain.

'The prisoners in this place are here for various crimes,' Yago said. 'Some stole from their royal masters. Some were caught plotting. Some, like my brother, failed in their royal duties. Some are killers and rapists. And then there is you: a man who dared to defy all four kings.'

The dark ooze around Jack was now entirely solid.

Yago gazed down at him, lying face-up in what was now a dark-grey slab, the entire back half of his body, including his arms, embedded in the stuff. His front half, including his bare chest, protruded from it.

Yago said, 'It feels like the liquid stone around you has set, but it is not done yet. It will cool further. And like everything that cools, it will *contract* and slowly squeeze you. First, it will squeeze your skin, causing it to burst in places. Then—very slowly, over the course of months and years—it will crack your bones. Your skull will feel it first—a steady, firm pressure—then your shoulders and your legs.

'You will be drip-fed water and just enough nutrients to keep you alive, if this state can be called living. If you excrete anything, you will do it over yourself. Don't worry, you will get used to the smell.

'For a sentence at the Prison at Erebus is a sentence to a lifetime of pain and agony. Listen to the screams of those around you. I adore that sound. It soothes me. Sends me to sleep at night. Soon, your screams will join theirs, Captain. Yours will be another voice in this choir of the damned.

'Sleep if you can. Dream of rescue, if you choose. But know that

such a thing will only ever be a dream. No-one knows the location of this place but me, and my guards cannot reveal it for they were born here.

'No, it is here that you will die, Jack West Jr. For in over five thousand years of recorded history, no prisoner has ever escaped from this place.'

Once the liquid stone had set, Jack's stone tub was raised into a vertical position and mounted on the Wall of Misery beside Hades.

From his own identical position on the wall—embedded in a slab, hands behind his back—Hades had watched the whole grim procedure. Once Jack was on the wall beside him and Yago was gone, he spoke.

'We meet again, Captain.'

'We do.'

'Got a clever plan to get out of here?' Hades asked.

'No. Hoping my friends might, though.'

'You shouldn't hope,' Hades said. 'Any attempt to rescue you is foolhardy. Anyone who tries to bust you out of this prison will only earn themselves a place on this wall. You overcame the Underworld, Captain. But this place is different. This isn't the Underworld. This is Hell.'

The prisoner on Jack's other side was the insane babbler.

And he never stopped. He muttered about his innocence and about 'the voices that made him do it'. Some of the other prisoners on the Wall called out, 'Quit it, Rubles!' 'Shut your fucking mouth, you mad bastard!'

The insane fellow—Rubles—merely replied, 'Come and fucking shut it, you miserable bastards.'

Then he started singing.

'*Ninety-nine bottles of beer on the wall, ninety-nine bottles of beer . . . !*'

Jack just closed his eyes and tried to tune it out.

Down in the depths of the ancient prison, one could not tell the difference between night and day.

Yago's silent guards, however, turned the cavern's lights on and off in a twelve-hour cycle, effectively creating a day-night rhythm.

In the last hours of his first 'day'—while Rubles sang—Jack gazed out at the cavern.

There was only one entrance: the wide circular hole in the ceiling from which the elevator descended into the cavern.

It was three hundred feet above the floor.

There was no ladder to it. No way to access it.

He could see why no-one had ever escaped.

Then, abruptly, the lights went out.

On that first night in the prison, Jack slept fitfully. The solidified liquid stone binding his body in place was hard and unforgiving. He could feel it contracting. The first couple of times he awoke, Rubles was still singing. Mercifully, by the third time, the insane man had himself fallen asleep.

Thank God, Jack thought.

He continued to doze unevenly until finally exhaustion overtook him and he fell into a deep sleep.

But then, at some point during that first night, while all around him slept, a blinding flashlight to his eyes woke him and, for a moment, Jack dared to hope someone had come to rescue him.

Two figures stood before his slab, shadows in the darkness.

One was Yago.

'Here he is,' he said.

Jack squinted against the glare of Yago's flashlight.

The second figure didn't move as he stared hard at Jack. He was about the same build as Yago, which was to say he was burly, tall and strong.

When he spoke, he had a deep, gravelly voice.

'So this is him,' the man said. 'The one who has caused so much trouble. The hero.'

'You don't have to talk about me in the third person,' Jack said. 'I'm awake.'

The man smiled at that: an indulgent smile. 'Given your reputation, Captain West, I thought you'd be . . . bigger.'

'Who are you?' Jack asked.

'I am but a humble lighthouse keeper,' the man said. He stepped forward so that his face came into the light inches away from Jack's.

He had broad leonine features and everything about his face was big: large eyes, large nose, broad mouth. He also, Jack saw, had two ghostly grey eyes.

'It's a pleasure to meet you, Captain,' he said. 'You may not know it, but by doing what you did at the Great Games, you upset the natural order of the royal world and created an opening for those of us who would like to institute a new kind of rule on this planet.'

'Who are you?' Jack asked again.

The man with the pale grey eyes seemed to ponder that question.

Then he smiled his wide leonine grin.

'My name is Hardin Lancaster XII. I am the Lord and Keeper of the Watchtower of the City of Atlas, the Third of the Trismagi. Those who know me call me Sphinx.'

He turned on his heel.

'Intriguing as you are, Captain, I must go. I have an appointment to keep with the gentleman who paid for the capture of your adopted daughter and with the Knights of the Golden Eight.'

Jack's eyes sprang wide at the mention of Lily. The man with the pale eyes seemed to enjoy the reaction.

'Enjoy the rest of your life, Jack West Jr, wretched as it will be. And know that this is what becomes of heroes.'

Then the flashlight went out and the two visitors' footsteps faded away into the darkness, and soon the cavern around Jack was silent once more.

AIRSPACE OVER THE ATLANTIC OCEAN
ORLANDO'S PRIVATE JET

Orlando Compton-Jones lay with his hands clasped behind his head on the sumptuous king-sized bed in the master suite of his Gulfstream private jet, naked, watching as Chloe Carnarvon, also naked except for a pair of red high-heeled shoes, strode into the bathroom.

They had just had hard passionate sex, up against the wall.

Orlando liked sex with Chloe. Still in her twenties, she was young and fit. Her body was firm and pert in all the right places. And the way she moaned with delight at his moves, he wondered if young men knew how to pleasure a woman any more.

And she was clever, too—

His computer pinged. The secure line. The monarch's line.

He threw on a robe and clicked on the keyboard.

On the screen, he saw the faces of two of the other kings, plus that of Yago, the royal jailer.

Both of the other kings on the screen were visibly younger than Orlando was, colts in their thirties.

Due to the chaos at the end of the Great Games, they were both new to their thrones.

The Caldwell lad from America was the new Sea King. His father had been cut down in the riot at the conclusion of the Games.

And the Xi fellow from China was the new King of the Sky.

Xi's Tibetan-born predecessor had been killed in the same melee; he had also died without an heir, his two sons having fought and died in the Great Games. His crown had passed, in accordance with his specific instructions, to Xi.

There was no King of the Underworld on the call. After Hades had failed in his solemn duty to produce a winning king from the Games, he had been stripped of his crown, but evidently no new King of the Underworld had been named yet.

'Your Majesties,' Yago said formally. 'I am pleased to report to you that, in accordance with the royal warrants issued for them, the fugitives Lord Hades and Captain Jack West Jr have been apprehended and taken into custody.'

Orlando grinned. This was excellent news. He didn't want West running around ruining his plans to get to the three cities.

Yago said, 'Both fugitives were taken to the prison at Erebus and I personally oversaw their entombment in the Wall of Misery. I was there until the stone fully hardened. I would like to extend my thanks to the Kings of Sea and Land who gave me full freedom of access in New York and London, and who also provided me with police and military resources. Thank you, sires.'

'A pleasure,' the King of the Sea said.

'Of course,' Orlando said.

Yago said, 'Then it is done. Order has been restored. Majesties, I remain your humble servant.'

They all hung up.

Orlando nodded with great satisfaction.

Chloe came out of the bathroom, grabbed a flimsy satin gown off a hook and began to put it on over her lithe body.

'Good news?' she said.

'Fantastic news,' Orlando said. 'West is imprisoned at Erebus. Our way is clear. When we land, you will continue on to Ra in South America, unhindered by West. And I will soon have the Mace and go to Atlas.'

Chloe nodded slowly. 'You will soon be the ruler of the world. As you deserve.'

She gave him a look . . . and slipped the flimsy little gown off, revealing her spectacular naked body once again.

'Would His Majesty like a reward?' she said coyly, slipping into his bed again.

'Indeed,' Orlando said. 'Oh, indeed.'

LONDON, ENGLAND
26–28 NOVEMBER

Zoe burst into the flat and went straight to Iolanthe. Mae was still there, watching over the battered princess.

'Where is the royal prison!' Zoe demanded. 'The Knights got Lily and then that Yago bastard turned up and grabbed Jack.'

Mae's face went pale. 'The royal jailer captured Jack?'

'Yes, and if we're going to rescue Lily and Alby, we need to get Jack back and we need to do it now. Where is the royal prison, Iolanthe?'

'Like I said before,' Iolanthe said, 'I don't know. No-one knows the location of Erebus except for the royal jailer himself.'

'You said it's believed to be somewhere in the Mediterranean Sea. Crete, Malta or even Troy,' Zoe said desperately. 'Can we try any of those? *Any* of them?'

'We can try,' Iolanthe said, giving Zoe a genuinely sympathetic grimace. 'But I don't want to give you false hope. Others have attempted this before and all of them failed.'

Putting aside for the moment their task of finding the coffin of Sir Francis Drake—and in the case of Zoe and Iolanthe, their prior battles—the three women spent the next two days chasing up every lead they could find on the location of the Prison at Erebus: from reading the entire history of Crete, to examining ancient family lines whose members had been royal jailers, to dissecting the Great Siege of Malta by Ottoman forces in 1565.

But, in the end, they found nothing.

No mention of a location. Not a single trace of information.

The location of the fabled prison at Erebus was indeed one of history's most closely guarded secrets.

After forty-eight hours of solid searching, Mae sighed. 'Zoe, it's hopeless. We can't find him.'

'We *have* to find him,' Zoe said. 'He'd do it for us.'

Iolanthe shook her head. 'If only it were that easy. Finding lost ancient places can be done when you have the information at hand and particular references to guide you, but not in this case. I'm sorry, Zoe, I really am, but if Jack's been taken to Erebus, he might as well have vanished from the face of the Earth.'

THE SECRET ROYAL WORLD II

THE CASTLE OF THE KNIGHTS

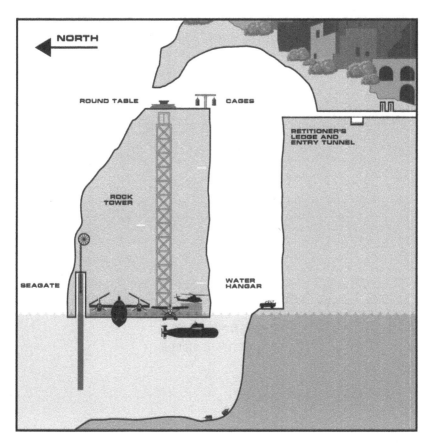

Cry 'Havoc!', and let slip the dogs of war.

WILLIAM SHAKESPEARE, *JULIUS CAESAR*

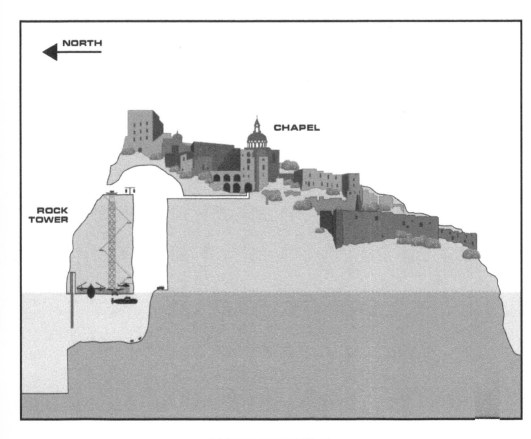

ISCHIA ISLAND &
ARAGON CASTLE

**THE CASTLE OF THE GOLDEN EIGHT
ISCHIA ISLAND, AMALFI COAST, ITALY**

It had taken the Knights of the Golden Eight two whole days to return with Lily from England to their castle on the west coast of Italy.

It could have been done faster, but on this occasion, given the value of their prize, the Knights opted for stealth over speed. Travelling by submarine was slower, but it made discovery exceedingly difficult.

Their initial escape from London, for instance, had been accomplished by travelling almost the entire length of the Thames underwater.

They had used an eight-man propeller-driven sled used by the British SAS and US Navy SEALs known as a wet combat submersible. The Knights had ridden on the sled in their scuba gear, clipped to it, gripping Lily in their midst, also in a full-face mask and also clipped on. Built by Lockheed Martin at a cost of about $80 million, the wet combat submersible was lean, fast, state-of-the-art and very, very quiet.

At the mouth of the Thames, they had linked up with a Russian-made Akula-class fast-attack submarine waiting in the Channel. After the sled had attached itself to the sub and the Knights had boarded it with Lily, the Akula had begun the slow journey back to Italy.

★ ★ ★

Two days later, on 28 November, in the middle of a gloriously sunny afternoon, it arrived off the western coast of Italy just south of the industrial port of Naples, cruising silently beneath the many supertankers and cargo ships that plied their trade at the port. The mighty bulk of Mount Vesuvius loomed in the distance, towering over everything.

The sub remained underwater as it came to a high island on which stood Aragon Castle, the home of the Golden Eight.

The castle is truly a wonder of the world: built in 474 B.C.E., it is an imposing fortress whose ramparts flow downward over six uneven levels from the island's high northern end to its lower southern end.

On every side where the towering fortified island meets the sea, its rocky walls have been shaped so that they are almost vertical and unscaleable. Ships cannot land on the island. An attacking force cannot get a foothold anywhere on it.

In medieval times, the island-fortress was unassailable. In the twenty-first century, despite the availability of air attack, it is still practically unconquerable, thanks to several concealed anti-aircraft emplacements.

The current colossal fortress that sits astride the island was built in 1441, but it is known as the *nuovo castello*, the new castle.

Over the centuries, castle upon castle has been built and rebuilt, new on top of old, but the only one that mattered to the Knights was the 'old castle', the most ancient one of them all, buried deep within the rock of the fortified island.

The Akula-class submarine entered the island via a seagate built into its northern tip: a giant rust-covered metal portcullis that came down to the water's surface but not below it, allowing the sub to enter the underground dock unseen.

To the world at large, the seagate was a decrepit relic: its rusted iron bars filled in with centuries of dirt and grime, its opening mechanism long broken.

This was not true.

The seagate worked just fine. It was just that the Knights only operated it late at night when no-one was around to see. Today, in broad daylight, they just cruised silently under it into the dock that lay behind.

Lily emerged from the submarine to find herself standing in a narrow superhigh stone cavern. Floodlights mounted on the walls lit the vast space.

The five Knights who had captured her—Jack had killed two others, while an eighth and final Knight had been in New Zealand murdering Sky Monster's parents—were met by eight younger men in combat fatigues.

'Squires!' Jaeger Eins called. 'Tend to your masters. Those of you who have lost your masters, rejoice, you are now Knights.'

The younger men—the squires, Lily guessed—hustled past her, leaping to assist the returning Knights.

Jaeger Eins added, 'Knights. Our employer has just arrived and is waiting for us upstairs.' He turned to Lily. 'And he is so *very* keen to see you again.'

Again? Lily thought.

A squire came up to Jaeger Eins.

'Sir!' He stood to attention.

'Speak, Squire Sechs,' Eins said.

'Jaeger Sechs arrived back from New Zealand two hours ago. He is upstairs in his quarters. He said to tell you that he quite enjoyed killing the old couple in Wellington.'

Jaeger Eins smiled knowingly. 'That is Sechs.'

'He also said to inform you that he has the extra package for the Lord of Atlas.'

Jaeger Eins nodded. 'I shall tell the good Lord it has been acquired. Thank you, Squire Sechs.'

Listening to them speak, Lily felt ill. The man who had killed Sky Monster's parents had enjoyed it.

She also noted their naming system. It was simple German.

Jaeger Eins translated as *Hunter One*.

Jaeger Sechs: *Hunter Six*.

'This way, please.' Jaeger Eins ushered her off the Akula.

Lily stepped onto a stone dock and took in the space.

The combat submersible was still mounted on the submarine's back. Next to the big Akula, also tied up to the dock, was another enormous vehicle: the massive Hercules seaplane Lily had fled from in Venice.

The Hercules's giant wings were folded back on hinges, a feature that had allowed it to fit through the seagate.

Other smaller vehicles were parked on adjacent docks: a Humvee, a jeep and a Mosquito helicopter.

A skyscraper-sized slab of rock stretched upward from the dock, disappearing into darkness high above the watery floor of the cavern.

The slab was absolutely huge: slick, rectangular and about three hundred feet tall.

An old switch-backing staircase scaled the perfectly sheer flank of the rock tower, but the stairs clearly hadn't been used in some time. A modern yellow gantry elevator like the kind found on a construction site had been bolted to the face of the rock tower, and it was into this that Lily was shoved by her captors.

The gantry elevator rose up the side of the rock tower, arriving at its summit.

The top of the tower was bare, polished to a sheen and rail-less at its frightening edges. The submarine dock lay far below it: three hundred feet straight down.

As Lily stepped off the elevator, surrounded by Knights, she beheld a large octagonal table mounted on an octagonal stage that sat atop a set of eight stairs.

A wide viewing balcony cut into the northern wall offered a panoramic view of Naples and Vesuvius, both gorgeous in the afternoon sun.

Two small medieval cages hung suspended from a T-shaped

wooden frame near the octagonal table, beside the vertiginous drop. One was empty, the other contained—

'Alby!' Lily cried.

She tried to run to him—confined within the tight little cage—but the two Knights on either side of her held her back.

'Now, now,' Jaeger Eins said. 'You were not brought here to be reunited with him. No . . .'

Eins nodded at a platform on the other side of the chasm.

Two men stood on it, waiting patiently.

'. . . you were brought here to be reunited with *them*.'

Lily gazed across the chasm at the two men on the platform.

The taller of the two was a man she had not met before: he was perhaps fifty, with a broad lion-like face and pale grey eyes.

The second man wore a translucent plastic medical mask over the lower right quarter of his face. Above the mask, his eyes blazed with hate and fury.

He was younger than the first man, and despite the mask on his face, Lily recognised him instantly.

She had most certainly met him before.

It was Dion DeSaxe.

Lily's mind raced.

The last time she had seen Dion was during the chaos at the end of the Great Games.

Dion had ambushed her, Jack and Scarecrow on the slopes of Hades's mountain-palace and aimed a pistol at Jack—only to be shot from behind, through the head, by Alby, who had appeared at the last moment from the other side of the mountain path.

The round had exited through Dion's face and Dion had fallen. Lily had assumed he was dead, and in the rush to flee the mountain, she certainly hadn't bothered to check.

'The bullet went through my cheek, Lily,' Dion said from across the chasm, as if guessing her thoughts. His voice was slurred. The bullet must have sheared off part of his upper palate.

Dion—once so handsome and rich, and full of himself for being both—was now the very thing he scorned the most: ugly and disfigured, with a mouth that couldn't speak properly.

'The bullet fired by *him*,' Dion pointed at Alby, trapped in the hanging cage. 'Your father ruined the Games and *he*'—he jabbed an accusing figure at Alby again—'ruined *my face*! You didn't think I would let these outrages go unavenged, did you?'

'Dion, I—'

'Soon you will call me by another name, you little bitch,' he said. 'Tomorrow, I will dial in to a conference call with the other three kings. And as the true and confirmed heir of the disgraced Lord Hades, I will be given my father's crown, title and kingdom. Then you will address me as Your Majesty.'

Dion, crowns, kings . . .

Lily's brain was still catching up.

So it had been Dion who had paid the Knights of the Golden Eight to kill Jack. But he'd wanted her and Alby alive. And now he would be a king. It all made her skin crawl.

But she wasn't going to let it show.

She jerked her chin at the older man beside Dion.

'Who are you?' she asked.

The man smiled, his eerie grey eyes glittering.

'You are so like your father,' he said evenly. 'Your *adopted* father, I mean. Captain West. You both have such grit, such *defiance*. It is nice to meet you at last, young Oracle. I have followed your progress for many years. I am Sir Hardin Lancaster, Lord and Keeper of the City of Atlas, but you may call me Sphinx.'

'Why are you here?' Lily demanded.

'For a long time, I have been something of a mentor to young Dion,' Sphinx said. 'I am also—how to put this?—obscenely rich, and before his formal coronation, Dion needed someone to put up the downpayment for the Knights' services. They do not come cheap, the Knights of the Golden Eight, but they do guarantee results.'

'What was the price?' Lily found herself asking, looking from Sphinx and Dion to Jaeger Eins.

'The downpayment was a Greek island that I own,' Sphinx said. 'When Dion is formally named King of the Underworld tomorrow, he will hand to the Knights ownership of the Indian states of Andhra Pradesh, Tamil Nadu and Kerala as well.'

Dion. A king, Lily thought fearfully. In the royal world, clearly it didn't matter if a new king was murderously insane.

'I thought my father was supposed to be killed as well,' Lily said. 'Wasn't that part of the commission?'

Sphinx said, 'Your father, it turns out, was also being pursued by the royal jailer. It's quite unseemly for the Knights to be acting in competition with a royal official, although this does sometimes happen. Thus we came to an arrangement with Yago in London and handed your father over to him. The Knights and the royal jailer have cooperated in this manner several times over the centuries. With West at Erebus and with your delivery here, the Knights have fulfilled their contract.'

'So what happens now?' Lily asked, trying to stop her lips from quivering. 'Why did we have to be captured alive?'

It was Dion who answered her.

'My life is now beset by constant pain, Lily. Pain that you and Albert caused. You both had to be taken alive so that I can return the favour and inflict upon the two of you similar pain. Physical pain for Albert. The torment of watching for you. Oh, Lily. What I'm going to do will probably make you physically ill. I'm going to torture Albert till he begs me—*begs me*—to die, and then I'm going to kill him right in front of your eyes.'

Lily shot a look at Alby up in the cage.

Only then, suddenly and to everyone's surprise, all throughout the castle, alarms began to sound.

Jaeger Acht came over to Jaeger Eins: 'Sir. A small helicopter just crash-landed in the woods on the eastern side of the island. According to its registration number, it's a rental chopper from Naples. Looks like a tourist pleasure flight.'

Jaeger Acht held up a small handheld security monitor for his boss to see.

On the screen, Jaeger Eins saw a crashed helicopter on the lower eastern slope of the island, half-buried in some stone fortifications, its landing struts twisted but its fuselage largely intact.

A lone figure lay slumped in the pilot's seat, head bent.

Jaeger Eins stared at the screen with hard eyes.

He threw a look at Sphinx. 'West is at Erebus?'

'I saw him there with my own eyes last night, sealed in stone,' Sphinx said.

Eins nodded to Acht. 'Send a couple of squires.'

The two squires approached the crashed helicopter cautiously, guns gripped and ready.

The chopper lay nose-down in some crumpled brickwork on the edge of the castle's eastern forest.

The two squires eyed the slumped figure in the pilot's seat. He did not move. He was still strapped in by his seatbelt and still wore his radio headset—

—and then he sprang, suddenly alive, whipping up two pistols,

firing quickly, and both squires dropped where they stood, shot in their chests.

The pilot unclipped his seatbelt and stepped out of the downed helicopter. He grabbed the guns of the two dead squires and strode in through the nearest gate leading to the multi-levelled castle.

'Who is it?' Eins said.

'It's an associate of West's,' Acht said.

Jaeger Eins raised an eyebrow at that.

Standing nearby, Lily heard Acht's words and her hopes lifted.

On Eins's monitor was a freeze-frame of the lone figure entering the castle, pistols gripped in his hands, glaring directly up into a security camera as he did so.

A matrix of facial recognition vector-lines had locked into place around the frozen image of the man.

Jaeger Acht said, 'Facial recognition confirms his name is Mr Julius Adamson.'

Julius Adamson walked quickly through the gardens and court-yards of Aragon Castle, his face locked in a dead-eyed stare.

It hadn't taken him long to reach the home of the Knights of the Golden Eight.

He had been in the room when Iolanthe had said that the Knights were based at Aragon Castle off the coast of Italy. A few extra searches on the flight there had confirmed some other relevant pieces of information.

The history of Aragon Castle, for one thing.

It had once been owned by the Catholic Church. A handwritten record from the Vatican—dated 26 May 1296, seven days after the mysterious death of Pope Celestine V—showed a transfer of ownership of Aragon Castle from the Church to the *Militum Sanguine Ischium*: 'the Blood Knights of Ischia'.

Ischia was an island off the coast of Italy, not far from Naples, and, indeed, was where one found Aragon Castle.

The term 'Blood Knights of Ischia' brought up matches with 'Knights of the Golden Eight', 'Merlin' and 'Knights of the Round Table'.

After that, the journey had been pretty straightforward. It was just the preparations—scoping out the island, buying weapons on the streets of Rome and finding a helicopter—that had required a little extra time.

Then he had rented the chopper in Naples, flown it directly to the island, and intentionally crashed it to get the Knights' attention.

Julius didn't care for the crumpled chopper.

He was beyond caring.

He had come for revenge. To avenge his dead brother and his family, murdered in their car above the Thames two days earlier.

Jaeger Eins stared in disbelief at the security monitor showing Julius Adamson striding through the outer courtyards of his castle.

Looking closely, he saw that Julius was gripping something *between* his right fist and the pistol it held: a scrunched-up piece of paper.

'Oh my God,' Jaeger Eins snorted. 'He's *attacking* us. How extraordinary. Jaeger Drei and Jaeger Fünf. Please kill that man.'

Two of the Knights standing nearby grabbed their guns and dashed away.

Julius came to a domed chapel on the third of Aragon Castle's six cascading levels, shot its padlocks and kicked in its door. The low afternoon sunlight lanced into the dusty space.

On the innermost wall of the chapel was an ornate arched doorway, sealed by an iron grille.

This was the entrance to the old castle, he had learned in his research, the original one that lay beneath the many newer ones.

Julius scanned the gorgeous chapel, saw a security camera up near the ceiling and calmly shot it to pieces.

Moments later, the two armed Knights sent by Jaeger Eins arrived in the chapel via a secret panel behind the altar.

They leapt out, their MP-9 submachine guns blazing, strafing every wall of the little church.

Julius wasn't there.

They frowned.

'Hello.' Julius emerged from a thick velvet curtain behind them and—*blam-blam!*—shot them both in the head.

He took one of the Knights' MP-9s and disappeared through the secret panel they had used to enter the chapel, forging relentlessly onward.

Behind the chapel, Julius entered a tight, long hallway that was lit by decaying yellow electric lights.

This hallway had a name—the Petitioner's Passage—since it was the one and only tunnel that led to the Petitioner's Ledge. All who came to employ the Knights had to pass through it.

The Petitioner's Passage was dead straight and about a hundred metres long.

Stone statues of Knights long gone were spaced along its length, eerie in the sickly light.

Julius—his face cold, his eyes dead, still gripping the sheet of paper between his right hand and the pistol in it—strode down it.

He saw the end of the tunnel and the wider, well-lit space beyond it.

That was his goal: the inner sanctum of the Knights of the Golden Eight. The men he was going to kill.

He was striding down the tunnel, glaring at the rectangle of light at its end, when—

Clang!

An iron-barred gate dropped into place in front of him.

Clang!

A second gate dropped into place behind him.

And suddenly he was trapped.

'*Drop your guns, Mr Adamson,*' a voice said over an unseen speaker in the ceiling.

'Screw you!' Julius shouted. 'Come and get them!'

'*As you wish.*'

There came a puff of yellow gas from a hole in the wall next to Julius's face and the next instant, he collapsed to the hard stone floor.

Julius fought the darkness engulfing him, but it was no use. The world around him shrank.

The last thing he saw was a shadowy blurred figure walking slowly down the length of the tunnel, growing larger as he neared, until he crouched in front of one of the barred gates trapping Julius and shook his head sadly.

'Mr Adamson,' Jaeger Eins said, 'your loyalty to your brother is commendable, but you, my friend, have just entered a world of pain.'

Night had fallen by the time Julius awoke . . . inside a barred medieval cage only slightly larger than his body.

He was upright, thanks to an iron neck-ring clamped around his throat, and his hands poked out the front of the cage through two manacle-like holes.

His cage hung suspended above an awfully high drop.

Blinking to his senses, Julius saw Alby imprisoned in an identical cage beside him: same neck-ring, same hands-through-the-manacle-holes, suspended from the same T-shaped wooden frame.

Julius closed his eyes. His mission was over.

'Fuck,' he whispered.

Lily stared in horror at Julius and Alby, strung up in their cages.

They were all inside the Hall of the Round Table, the heart of the old castle, deep within the island.

Julius's cage hung a foot out over the drop. Alby's hung over the platform, over solid ground, at least for now.

The remaining Knights stood arrayed around the two cages, their eyes deadly.

Dion and Sphinx stood a few steps behind them.

Ominously, Lily saw a squire step out onto the platform carrying a purple velvet box with gold buckles. It was about the size of a thick hardback book and he carried it with great reverence.

'Mr Adamson.' Jaeger Eins stood in front of Julius's cage.

'We know why you're here. You suffered a terrible loss, the death of your brother, and you came here to avenge him.'

Julius said, 'Yup.'

Jaeger Eins smiled wanly, and raised a rumpled sheet of paper.

'You were holding this when we gassed you in the tunnel,' he said. 'It's a printout of an email.'

Jaeger looked down at the sheet and, standing close to Julius's cage, read it in a calm, even voice:

'Dear Jack, dear everyone.

If you're reading this, then I guess I'm dead. To be completely honest with you, I'm not sure what to write right now. Sending a message from beyond the grave is not something you ever really think about.

First, I hope you're all okay. Second, I hope I went out fighting. A good death, as the Vikings said. And if some evil shithead killed me, avenge me!

But seriously.

I guess, more than anything, I just want to say this to my brother, Julius: Jules, you were never just my brother. You were my best friend. I love you, man, with a love so strong it can cross time and space and the wall between the living and the dead. Brothers forever. I'll see you again.

Lachie.'

Trapped inside the tight cage, Julius clenched his teeth. His eyes welled with tears.

'Oh, Julius . . .' Lily sobbed, her heart going out to him.

Jaeger Eins crushed the sheet of paper into a ball and tossed it into the chasm.

'You will be seeing your brother again much sooner than you think,' he said.

Jaeger Eins turned to face Lily. 'Having said that, Mr Adamson has inadvertently given us the means to provide a demonstration of what will happen to Mr Calvin shortly.'

He held out a hand and the squire handed him the purple velvet box.

Jaeger Eins opened it and took from it a curious ancient weapon.

It looked like a harp, but a very small one, handheld, and with only a single string.

Its lone ultra-narrow thread glistened in the light, a filament no wider than a fishing line. What exotic metal it was made of, no-one alive now knew, but it looked sharper than any human blade.

Jaeger Eins gripped its curved handle in his fist, so that the filament-string lay outside his knuckles.

Then, so quickly it was shocking, he casually waved the string-weapon in front of Julius's cage and, just like that, one of Julius's hands, sticking out the front of his cage, went tumbling into the abyss.

Julius roared in pain, staring in horror at the stump that was now his left wrist.

He started hyperventilating.

Blood gushed from the stump, still in its iron manacle.

Lily gasped in horror.

'What the . . .' Alby whispered.

Jaeger Eins had hardly applied any pressure at all, she thought. That filament in the harp must have been—

'This is a weapon from another time,' Jaeger Eins said. 'Elegant yet severe. A razor-sharp filament that will cut through just about any organic thing: wood, bone, human flesh. *You killed two of my Knights, motherfucker.* Such an outrage cannot go unpunished!'

He slashed again with the string-weapon and Julius's other hand was severed, and suddenly poor Julius was standing there, in the cage, held upright by the iron neck-ring, *with both of his hands cut off.*

He wailed. The veins on his forehead bulged.

Jaeger Eins stepped in front of Julius so that they were only inches apart.

Julius's face was covered in sweat.

Jaeger Eins was impassive and cold.

'You did your best, Mr Adamson, but your best was not good enough.' He began to turn away.

'Hey,' Julius gasped abruptly, making Eins stop.

'Yes?'

Julius heaved for breath.

Through the sweat and spittle on his lips, he said, 'His wife's name was Eriko . . .'

Jaeger Eins frowned.

'She was an astrophysicist. Their kids were named Caleb and Willow. The boy liked Lego and *Minecraft*. The girl liked soccer and dressing up as Wonder Woman . . .'

Lily began sobbing.

Alby clenched his teeth. 'You tell 'em, Jules!' he shouted, trying to send some defiant strength to Julius.

'They were ordinary decent people,' Julius said, glaring at Jaeger Eins. 'And you're just a sick fuck.'

Eins said nothing.

He just turned and nodded to a squire by the wall and the squire released a lever and suddenly Julius's cage dropped from the timber frame and fell, soaring through the air, three hundred feet straight down the side of the rock tower before it plunged with a splash into the water at the bottom of the cavern, beside the Akula submarine parked there.

Julius—handless and in agony—shot underwater amid a mass of bubbles.

The water wasn't actually that deep and within moments, he hit the bottom, where he saw at least six other cages just like his, each with a figure in it, all of them without hands, all of them long dead.

It would be the last thing Julius Adamson saw.

He closed his eyes and inhaled the water into his lungs, and in that very last instant before everything went black, Julius found peace because he knew that he would soon be reunited with the brother he loved.

Lily screamed at Jaeger Eins. 'You bastard! You're all bastards!'

'No!' Eins turned, his eyes flaring. '*You* did this! *Your father* did this! *You have entered a world you do not understand and you are paying the consequences for your ignorance!* You think I am just a mercenary? My Knights and I are well aware that the fate of the world hangs in the balance. We have made our alliances for the times to come; we have prepared. Have you? No, because you do not understand. But you will.'

He handed Dion the filament-blade weapon. 'My prince . . .?'

Eins nodded to the squire by the wall. The squire swung Alby's cage into place above the drop, putting it in the same spot where Julius's cage had been moments before.

'Oh, God, no . . .' Lily said. 'Dion, please, I'll do anything. Please don't hurt him—'

'Hurt him?' Dion snarled through his half-mask.

He came over to Lily and removed the mask, revealing his face.

It was hideous. Horribly disfigured. The skin of Dion's right cheek was twisted in an impossible way. His cheekbone sagged like melted wax and his mouth drooped in one corner, revealing teeth that are not usually visible.

Dion grinned through his gnarled face. 'Oh, I'm gonna hurt him. Repay him for doing this to me.'

Dion strode over to Alby's cage, lazily twirling the string-weapon.

Lily struggled against the two Knights holding her. 'No . . . !'

Dion stood before Alby, helpless in the cage.

'Hello again, Albert,' he said. 'I am giving away a sizeable portion of my kingdom for this, so I plan to enjoy every second of it.'

Dion raised the filament between their faces.

The ultra-thin string shimmered in the light.

'Every last second.'

Then, quick as a rattlesnake, Dion brought the filament-blade down hard and Alby yelled in pain as his left hand came away at the wrist and fell into the abyss.

Lily screamed, but her guards held her tightly.

Her eyes searched the area, looking for someone, anyone who would stop this.

Her gaze found Sphinx: he was just watching Dion with a cool evaluating stare.

She glared at Jaeger Eins.

He shrugged. 'Are you beginning to understand now?'

And then, in that horrible place, while Alby gazed in horror at his missing left hand, something very weird happened.

A phone rang.

A cell phone. Sphinx's phone.

Sphinx frowned and answered it. 'Yes?—When?—Okay, we are on our way.'

He hung up, looked at Dion and Jaeger Eins. 'King Orlando has found the city of Thule. He has sent men into it and is now heading for Atlas. I must go and be there when he arrives. Is the other package on my boat?'

'It is,' Jaeger Eins said.

To Lily's great surprise, Sphinx grabbed her firmly by the hand and pulled her with him. Was she *his* prize?

'Let's go,' he said.

She resisted. 'No—'

'Lily!' another voice called.

It was Alby.

'Lily, go! Please'—he gasped—'Please, go. Don't see this. I don't want you to see this.'

'A nice sentiment,' Sphinx said. 'But in truth you don't have a choice.'

Jaeger Eins and two other Knights dragged Lily to the gantry elevator leading down to the water hangar.

Joined by Dion, she, Sphinx and the Knights stepped into the elevator. Jaeger Eins closed its sliding grille.

'Alby!' Lily called. 'I love you!'

In his cage, with sweat dripping off his face and one of his hands missing, Alby locked eyes with her.

'I always loved you, Lily,' he said.

And then Alby vanished from her sight as the elevator whizzed down the side of the rock tower.

The elevator arrived at the water hangar thirty seconds later.

There, Lily was taken to a huge, sleek, 130-foot Princess motor yacht parked beside the Hercules. The luxury boat was almost as big as the plane.

Sphinx had two bodyguards of his own waiting there and the Knights handed Lily off to them.

Pausing on the dock, Sphinx shook hands with Jaeger Eins. 'Till we meet again, Hunter One.'

'It is always a pleasure doing business with you, my Lord,' Jaeger Eins said.

Sphinx then clasped Dion's hand. 'You have grown into a fine young man, Dionysius. You will be a great king, greater than your father, of that I have no doubt.'

Dion beamed. 'I will not forget this; the aid you gave me in my time of need.'

Sphinx bowed.

Then he boarded his yacht after Lily, the seagate opened and the massive motorboat powered out through it into the night and was gone.

LONDON, ENGLAND

It was evening in London.

While Zoe and Iolanthe ate some dinner and Sky Monster dozed, Mae Merriweather sat in front of a computer, illuminated by the glow of its screen, still searching doggedly for anything that might reveal the location of the Prison at Erebus.

After two whole days of failed searches, the mood in the flat at Vauxhall was grim. Despair had set in.

And then, as she scanned some sixteenth-century royal Portuguese correspondence, Mae saw it.

She hurriedly grabbed the others and excitedly brought them to her computer.

'I think I might've found something,' Mae said. 'I mean, it's just a theory, but . . .'

'Let's hear it,' Zoe said.

Mae took a breath. 'Okay. The royal prison is called *Erebus*. In Greek mythology, Erebus was a region of the Underworld, its most forbidding depth, a place of pure darkness where death and misery were said to dwell.'

She turned to her computer and pointed to a note on it, an old parchment written in Portuguese.

'I just saw this note about the famous missing King of Portugal. It mentions a place not unlike that. It was written to his cousin, Isabella, Queen of the Spanish Netherlands.'

'Oh, my . . .' Iolanthe said. 'There's a connection to the royal world there, too—'

'Wait, there was a *missing* King of Portugal?' Zoe asked.

'Yes, King Sebastian I of Portugal,' Iolanthe said, nodding. 'It's one of history's most famous and peculiar vanishings.'

Mae explained. 'King Sebastian disappeared after the Battle of the Three Kings in northern Morocco in 1578. His forces were routed in the battle, but despite much searching, Sebastian was never seen again. He just vanished from the face of the Earth.'

Iolanthe added, 'In royal circles, that battle is seen as a struggle between rivals for the Land Kingdom's African governorship. Sebastian tried to kill his rival and lost. He didn't go missing. For his impertinence, he was sent to Erebus.'

Mae said, 'Sebastian was very close to his cousin Isabella. Later, she would marry into the Habsburg line and become a minor queen. In that capacity, she employed a servant to find out what had happened to Sebastian. When the servant finally wrote back to her, he used some very specific and peculiar language—ah, here it is.'

Mae enlarged an image of a scroll, written in Portuguese. She translated it:

> '*Your Majesty,*
>
> *I have discovered the location of your beloved cousin. He lives, but in wretchedness, in a realm of ultimate darkness, in the company of Death and Misery, far beneath an ancient mine on the dreaded Barbary Coast, fifty miles east of the great slave market at Al Jazaer.*
>
> *I dared not attempt a rescue. To have done so would only have resulted in my sharing his terrible fate.*'

'"*In a realm of ultimate darkness, in the company of Death and Misery*",' Mae quoted. 'I read this as a reference to Erebus.'

'"*Fifty miles east of the great slave market at Al Jazaer*",' Zoe said. 'So where is Al Jazaer?'

'That's easier,' Mae said. 'The city of Al Jazaer is actually still known by the same name, only the spelling has changed. Al Jazaer is Algiers.'

They did a land-records check of the region east of Algiers.

Sure enough, there was a vast plot of privately held land there containing a gigantic open-cut mine. According to the records, it was owned by an Anglo-French mining company called Briparisi.

'A company whose board of directors is stacked with shadow royals,' Iolanthe said. 'Ladies, we may have just found Erebus.'

Zoe didn't waste any time after that.

First, she instructed Mae and Iolanthe to continue with the task Jack had originally given them: finding Sir Francis Drake's coffin based on his note to Queen Elizabeth I.

Then Zoe called Stretch and Pooh Bear in India and met them eight hours later in Malta, in the heart of the Mediterranean Sea and only a few hundred miles from Algiers.

They weaponed up and looked at some satellite scans of the coast fifty miles to the east of the Algerian capital.

Zoe eyed the satellite images, zeroing in on the mine and some cement trucks that moved constantly up and down its road.

It was still dark, 4:45 a.m.

'We don't have a moment to waste,' she said. 'We go in now, before sunrise.'

And so, nearly three days after Jack had been taken in London— under cover of darkness, dressed in black scuba gear and wearing night-vision goggles and face-paint, and gripping silenced MP-7 submachine guns—Zoe, Stretch and Pooh Bear crept ashore on the barren coast of Algeria, a few miles from the mysterious mine.

Once on dry land, they ditched their scuba gear and made the rest of the journey on foot, heading for the ancient impregnable prison that held Jack.

The vast crater was silent in the darkness, but it was not still.

Its automated cement-mixer trucks did not sleep, so they just kept labouring through the night, rumbling up and down the mine's curving dirt ramp, going back and forth to the dock on the coast.

The three figures of Zoe, Pooh Bear and Stretch moved in perfect sync as they swept toward the mine, leapfrogging one another.

There were guards stationed at two watch-houses on the land-ward and seaward sides of the mine.

They never saw the three figures leap aboard one of the cement trucks as it returned from the dock, empty, and headed back toward the mine; never saw them scamper up onto its back and into its mixer.

The truck rumbled down the ramp and into the circular shed at its base.

Ten minutes later, that same truck was lowered into the prison cavern.

As it came down into the cavern on the extending arms of the elevator platform, Zoe, Pooh Bear and Stretch peered out from the cement mixer on its back and beheld the gigantic cavern one mile beneath the surface.

They saw the multi-levelled castle protruding from one wall, dominating the space. Then they saw the bridge over the pool of liquid stone leading to the Wall of Misery.

'Lord in Heaven,' Zoe breathed as she took in the full horror of the Wall.

'There,' Stretch whispered, pointing. 'Bottom row. In the middle.'

Through her NVGs, Zoe followed Stretch's finger and saw him, half-sunk into a stone slab, his eyes closed in sleep.

Jack.

Six black-clad guards stood in a silent circle in the centre of the cavern, waiting for the elevator platform with the cement truck on it to touch down. A few safety lights on the platform's rim gave off a dim glow, sending long shadows into the cavern.

The elevator came to a halt—

—and Zoe, Stretch and Pooh sprang from its rear mixer, unleashing a stream of silenced bullets that cut down all six guards in an instant.

The three rescuers leapt down from the cement truck and ran across the bridge leading to the Wall of Misery.

Zoe came to Jack and touched his forehead gently.

'Jack,' she whispered. 'It's me.'

Jack's eyes opened, groggy and weary, and then they burst wider in hope.

'Zoe!'

'Shhh. We're going to get you out of here,' she hissed.

Beside Jack, the madman named Rubles awoke. 'Why, hello—' Stretch slammed a hand over his mouth.

Zoe scanned Jack's liquid stone slab and frowned. 'I wasn't expecting this. Shit. How do we extract you from the stone?'

'You need to heat it very carefully,' a distant voice called from the darkened castle overlooking the cavern.

Zoe, Stretch and Pooh all spun . . .

. . . as every light in the mine, both on the surface and in the cavern, came on.

Their eyes stinging, they yanked off their NVGs . . . and saw Yago standing on the main balcony of his subterranean castle, surrounded by twenty armed guards, all of their guns aimed at the three intruders.

Yago smiled. 'But you needn't worry about that. Soon, you will be joining Captain West in his misery. Please, drop your weapons. Your foolish rescue attempt is over.'

Zoe, Stretch and Pooh dropped their guns.

'Oh, you're in trouble now, so much trouble,' Rubles said. 'Trouble, trouble, trouble.'

Flanked by a pair of guards, Yago calmly strolled down the stairs of his castle and across the bridge until he stood in front of the three rescuers and Jack.

His other men—eighteen of them—took up positions on the main bridge, blocking any possible escape.

Zoe sighed inwardly.

They were screwed.

Yago stopped in front of her. 'Ms Kissane, I presume? Ms Zoe Kissane, wife of Captain West? You are truly loyal to your man.'

He snorted. 'We saw you on our underwater thermal cameras when you were a mile offshore. Out of curiosity, we watched you three come all the way in.

'I must admit, you have actually done me a favour. It was very helpful to observe your method of entry. I shall know what precautions to take in the future. The perimeter guards who missed you slipping past will, of course, be shot.'

Yago turned to Jack.

'Oh, Captain. I told you: no-one escapes from this place. You had hoped for a rescue from your friends, but it would appear that you are now officially all out of friends.'

★ ★ ★

At the exact same moment that Yago was saying this to Jack, a lone plane was flying high above the northern coast of Algeria.

It was a Russian-built fighter-bomber, a hover-capable Sukhoi Su-37, but it was not owned by any Russian.

Nor was it owned by any friend of Jack's.

Thanks to a layer of black radar-absorbent material, it was invisible to radar.

As it shot above the coast, the plane loosed a small missile that streaked away into the night.

Then the sleek black plane accelerated across the hazy star-filled sky and turned upward until it was soaring almost vertically.

It was only then that a tiny figure leapt out of the plane's bomb bay.

He was dressed entirely in black—black helmet, black fatigues, black gloves and a black utility vest covered in unusual tools and devices—plus a high-altitude oxygen mask and a parachute pack. He also had something compact and tubular strapped to his chest.

And one other thing: he and Jack West had never met.

Thanks to the plane's near-vertical flight-path, the figure dropped perfectly vertically, with no sideways movement. This was important.

The man-in-black plummeted toward the Earth, his body stretched out like a spear, flying feet-first, reaching terminal velocity, his target . . .

. . . Yago's open-cut mine, or, rather, the rusty shed in its middle.

As the man-in-black shot toward the mine like a human bullet, the missile his plane had fired moments before struck the mine.

It slammed into the iron shed that housed the mine's elevator and blew it to smithereens. The shed's walls and roof flew outward, exposing the wide round mouth of the mile-deep elevator shaft.

A few seconds later, the man-in-black—falling at close to two hundred kilometres per hour and perfectly vertically—shot straight *into* the elevator shaft and the real rescue began.

Down in the cavern, Yago felt the shudder of the explosion on the surface.

He spun. 'What the hell was that?'

The man-in-black shot down the elevator shaft at blistering speed, its walls whipping past him in a superfast blur.

With three hundred feet to go, he activated his parachute, and in the confines of the wide cylindrical elevator shaft, it blossomed to life, arresting his fall.

He glided the rest of the way down the shaft, still moving quite fast, while unclipping four small objects attached to the black utility vest he wore.

In the cavern, Yago gazed around, unnerved. It was perhaps the first time he had ever felt uncomfortable in this place.

His guards on the bridge raised their guns.

All was silent.

And then, without warning, four small objects dropped out of the hole in the ceiling.

With metallic clinks, they landed on the steel elevator platform parked on the floor of the cavern with the cement truck still standing on it.

Grenades.

They detonated.

★ ★ ★

A zillion flakes of white chaff blasted out from the four grenades, filling the cavern with a wafting snow of the stuff.

The sticky flakes adhered to the uniforms of Yago's guards and drifted into the barrels of their guns.

Zoe was totally confused.

She glanced at Stretch. 'Chaff grenades?'

A second later, the man-in-black burst out of the circular hole in the ceiling of the cavern, hanging from his parachute . . .

. . . now with the compact tubular object he'd been carrying mounted on his shoulder.

A Predator rocket launcher.

The guards opened fire at him—only to see their guns lock up after a single shot, jammed by the chaff.

Still wearing his high-altitude oxygen mask, the man-in-black took in the scene in an instant: he saw Yago and his two guards standing with Zoe, Stretch and Pooh Bear in front of the Wall of Misery; and the eighteen other guards on the bridge.

He didn't hesitate.

He fired the rocket launcher at the guards on the bridge.

The RPG streaked out from the launcher and detonated right in the middle of the group of guards, exploding violently and sending them flying through the air into the pool of liquid stone.

As smoke billowed and the guards landed with dull squelches in the liquid stone, the man-in-black landed on the elevator platform and with frightening speed, jettisoned his chute and drew two short-barrelled Remington 870 auto-reload pump-action shotguns from holsters on his thighs—both guns, of course, were fitted with anti-chaff valves on their barrels—and sprinted across the bridge toward the Wall of Misery.

Jack watched the man in silent awe. The guy fired his silver-barrelled shotguns as if they were pistols, one in each hand, their auto-reloading actions allowing him to fire repeatedly as he ran—*blam-blam-blam-blam-blam!*

Beside Jack, Rubles started screaming—with pure joy. 'Wahoo! Fuck yeah! Shoot 'em up! Shoot 'em all up! Fuck *yeah*!'

It was an absolutely blistering barrage of gunfire. The man-in-black was a one-man army.

The two guards covering Zoe and her team dropped, hit in the chest, their torsos exploding with blood.

A couple of guards who hadn't been thrown into the pools of liquid stone were nailed in their heads.

Yago drew a pistol but the man-in-black shot his gun hand, turning Yago's forearm to mush and making him spill the gun, fall, and clutch what remained of his arm.

And then suddenly the man-in-black was standing in front of Zoe, Stretch, Pooh Bear and Jack.

He was tall, easily six feet, and well built. Over his black combat fatigues, Jack saw his SWAT vest covered in curious devices: handcuffs, knives, pliers, rope, mountain-climbing pitons, two scuba breathers and—Jack did a double-take—a blowtorch.

The man-in-black wrenched off his high-altitude oxygen mask to reveal a rugged weathered face, hard and unshaven. He had dark hair and a pair of eyes that glistened with mischievous intelligence.

And that was the final thing about this man.

His eyes.

They were covered by wraparound anti-flash glasses with black frames and yellow-tinted lenses.

'Jack West?' the man-in-black said. 'I'm a friend of Scarecrow's. He saw you on TV in London and sent me to rescue you. My name is Captain Aloysius Knight.'

Getting Jack out of his stone slab took a little time.

Yago had a heating unit nearby for use when a prisoner died or if a person needed to be removed from the Wall of Misery for some reason.

The heating unit was basically a set of red-hot heating elements that were lowered onto the grey slab and which gradually returned the solidified stone to a liquid state.

Jack's slab was placed under a heating unit and, slowly, very slowly, the hard stone around his body began to turn to goopy fluid again, releasing him from its vice-like grip.

As this was happening, Aloysius Knight stood over Jack, scanning the cavern: the Wall of Misery, the castle, the whole incredible place.

'Scarecrow said to be ready for some fucked-up ancient shit,' he said. 'But this is seriously fucked up.'

'Better believe it,' Zoe said.

'I've seen weirder.' Knight shrugged. 'You wouldn't believe what you'll find in the darkest corners of Siberia.'

The stone gripping Jack was now fully liquid again.

Stretch and Pooh Bear yanked Jack out of the thick ooze with a loud squelching sound. They cut the leather straps that bound his arms and wiped away any remaining dollops of greystone clinging to his skin.

The first thing Jack did was embrace Zoe. 'Thanks for coming to get me.'

'Wasn't much of a rescue,' she said.

'It's the thought that counts. Busting into an ancient prison from which there has never been an escape? When you find a girl willing to do that, you marry her.'

'Which you did,' Zoe said.

Jack kissed her. Then he said to Stretch and Pooh Bear, 'Hey, guys. Get Hades out, too, please. We're gonna need him.'

As they set about that task, Jack turned to Aloysius Knight.

'I owe you a significant debt, Captain Knight.'

'Call me Aloysius.' He pronounced it *allo-wishus*.

'So, who are you?' Jack asked.

'I'm a bounty hunter. Ex–special forces. Worked on a mission with Scarecrow a while back. Saved his ass. I also have a pilot circling above us in my plane right now. His name's Rufus. You'll meet him later.'

What Knight didn't say was that when he'd been a member of Delta Force, he had been framed by his own government and ended up on the Defense Department's Most Wanted List. He'd gone underground and become one of the best bounty hunters in the world, albeit one with a price on his own head. Cold, hard and dry, he was the closest thing to a one-man army you could find.

'Well, thank you,' Jack said. 'As I said, I owe you a debt that I'm not sure I can ever repay.'

'Forget it. I owe Scarecrow a debt,' Knight said. 'That guy showed me what real loyalty is and reminded me who I was. So let's call it even. Now, if you don't mind, can we get your buddy out of his slab and get the fuck out of this creepy place?'

Hades was removed from his slab the same way Jack had been, slowly and carefully.

As this was happening, Jack said to Aloysius Knight, 'How did you find me?'

'Scarecrow forwarded your text to me about some bounty hunters called "The Knights of the Golden Eight". I'd heard that name before, once, a few years ago.

'It was during a bounty hunt. I heard it over a supposedly secure radio frequency. They swooped in on a big hunt to nab a wealthy Swiss banker from Geneva. Apparently, this banker had embezzled money from some European royal families. He was never seen again and I never heard of those Knights again.

'But before the Knights grabbed the banker, I'd managed to spray some GPS MicroDots on him, so I saw where they took him. First, they took him to some Italian island and then he was brought here, to the coast of Algeria. And this is where he stayed.

'Rufus and I did a fly-by and we saw the mine crater. Also saw that, according to the MicroDots, our banker was *a mile* below the surface. I let it go. In bounty hunting, you gotta know when to cut your losses.

'Anyway, right after that shit went down in London a couple of days ago—live on television—Scarecrow called me and said it was you, his friend, in the middle of it all. Said you were a decent dude. Asked me to find you and help you.

'I remembered the Knights and immediately thought of this place. So I flew out here and patched into a Russian spy satellite surveying the African coast. Watched it for a whole day, looking for anyone coming or going.'

He nodded at Zoe. 'Sure enough, in the dead of night, I saw three heat-signatures creeping in from the coast: her and her two buddies. Watched 'em come all the way in and go down in the elevator. Waited to see if they came out with you. But then I caught radio chatter on the airwaves between the security posts here: your rescuers had been caught. Given that the elevator was down at the bottom of the shaft—leaving the shaft wide open—I figured it was time to do my thirty-thousand-foot swan dive and make an entrance.'

Jack nodded. 'I'm glad you did.'

'So are we,' Pooh Bear said from the heating unit.

'So what's the deal?' Aloysius said.

Jack said, 'We have a lot to do: we have to find three lost cities and three fabled weapons or else everyone on this planet is going to die. But before we do that, I need to bust my daughter and a good

kid named Alby out of the stronghold owned by those Knights.'

'*Another* stronghold?' Knight arched an eyebrow. 'You know, I normally have a policy of breaking into only one stronghold per day. One. You better be fucking worth it.'

While Pooh Bear and Stretch continued to work on Hades's slab, Jack gave Aloysius a brief summary of the royal world: the four kingdoms, his harrowing time with Scarecrow at the Great Games, and the prison they now found themselves in.

'It's a shadow royal world that exists behind the real world,' Jack said. 'A world of incredible wealth and influence, with its own history, its own aristocracy, its own rules. Occasionally, though, it reaches out into our world.'

Hades came fully out of the slab. He was weak with hunger but okay. Pooh and Stretch gave him water, cleaned him and dressed him in some of Yago's clothes they'd fetched from the castle.

Knight said, 'So why did they imprison you and grab your daughter?'

Jack said, 'At the end of the Great Games, I did something that tore their world apart. I should've remembered the old saying: no good deed goes unpunished.'

'That's why I usually avoid good deeds,' Knight said sourly. 'So the Knights of the Golden Eight have your daughter and her friend?'

'That's right. They're formidable. Soldiers-for-hire who serve these royal families and who exist completely outside the law,' Jack said. 'I imagine that Swiss banker you were chasing wronged members of the royal world and the Knights were dispatched to get him. They turned him over to the royal jailer and he was brought here.

'Like I said, every so often, the royal world reaches out into our world. It was they who trashed New York, Venice and London trying to kill me and grab my daughter.'

Aloysius pondered that for a moment.

Then he stood. 'These assholes who have your daughter were the ones who trashed London? Did all that shit with that family in the van, the bus, the choppers and the tank?'

'Yes.'

'And it's their base that's in Italy?'

'Yes.'

'I have one question,' Knight said.

'Shoot.'

'It's for him.' Knight nodded at Hades.

He asked his question and Hades answered it.

'Then let's roll,' the Black Knight said. 'We just need to make one stop on the way.'

They retrieved Jack's personal possessions from inside Yago's castle: his fireman's helmet, phone and weapons.

'Jack,' Zoe said, eyeing the wall of prisoners. 'What about them? Should we release them?'

'The beautiful lady has a point,' Rubles said quickly from his slab. 'Beautiful lady. Smart lady. Kind lady.'

Jack glanced from Rubles to all the other pathetic prisoners embedded in the Wall.

Jack threw a look at Hades. 'We don't know what crimes they committed to get sent here. We could be releasing killers or worse.'

Hades nodded. 'Worse. For example, Mr Rubles here is quite notorious. He was the butler of a minor royal family in Luxembourg. While the head of the family was away, Rubles killed and ate his master's wife, two young children and dog.'

'He ate them?' Jack stared in horror at Rubles.

Rubles rolled his eyes bashfully. 'I liked the meat of the children best. It was very tender.'

Jack just shook his head. 'Let's go.'

They did, however, do one more thing before they left.

A final act regarding the Wall of Misery. They left someone in the very same spot that Jack had occupied, in a new slab of liquid stone.

Yago.

Embedded in the dreadful stuff and mounted on the wall.

Jack stood in front of the royal jailer, now pinned and furious. 'Hope you like this new view of your realm.'

Then Jack turned on his heel and walked away, his footfalls echoing in the enormous cavern.

Beside Yago, Rubles started speaking quickly. 'Well, well, what an honour this is, what a remarkable honour, the Slave King himself, by my side, by my very side . . .'

Yago wailed in protest as Jack and the others left, turning off the lights as they did so, plunging him and Rubles and the Wall of Misery into darkness.

**THE CASTLE OF THE GOLDEN EIGHT
ISCHIA ISLAND, AMALFI COAST, ITALY**

After Sphinx had left Aragon Castle with Lily the previous night, Dion and the Knights had retired for the evening.

But before he'd taken his leave, Dion had stood before Alby in his cage and suddenly snatched his bleeding wrist. Then, shockingly, he'd seared it with a cigar lighter, cauterising the wound. Alby screamed in pain.

Dion smiled. 'Now, now. We can't have you bleeding out before the real fun begins. We shall resume this invigorating conversation tomorrow evening.'

Then he left and Alby slumped, breathless and sweating, against the bars of his hanging cage.

Alby spent a long, painful and sleepless night in the cage after that, his wrist pressed into his t-shirt, his right hand still trapped in its manacle-like hole.

The next morning, Dion and the Knights went to the mainland and stayed there for most of the day, saying something about a coronation for Dion.

Some squires were left to guard Alby and the castle. At irregular intervals one of them would come over and shove a wet sponge against his mouth. Alby sucked in whatever drops of water he could.

He also heard the squires mention the celebratory feasting that Dion and the others were partaking of in nearby Naples—with

beautiful models filling their glasses and 'tending to their needs'.

Then, as evening fell, Dion and the Knights returned to the castle's dock by boat. The Knights were not the kind of men to get roaring drunk. Jaeger Eins wouldn't stand for that. Dion, though, was a little off-balance.

The seagate closed and Eins turned to Dion. 'Shall we return upstairs, *Your Majesty?*'

He emphasised the title. Terms like 'Your Highness' were used for lesser royals: princes and princesses, queens who had married to get their crowns. 'Your Majesty' was reserved only for kings.

The coronation had been performed at a verified, and very old, royal estate on the mainland, with the three other kings—Orlando and the Kings of Sea and Sky—attending via videolink, since the ceremony could only be performed in the presence of the other kings.

Dion was now, officially, the King of the Underworld.

'I imagine you are very keen to reconvene with Mr Calvin,' Jaeger Eins said.

Dion clapped his hands together. 'Absolutely.'

Then Jaeger Eins's earpiece beeped.

'Yes?' he said into his radio.

'*Sir, this is radar control. We just detected an incoming airborne signal. Vertical signal. Coming in fast.*' Radar control was a state-of-the-art communications and command centre at the very summit of the island that was manned by two senior squires.

'What kind of signature?' Jaeger Eins asked, concerned.

'*That's the thing, it's not a plane or a man,*' the squire said. '*It actually looks like a—wait—it's slowing. Okay. Parachute signature. It's a parachute, all right. But it's not a paratrooper. Looks like it's going to miss us to the north.*'

Jaeger Eins turned, thinking. 'To the north . . .'

He spun to face two of his Knights: 'Come with me.' Then to Dion: 'Your Majesty. For your own safety, please wait here a moment.'

Eins leapt into the gantry elevator with his two Knights and rode it up the rock tower.

They emerged in the Hall of the Round Table and charged over to the wide viewing balcony cut into the northern flank of the island.

Still imprisoned in his tiny cage, Alby watched them.

Arriving at the balcony, Jaeger Eins saw the lights of the Italian mainland glittering in the distance. Off to his right, he saw the usual lines of supertankers and container ships cruising in and out of the busy port of Naples.

Then he peered upward.

And he saw it.

A parachute, high in the sky, passing in front of the stars, drifting downward.

His radar operator had been correct: the object hanging from the chute wasn't a paratrooper. If it had been, they'd have shot him on sight.

'What *the fuck* . . .?' the Knight beside Eins said.

As the parachute drifted down in front of the viewing balcony, Jaeger Eins blinked to make sure he wasn't seeing things.

Hanging from the parachute was *a tank*, a main battle tank.

Scrawled crudely on its side in stark white paint and lit by a carefully-aimed flashlight attached to the exterior of the tank were the words:

RETURN TO SENDER

Hanging from its chute, the tank glided past the viewing window and dropped gently into the sea below it, where it silently sank from view.

'It missed,' Jaeger Acht said.

Jaeger Eins stared open-mouthed at the strangeness of it all.

'It wasn't meant to hit us,' he said. 'It was meant to send us a message.'

For it wasn't just any old tank.

It was *his* tank.

The Challenger 2 main battle tank he had used in London to lure Jack West into the open.

And as the realisation dawned on him, a sudden explosion shook the entire island and Jaeger Eins's world went crazy.

Eins spun as the castle around him shuddered.

'What was that?' he demanded.

'*Jesus Christ!*' the radar operator said in his ear. '*A supertanker just ran aground on the southern shore of the island!*'

From his position at the higher northern end of the island, Jaeger Eins couldn't see it, but had he been outside he would have been stunned by the sight.

A gigantic supertanker—previously steaming out of Naples in a long line of other slow-moving ships—had turned suddenly, and without slowing in any way, had ploughed into the fortified southern wall of the castle's island.

The impact sent bricks flying every which way. The ship's bow came fully out of the water and it ended up resting on the wall, beached.

'Put it onscreen,' Jaeger Eins commanded.

A set of large flat-screen TVs came to life, displaying security feed from cameras all over the island, and there, shockingly, on the main screen, Eins saw it.

A fucking supertanker, mounted on the island's southern flank.

'What is going on?' Jaeger Acht said.

That was when a *second* supertanker powered out of the

night and rushed toward the cliff beneath Jaeger Eins's viewing window . . .

. . . and crashed right into the seagate at the base of it.

The castle shook again.

Alarms sounded.

The other Knights peered out over the edge of the rock tower and saw the bow of the second supertanker now *inside* the water hangar at its base.

In addition to the surreal sight of a tank drifting down past their main hall, they now had two supertankers lodged at both ends of their island-fortress.

'Gentlemen,' Jaeger Eins said. 'Arm yourselves. Extraordinary as it may sound, we are under attack.'

Down in the water hangar, Dion saw the second supertanker smash through the seagate from up close.

The ship's huge bow just mowed down the gate, thrusting itself into the hangar, pushing aside the floating Hercules seaplane with ease.

Dion didn't need to be told what was happening.

The island was under attack.

Get the fuck out of here.

Dion leapt into an inflatable dinghy and gunned the engine, shooting quickly out of the hangar into the night.

Up in the Hall of the Round Table, Jaeger Eins was reeling.

This simply couldn't be.

No-one in all of history—no prince or duke, not even a king— had been brazen enough to launch a full-scale assault on the Castle of the Golden Eight, no matter who the Knights held in their custody.

'Who would be insane enough to do this?' he asked aloud.

It was then that two figures came swooping out of the night-time sky, each on a set of carbon-fibre gull-wings, landing perfectly on the rim of the viewing balcony, jettisoning their gull-wings as soon as their feet hit the polished stone floor.

The first man wore a tan miner's jacket and an FDNY fire helmet. In his hands, he gripped a pair of MP-7 submachine guns.

Jack West Jr.

Jaeger Eins was beyond shocked to see him. Last he'd heard, West had been sent to Erebus, from which there was no escape.

The second man he didn't recognise, but Eins had fought enough dangerous men to know, on sight, that this man was even more lethal than West.

The second man was dressed entirely in black, including a black hockey helmet that screamed Special Forces and yellow-lensed glasses, and he held on his shoulder a Predator rocket launcher.

Without missing a beat, the second man fired his rocket launcher *into* the Hall of the Round Table.

Jack West had brought a knight of his own to take on the Knights of the Golden Eight.

A black knight.

One of the Knights of the Golden Eight exploded.

One second he was standing there, the next he was gone, hit by Aloysius's RPG and vaporised.

Aloysius ditched the Predator and drew his two short-barrelled Remington shotguns from his thigh holsters and started firing them ruthlessly as he advanced.

He shot another Knight, who went sailing off the edge of the rock tower, plummeting down its side. Previously, the man would have landed in water, but today he landed with a foul thud on the bow of the supertanker that had penetrated the hangar down there.

Jack strode along beside him, firing repeatedly with his sub-machine guns. Three squires fell in hails of bullets.

Glaring in disbelief, Jaeger Eins barked two orders.

'Drop the boy!' he called to the Knight nearest to Alby.

The Knight obeyed at once and hit the release catch on the frame holding up Alby's cage and . . .

. . . the cage dropped, with Alby in it.

Jack gasped as he saw Alby disappear from view.

Alby's cage fell through the air, speeding down the sheer side of the rock tower before it splashed into the water at its base.

It bobbed for a moment and then—still with Alby in it, his remaining hand still pinned in the cage's manacle-hole—it went under.

Jaeger Eins's second order was to Jaeger Acht. 'The railgun!'

Acht dived into a compartment near the Round Table and hurled open its door to reveal a full-sized long-barrelled anti-aircraft turret inside it, complete with gunner's chair. He sat in the chair and swung the immense gun around to face Aloysius.

Jaeger Eins grinned. This was why no-one ever attacked the Castle of the Golden Eight.

Silhouetted by the wide viewing window, Aloysius saw the big gun come around toward him, but he just kept firing in a different direction.

Jaeger Acht brought the railgun around . . .

. . . just as a fearsome shape swung into a hover outside the viewing window . . .

. . . the shape of a Sukhoi Su-37 fighter-bomber, *its* guns aimed into the hall.

It was Aloysius Knight's plane, the *Black Raven*, flown by his loyal pilot, Rufus.

The Sukhoi's guns blazed to life, spitting tongues of fire. A shitload of tracer rounds sizzled past Jack and Aloysius, right into Jaeger Acht and his railgun.

Acht and the railgun were cut to pieces, literally blown apart.

Seeing the Sukhoi and its incredible firepower, Jaeger Eins scurried for the edge of the rock tower. 'Knights! Squires! Effect Escape Plan Delta!'

He glared at Jack. 'You came for your daughter and the boy! She has already gone and now he is dead! You have failed, Captain! Failed!'

Then Eins simply stepped off the top of the rock tower and dropped down its side, falling three hundred feet before splashing feet-first into the water at its base.

He surfaced in the hangar at the bottom of the rock tower and clambered into the Akula-class submarine parked there.

The water hangar looked like a bomb-site: pieces of the shattered seagate lay everywhere and the supertanker had shoved the Hercules up against the Akula.

It was also blocking the exit.

Eins followed Escape Plan Delta, a plan that had been prepared in the event of an attack that blocked the seagate.

He hurried into the torpedo room of the Akula, prepped three torpedoes, and launched one of them.

That first torpedo hit the supertanker at point-blank range and detonated.

The front half of the supertanker exploded spectacularly.

The giant ship lurched backwards like a boxer being punched, erupting along its long bow with billowing fireballs, emitting a deep metallic groan as it recoiled.

The blast knocked it completely out of the seagate and suddenly the exit was clear.

Then Eins launched two more torpedoes.

They *shoom*ed out through the seagate and lanced into the sea beyond it, their timers ticking downward.

Then he hurried up onto the hull of the sub, to be met by the surviving Knights and squires. They swung the underwater combat sled that sat on top of the Akula into the water and zoomed off on it into the night.

It was only once they were clear of the island that the other two torpedoes turned around and came back toward Aragon Castle.

That was the final part of Escape Plan Delta: destroy the island and whoever had attacked it.

When those torpedoes hit the base of the cliff—armed as they were with powerful RDX explosive charges—they would bring down the entire northern end of the island, including the new castle, the old castle and the Hall of the Round Table.

The two torpedoes rushed toward the island, gaining speed, when suddenly a pair of decoys dropped into the water in front of them, released from the hovering Sukhoi.

The torpedoes slammed into the decoys and detonated a hundred metres offshore, sending two huge but harmless geysers of water shooting into the air . . .

. . . leaving the Castle of the Golden Eight intact and in the hands of Aloysius Knight and Jack West Jr.

Minutes later, Zoe, Hades and Sky Monster arrived in the water hangar, after disembarking from the two supertankers they had commandeered and slammed into the island.

Sky Monster had driven the one that had run aground on the southern end of Ischia Island; Zoe had been at the wheel of the one that had speared into the seagate with the still-weakened Hades by her side. They'd been thrown around the tanker's stern-mounted bridge as their ship had been blasted back out of the hangar by Jaeger Eins's torpedo, but had survived well enough to board a lifeboat and drive it here now.

After they had secured the Hall of the Round Table, Jack and Aloysius went down in the gantry elevator to join the others in the water hangar.

They saw the Hercules and the Akula, askew in their berths, plus a few other vehicles parked on the docks. The broken seagate lay open, and beyond it, they saw the waters of the Mediterranean and the coast of Italy, glittering in the night.

The water in the hangar was still, like glass.

Zoe looked at Jack, worried. 'You don't think . . .?'

The stillness of the water was shattered by two figures in scuba gear bursting up from it, holding a third.

It was Pooh Bear and Stretch . . . with the sagging figure of Alby held between them.

'Is he okay?' Jack hurried to the edge of the dock to meet them.

Stretch yanked off his scuba mask. 'The bastards cut off one of his hands. But he's alive.'

Pooh Bear glared at Aloysius Knight. 'I can't believe you convinced us to parachute to Earth inside that tank. They could have shot us out of the sky.'

'I figured they'd be too shocked to see their own tank right in front of their eyes to shoot it down,' Aloysius said as Zoe and Jack pulled the three of them out of the water.

That wasn't entirely true.

It wasn't the Knights' *actual* tank. Jack and Aloysius had grabbed this one in Malta on the way here.

In response to Aloysius Knight's single question to him—'Does Malta own any tanks like the one that was used in London?'— Hades had informed them that, yes, the Republic of Malta did indeed own several Challenger main battle tanks just like the one the Knights had used in London. It didn't have to be the exact same tank, just a lookalike.

'It was worth a quick detour to Malta,' Aloysius said. 'Shock value has great value.'

Pooh Bear shook his head and turned to Jack. 'Where did you find this guy?'

'He found me. Scarecrow sent him.'

Inserting Pooh and Stretch via the tank had actually served two purposes. The first was to put them in the water hangar in the event that the fighting went down there.

The second was something that Hades had warned them about: if attacked, the Knights might drop any prisoners into the water to drown. Pooh and Stretch were also there for that eventuality.

Jack examined the stump that was Alby's left hand. Stretch and Pooh had hastily wrapped some moist bandages around the cauterised wound, but it would need to be properly dressed.

Alby shivered, in shock.

'L . . . L . . . Lily . . .' he stammered. 'A guy named Sph . . . Sphinx took her . . . and they . . . killed Julius.'

'Julius was here?' Jack said.

'He wanted payback for Lachie. But he was too obsessed, too intent on revenge, and they caught him and killed him.'

'Oh, Julius,' Jack whispered. He hadn't seen that coming, but he should have known that Julius would come after the men who had so brutally killed his brother. He'd come after them, all right. 'Rest in peace with Lachie.'

'But no rest for us,' Zoe said to Jack. 'Your mother and Iolanthe should be in South America by now. Iolanthe spotted something in that letter from Francis Drake to Queen Elizabeth. They went to join up with Nobody down there while we came for you.'

'You and Iolanthe were working together?' Jack said.

'Even I can forgive someone. Eventually,' Zoe said.

'Jack. Please! We gotta find Lily,' Alby said fretfully. 'And that guy called Sphinx.'

'Sphinx,' Jack said softly, recalling the shadowy figure who had visited him at Erebus.

Alby said, 'We can't wait. We have to catch up with them—'

'Easy, son. Easy,' Jack said, wrapping his arms around him. 'If someone took Lily, it means he plans to use her talent and that keeps her alive. Right now, we gotta take care of you.'

As Jack held Alby close, Aloysius Knight took in the space around them: the spectacularly high cavern with the dock at its base and the Hall of the Round Table at its top.

'I like this place,' he said. 'It's got a nice evil-lair feel to it. I've been looking for a new European base of operations. I think I'll take it.'

FIFTH PURSUIT

FRANCIS DRAKE'S COFFIN AND THE TOMB OF POSEIDON

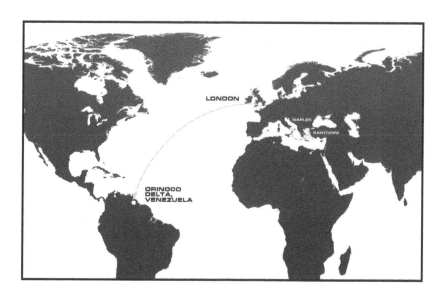

'Ride, boldly ride,'
The shade replied,
'If you seek for Eldorado!'

EDGAR ALLAN POE, *ELDORADO*

THE ORINOCO DELTA
NORTHEASTERN COAST OF VENEZUELA
29 NOVEMBER

The Orinoco Delta is one of the most remote, beautiful and dangerous bodies of water on our planet.

Situated on the Venezuelan coast at the extreme northeastern tip of South America, it is where the mighty Orinoco River discharges into the Atlantic at the astonishing rate of over twenty-five million litres per second.

It is also vast.

Really vast: over fifteen thousand square miles of marshy islands and countless interconnected waterways created by the outward-flowing waters of the Orinoco. Seen from the air, it is a carpet of limitless green shot through with hundreds of twisting canals.

This maze-like network of natural canals actually gave Venezuela its modern name. When they saw them, the Spanish conquistadors named the new land 'Little Venice': Venezuela.

But it is a long way from anywhere. Owing to the lack of firm ground, few people live on the delta. It is far from the strife that has riven Venezuela's major cities in recent years. It is so remote, it has no cell phone coverage.

The delta is also home to all manner of dangerous animal life, from tarantulas and swarms of *Pygocentrus nattereri*—the notorious red-bellied piranha—to the Orinoco crocodile, known for its immense size and tan colour.

It was into this huge natural maze that Dave 'Nobody' Black's boat, the *Betty White*, cruised slowly and silently.

It had been a day since Mae and Iolanthe had arrived from London and met up with Nobody in Barbados.

In the time they had been away, Jack had been broken out of Erebus and had successfully attacked the Castle of the Golden Eight.

While that had been happening, they had been down here, on the edge of South America, virtually incommunicado, searching for the final resting place of Sir Francis Drake.

And the clock was ticking. It was now 29 November so they only had two days to perform the ritual at the Altar of the Cosmos to avert the end of the world.

The *Betty White* moved slowly around the outer reaches of the delta, where the fresh water of the river met the salt water of the Atlantic Ocean, her depth-sounding radar pinging constantly.

Giant flat-topped mountains known as *tepuis* loomed in the distance to the south, rising out of the endless swamp, immense behemoths against the hazy sky.

Mae and Iolanthe stood on the bridge of the boat with Nobody.

The *Betty White* wasn't exactly a sleek ship.

Based in Barbados, it was a submersible support vessel: a utilitarian-looking boat with a crane on its stern—from which hung a three-person deep-sea submersible—and a small white floatplane tied down on its bow.

At seventy feet in length, the *Betty* was actually rather small for a support vessel, but what she lacked in size, she made up for in tech: glistening white, the *Betty* was brand-new and state-of-the-art.

'I bought *Betty* with the proceeds of a wreck I found,' Nobody said as they patrolled the edge of the delta, the ocean behind them.

'What kind of wreck?' Iolanthe asked.

'A Spanish treasure galleon,' Nobody said. 'Filled with silver bars.'

'I thought you were some kind of do-gooder oceanographer,' Iolanthe said, squinting at him. 'Not a treasure hunter.'

Nobody grinned. He was a handsome guy: tanned and lean. In his Johnnie-O t-shirt, sun-bleached shorts, deck shoes and sailing sunglasses, he cut a cool figure. He looked like he lived on the sea, which he kind of did.

'A collateral benefit of spending a lot of time on the ocean floor. I love my *Betty*. She's got all the mod cons: seabed scanning radar, four berths with private bathrooms, and that little floatplane has a watertight engine that could stay dry in a hurricane, which is necessary these days in the Caribbean.'

Iolanthe gazed at the radar scanning the ocean floor ninety feet below them.

It was her idea that had brought them here and, after a day of fruitless searching, she was starting to doubt if she'd been right.

She looked again at the five-hundred-year-old letter from Sir Francis Drake to Queen Elizabeth I:

> *My Queen,*
> *I have taken ill with the fever. I cannot get back. I doubt I will survive the next five days.*
> *But know that I found them—all three of them—as you commanded. Their locations will be buried at sea with me in a lead coffin here in Portobelo.*
> *As I approach my last sunrise, I remain forever,*
> *Your loyal servant,*
> *Drake*

Codes, Iolanthe thought.

Like all monarchs of her time, Queen Elizabeth I—a canny ruler who for almost her entire reign was at war with the Spanish—had had many codes with her sailors, men like Francis Drake and Walter Raleigh. As a historian with special access to British royal records, Iolanthe knew the key elements to Elizabeth's main codes.

Codes concerning locations had four elements: a starting point, a number, a direction and a distance. The first three would be threaded into a message; the last element, the distance, would be prearranged.

The starting point here was obviously Portobelo. The Panamanian town was not, as many had surmised, the end point. It was the launching point from which their coded calculation would begin.

Drake had written that he would not survive five days. That was the number. *Five*.

The direction was the direction one had to go from the starting point, Portobelo.

In his note, Drake mentioned his *last sunrise*. Sunrise meant *east*.

The final element of the code was the distance, a prearranged distance known only to Drake and the queen that was not in the letter.

Fortunately, in over a decade of working in the Hall of Royal Records, Iolanthe had found many of Elizabeth's personal diaries.

They were quite stunning documents, actually. One of them recounted an extraordinary trip Elizabeth had taken as a child with her famous teacher, Roger Ascham, to a chess tournament in Constantinople that for some reason had been lost to history.

In another of the diaries, however, was an entry written in Elizabeth's own hand that simply read: *Drake 250 miles*.

And so here they were, 1250 miles—five times 250—east of Portobelo, Panama, scanning the seabed for a coffin made of lead.

Looking out over the vast Orinoco Delta from the deck of the *Betty White*, Iolanthe began to worry. What if she'd been mistaken? What if the distance was wrong? They hadn't found anything yet. Christ, they could have been hundreds of miles off course.

Nobody saw the look on her face. 'We'll find it. My depth sounders are good and in a place like this, if we can get vaguely close to it, a big hunk of metal will send a strong signal back. And, hey, I'm digging the punk-rocker look.'

Iolanthe gave him a sideways frown, until she realised that with her shaved hair and wounded nose, she probably did look like a punk-rock fan.

She touched her almost bald head self-consciously. 'It'll grow back . . . I mean . . .'

'It's okay,' Nobody said kindly. 'Mae told me what happened to you and it sucks. Your brother sounds like an asshole. But I mean it. The look works on you.'

Iolanthe smiled.

And then, suddenly, the ship's depth sounder began pinging.

Nobody checked it.

'It's half a kilometre that way,' he said, grabbing the wheel and hitting the gas.

A few minutes later, the *Betty White* pulled to a halt near some reeds at the edge of the delta.

According to the depth sounder, it was a hundred feet below them, buried a few feet under the silty seabed . . .

. . . a six-foot-long rectangular object made of lead.

Nobody leapt into action, dropping anchor and prepping the *Betty*'s submersible: a spindly thing with many domes, lights and mechanical arms that he had christened the *Spider*.

Using the boat's crane, he lowered the *Spider* over the side.

Then he, Mae and Iolanthe all got in and, using its interior controls, Nobody guided their descent under the surface.

They entered a world of green gloom.

Seaweed swayed in the current. The trunks of marshy trees stretched away into the haze like pillars in a temple. Schools of fish darted by, moving hurriedly when they spotted an incoming swarm of piranha.

They came to the seabed: a flat silt plain.

Nobody used the *Spider*'s extendable drill to burrow into it and a cloud of silt and dirt billowed up all around them as it did its work.

An hour later, when it was six feet down, the drill struck metal.

When the silt and dirt settled, they saw on their viewscreen a newly created hole in the seabed and in it . . .

. . . an old lead coffin caked in five centuries of lead oxide.

Nobody whistled. 'Smile, Ms Compton-Jones. Historians and

treasure hunters have been searching for this for five hundred years. You just found the resting place of Sir Francis Drake.'

Iolanthe grinned, just as a muffled *boom* rang out from somewhere above them.

Nobody whirled. 'What was that?'

He pressed some buttons, bringing up an image on a monitor: feed from a security camera up on the *Betty*.

A naval vessel could be seen on the eastern horizon, powering toward their position.

A destroyer.

The flag on it showed it to be Brazilian in origin.

'A Brazilian navy ship?' Nobody said.

'The Catholic Church must have called them in,' Mae said. 'Cardinal Mendoza—'

The destroyer's main gun boomed and a shell landed near the *Betty*, sending a geyser of water showering into the air. Then the destroyer's gun fired again and the image on the screen crashed to hash.

'Jesus . . .' Mae said, pointing out through the *Spider*'s port-side dome.

Iolanthe and Nobody followed her gaze . . .

. . . to see the *Betty White*, Nobody's brand-new support ship—complete with the crane on its stern and the floatplane still tied to its bow—drift down through the gloom, a great gash in its side, flying downward in eerie slow motion, before it landed on the seabed a short distance from them with a dull underwater thud.

'Oh, damn, damn, *damn* . . . !' Nobody said.

Iolanthe just stared. 'We're stranded down here.'

A second later, the three of them heard a low whining sound and suddenly—*fzzzz!*—something whizzed past them at incredible speed, leaving a long tail of bubbles behind it.

'Was that a—?' Iolanthe breathed.

'Yes,' Nobody spun. 'That was a torpedo. Goddamn it, they're firing torpedoes at us!'

With their support vessel on the bottom of the delta and the Brazilian destroyer coming in fast and at least one torpedo having been fired at them, Nobody Black sprang into action.

He started flicking switches on his console and their submersible lowered over the now-exposed lead coffin.

'What are you doing?' Mae asked.

'I'm doing what Jack wanted us to do,' Nobody said. 'Getting what we came for and then trying to get out of here with it.'

The submersible's belly came to a halt directly above the coffin.

'I'm going to create a little air pocket around the coffin's lid,' Nobody said.

Hitting some more switches, he extended a small inflatable skirt from the belly of the *Spider* until it covered the coffin and its hole completely.

Next, he hit some switches marked 'INITIATE AIR SEAL' and Mae and Iolanthe heard the hiss of air passing through hoses.

A moment later, a green light on Nobody's console pinged to life: 'POSITIVE PRESSURE ACHIEVED — AIR SEAL INITIATED.'

Then, without so much as a blink, Nobody yanked open the *Spider*'s lower hatch and instead of water rushing in, there it was, right below them . . . in its grave, in a little pocket of air . . . its smooth, dark, slightly domed surface dripping with water.

The long-lost coffin of Sir Francis Drake.

★ ★ ★

It was oddly beautiful in its sturdiness. Long, black and hard, it even *looked* heavy. This coffin had been designed to sink and stay sunk.

Beads of water speckled its dark lid.

'We don't have much time,' Nobody said as he jumped down into the hole beside the coffin. He was now actually standing on the muddy seabed.

With a deep grinding sound, he slid the coffin's heavy domed lid at an angle to the side, opening it partially.

The pale dry corpse of a portly red-haired man in a sixteenth-century British naval uniform stared up at them.

'Sir Francis Drake,' Mae breathed. 'The greatest seafarer in British history.'

Iolanthe was looking the other way, out the window: on the lookout for more incoming torpedoes. 'I appreciate the awe, people, but let's not dawdle.'

Thanks to the airtight coffin, Drake was in remarkably good condition: his skin and hair, while dry and brittle, were still intact. His closed eyes had sunken into their sockets, creating a skeletal look. But apart from that, Sir Francis Drake looked just as he had the day he'd died.

Gripped in his fingers across his chest was an envelope marked: *E.R.*

'Elizabeth Regina,' Mae said. 'That's it. That's the location of the three secret cities.'

Nobody snatched the envelope from Drake's dead hands and opened it.

Inside was a sheet of linen-based parchment.

A quick glance at it showed three coordinates written in Drake's flowing handwriting, each with an annotation:

R: 8°6'N 60°30'W of London
Follow the hidden river to the base of the tabletop mountain.

T: 63°30'N 18°01'W of London

Enter through the tunnel at the tideline below its watchtower.

A: 35°48'N 5°36'W of London
Enter through its watchtower.

'This is incredible,' Mae gasped. 'The exact locations of all three—'

'Look out!' Iolanthe called suddenly.

Fzzzzz!

Another torpedo. It passed so close, this time the *Spider* rocked.

Nobody began to climb back up into the submersible.

'Let's go,' he said. 'We might still have a chance to get out of here—'

He never finished the sentence, for right then a third torpedo arrived at full speed and hit the *Spider*.

The *Spider* lurched wildly as the torpedo detonated.

Everyone was thrown sideways.

Two of the *Spider*'s glass domes shattered and blew inward. Green water began spraying into the submersible.

It would fill in seconds.

Mae stared about herself with panicked eyes. There was nowhere to go.

They were stuck on the bottom of the seabed with their support ship sunk and their submersible taking on water.

They were dead. There was no way out of this.

'Quick! Protect the parchment!' Iolanthe took the parchment from Mae and sealed it inside a waterproof Ziploc bag.

'This way!' Nobody yelled, hauling the two women down into the air-skirt ringing the coffin and its hole, at the same time as he grabbed two scuba tanks from the wall nearby.

'What are you doing?' Mae yelled above the roar of inrushing water.

'No time to explain! Just hang on to me and hold your breath! I'll guide you.'

And so Mae took a deep breath, closed her eyes and dropped through the wide hatch as the *Spider* filled completely with water.

A moment later, with her eyes shut and guided by Nobody, Mae's feet touched solid ground and suddenly—to her surprise—she felt dry air on her face.

'You can open your eyes,' Nobody's voice said, echoing slightly. Mae opened her eyes . . .

. . . to find herself crouched inside Sir Francis Drake's lead coffin, standing rather unkindly on top of Drake's long-dead body, her head poking up inside the domed lid of his coffin.

The lid was still turned slightly askew . . . but its concave inner dome was now filled with a pocket of air, air from one of the scuba tanks Nobody had snatched on the way out of the *Spider* and which he had blown up into the lid.

Nobody and Iolanthe were in the tight space with Mae, the water up to their necks, the only light the pale glow from Nobody's dive watch.

'Nice air pocket,' Iolanthe said, impressed. 'Tell me, how are you single? You're a genuine unicorn.'

'We're standing on Sir Francis Drake,' Mae said.

'I think he'd be okay with it,' Nobody said. 'He was a cool cat.'

'What do we do now, smart guy?' Iolanthe said. 'Our boat is sunk and so is our submersible.'

Nobody looked at her.

'I have a last-ditch plan.'

Ten minutes later, the Brazilian Navy destroyer arrived at the spot where the *Betty White* had gone down.

Sailors peered over its sides, searching for the sunken boat, its submersible and any survivors.

But then, off the stern of the destroyer, amid a sudden flurry of roiling white bubbles, like a cork popping out of a champagne bottle, a floatplane burst up out of the waves.

It practically sprang out of the water, lifted by the buoyancy of its two pontoons.

It had taken Nobody, Iolanthe and Mae five minutes to swim across the seabed to the sunken *Betty White*, taking turns with the two scuba breathers. Then they'd boarded the floatplane tied down to the sunken boat's bow.

Nobody had then leaned out and, with his knife, slashed the ropes tying down the plane.

The floatplane—with its buoyant pontoons and watertight engine bay—*whoosh*ed up toward the surface.

No sooner was the plane out of the water than Nobody hit the starter and the plane's nose propeller burst to life and in moments the aircraft was moving, powering away from the rear of the destroyer, accelerating quickly to take-off speed and lifting off into the sky before the bulky naval ship could turn even halfway around.

'Iolanthe! Send Jack the coordinates of the three cities!' Nobody yelled above the din of the engine when they were safely in the air. 'Mae! Figure out which of the three sets of coordinates gives the location of the City of Ra. That's our mission!'

Iolanthe quickly snapped off a photo of Drake's note and sent it as a text message on her satellite phone.

'Message is away!' she called.

'Mae?' Nobody asked.

Mae was punching some coordinates into the plane's dashboard GPS.

'It's this one,' she called, pointing at Drake's note.

R: 8°6'N 60°30'W of London
Follow the hidden river to the base of the tabletop mountain.

'The "R" must stand for Ra,' she said. 'It's not far, about eighty miles south of here. By the look of it, it's at the extreme southern end of the Orinoco Delta, at the base of one of the *tepui* mountains there.'

Nobody banked the little floatplane around and headed for the cluster of giant *tepuis* on the southern horizon.

Somewhere in there was the secret city of Ra.

As he sat in the rear bomb bay of Aloysius Knight's plane, the *Black Raven*, Jack West tapped out a text message:

> Hey Scarecrow,
>
> Thanks for sending your friend. He got me out of a real jam.
>
> Colourful guy, but very effective.

Jack looked forward at Aloysius Knight as he hit send on the text. A few moments later, his phone pinged with a reply:

> Jack,
>
> Mark Twain said, 'It's not the size of the dog in the fight, but the size of the fight in the dog.'
>
> Not always. Sometimes you just need the biggest, baddest dog you can get.
>
> I asked him to help you for as long as you need.
>
> Good hunting.

Jack snuffed a laugh and went forward into the cockpit.

'What's so funny?' Aloysius Knight asked.

'Nothing.'

Knight's tall and big-bearded pilot, Rufus said, 'Coming up on Santorini.'

Jack peered through the cockpit window.

Below them was the immense water-filled caldera that the world knew as the island of Santorini. A few cruise liners were parked in the lagoon in the middle of the caldera, looking positively tiny against its gargantuan curving cliffs.

Just then Jack's other phone, his chunky satellite phone, pinged.

'It's a message from Iolanthe. With a photo attached.' Jack opened it. 'Oh, nice work.'

'Who's Iolanthe and what's she got to say?' Aloysius asked.

'Royal princess. Smart but ruthless, and not entirely trustworthy. I think you'd like her. She just sent us the coordinates of the three cities as found by Sir Francis Drake.' He held the photo up for Aloysius to see.

'Amazing,' Aloysius said, deadpan. 'I'm overwhelmed with fucking joy.'

Jack immediately called the others. They were still at Aragon Castle.

'Pooh, Stretch, Sky Monster,' he said. 'I need you guys to get to Thule ASAP. Orlando's people are already there, but if Orlando didn't know that opening the first city would open the others, we can't be sure his people will be able to empower the Sword. We have less than thirty-six hours left. I need you to make sure that if they don't do it, someone does. Sending you the coordinates now.'

'*You got it,*' Stretch said.

'Zoe? You almost done there?'

Zoe's voice came on the line. '*We've gone through the Knights' private quarters and offices, and grabbed all the documents and computers we could find. Alby and I are about to leave for Hades's little safehouse in Rome. We'll go through them there.*'

'How is Alby doing?' Jack asked.

'*We patched him up good and tight. Also gave him some pretty potent painkillers,*' Zoe reported.

Alby's voice came on the line. '*Those assholes cut off my hand, but I'm alive. Pooh said I should ask if I can borrow one of your old bionic hands.*'

'Alby, when this is all done, we'll build you one of your own. Before Pooh and Stretch go to Thule, be sure to show them that scroll you found written by Plato about the cities. The one that talks about the entry avenues and the cities' guardians.'

'*I can make it to Thule, Jack,*' Alby said.

Jack grimaced. He didn't want to do this but he had to.

'Kid. No. You've got guts, I know that, but right now your body needs to rest and mend. Go with Hades and Zoe to Hades's hideaway in Rome. You can help me by finding the location of the Altar of the Cosmos and figuring out the ritual that has to be performed there.'

'*Okay,*' Alby said resignedly.

Jack hung up and turned to Aloysius.

'As for us, you and I need to find Poseidon's Mace.'

After attacking Aragon Castle and annihilating the Knights of the Golden Eight, Jack had sat down at the head of the Round Table and assessed the situation.

He was running out of time.

They had less than two days till Sagittarius A-star—the supermassive black hole at the centre of the galaxy—appeared over the sun and gave them a twelve-minute window to save the world.

Jack's problems lined up in his mind like aeroplanes waiting to land at an airport:

He hadn't laid eyes on the Three Secret Cities yet.

And by the look of it, Orlando may have jumped the gun and, by entering the first city, Thule, set in motion the defences of *all three* of the secret cities.

He didn't know what kind of miserable wasteland the world would become.

Nor did he know the location of the Altar of the Cosmos or the nature of the ritual that had to be performed there—a ritual that Iolanthe suggested may involve human sacrifice. Hopefully Alby could find that out.

And Sphinx had Lily. Hopefully, her gift was keeping her safe. Hopefully.

He thought about the three weapons.

Orlando had two of them: the Sword, Excalibur, and the Helmet of Hades. The third weapon, the Trident/Mace of Poseidon, had to be found and found fast.

'But it's been lost since antiquity,' Hades said to Jack. 'How can you hope to find it quickly when so many others have failed?'

Jack said, 'History leaves us clues, breadcrumbs, random lines of breadcrumbs, so to speak. Somebody, at some time in the past, wrote about the Mace and its final resting place. In my experience, it's not the *amount* of research you do that unearths an ancient place. It's the quality: finding relevant clues. Two of them, in fact. They can have been written centuries apart, but if you can find two clues about something and you can connect them—and let them help you zero in on your target—then you *can* do in a day what others have failed to do for centuries.'

'You just have to find the two clues,' Hades said, 'in a mountain of historical data.'

'Yes,' Jack said. 'Fortunately, having people like you and me around with lifetimes of historical expertise in their heads helps.'

And so, with Alby's and Hades's help, Jack had settled in for some intense research, reading deep into the night, research that had led him here, to Santorini.

THE CLIFFS OF OIA
SANTORINI, GREECE

The glaring noonday sun pounded down on the island of Santorini.

Jack squinted up at the many white-painted hotels and homes that cascaded down the wild cliffs of Oia above him.

Santorini—the Isle of St Irene, or, as it was known to the ancient Greeks, Thera—is a member of the group of islands called the Cyclades.

It is actually a gigantic water-filled crater left by one of the greatest volcanic eruptions of all time, the Minoan Eruption that occurred sometime between 1650 and 1550 B.C.E. The earth-shaking eruption caused two sections of the caldera's walls to collapse, allowing the waters of the Mediterranean to flood into it.

What remains is a devastatingly beautiful island shaped like a reverse-C, with dramatic thousand-foot-high cliffs ringing its seven-kilometre-wide central lagoon.

It is a wildly popular tourist destination. Every day, a dozen cruise liners stop in the lagoon. On the island's many steep cliffs one finds a chaotic jumble of chapels, homes and hotels (many of which burrow *back into* the cliff in search of coolness and almost all of which are painted white). Some of the chapels, famously, have gorgeous sky-blue domes.

The structures tumble down the cliff faces in no discernible order, never quite reaching the water's edge, since at their lower levels the cliffs become vertical and unstable. Crumbling staircases and dangerous old ladders give access to the few docks and jetties at the bases of the cliffs.

It was on one of those jetties that Jack and Aloysius now stood, gazing upward.

In his search for Poseidon's Mace, Jack had trawled through all manner of references to Poseidon and his trident and places devoted to him.

A scroll by the famed Greek historian Herodotus written in 430 B.C.E. stood out. It claimed that *'the Great Mace of the Sealord was buried with him, in a tomb defended by his son and the Sealord's cursed lover'*.

'Who was Poseidon's son?' Aloysius asked.

'Triton,' Jack said. 'Poseidon's son was named Triton. He's a relatively obscure god. In the myths, he's always been depicted as a merman: a man with the tail of a fish.'

'And Poseidon's cursed lover?'

Jack's eyes narrowed. 'That's another story entirely. She was a very famous woman, one of the most famous women in all of mythology. Her name was Medusa.'

'The chick with snakes for hair?' Aloysius said. 'The one who turned people to stone when they looked at her?'

'The very same,' Jack said. 'One of the three Gorgons. Although, to be fair, she may not have been the vicious monster history has made her out to be.'

'How so?'

'Well, for one thing, Medusa wasn't always ugly. According to the original Greek texts, she was a beautiful young virgin. But she was seduced by Poseidon and they made love inside the temple of Athena, thus angering Athena.

'As punishment, Athena made Medusa hideous to look upon, with a wrinkled face and snakes for hair. And then, of course, there was the whole turn-them-to-stone thing, which kept Medusa from any kind of human contact.'

Jack gave Aloysius a look. 'A modern interpretation of this would be that after sleeping with King Poseidon, young Medusa caught some kind of skin disease, probably leprosy, and was banished by the queen of the time—Poseidon's furious wife—who was named Athena.'

During his late-night research session, Jack had followed up on the Herodotus lead, but he couldn't find other references to any such tomb or its location. He briefed Alby and Hades on what he needed and they went off, searching.

Then, long after midnight, Hades brought Jack something.

It was a letter from a Venetian noble who had gone to the Holy Land during the Fourth Crusade in 1204.

It was a note from the noble to his wife back in Venice and it said:

> As payment for my participation on this foolish Crusade, I was given land on the island of Thera, which the Franks call the Isle of St Irene. My parcel of land is at the northern end of the crescent-shaped island.
>
> It is useless. Barren, rocky and steep, all high cliffs and gorges. It is most unpleasant, fit for nothing of use: not grazing, not planting, nothing.
>
> It is dotted with the crumbling ruins of native huts and old pagan temples that delve into the cliffs to hide from the punishing sun.
>
> One such temple down by the waterline bears a cracked inscription of a man with the tail of a fish and the fearsome visage of snake-headed Medusa.
>
> What a miserable place. I have been duped by the Pope. This grant of land is entirely unworthy of my efforts on his behalf.

Jack had zeroed in on the line:

> One such temple down by the waterline bears a cracked

inscription of a man with the tail of a fish and the fearsome visage of snake-headed Medusa.

Triton and Medusa.

Jack gave Hades a look. 'Two clues, on the surface entirely unrelated, written 1600 years apart, both referring to an ancient structure with a singular image on its entrance. Thanks, Anthony, you just gave me the crucial second clue that I needed.'

Within ten minutes, Jack and Aloysius were in the air, heading for Santorini.

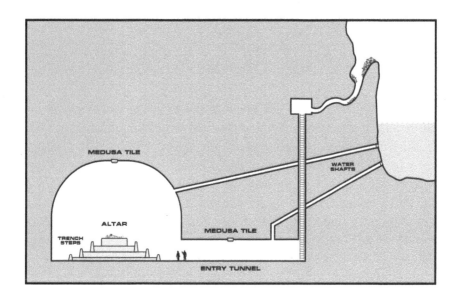

MEDUSA TILE

WATER
SHAFTS

ALTAR

TRENCH
STEPS

MEDUSA TILE

ENTRY TUNNEL

THE TOMB OF POSEIDON
SANTORINI, GREECE

They found the tomb's entrance at the extreme northern tip of Santorini, in a steep V-shaped gorge below the clifftop town of Oia.

When he saw the little temple's faded stone entrance, Jack could see why it had never been found.

It lay in a cleft a short way up from where the waves battered the cliff's rugged vertical base: one natural defence. And the water here was deep, meaning small boats could not lay anchor. To stray too close meant being dashed against the cliff: a second natural defence.

But the ancient tomb's main defence against discovery by explorers and archaeologists was actually far more mundane than that.

Rubbish and debris.

Decades worth of modern trash—cola cans, chairs, doors and dirty plastic bags, all of it faded by many years in the sun—had been tossed into the gorge from above, concealing the passage in it.

Amid that tangle of rubbish, Jack and Aloysius found the temple's entrance with the carving of a merman and Medusa on it, and thus the long-lost tomb of Poseidon.

After penetrating the tomb's entrance, they climbed down a tight vertical shaft cut into the rock.

Crude ladder-holds had been chiselled into its rough stone walls. Using them, they descended for a good hundred feet—well below sea level, Jack guessed—before they arrived at a horizontal tunnel.

This tunnel was dead straight, perfectly square in shape, and it ran away from them for maybe thirty metres before opening onto a wider, darker space.

It was high enough for them to stand in and wide enough for the two of them to walk down side-by-side.

Guided by the beams of their flashlights, they ventured into the tunnel, Jack leading the way.

A short way down the tunnel, he stopped, peering upward.

There was a square hole in the ceiling. It spanned the entire width of the passageway.

'A problem?' Aloysius said.

'In my line of work, booby traps are an occupational hazard,' Jack said.

He peered at the floor below the hole in the ceiling, searching for any kind of trigger stone, but found nothing.

He jumped across the section of tunnel underneath the ceiling-hole.

Nothing happened.

No trap. No death.

Aloysius shrugged and followed him.

About halfway down the passageway, they found something else in the ceiling.

Jack raised his flashlight to examine it.

It was a circular tile the size of a dinner plate. It protruded a couple of inches from the tunnel's otherwise flat roof, like a modern ceiling light.

Painted on it was the face of Medusa: snarling and angry, with her trademark snakes for hair.

Looking closely, Jack saw that the *pupils* of Medusa's furious eyes were made of a pair of small raised stones the size and shape of two tiny pills or pellets.

'Friendly, isn't she?' Aloysius said wryly.

'Careful,' Jack said. 'That gaze can turn you to stone.'

They pressed on.

At the far end of the passageway, they emerged into a wide

circular chamber with a high domed roof and beautifully curving walls, all cut from solid grey stone.

The round walls of the space were covered in gorgeous blue bas-reliefs: raised images of Poseidon wielding his three-pronged Mace, causing the seas to rise and cities to fall.

In the exact centre of the chamber was a high round platform that rose like a wedding cake in four broad steps.

The steps were themselves unusual: they were each cut in the shape of a trench, a circular trench, sort of like the pool at the base of a fountain. One climbed them by leaping from edge to edge.

And on the platform atop the steps was the centrepiece of the place.

A waist-high oblong stone tomb covered in three thousand years' worth of dust and stone flakes.

It looked like an altar: squat, sturdy and old.

'Captain, what is that?' Aloysius said, looking up.

He shone his flashlight at a round hole cut into the curving wall of the ceiling. It was maybe three feet in diameter.

'Looks like a light shaft,' Aloysius said. 'Seems to go up at an angle. But no sunlight is getting through.'

'I'd guess it's more likely a *star* shaft,' Jack said. 'Like the ones inside the pyramids at Giza. They tend to get blocked up over the years with dirt and sand, but thousands of years ago, you might have been able to look up through that shaft at night and see a certain constellation.'

Jack took in the rest of the dome-shaped chamber.

And he spotted something.

It was at the highest point of the chamber, at the very peak of the domed ceiling: a single round tile just like the one back in the passageway.

On it was painted the snarling face of Medusa, complete with the small dark pills as her blazing eyes.

Slowly, reverently, by the light of their flashlights and beneath the angry glare of Medusa, Jack and Aloysius strode up the odd-looking steps and onto the platform at their summit and beheld the ancient tomb.

Jack risked a smile.

Cut into the top of the oblong slab, caked in a thick layer of grit but clearly visible, was a raised life-sized carving of the Mace of Poseidon.

Jack gazed at the carving, entranced.

The Tomb of Poseidon, he thought.

As he looked at the raised image of the Mace more closely, he saw that it was very detailed, amazingly detailed, in fact.

'Nice carving,' Aloysius said.

'Sure is,' Jack said, and suddenly he realised. 'Only it's not a carving.'

'What?' Aloysius said.

'It's the Mace.' Jack leaned close and gently blew the dust off the 'carving'.

The layer of dust and stone flakes that had landed on the tomb over the millennia scattered, revealing slivers of glimmering gold.

Ever so delicately, Jack brushed away the remaining dust layer with his fingers.

And there it was.

Resting in a recess that had been perfectly shaped to accommodate it.

The Trident of the Sealord, the Mace of Poseidon, the King of the Sea.

It was simply stunning to behold.

Its thick handle was made of burnished gold and its three blades—all pointed slightly inward—were made of silver. They looked as sharp as daggers.

The three blades, however, were not laid out laterally like a fork or trident, but rather they were arrayed in a circle—officially making the weapon a mace, not a trident.

'It really is a mace,' Jack said softly. 'A sceptre.'

The Mace's golden handle was inlaid with six glistening gems: two rubies, two emeralds and two sapphires. The gems alone would have been priceless.

In between the three blades was an empty setting.

In it would be placed another gem of some sort, a blue gem, Jack knew, that would be found in the sacred vault of the third secret city, the City of Atlas.

Aloysius reached forward to grab the Mace. 'Well, what are we waiting for—'

'No!' Jack pushed Aloysius's hand away before he could touch the sceptre.

'Wait now,' Jack said. 'Let's just go about this very carefully—'

The cocking of a gun made them both spin.

By the time he'd turned around, Aloysius had one of his sawn-off Remington shotguns drawn, raised and aimed . . .

. . . at the three men armed with AK-47 assault rifles standing in the entryway to the chamber behind them.

'Now, now, let's not be like that,' the lead man said amiably. He was an overweight Pakistani, with wobbly jowls, sweaty armpits, and in addition to the gun, a glowing lantern hanging from his forearm.

Sunny Malik grinned, revealing his sickly yellow teeth. 'Well, not yet.'

'Drop the gun, Captain Knight,' Sunny said.

'Do I know you?' Aloysius asked.

'No, but I know you,' Sunny said. 'You caught a friend of mine during a bounty hunt last year, a very perverted but reliable gun runner from Kabul who was slipping me American weapons. You collected the price on his head and in doing so, you ruined my supply line.'

Aloysius lay his shotgun on the ground beside the tomb.

'I'd say I'm sorry but I'm really fucking not,' he said.

Jack stepped back as Malik's two henchmen ascended the broad trench-like stairs, their guns trained on him and Aloysius. They also appeared to be Pakistani and they both wore bullet-proof vests.

'I met your mother in Karachi,' Sunny Malik said to Jack. 'I liked her. Feisty. When I see her next, I'll be sure to tell her that I shot you like a dog. Then I'll kill her, too.'

Jack noticed that Malik remained down near the entryway. He had the feeling Malik was staying down there just in case there were any close-range traps near the altar.

'Grab the trident,' Sunny Malik called to his men.

The first henchman snatched up the golden Mace and held it aloft.

Jack waited.

Aloysius waited.

Sunny Malik waited.

Nothing happened.

The henchman grinned . . .
. . . and then the trap went off.

It came blasting into the chamber through the sloping shaft situated near the top of the dome.

Seawater.

A gushing torrent of the stuff.

It roared down all around Jack and Aloysius, pouring into the chamber with such ferocious force that it knocked Sunny's second henchman clear off his feet.

Down on the floor, Sunny Malik spun as more water came surging out of the entry passageway *behind* him—smashing into his knees so powerfully it caused him to fall to the ground.

This body of water was thundering in through the wide square hole in the ceiling of the tunnel back near the ladder-shaft.

Aloysius Knight was not a man to miss an opportunity.

As the trap was triggered and the water came blasting into the chamber, he kicked his shotgun, bouncing it off the tomb and up into his hands and from point-blank range, he shot the distracted henchman gripping the Mace.

The henchman was hurled through the air by the powerful blast, the front of his bulletproof vest absorbing the shot and saving his life.

He flew down the trench-steps, splashing into the swirling water at the bottom, winded but alive, leaving Aloysius Knight standing at the top of the platform, gripping his gun in one hand . . . and the Mace in the other.

Jack reacted in his own way, too.

He was trying to figure out the trap.

His mind raced, putting the pieces together.

He saw the water rushing in through the ceiling-shaft. When combined with the water coming in through the entry passageway, it was rapidly filling the chamber. It was already thigh-deep and pouring over the rim of the platform's first trench-like step, filling it.

In the nanoseconds of time in which the mind operates, Jack made some deductions:

Removing the Mace must have released gates in the shafts, allowing seawater to rush in.

So what happens next?

The entry tunnel is going to fill completely with water.

Then this chamber is going to fill with water.

The vertical ladder-shaft will fill with water.

And we'll drown.

The water rose quickly, cascading into the next trench.

Sunny's second henchman sloshed desperately back toward the entry tunnel, fighting against the inrushing torrent, fleeing for his life, pushing past the still-kneeling figure of Sunny who had apparently lost his gun when the sudden flood had felled him.

As he watched the chamber fill with seawater, Jack realised that the weird trench-shaped nature of the steps *slowed* the rising of the water. Without the trenches, the water would have just risen fast, unimpeded.

And then Jack saw that *the very top step* of the platform *was perfectly level* with the roof of the doorway to the entry tunnel.

To anyone else, it was a meaningless detail, but to Jack West Jr, it was pivotal.

'Oh no . . .' he breathed.

He snapped to look up at the Medusa tile set into the uppermost point of the dome, his gaze falling on . . .

. . . the small black-grey pills set into Medusa's eyes.

Black-grey pills.

Those pills are made of grey matter, greystone, Gorgon Stone, the powder that creates liquid stone.

'Guarded by Medusa . . . one of the Gorgons,' Jack said to

himself as Medusa's famous mythical power suddenly became very real. 'Her gaze turns people to . . .'

And suddenly the full terrifying extent of the chamber's trap system became clear to him.

In his mind, he saw the other Medusa tile attached to the roof of the entry tunnel.

The inrushing water wasn't designed to drown them.

First, it would fill the entry tunnel, which was the exact same height as the top step of the platform.

Thus, as the entry tunnel was completely filled . . .

. . . thanks to the trench-steps, for at least a few short minutes, a level lake would be created in the chamber, ringing the platform with the tomb on it . . .

. . . at which point, inside the entry tunnel . . .

. . . the rising water would touch the two small black-grey pills in Medusa's eyes . . .

. . . the pills made of grey matter . . .

. . . *which would turn all the water in the tunnel and the chamber to stone.*

The immediate ramifications of that hit Jack.

The exit would be closed forever: the thirty-metre-long entry tunnel, plus the bottom of the ladder-shaft, would be clogged with solidified liquid stone.

But that wouldn't be the end of it.

There was still the *second* tile with Medusa painted on it at the peak of the chamber's dome.

After pausing for a few minutes at the platform—thanks to the trenches—the inrushing water would resume its rise, now quickly filling the rest of the chamber!

First it would drown anyone still in it—like Jack and Aloysius—but then as a final punishment for trying to steal the Mace, when the rising water finally filled the chamber completely and touched the two dark grey eyes on the second Medusa tile, all the water in

the chamber would also turn to stone, sealing Jack and Aloysius in it forever.

Jack gazed in stunned awe at the scene around him.

'Oh, we are so screwed,' he gasped.

He turned to Aloysius and yelled above the din, 'Keep hold of the Mace and follow me!'

Jack sloshed through the chest-deep water to the wall of the chamber and started climbing up it, using the raised protrusions of its gorgeous bas-reliefs as handholds.

Aloysius jammed the Mace into his belt and chased after him. 'Where are you going?'

'We have to push our way out through that shaft!' Jack said, pointing at the shaft immediately above them: the one allowing seawater to pour into the chamber in a powerful gushing stream.

'Are you crazy!' Aloysius protested.

'It's the only way we don't die here!'

'Then let's move!'

As for Sunny and his men, several things happened at once to them.

The fleeing henchman had made it almost all the way down the entry tunnel, pushing through the neck-deep water there.

Sunny, his search for his gun now abandoned, had remained in the chamber and clambered up the trench-steps to get out of the raging, swirling waves.

Beside him was the thug who had been shot in his bulletproof vest by Aloysius. Groaning and staggering—he didn't know it, but two of his ribs were broken—this thug fell back into the water from the bottom step.

And then it happened.

Inside the entry tunnel, the rapidly rising water hit the ceiling and touched the two tiny black-grey pills that were Medusa's eyes.

As long as he lived, Jack would never forget the sight.

He'd been right about the trench-shaped steps.

As the incoming water completely filled the tunnel, the trenches created—at least for a few short minutes—a kind of level *lake* inside the chamber.

Halfway up the wall, Jack looked down behind him and saw the body of clear flat water ringing the platform turn a dense, dark grey.

It was like watching a virus take over the water: creep through it and infect it, and rob it of its essential nature.

The entire 'lake' went grey and then . . .

. . . *craaaaack*.

It was the same sickening sound Jack had heard when he'd been entombed in the liquid-stone tub at Erebus.

The sound of the infected water *hardening*.

The thug inside the tunnel had no hope.

He'd managed to take a deep breath just as the water had filled the tunnel completely.

Then he'd opened his eyes and seen the ladder-shaft ahead of him . . .

. . . only for the water all around him to suddenly darken and he could see nothing.

Then, to his horror, that same dark water abruptly *hardened around his entire body*. At first it felt like jelly but then it started

cracking and crunching, and abruptly, to his complete confusion, he found himself *suspended* in the stuff like a fish caught in ice, entirely encased in it and unable to move.

It actually hardened quite quickly and to his surprise, he didn't drown. In fact, he could actually breathe, because he was now entombed in a little pocket of solidified stone perfectly form-fitted around his body.

He would not die of drowning.

No, it would be worse than that.

First, the stone, as it set, would contract little by little, slowly crushing his limbs, and then, as he groaned in abject agony, unheard by anyone in his claustrophobic little tomb, he would suffocate as with his desperate wails, gasps and pants, he would eventually run out of air.

In the chamber, it wasn't much better for the thug with the broken ribs.

Having fallen into the darkened water, he was halfway out of it when it solidified around his legs.

He was trapped half-in, half-out of the hardening stone. As it cracked and crunched around his waist, locking him in its unbreakable grip, the man screamed in terror.

He couldn't get out of the stuff.

He scratched and reached for his boss, begging him for help, but Sunny Malik just recoiled, wide-eyed, at the man's predicament.

Even Malik—a cruel gangster who had executed and tortured both the wicked and the innocent—was struck dumb with fear at the situation in which he now found himself.

In this way, the temporary lake of water ringing the platform solidified into hard greystone, essentially creating a new, higher floor for the space.

But seawater kept gushing into the chamber through the shaft high up on its wall.

Jack and Aloysius kept climbing for the shaft.

Sunny Malik sat frozen on the platform, in front of his screaming henchman.

But it wasn't over.

Now the second phase of the trap began.

For as that first flat layer of water became a new solid floor, the chamber began to fill even faster; the water now clear once again and rising toward the *second* Medusa tile at the top of the dome.

Aloysius Knight saw it all.

'What is going on here?' he called to Jack above him. 'The water just turned to fucking stone!'

Jack said, 'Keep climbing! When this new body of rising water touches that Medusa's eyes, *all* the water in this chamber and in this shaft will also turn to stone!'

Aloysius Knight stared in shock at the scene. 'Then climb faster!'

And so they climbed.

Up the bas-reliefs on the wall, toward the shaft from which the seawater cascaded.

When they arrived at it, Aloysius stopped beside Jack.

'Here, you'll need this,' he said, handing Jack a small mouth-piece. It was a portable scuba breather, good for about ten minutes underwater.

'No slips now, or we go sliding back into that chamber,' he added.

'Right,' Jack nodded.

Then Jack led the way, shoving himself into the torrent of water coming out of the shaft. The walls of the shaft were rough and uneven, causing the incoming water to slosh and bounce around them.

Jack leaned into it with his fireman's helmet, pressing his hands and feet against the shaft's walls, straining against the flow.

Behind him, Aloysius risked a look back into the chamber.

He saw Sunny Malik and his trapped henchman down on the platform.

The henchman was gripped to his waist in the layer of solidified stone. He screamed as the inrushing water consumed him, rising around his face. He went under with a final desperate shriek.

As for Malik, he was carried up on the rising water, thrashing and panicking.

The last thing Aloysius saw of him before he followed Jack into the shaft were his wild terrified eyes.

★ ★ ★

And then the two heroes were in the shaft, forcing their way up its sloping length, fighting with all their might against the water rushing in at them.

Jack moved doggedly, one foot at a time: planting his feet against the shaft's walls, then shifting his hands upward and repeating the process, all while water relentlessly slammed against his helmet from above.

He gripped his breather in his teeth, sucking in air.

He saw Aloysius below him, shouting through the mouthpiece gripped between his teeth: 'Keep going, Captain! You gotta keep going!'

And then Jack slipped . . .

. . . and fell.

And in a single split second, Jack knew he was going to die.

But Aloysius caught him: caught one of Jack's boots one-handed while somehow managing to keep himself from falling back down the shaft, and with incredible strength, he held Jack up.

'I got you!' Aloysius called over the roar of the water. 'Grab hold again! Keep going!'

Jack grabbed another handhold against the wall and soon he was moving again, against the ceaseless flow, inching his way upward.

Below him, Aloysius Knight looked fearfully behind them.

They had climbed maybe eighty feet up the shaft.

In the chamber, the main body of water wouldn't be far from the summit of the dome and the two black-grey pills that were the eyes of Medusa.

They had to get up this shaft.

'Faster, Jack!' he shouted. 'We can't let the water catch us!'

Jack strained against the powerful flow.

Through the breather clenched between his teeth, he called back, 'We didn't come this far . . . just to come *this* far!'

Down in the chamber, Sunny Malik had indeed missed his opportunity to escape.

Floating on the surface of the rising body of water, he hadn't been able to flee into the shaft like Jack and Aloysius had.

And so he had just risen with the water, riding it to the domed ceiling of the chamber, resigned to his fate.

He came to the top of the dome, saw the snarling face of Medusa painted on the round tile there.

Unaware of the workings of liquid stone, he didn't know the importance of the pills set into her eyes.

It didn't matter.

With nowhere else to go, the water flowed over Sunny Malik's face and filled the chamber entirely . . .

. . . and touched Medusa's eyes.

The reaction was instantaneous.

The water filling the chamber instantly turned dark, infected by the grey powder.

It solidified around Malik, encasing him as it had his first henchman, entombing him alive in his own personal nightmare.

It also solidified inside the entire chamber. As far as any future generation would know, that chamber had never existed. It was now solid black-grey stone.

In the shaft, Jack West Jr and Aloysius Knight climbed desperately.

Incoming water pounded Jack from above.

Aloysius peered fearfully behind him.

He saw the body of water rising up the shaft below them, ravenous and relentless . . .

. . . and then to his horror he saw it turn a deep grey.

'Jack . . . !'

It was barely fifteen feet below them and rising fast.

Then, without warning, Jack's feet leapt out of Aloysius's view to be suddenly replaced by Jack's hand, gripping his around the wrist and hauling Aloysius out of the shaft and onto the seabed at the base of an underwater cliff.

Biting into their breathers, Jack and Aloysius pushed off the sea floor and swam for all they were worth away from the shaft-hole cut into the underwater cliff's base.

They swam and swam, with broad powerful strokes, until they were twenty, then thirty feet clear of the cliff-base.

And then, with a foul, explosive sound, like a supersized snake reaching out for them, a great black-grey finger of semi-solid stone extended out from the shaft-hole, lancing out into the water for a full twenty feet.

But it wasn't strong enough to reach them and, as it hardened, it fell, drifting in slow motion to the sea floor until it looked no different from the many other rocks and stones that lay there.

Jack and Aloysius surfaced moments later.

They bobbed in the water off the northern tip of Santorini, gasping and heaving for air, but alive.

A giant luxury cruise liner rumbled by, sounding its horn as it headed into the caldera. Throbbing dance music could be heard.

Aloysius pulled the Mace from his belt and held it in one fist.

He glared at Jack. 'Honestly, I'm gonna kill Scarecrow for introducing me to you.'

HADES'S APARTMENT
ROME, ITALY

Alby Calvin sat alone in a study filled with computers and communications gear, the stump that was his left wrist bandaged, typing with his right hand.

He was in Hades's secret apartment in Rome.

Of course, Hades's 'little' hideaway wasn't that little at all. It took up a whole floor of an old building and through the window beside him, Alby could see the Coliseum and the Roman Forum and, in the distance, the Vatican.

Zoe and Hades were working away in other rooms, keeping track of Jack and the others around the world.

Wounded as he was, Alby was restless—restless to help in the quest—so he buried himself in the task Jack had set him: finding the Altar of the Cosmos and discovering the nature of the ritual that needed to be performed there.

He started with the documents Iolanthe had taken from the Hall of Royal Records.

The first was a very old scroll written in Hebrew with a translation attached. It was titled: *THE REAL GENESIS 22.*

'The *real* Genesis 22?' Alby said aloud.

As Alby knew, the book that people know as the Bible was not really one complete homogenous text.

In truth, it was a disparate compilation of writings, gospels and scrolls written by many—often unknown—authors that had been assembled over a period of three hundred years both before and after the birth of Christ.

And that wasn't even mentioning the many changes to the text that had occurred in Arabian libraries and European monasteries over the next thousand years.

This scroll appeared to be a chapter from the first book of the Bible, the Book of Genesis.

Genesis 22.

Alby knew of it: it was the chapter where God tested Abraham by asking him to kill his son, Isaac. Abraham obeyed, but, as everyone knows, God stepped in at the last moment and stopped him.

Alby read this version:

> And it came to pass that God said unto Abraham, Take thyself or thy son Isaac, whom thou lovest, to the mountain-altar at the end of the world; and there, in the altar's bath, offer one of you to me.
>
> After five days' sail, Abraham lifted up his eyes and saw the place afar off.
>
> There Abraham laid his son Isaac in the sacred bath and plunged the holy blade deep into his son's breast, spilling his sacred blood into the water, slaying him.

'Oh, that is messed up,' Alby said. 'No wonder they rewrote this.'

The pious and noble Abraham, father of the three great religions of the Middle East, had killed his own son instead of himself.

Alby re-read the chapter, zeroing in on the details:

A mountain altar. With a sacred bath. Five days' sail from Judea. And a choice for Abraham: either kill himself or his son. So Abraham had killed his son.

Alby went to Iolanthe's next document: a parchment written in Spanish by King Alfonso X of Castile. Iolanthe's translation of it read:

> *From my summer palace here in San Roque, I watch over*
> *both flooded Atlas and the glorious Altar for the Rebirth*
> *of the Cosmos every day.*

Alby looked up San Roque. It was a small town in the south of Spain, near the Mediterranean.

Then he came to the last document.

It was the report labelled *K.E.O.—King's Eyes Only*. It had a notation from Jack saying that the Altar was 'the size of a mountain'.

'Like Abraham's altar,' Alby said aloud.

He read the report:

K.E.O. REPORT
CORPS OF ROYAL ENGINEERS
178th TUNNELLING COMPANY
12 May 1942

Your Majesty,
    During our excavations of Arrow Street an unusual chamber was found. It appears to be the holy chamber of the Altar. Photographs are enclosed.
    The men who found it were duly executed.
Brigadier James Conn Jr
Chief Royal Engineer

Alby had not been in London when Jack and the others had gathered there with Iolanthe, so he hadn't seen this document till now.

If he had been in London then, he would have spotted the telltale words right away: 178TH TUNNELLING COMPANY and Arrow Street.

'Oh, no way,' Alby said to the empty room around him. 'They spelt the street name wrong . . .'

He grabbed his iPhone and pulled up, of all things, some holiday snaps from his European vacation; the solo trip he'd taken on summer break during which he'd visited a bunch of European destinations: Venice, Rome, Paris and the Rock of Gibraltar.

Alby had loved the Rock.

He had marvelled at its sheer bulk—four hundred metres of towering solid rock rising up from the Mediterranean Sea—and its singular shape. Its western flank was gently slanted while its eastern face was almost perfectly vertical, giving it the shape of an enormous sundial.

Alby had also loved reading about its long and rich history.

Dangling off the bottom of Spain—in sight of Alfonso X's summer palace in San Roque and about five days' sail from Judea—looking out over the Strait of Gibraltar to Africa on the far shore, for five thousand years it had marked the end of the known world.

Over the millennia, it had been held by the Carthaginians, the Romans, the Visigoths, the Moors and the Spanish, until finally, under the terms of the Treaty of Utrecht in 1713, it was granted to the British Crown in perpetuity.

To the fury of Spain, it remains British territory to this day, complete with British immigration personnel and passport kiosks at its little airport and land entry. Britain interprets the words *in perpetuity* literally.

While everyone had heard the phrase 'as solid as the Rock of Gibraltar', what few people knew was that the Rock of Gibraltar was not that solid at all.

It was honeycombed with tunnels: *thirty-five miles of them.* While many of the tunnels went back to Roman times, it was the British who had tunnelled the most beneath and through the Rock. The peak of their tunnelling activity had been during World War II when the prospect of the Nazis storming Gibraltar had been a very real one.

Alby brought up one of his photos: it showed him smiling as he stood in front of an underground street sign: AROW STREET.

AROW Street was a tunnel at Gibraltar, a long supply tunnel dug by the 178th Tunnelling Company of the Royal Engineers in 1942.

It was named after the initials of the commanding officer of that company, Lt Colonel Arthur Robert Owen Williams—A.R.O.W.—hence the unusual spelling.

But somewhere along the way—maybe when the letter was retyped for presentation to the king—the word had been respelled... *incorrectly*. Only someone who had been there would know this.

Alby leaned back in his chair.

During the digging of AROW Street, the Royal Engineers had evidently come across a strange chamber, a chamber the Chief Royal Engineer called 'the holy chamber of the Altar'. And then he'd executed the poor troops who'd found it.

An altar the size of a mountain.

The Rock of Gibraltar was almost five hundred metres tall . . .

. . . *above* the surface of the sea.

Alby scrambled to find some kind of cross-section of the Rock, showing its full shape both above and below the water's surface.

He found one and he gasped.

The immense landform the world knew as the Rock of Gibraltar was literally the peak of a much larger mountain that plunged underwater for at least another kilometre. If, at some time, the Mediterranean Sea had been lower, or even dry, the Rock would have been a towering mountain dominating the area.

'No wonder the Altar hasn't been found,' Alby said to himself. 'It's been covered over by the sea for thousands of years. The Rock of Gibraltar is the Altar of the Cosmos.'

SIXTH PURSUIT

THE THREE SECRET CITIES

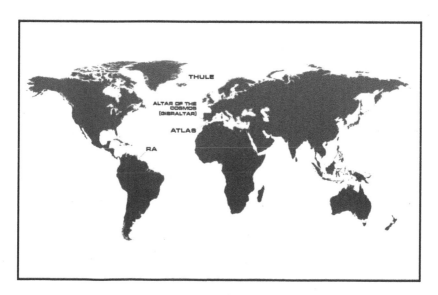

Who watches the watchmen?

JUVENAL, ROMAN POET

**SPHINX'S MANSION &
THE ANCIENT LIGHTHOUSE**

THE NORTH COAST OF MOROCCO
MEDITERRANEAN SEA

As the day of the ritual dawned, Lily awoke in a multi-levelled mansion looking out at a stunning and most unique view.

The mansion belonged to Sphinx and it sat in a commanding position atop a high cliff on the Moroccan coast, facing both north and west.

As for the view, it was unique because it took in two continents: Africa and Europe.

Sphinx's luxurious home had been positioned—long, long ago—in such a way that it looked out over the Strait of Gibraltar, the gateway to the Mediterranean Sea, where Europe was separated from Africa by only ten miles of water.

The mansion had a helipad, a short airstrip, a six-car garage and, down at the water's edge, a dock that housed Sphinx's 130-foot cruiser.

There was one other feature of the remote mansion worth mentioning: standing a short way out from the high rocky cliff, rising out of the sea, was a stupendous tower of greystone easily three hundred feet high.

To the uninitiated, it appeared to be a natural rock formation, but to those with royal knowledge it would be instantly recognised as having been fashioned by hands of old from the curious substance known as liquid stone.

The towering finger of rock had been moulded into the shape

of a lighthouse, with a lantern room at its summit. In the lantern room, a modern electric light rotated at night, keeping ships—and the curious—away from the shore.

Around noon, Sphinx sent for Lily and she joined him in the main lounge of his mansion.

She gazed out at the view: to her left was Morocco, the tip of Africa; to her right, Spain, the southern edge of Europe.

The mighty Rock of Gibraltar could be seen on the other side of the strait, even though it was ten miles distant. Its hazy bulk loomed on the horizon, half a kilometre high.

'For nearly five thousand years, this strait was the most strategic body of water in the world,' Sphinx said, standing beside Lily, also taking in the view. 'It was only with the advent of flight and aerial warfare that its significance waned.'

Lily said nothing.

'Today we call it the Strait of Gibraltar, but it has gone by many names. The Great Dam of the Ancients. The Gateway of Atlas. Atlantis.'

Lily cocked her head at the word.

The most famous lost city of them all.

'People have the wrong idea about Atlantis,' Sphinx added. 'It wasn't, as Plato wrote, an island city ruled by a proud and arrogant people that was destroyed in a cataclysmic flood because of its hubris.

'It was a society of proud and arrogant people that managed a dam, the greatest dam ever built.

'For it wasn't *one* dam, it was actually five, a series of five cascading dams that stretched across this strait, holding the Atlantic Ocean at bay. Strangely enough, in the 1920s, a German architect named Herman Sörgel proposed building a dam across the Strait of Gibraltar to dry up the Mediterranean and create more land. His five step-dams were surprisingly similar to the actual Atlantean Dam. I have a sketch of Sörgel's dam here.'

Sphinx guided Lily to a framed picture on the wall of the lounge.

Lily peered at the image.

She saw five dams spanning the Strait as broad step-like weirs. At the bottom right-hand corner of the image, she saw the Rock of Gibraltar with its massive underwater bulk exposed.

The German architect's concept was a project of mind-boggling scale. If the Atlantean dams had been anything like it, then they must have been simply astonishing.

Sphinx said, 'If you look at scans of the seafloor here, you can see the outlines of the five Atlantean dams. Gigantic waterfalls flowed down their spillways into the dry bed of the Mediterranean Valley.

'But then came the day the top two dams cracked in their middles and the ocean exploded through their walls, flooding the Mediterranean and creating the twin myths of the end of Atlantis and of the Great Flood that is found in every major religion on Earth.'

'When exactly was that?' Lily asked. 'Atlantis myths talk of the Atlanteans lording over Egypt and Athens.'

Sphinx shrugged. 'Best guess? Around 12,000 years ago. Stone

sampling dates it to around the same time as the carving of the Great Sphinx in 10,000 B.C.E.'

Lily turned to face him. 'I was told that you were the guardian of the City of Atlas. Doesn't that mean you're supposed to live in its watchtower?'

'It does.'

Lily looked at the mansion around her again. Her eyes landed on the stone lighthouse outside.

'*This* is the watchtower?' she said. 'This mansion is the entrance to Atlantis?'

Sphinx smiled, his pale eyes shining.

'My dear girl, this mansion and its lighthouse, as they say, are but the tip of the iceberg.'

As one would expect of a man as wealthy and aristocratic as Sphinx, his home was both luxurious yet understated.

The floors were of Italian marble, the décor was from Paris and the artwork hanging on the walls would have been the envy of any museum: Rembrandts, Picassos, original sketches by Michelangelo, and not a few ancient artefacts including a glorious fifteen-foot-tall sandstone sphinx that looked like an exact replica of the Great Sphinx at Giza.

On one wide marble pedestal stood four scale models made from greystone.

Three stood together.

The first looked like a funnel; the second resembled a round-sided pyramid pressed up against the base of a square mountain; and the third, an hourglass. All three were intricate in their details: they were dotted with tiny staircases and swooping bridges.

Lily recalled the symbols she had seen representing the three secret cities:

These models were three-dimensional representations of them.

'The three cities,' she said.

'Yes,' Sphinx said. 'Thule, Ra and Atlas.'

The fourth model was different.

It was much larger than the models of the three secret cities, easily four times their size.

It was a sharp, triangular blade of rock, spiking into the air. It looked like a right-angled triangle, with one sloping side and one vertical side. A flat niche made a slight indent in the vertical side.

'What is that one?' Lily asked.

'The Altar of the Cosmos,' Sphinx said. 'Like Lord Hades's mountain-palace in the Underworld, the entire mountain has special properties. It is not one of the five iron mountains, although many over the centuries have mistakenly thought it was.'

'It must be enormous . . .' Lily said. 'Why haven't I seen it before?'

Sphinx gave her a knowing smile. 'You have seen it. It hides in plain sight.'

He nodded at the view . . . at the Rock of Gibraltar on the far side of the Strait.

Lily looked from the model to the Rock: they were the same.

'The Rock is the Altar of the Cosmos . . .' she whispered.

'Indeed it is.'

Sphinx and Lily sat down for lunch on a broad balcony overlooking the view.

It was a pleasant North African afternoon, warm and dry. On any other occasion, Lily thought, it would have been a postcard moment.

But the fact that Sphinx had brought her here against her will gave it an entirely different feel. She had goosebumps on her arms and neck. Her skin was literally crawling, she was so uncomfortable.

A silent butler attended to their every need: food, a glass of thousand-dollar Spanish wine for Sphinx, water for Lily.

As they ate, Sphinx occasionally glanced at a laptop beside him.

Then he said softly, 'I knew your father, you know.'

Lily's brow furrowed, confused. So far as she knew, Jack and Sphinx had never crossed paths. 'How?'

'I'm sorry, I should be more specific,' Sphinx said. 'Your *real* father. Your birth father. The previous Oracle of Siwa. I was actually with him on the day of your birth, twenty years ago.'

The day of her birth.

Lily had heard about it many times in her youth.

Kidnapped by a gang of fanatical Catholic priests led by Father Francisco del Piero, her mother—a sweet, gentle, unmarried woman named Malena—had been taken to a sacred volcano in Uganda.

There, in a holy chamber ringed by lava, by the light of a beam of noonday sunlight and to the beat of drums, surrounded by masked priests and armed paratroopers, Malena had given birth to Lily's twin brother, Alexander, and in the doing, had tragically died.

The priests didn't care for Malena one bit. They swept out of the chamber with their prize, Alexander, the new Oracle.

Moments later, Jack West Jr and his friend, Wizard, had entered the chamber. Jack had wept for Malena; he had promised to keep her safe and he'd failed.

And then, as he'd slumped beside her and touched her belly, he'd felt the kick.

Thus Lily had been born—extraordinarily, by Caesarean section, in an impromptu operation performed by Wizard and Jack, lifted from the dead body of her mother—an act unknown to the men who had abducted her brother.

Lily had seen pictures of her mother in happier times. She had been young and beautiful, with kind, innocent eyes.

But Lily had not known her father.

By all accounts, he had not been gentle or innocent.

He'd been a spoilt petulant drunk. His status as the Oracle had turned him into an entitled ass. He had died two months after Lily's birth in what had been described to her as a 'drunken accident'.

'It's strange how lives cross,' Sphinx said. 'Jack West was with your mother on the day of your birth and I was with your father. Getting drunk at a casino in Monaco with two-thousand-dollar-an-hour prostitutes on our laps.'

Lily bit her lip. While she didn't like being here, she was

curious now. 'I was told he died soon after I was born in a "drunken accident". Is that what really happened?'

'It *was* a bar fight, yes,' Sphinx said. 'In a grubby bar near Wembley after the Cup final. Your father was drunk and dressed in the wrong team's colours. He propositioned another man's wife and the fellow—a huge bald ironworker—objected. Milo called him an uneducated peasant and the man headbutted him. Killed him with a single blow.'

Sphinx looked away.

'But that's not really right, is it? It was his gift that killed him.'

Lily remained silent; let him go on.

'A man needs a purpose in life, a goal. Your father's name was Milo Omari. *Milo* meaning grace, and *Omari* being the Egyptian name for one of high birth. Grace, though, was not his strong suit.

'Like you, he was born with the ability to read the mysterious Word of Thoth. This gave him great status in the world of the four kingdoms. He was feted in palaces, toasted at dinners. But he never had to work a day in his life and it made him a spoilt man-child. Boredom led him to gambling, whorehouses and alcohol, and alcohol made him violent. He beat women, especially the prostitutes he paid for. I had to intervene a couple of times.'

Lily said quickly, 'Did he love my mother?'

'No,' Sphinx said firmly. 'Not at all. She was a means to an end.'

'I don't understand.'

Sphinx explained. 'Milo was entirely uninterested in having children, until he discovered the Oracle's *other* purpose. I told him that that . . . event . . . may not even happen in his lifetime, but he would not be swayed. And so he quickly seduced Malena—a sweet impressionable maid on his household staff—and got her pregnant. His sole goal: to create a new Oracle who would take his place on the Altar of the Cosmos if it became required.'

Lily felt a chill crawl up her spine.

'What's this other purpose of the Oracle?' she asked cautiously.

'That,' Sphinx smiled, 'is for Kings' Eyes Only, and you and I are not kings.'

Sphinx shrugged. 'Your adopted father, however, is the polar opposite of your birth father. Captain West is a most impressive man. A warrior foretold in prophecy and winner of the Great Games—'

'He's also pretty good at Scrabble and loves animals,' Lily said. 'But his taste in music stinks.'

Sphinx caught himself, chastened.

'He raised you and you love him.'

'Best dad in the world. And he's got the t-shirt to prove it.'

'He has also altered history,' Sphinx said. 'Although to correct myself, to be perfectly accurate, it was not your father who won the Great Games, it was my cousin, King Orlando.'

'My dad did all the work.'

'Yet it was Orlando, as his sponsor, who was to receive the prize for winning. And by depriving Orlando of his due reward, your father has created a unique situation whereby the entire world is now there for anyone willing to seize it.'

Sphinx fell silent for a moment.

'My own father was not so impressive,' he said softly.

Lily waited for what came next.

'As you may know, Orlando is my cousin,' Sphinx said. 'Our fathers were brothers. In fact, my father was his father's *older* brother.'

Sphinx paused, letting the fact sink in.

Lily got it straight away. 'But that would mean . . .'

'That's correct,' Sphinx said. '*My* father was supposed to be the King of Land. But he was a timid man, anxious, worried by the

slightest thing, woefully indecisive. After the death of Carnivore—who was childless—my father was next in line for the throne.

'But he fretted in his anxiousness, awed by the responsibilities of being king, and he was convinced to abdicate. In the shadow royal world, abdication is total: it wipes out that man's entire line. I was thrown out of the line of succession and Orlando's father became King of Land. He died of a heart attack within a month and Orlando, as his son, became King.

'Shortly after, it was arranged for me to assume *this* posting: this ghastly posting at the ends of the Earth, on the tip of Africa, watching over a dead city and its watchtower, observing the machinations of the royal world from afar, hearing about events like the Great Games but generally not attending them.'

Sphinx gazed out at the magnificent view with unseeing eyes, staring at his memories.

Then he blinked.

And turned back to face Lily with his deadly grey eyes.

'I like to think I have a special kind of patience, an unsentimental patience that now, finally—thanks to your second father, Captain West—is about to be rewarded.

'For by denying Orlando, your father has opened the door to someone with superior *knowledge*, not blood. Have no illusions, Orlando is both cruel and clever and a very dangerous man. But he is not half as cruel as I am or a tenth as knowledgeable in matters of the ancient world.

'We are all the products of our parents,' Sphinx said wistfully. 'Your callow birth father gave you life in order to save his own. My anxious father forfeited his crown and, in doing so, condemned me to a life of exile in the service of lesser men. And your adopted father, Jack West Jr, through what seemed a well-meaning and noble act, could well have changed the course of history.'

As Lily tried to absorb Sphinx's words, he went on.

'In my exile here, I have spent my time learning. Studying,

collecting, researching and understanding everything I can about the Omega Event, the end of all things.'

As Sphinx spoke, Lily looked at him closely, evaluating him.

She saw a brilliant yet frustrated man, denied his royal birthright and sent out here to stew.

Sphinx nodded at a sketch on the wall: a framed pencil sketch of a planet and its moon.

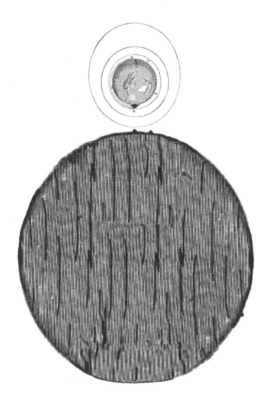

'Take this sketch, drawn by Sir Isaac Newton himself. He only put *half* of this image in his masterwork, the *Principia*, and even then he put it there upside-down. It was far too dangerous to reveal in its entirety. There are maybe three people in the world who have seen this full image and understand its terrible meaning.'

Sphinx stepped over to another framed sheet of paper, this one depicting a handwritten mathematical formula:

$$\left(H^2 - \frac{8}{3}\pi Gp\right)R^2 = -kc^2$$

$$\left[\left(\frac{1}{2}\frac{dR}{dt}\right)^2 - \frac{8}{3}\pi Gp\right]R^2 = -kc^2$$

$$k > 0$$

'Do you know this equation?' he asked.

'Of course. It's the Friedmann Equation,' Lily said. 'The mathematical model of the expanding universe.'

Sphinx did a double-take. 'Goodness me. You *are* more than just a pretty face.'

He gazed at the framed equation.

'It is indeed Alexander Friedmann's famous mathematical equation, written in his own hand. I find it beautiful, elegant in its brevity.

'But this version of his formula comes with a single handwritten annotation by no less a titan than Albert Einstein himself; this small notation at the bottom: $k > 0$.'

Lily saw the little addition at the bottom right of the framed sheet.

Sphinx said, 'This tiny addition by Einstein is nothing short of earth-shattering. It is monumentally important, for when k is greater than zero, gravity will eventually stop the universe from expanding and the whole universe will collapse in a single cataclysmic moment: The Big Crunch, as some have coarsely put it. The ultimate singularity.'

'The Omega Event,' Lily said in a low voice.

'Yes.'

'I have a question for you,' she said suddenly.

'Please.'

'The Zeus Papyrus contained a poem about the Trial of the Cities. It talked about no oceans, no clouds . . .'

'. . . no rivers, no rain. The world a wasteland of misery and pain,' Sphinx finished for her. 'I know it well.'

'Do you know what it means?' Lily asked. 'Is it referring to some kind of punishment for failing to complete the trial?'

'Oh, Lily, punishment does not even begin to describe what that poem warns of.'

Aloysius Knight's Sukhoi Su-37 shot over the Mediterranean, heading away from Santorini.

Aloysius's loyal friend and pilot, Rufus, flew up front while inside its rear hold, Jack and Aloysius were bent over a map of the world.

They had the photo of Drake's note in front of them, with its three sets of coordinates, the locations of the Three Secret Cities:

> R: 8°6'N 60°30'W of London
> *Follow the hidden river to the base of the tabletop mountain.*
>
> T: 63°30'N 18°01'W of London
> *Enter through the tunnel at the tideline below its watchtower.*
>
> A: 35°48'N 5°36'W of London
> *Enter through its watchtower.*

Jack grabbed a grease pencil and made three markings on the map based on Drake's coordinates:

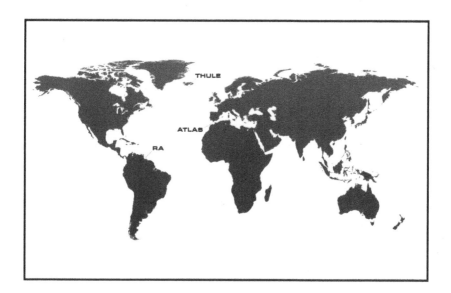

He paused, thinking.

Pooh Bear, Stretch and Sky Monster were on their way to Thule.

Mae, Iolanthe and Nobody were very close to Ra.

And Zoe, Alby and Hades were in Rome figuring out the location of the Altar and the ceremony to be performed there.

Getting to Atlas and empowering the Mace was his job.

Jack stared at the map, biting his lip as he assessed the positions of the three cities.

'Iceland, Venezuela and the Strait of Gibraltar . . .' he said aloud.

'What are you thinking?' Aloysius asked.

'I'm thinking about punishment.'

'Punishment?'

'We found a poem about all this.' On his phone, Jack pulled up his copy of the Zeus Papyrus, pointed at the ode on it:

THE TRIAL OF THE CITIES

No oceans.
No clouds.

No rivers.
No rain.
The world a wasteland
of misery and pain.

'That last line,' Jack said. '"*The world a wasteland of misery and pain*". Zoe and my buddy, Nobody, found those same words carved into a sealed underwater doorway in the Mariana Trench. But I still can't figure them out.'

Aloysius shrugged. 'Well, take the whole poem to its logical conclusion: no oceans means no moisture-evaporation, which means no clouds. No clouds means no rain or snow, which means no rivers. No rivers means no fresh water. And no fresh water means no life on Earth: not for plants, animals or humans. I'd say seeing every creature on the planet dying of thirst would definitely amount to "misery and pain".'

Jack was staring off into space.

He spun to face Aloysius. 'Say that again.'

'I said, seeing every creature on the planet dying of thirst—'

'No, the first part: no oceans means . . .'

'No oceans means no moisture-evaporation, which means no clouds,' Aloysius said. 'As the sun warms the oceans, they send evaporation up into the sky which forms clouds.'

Jack gazed at his map again, a vague yet terrible thought forming in his mind.

'When I was imprisoned at Erebus in that tub of liquid stone, Yago said something to me: he said Erebus was one of six mines in the world that mined greystone powder, the main component of liquid stone. The Underworld was another. He said that, chemically, greystone powder is often mistaken for volcanic soils like picrite basalt.

'Behind that door in the Mariana Trench, Nobody and Zoe detected a massive deposit of what appeared to be picrite basalt. A deposit in the shape of a vast cube, with dozens of other false doorways . . .'

Jack added the locations of Erebus, Hades and the Mariana Trench to the map:

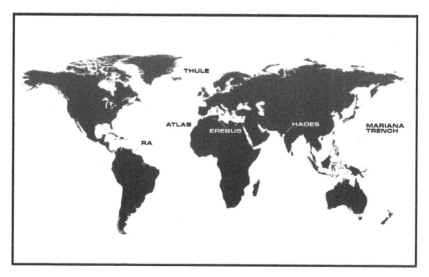

Jack gazed at the map—at the spacing of the six locations around the world's three great oceans, the Atlantic, the Indian and the Pacific—and the terrible thought in his mind became clearer.

'Six massive deposits of dry greystone . . .' he said. 'Arrayed around the planet. A few specks of that greystone dust turned my tub in Erebus to solid stone.'

'And a couple of pills of it turned that whole chamber in Santorini to rock,' Aloysius added.

Jack stared at him. 'So what would happen if six massive deposits of it were exposed to the world's oceans?'

'They'd turn large swathes of them to stone,' Aloysius said.

Jack said, 'The oceans would go dry. And as you said, *no oceans mean no moisture-evaporation, no clouds and ultimately, no fresh water*. Good Lord. That's what the world's punishment will be for failing to complete the trial: the oceans turn to stone and we all die in pain.'

Jack added some expanding lines to his map and the great global punishment became clear:

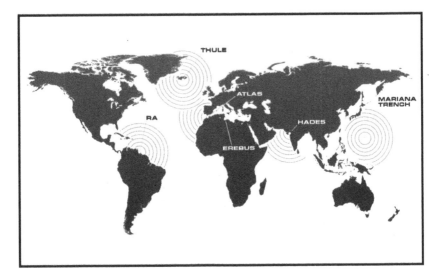

He and Aloysius exchanged worried looks.

'We have to get to Atlas and complete this trial,' Jack said, 'or else the whole world will become a lifeless rock and everybody on it will die.'

THE WATCHTOWER OF THE CITY OF ATLAS
THE STRAIT OF GIBRALTAR (MOROCCAN SIDE)

At almost the exact same time Jack was figuring it out for himself, Sphinx finished telling Lily about the punishment that would befall the Earth if the Trial of the Cities was not completed.

He finished his explanation by dropping a couple of grains of black-grey powder into Lily's glass of water.

The water turned black before thickening into a foul ooze, and then—*crack*—it hardened and became solid and suddenly Lily's glass was filled with dry black-grey stone.

Lily was silent for a long moment.

'And this will happen on a planetary scale?' she asked.

'Yes.'

'A dead dry planet . . .'

'We should not get too down. I am certain that the Trial of the Cities can be overcome and all will be just fine.'

Sphinx glanced at his computer, pressed an intercom button beside it.

'*Yes, sir?*' came a voice.

'Is Dion DeSaxe on his way to the Altar?'

'*He is, sir. We sent a plane for him shortly after he called from Naples.*'

'Dion?' Lily said in horror.

'Send out the invitations to the other kings,' Sphinx said.

'*Yes, sir.*'

'And what about Captain West's plane?'

Lily perked up at that.

'*Still heading this way, sir. Thirty miles out. We're monitoring it.*'

'Thank you.'

Sphinx abruptly stood.

He stepped inside the balcony's door and walked over to his replica of the Great Sphinx. For a moment he seemed to retreat into his own mind.

He gazed at the fifteen-foot-tall sandstone statue. It loomed before him: the world-famous reclining lion with the face of a man staring with unblinking eyes.

'My namesake,' Sphinx said, turning to Lily. 'Since I was a boy, I have loved the Great Sphinx. All my life, it has been my obsession. It is the most mysterious structure on Earth. For thousands of years it has confounded man. Why is it there? What is its purpose? There are three pyramids at Giza, but only one sphinx. The Egyptians carved many sphinxes, but they were all small. Why is there only one *giant* sphinx, one Great Sphinx? It is the question of questions.'

He smiled at Lily: a thin sinister smile.

'But that is another part of my studies, to be used at another time,' he said. 'Right now, the world stands on a precipice—facing painful destruction—and thanks to your second father, *any* man can complete the two trials and become the overlord of the world. Which means it is time for me to make my move and make use of my singular knowledge.'

As she listened to Sphinx, Lily suddenly felt very uneasy.

Why is he telling me this? she thought. *He shouldn't be telling me this . . .*

Then Sphinx rounded on her, his eyes flaring.

'I imagine you're wondering why I would tell you all this,' he said, as if reading her thoughts.

His look became deadly.

'I am unlike anyone you have ever met, Lily. I don't need your talent at translating the Word of Thoth. I have my plan to take advantage of this new state of affairs that your father has created and it is playing out exactly as I had hoped. I just needed to tell someone who would understand. But the fact that I have told you this means that you cannot be allowed to live. You will die, young lady, very soon.'

THE ORINOCO DELTA
ATLANTIC COAST, VENEZUELA
1 DECEMBER, 0800 HOURS LOCAL TIME (FOUR
HOURS EARLIER)

Following the coordinates laid down by Sir Francis Drake five hundred years previously, Dave 'Nobody' Black—with Iolanthe and Mae by his side—landed his floatplane on a short stretch of open water at the southern edge of the vast Orinoco Delta . . .

. . . to find himself facing something most peculiar.

An archway of bent-over swamp trees that formed a natural roof over a placid river.

Not from any other angle—not from the ocean or the air or the nearest cliff a few miles to the south—would you have seen it.

Driving it like a boat, Nobody brought his little floatplane up the hidden river. It was eerily dark. The branches of the trees overhead closed above the plane so tightly they all but blocked out the sun.

To the south, rising like behemoths from the jungle, were several awesome *tepuis*, the iconic flat-topped mountains for which Venezuela is famous.

After a time, the little plane rounded a bend in the hidden river and Dave, Iolanthe and Mae saw two seaplanes tied to a crumbling stone dock jutting out from the left-hand bank.

The dock was covered in moss and mud. Fanning out from the two seaplanes parked at it were many muddy boot prints.

'Orlando's people are here already,' Iolanthe said.

At the dock's landward end, shrouded by trees and branches,

was a small modern structure that contrasted markedly with the ancient dock: a cabin on stilts, made of shiny steel.

And calmly standing in front of it was a lone man.

A sign on the cabin read 'INPARQUES', denoting it as the property of the Venezuelan National Parks Institute, the government department in charge of protected lands.

The man in front of it wore a park ranger's uniform. He looked about sixty and he watched them silently.

'That's a nice cover for a watchman,' Mae said, nodding at the man's uniform. 'A government ranger. Keeps poachers and the curious away. And he can live out here and guard the City of Ra.'

Nobody parked the plane and the three of them stepped out onto the dock where the 'ranger' waited.

'Greetings,' he said. 'My name is Sir Inigo Defenestra. Who might you be?'

Iolanthe said, 'I am Iolanthe Compton-Jones, Princess of the Kingdom of Land, Keeper of the Royal Records. These are my companions. We've come to enter the secret city.'

'Others are already in there,' Sir Inigo said. 'With the weapon.'

'They don't know what they are doing. We are here to ensure the weapon is properly empowered.'

The ranger's face was impassive. 'Like my father and his father before him, I have watched over this city for most of my adult life, keeping the unworthy away, waiting for this time. On this day of days, it is not for me to prevent anyone versed in the ancient ways from entering, if you are willing to brave its avenue.'

He stepped aside, revealing a small hemispherical structure hidden under the stilts of his little steel cabin.

Nobody stopped.

'Geez, Louise . . .' he gasped.

A creepy-looking structure yawned before them. It had a cracked vine-covered dome for a roof.

On closer inspection, they saw that the structure had been carved in the shape of a giant human skull, and in such a way that its crumbling doorway was the skull's mouth, gaping in an eternal scream. It looked like the entry to Hell.

As they approached the huge stone skull, Iolanthe, Mae and Nobody peered inside it and saw a tunnel stretching away into darkness with three archways spanning its width.

If the tunnel continued in a straight line for about a kilometre, it would end at one of the *tepui* mountains to the south.

'Wait. Is that floor made of—?' Nobody began.

'Yes, it is,' Mae said solemnly. 'It's made of gold.'

It was true. While they were covered in a layer of grit and grime, the floorstones of the tunnel before them glimmered dully. The streets of El Dorado really were paved with gold.

Mae, Nobody and Iolanthe gazed at the first triple-archway.

A line of muddy boot prints—smearing the golden surface—led into the right-hand arch.

In front of the middle arch, however, was something else entirely: a mouldy, moss-covered skeleton.

It had been cut cleanly in two, diagonally across the ribcage.

A distinctly European helmet lay beside the skinless skull. The helmet was bowl-shaped and made of brass with curving upswept brims that created sharp points at the front and back.

Mae crouched in front of it.

'This is a *morion*,' she said. 'The classic Spanish infantry helmet worn by the conquistadors in the 16th and 17th centuries. This poor fellow found El Dorado.'

'Sure did,' Nobody said, looking up at the archway above the split-skeleton. He threw Iolanthe a look. 'Thoughts, Ms Royal Expert?'

Iolanthe said, 'Only the obvious one: these arches are booby-trapped.'

She nodded further down the tunnel, where several more triplets of arches could be seen.

'As, I suspect, are those ones. This is the city's Grand Avenue. At each set of arches, you need to know the correct one to pass through . . . or else you die like this guy did.'

She nodded at the line of muddy boot prints passing through the right-hand arch. 'It would seem our adversaries knew exactly which archway to choose.'

A sudden noise made them all snap up.

The clatter of gunfire.

Automatic gunfire.

But it was muffled, distant. Coming from deep within the tunnel. In the gaps between bursts, they heard desperate shouts.

Nobody said, 'They may have got past the arches, but they haven't outwitted the city yet. We still might have a chance.'

Following the muddy boot prints through the arches, they hurried down the tunnel—its incredible golden footstones instantly forgotten—leaving the quiet Sir Inigo, the humble keeper of the Great City of Ra, out on the dock.

**THE CITY OF THULE
ICELAND**

Deep inside the underground city of Thule, Cardinal Ricardo Mendoza was getting frantic.

'Send another one in!' he yelled to the commander of his squad of Swiss Guards.

Gripping the fabled sword known as Excalibur in one hand, Mendoza peered worriedly behind him.

He and his team of Swiss troops were standing on the high bridge in the heart of Thule, hopelessly trapped.

The guardian army of the city—three hundred faceless bronzemen—loomed behind them, filling the curving path that led back out of the city, blocking their retreat.

And every few minutes, the entire army, in perfect robotic unison, took a single step closer. If Mendoza and his men didn't get across this bridge soon, the army would be on them and it would be all over.

'Fucking hell!' Mendoza swore.

It was the bridge that was the problem.

When they had arrived at it a few days ago, it had seemed to be a simple enough structure: an open-sided square cupola, with four silver man-shaped statues standing silently in its corners.

But as soon as Mendoza's first Swiss Guardsman had set foot on it . . .

. . . the statues had come alive.

It had happened so fast.

The four silver statues—six feet tall and faceless, but with long claw-like fingers—stepped forward, revealing their fingers to actually be pointed blades.

The lead Swiss Guardsman was beheaded in an instant, the force of the blow sending both his head and his body sailing off the bridge into the abyss below.

Then the four faceless silver 'men' silently resumed their positions in the corners of the open-sided cupola and were statues once more.

That had been several days ago.

They had been stuck here ever since.

At various intervals, Mendoza had commanded more of his men to enter the bridge. The devout Swiss Guards had obeyed: obedience that had seen them march to grisly deaths.

Each time a guardsman set foot on the bridge, the four silver statues stepped forward to block his way.

One Swiss trooper had fired his gun at the silvermen. His bullets had pinged off their shiny alloy skin without leaving so much as a scratch and the silver statues had cut him to pieces and thrown him into the abyss.

The next man tried his knife. It bounced off their metal throats and he was thrown into the abyss.

The next trooper tossed a grenade at the nearest silver statue. The grenade detonated, enshrouding the silverman in fire and smoke . . . only for the automaton to emerge from it, unscathed. That trooper was also cut to pieces.

And all the while the three hundred bronze-coloured automatons closed in behind them—slowly and steadily stepping down the curved descending road of the city, one ominous step at a time—until now they were almost on them.

Mendoza had entered the lost city of Thule with twenty Swiss troopers.

Now he had only four left.

Their supplies were fine. They'd prepared for three days and

dead soldiers didn't eat or drink, so they had their rations and water. When each soldier entered the cupola, he left his personal canteen behind with the others.

The Swiss commander despaired. 'My lord Cardinal, please . . .'

'I said send another one in, damn it!' Mendoza shouted in his face.

The commander bowed and nodded to the next trooper who, taking a deep breath, placed his water bottle on the ground, drew his gun and stoically stepped onto the bridge to face certain death.

SPHINX'S MANSION
THE STRAIT OF GIBRALTAR

Sphinx's intercom pinged.

A voice came from its speaker. 'Inbound aircraft, sir. Satellite scans indicate it's a Sukhoi Su-37 fighter-bomber. It's the same plane we monitored leaving Aragon Castle. It belongs to the bounty hunter who turned up there with West: Captain Aloysius Knight.'

Sphinx stepped onto his balcony and gazed out at Aloysius Knight's Sukhoi Su-37 as it approached through the heat haze.

'Somehow, your father escaped from Erebus,' he said to Lily. 'Then he attacked Aragon Castle, I assume to rescue you. Now he is coming here to enter the City of Atlas. This is most fortuitous.'

Two guards suddenly appeared on either side of Lily, grabbing her roughly by the arms.

Sphinx said, 'Come, dear girl. It is time to put you on display.'

Aloysius Knight's plane landed vertically on Sphinx's helipad.

Aloysius and Jack emerged from it cautiously. Aloysius gripped his Remington shotguns. Jack gripped the Mace of Poseidon and a pistol.

The lone figure of Sphinx stood a short distance away from them, waiting politely at the helipad's exit stairs, unarmed, his hands clasped in front of him.

'Why, hello, Captain West, Captain Knight,' he said.

Jack's eyes narrowed. 'I've seen you before. In Erebus. You came to see me while I was imprisoned there. You're Sphinx.'

'I did, and I am. I must say how impressed I am that you managed to escape. You are impressive in many ways, Captain West.'

'You're the keeper of the City of Atlas,' Jack said. 'The Trismagi who watches over it.'

'Like I told you at Erebus, I am but a humble lighthouse keeper.'

Jack cocked his pistol and aimed it at Sphinx's head. 'I've had a really shitty few days, pal. Some of my closest friends have died, so I'm not in the mood for smart-asses.'

He held up the Mace. 'Orlando has screwed this up for everybody. He didn't have the entire triangular tablet, so when he entered the first city, he triggered the defensive mechanisms at the other two. He should have waited until he had people at *every* city and entered them at the same time. I've sent people to each city to fix his mess. We're here to penetrate Atlas, empower the Mace and get it to the Altar.'

'A laudable mission, to be sure,' Sphinx said. 'One I shall be more than happy to see you perform on my behalf.'

'On your behalf—?' Jack said.

Sphinx threw Jack an iPhone.

Jack caught it and looked at it.

A live FaceTime video was on it . . .

. . . showing closed-circuit camera footage of Lily inside a stone cell with iron bars . . .

. . . and with rising seawater sloshing around her. It was currently at knee-height.

Sphinx locked eyes with Jack. 'She is in a tidal cell, Captain. And the tide comes in fast in these parts.'

'What do you want?' Jack demanded.

'I want to break you,' Sphinx said.

'What do you want me *to do!*'

'I want you to take the weapon into the city and empower it, just as you wish. But then I want you to *bring the Mace back to me*. Only when that is done will I spare your daughter. Take Captain

Knight with you—I'll be happy to take advantage of his skills as well. I shall even guide you to the entrance to Atlas myself. That said, Captain Knight's pilot will now fly his plane one hundred miles from this place or be blown to pieces. Tick-tock, Captain West, the tide is rising in that cell. It takes perhaps an hour to fill so you really should not delay.'

Jack swallowed hard.

Aloysius glowered at Sphinx. 'Asshole.'

Jack clenched his teeth. 'Take us to the entrance. Now.'

Sphinx smiled as he kicked open a trunk behind him.

Diving gear—scuba facemasks, fins, flashlights, air tanks, even two harpoon guns—tumbled out of it.

'You're going to need this,' he said.

Within minutes, Rufus had flown the *Black Raven* away and Jack and Aloysius—calmly led by Sphinx—had crossed a short bridge leading to the ancient stone lighthouse that stood apart from the mansion. They descended a corkscrewing stairwell within its cylindrical body.

The stone steps wound downward, with no rail, around the empty core in the tower's middle.

Then abruptly the spiralling stairs plunged into water. They just kept going down into the sloshing waves.

'The City of Atlas experienced an unfortunate *flooding incident* some time ago,' Sphinx said. 'Perhaps you've heard of it? I shall leave you to your mission.' He went back up the stairs.

Alone now, Jack and Aloysius kicked off their boots and donned the scuba gear.

The facemasks that Sphinx had provided them with were sturdy full-face helmets that allowed them to communicate via radio. As he put his on, Jack kept his satellite earpiece lodged in one ear.

Jack also jammed the Mace into his weight-belt. Then he looked at an image on his phone.

'What's that?' Aloysius asked.

'It's a translation of a scroll written by Plato. It refers to the three cities and how to get into them.'

Jack read it aloud:

> 'To enter each city, you must first pass through its watchtower and navigate its sacred avenue. At its bridge

you must overcome its silver guardians. Only then can you advance to its innermost vault and empower the weapon.

'But beware, the three cities are well defended. Woe betide he who awakens their silent bronze armies. For the armies will only allow one versed in the Mysteries to pass and keep his life. False claimants and intruders will suffer only death.'

'Sounds like a fucking cakewalk,' Aloysius said. 'Is *anything* you do easy?'

'No,' Jack said.

He dropped into the water and by the light of a Princeton Tec flashlight, began swimming straight down through the core of the corkscrewing stairwell. Aloysius followed him.

Down they swam.

Down and down, past the many steps of the spiralling stairwell, their flashlights carving sabre-like beams through the murk. Schools of fish fluttered away.

At length, they came to the bottom of the stairwell and found themselves hovering in the water at the entrance to a very long and very old tunnel.

At the mouth of this tunnel, spanning its width, were three ominous arches.

Aloysius peered at the arches. 'So, what, we have to pick the correct one?'

'Yes. This must be the sacred avenue.'

As he said this, a school of fish swam past them, through one of the arches—

A flash of silver.

Faster than the eye could see.

And suddenly the school of fish scattered, leaving three fish drifting in the flooded archway, *cut cleanly in half*, blood wafting from their bodies.

'What in the world was that?' Aloysius said.

Jack hovered cautiously in the water-filled tunnel.

'The arches are booby-trapped. As Plato said, we have to *navigate* this tunnel, which means negotiating the archways: going through the right one each time.'

Beyond the first triplet of arches, Jack saw more stretching away down the long flooded tunnel.

'Maybe we could just float something through each arch till one doesn't react,' Aloysius said.

He unclipped a shuriken throwing blade from his utility vest and tossed it through the middle arch.

It drifted harmlessly through the flooded archway, floating gently to the stone floor on the other side.

'See?'

Jack shook his head. 'No. These places were built by an advanced civilisation. I'm guessing the arches can sense when something organic passes through them, like the fish. Your throwing knife won't set them off. Only something that lives and breathes will.'

At that moment, another school of fish swam past them, heading for the middle arch.

This time, Jack was ready, and he watched closely as—

Another silver flash.

Two more fish were cleaved in two.

And this time, Jack saw it: a silver filament had whizzed down the length of the archway, an ultra-fine and ultra-sharp thread of some kind; so sharp that it had sliced through the fish in an instant.

'Fuck me . . .' Aloysius gasped.

'Damn it,' Jack said. 'We're not going anywhere till we figure out the safe way through these things.'

THE CITY OF THULE
ICELAND

At the same time as Jack had been arriving at Sphinx's mansion and Nobody had discovered the entrance to the City of Ra, one other team of his friends was approaching the secret city of Thule in Iceland.

Stretch and Pooh Bear, also guided by the Drake coordinates, were touching down on a forbidding black-sand beach on the remote southern coast of Iceland in Jack's plane, the *Sky Warrior*.

As Sky Monster—with one arm still in a sling—brought the plane in to land, Stretch gazed out at the black volcanic soil of the cliffs, beach and mountains.

'It looks almost prehistoric,' he said.

'Other-worldly,' Pooh Bear agreed.

Within minutes, they found the watchtower and Sir Bjorn.

Stretch said, 'We've come to fulfil the requirements of the trial.'

Bjorn frowned. 'You are aware that King Orlando has already sent a delegation to do this?'

'We know,' Pooh Bear said. 'But we have reason to believe that they are not fully aware of what must be done. We are here to make sure the trial is completed properly.'

Sir Bjorn shook his head, befuddled. 'These are unprecedented and puzzling times. As there is no clear emperor, who am I to deny you if you wish to brave the avenue and its defences? Proceed, by all means, but at your own peril.'

And so they ventured down the staircase within the wave-battered cliff.

As they descended the stairs, Pooh Bear noticed something wrong with his sat-radio, something that Mendoza's team hadn't realised until it was too late.

'Satellite signal is cutting in and out,' he said. 'Must be from all the seismic activity. We better lay some repeater units along the way to boost our signals.'

They came to the cave inside the cliff and climbed the short flight of stairs at its rear.

The long straight avenue receded into the distance before them. It felt ten degrees colder than the outside air.

And just like Mae's team had found at Ra, and Jack and Aloysius had experienced at Atlas, Pooh and Stretch found themselves confronted by three arches.

Their arches were slick with icy wetness. Peering through them, Pooh and Stretch saw more sets of arches vanishing down the avenue.

A small pile of six dead seagulls lay before the first set of arches: bloodied or decayed or both. All had been cut cleanly in half.

'Booby-trapped,' Stretch said, gazing at all the other sets of arches further down the tunnel.

'Damnation!' Pooh Bear spat.

He keyed his satellite radio. 'Jack, Mae? It's us. Any idea how to get safely through these archways?'

THE CITY OF RA

Mae, Nobody and Iolanthe were more than halfway down their mud-and-vine-covered tunnel when Pooh Bear's call came in.

Jack's voice also came on the line, slightly garbled by the long-range satellite link: 'We've got a similar problem at Atlas.'

'We had some help here at Ra,' Iolanthe said into her radio. 'Someone got here before us and left a trail to follow.'

Mae's eyes narrowed. 'Then let's try to figure this out.'

She looked back at the way they'd come. Following the muddy path of their rivals, she, Nobody and Iolanthe had passed safely through five sets of arches.

At the first triplet of arches, the right-hand one had been safe.

At the second set, it was the left-most one.

Then right, left, then the middle one.

Mae cocked her head. 'Wait a second . . .'

'What is it?' Iolanthe said. 'Do you see a pattern?'

'No, I see an order . . .' Mae said. 'An order I've seen before.'

She pursed her lips in thought, then suddenly it hit her.

'Of course. Three options. Why didn't I see it earlier?' Mae hurriedly pulled something from her jacket pocket: her now slightly soggy printout of Hades's triangular tablet with Lily's added translations.

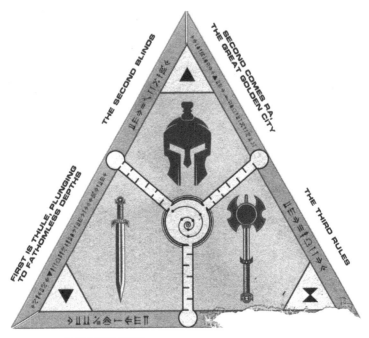

THE FIRST KILLS

'There!' she pointed at one of the three straight arms extending from the sides of the triangle to its centre.

'Can you see it?' Mae said excitedly.

'Uh, no,' Nobody said.

'Look *closer*. This tablet has told us all we need to know about the three cities. I think it includes *how to get into the cities*. Those three straight "arms" reaching into the middle of the triangle represent the three Grand Avenues of the cities.'

She was grinning like someone who had just solved a fiendish riddle. 'Look closely at the right-hand arm, the one between the Helmet and the Mace, beside the description of Ra, "the Great Golden City". Look at these little black lines along it, jutting into it.'

Iolanthe and Nobody leaned in closer and saw them.

'I'll be damned,' Iolanthe said. 'I never even noticed them before.'

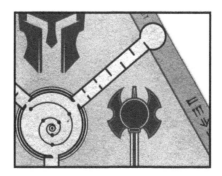

Mae said, 'That arm represents this avenue and those tiny gaps along it indicate the *safe* arches: the first safe archway was the right-hand one, then the left, and so on. It matches perfectly.'

'You're absolutely right . . .' Nobody said, looking from the printout to the archways around them.

Mae grabbed her radio. 'Pooh, Jack. The tablet tells us every-thing we need to know about the cities. It shows you the safe path through your boulevards.'

She relayed to them what she had just explained to Nobody and Iolanthe.

In the flooded tunnel at Atlas, Jack clicked off his radio and brought up the image of the triangular tablet on his smartphone. He was glad Nobody had given him the waterproof casing for it.

He scanned the tablet, focusing on the vertical arm to the left of the Mace:

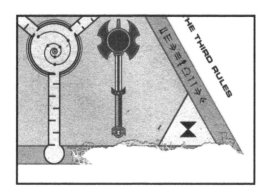

According to it, the right-hand arch in front of him was the safe one.

Aloysius gave him a look. 'She's your mother. You first.'

'Talk about a trust exercise,' Jack said as he swam in front of that archway.

He keyed his radio. 'Folks, I'm going to swim through my first arch. Stand by.'

Then, more quietly to himself: 'I hope you're right, Mum.'

With those words, he kicked his fins and entered the right-hand arch.

Nothing happened. No trap was triggered.

Jack emerged safely on the other side of the arch.

He exhaled in relief and said, 'Nice work, Mum. I'm through.'

Aloysius joined him a few seconds later. 'Damn, I wish I trusted my mom as much as you trust yours.'

Using the path shown on the left arm of the tablet, Pooh Bear and Stretch did the same at Thule.

And thus at the Three Secret Cities, Jack's teams penetrated the Grand Avenues simultaneously, wending their way through the triple-archways, advancing down the deadly tunnels.

THE CITY OF ATLAS

ATLAS

Guided by the tablet, Jack and Aloysius swam down their flooded tunnel, choosing the correct arch each time.

Lighting the way with their flashlights, after a while they saw the end of the avenue up ahead.

Dim blue light framed by a square doorway.

But there was also something else.

Man-shaped figures—dozens of them, eerie shadows in the underwater haze—stood on the seafloor just beyond the doorway, partially blocking the light.

Jack and Aloysius came to the end of the tunnel and shone their flashlights out into the gloom.

Three hundred faceless, beaked bronze figures stood between them and the City of Atlas, erect and silent, in perfect ranks and rows, like soldiers standing to attention.

They filled the whole area between Jack and Aloysius and the city, plus the last few metres of the tunnel—stopping them from exiting it.

They looked like the renowned army of terracotta warriors at Xian, China: silent man-sized bronze statues, each one six feet tall and standing deathly still in their ordered lines.

Behind them, soaring into the watery blue void, was an hour-glass-shaped rock formation covered in towers and domes, bridges and battlements. On the upper half of the hourglass, the towers hung suspended from the rock, dangling spectacularly.

It was a colossal thing, several hundred feet high. A path ran up its lower half, pausing at one point at a bridge with an open-sided square cupola on it.

'The City of Atlas . . .' Jack breathed.

It was truly magnificent.

In its time, it must have been extraordinary: a towering city on this singular rock formation. Until the day of the flood, the greatest flood in history.

Off to his left, Jack saw something that did not belong to the City of Atlas.

A wreck lying awkwardly up against the base of the ancient city.

The wreck of a plane.

It was an old plane from the 1960s, a DC-3 or maybe a Boeing 707. It looked like a cargo plane and it was covered in coral and barnacles: the accumulation of years of undersea growth. It must have crashed long ago and been washed here on the current.

Jack turned to face the incredible sunken city in front of him. His gaze found the tiny bridge halfway up the lower slope.

'*At its bridge you must overcome its silver guardians . . .*' he said.

Aloysius, however, only had eyes for the army of bronze figures blocking their way.

'Statues?' he said. 'That's all there is guarding this place? I was kind of expecting something more . . . *elaborate.*'

And then the statues moved.

Aloysius's jaw dropped.

'Oh, fuck me . . .' he gasped as he raised his harpoon gun and fired it.

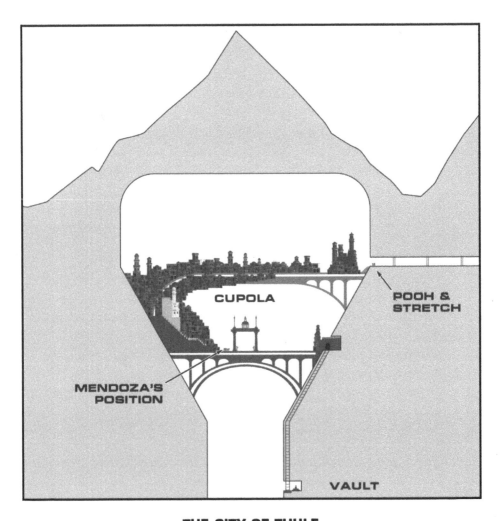

THE CITY OF THULE

THULE

In Iceland, Pooh and Stretch heard the gunfire before they reached the end of their frigid avenue.

Their tunnel had its own singular feature: its ceiling and floors had been comprised of stone coffins . . . which had evidently opened sometime before their arrival. This had meant they'd had to walk along the narrow flagstones between the opened coffins.

'There's an awful lot of these things . . .' Pooh Bear said worriedly.

At the sound of gunfire, they started running, eventually emerging from their avenue at the top of a vast funnel-shaped city that plunged into the Earth.

It was an awesome sight.

The Icelandic chill had caused a layer of frost to cover everything, so the entire city gleamed white.

Clusters of frost-laden buildings hung off a wide spiralling path that swept in a descending curve around the cavern's walls. Then the path reappeared from the structures to spring across the cavern's central abyss via a narrow bridge that had a square opensided cupola in its middle.

The shouts and gunfire had come from Cardinal Mendoza and three Swiss Guards who were standing before the cupola on the bridge.

Behind Mendoza and his men, blocking their escape, filling the

curving main roadway of the underground city, was a veritable army of faceless bronze automatons that were identical to the one Pooh and Stretch had seen at the Underworld.

The bronzemen stood like silent statues on the curving road, in perfect ranks.

Every few minutes, in unison, the entire army would take a single collective step forward, the echo of their move resounding in the space.

One of the Swiss soldiers fired back at them, but his bullets pinged harmlessly off the bronzemen's metal bodies and a minute later the army just took another inexorable step forward.

'There've got to be hundreds of them,' Stretch breathed.

Pooh, however, was looking at the bridge. 'I don't think they're the real problem.'

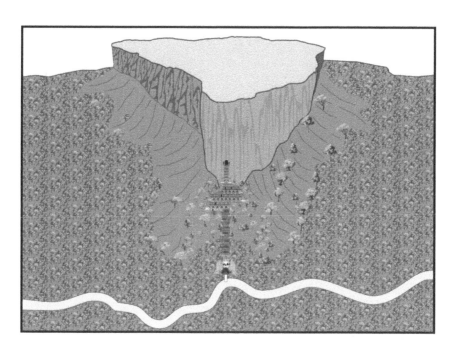

THE CITY OF RA (X-RAY THROUGH JUNGLE)

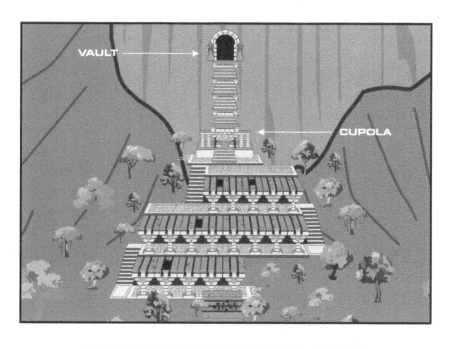

CLOSER VIEW (X-RAY THROUGH JUNGLE)

RA

Mae, Nobody and Iolanthe stood at the end of their tunnel at the edge of the Venezuelan jungle, also frozen in shock.

Their golden-floored avenue had ended at the base of a colossal *tepui* mountain that covered them in deep shade.

The lost city of Ra rose before them.

El Dorado.

The city appeared to be made up of three wide step-like levels that had been cut into the slanting lower face of the *tepui*.

Rising up through those levels was a single partially-enclosed street that switched back and forth. Widely-spaced Y-shaped uprights held up a ceiling of long slats that covered the roadway. Through gaps in the uprights, one could see doorways on the inner walls of the street.

The whole city, however, had been consumed by the encroaching jungle: it was shrouded in a foul tangle of trees, moss, mud and vines.

Architecturally, it wasn't particularly remarkable. It was squat and low, and mainly square in shape. It had no soaring spires or dominating ramparts. In fact, the three winding switchbacks seemed to have only a hundred or so doorways. As a 'city', it was kind of unimpressive.

Except for one thing.

Every surface was made of gold.

Not just the floorstones. Every wall, every upright, every step, everything.

Nobody gasped. 'If it weren't for the jungle and all the grime strangling it, in daylight this place would shine like the sun.'

Mae nodded. 'It *is* the Great City of Ra, and he *was* the Sun-god.'

They could now see that the slat-like roof of each level was composed of thick gold beams.

They had not survived the ages well. There were wide gaps between the golden slats and, over the centuries, some of them had fallen in on the street.

This had allowed even more jungle weeds to invade the city. Now the porous roofs of the levels were shot through with unchecked vegetation.

To anyone in an aeroplane flying overhead or looking down via satellite, it would've looked like just another jungle-covered slope at the base of a *tepui*. Only someone who came here specifically looking for it and who got close enough would spot the city amid the dense jungle that had swallowed it.

Through gaps in the gold uprights of the three lower levels, spaced between the doorways on the internal walls, Mae and the others could see dozens of horizontal coffin-shaped recesses carved into those same walls.

The coffins were open.

Their former occupants—three hundred bronze automatons—now filled the rising golden street of the city of Ra.

At the top of the enormous mountainside city was a section that was almost open to the sky.

Here a stepped gold bridge leapt across a wide ravine in the cliffside. At its near end, the bridge had a square opened-sided cupola and it was at this cupola that their rivals—a young woman and a squad of six Brazilian special forces troops—had stalled in their quest to reach the city's innermost vault.

'Chloe,' Iolanthe said, recognising the woman.

'Who?' Nobody said.

'Chloe Carnarvon,' Iolanthe said. 'My former assistant. She sold me out to my brother and left me in the hands of his torturer.'

Standing in the midst of the Brazilian troops, Chloe held the Helmet of Hades.

The reason for her team's delay wasn't immediately apparent: as Chloe and her men waited on the near side of the bridge, one of the Brazilian soldiers stepped tentatively into the cupola and began fighting with several glistening man-shaped silver figures inside it.

The soldier fired his gun at the figures from point-blank range but it didn't seem to have any effect on them. Then one of the silver figures stabbed him with its right hand and hurled the Brazilian trooper off the bridge.

Making matters worse for Chloe and her men was the three-hundred-strong army of bronze automatons packed into the main street of Ra below them.

They were stuck between a rock and a hard place: they either fought the four silver figures on the bridge and got past them . . . or they faced the army of bronze ones behind them.

Abruptly, with a loud *boom*, the entire bronze army took a single step in unison, closing in on Chloe and her team.

Mae pulled up an image of the Plato scroll on her phone: '*At its bridge you must overcome its silver guardians,*' she read.

She turned to Iolanthe. 'Your protégé evidently doesn't know how to get past the guardians on that bridge.'

Iolanthe said, 'True. But as of right now, neither do we.'

ATLAS

Aloysius Knight's harpoon bounced harmlessly off the chest of the first bronzeman striding slowly across the seabed toward him and Jack.

'*Kushma alla?*' the assembled army intoned, muffled by the water.

Jack recalled Lily's translation of the phrase from before: *Are you my master?*

He figured the answer to that question was one of the Mysteries that would have been revealed to Orlando had he stepped inside the obelisk after the Great Games.

The army of bronzemen closed in on Jack and Aloysius.

Their collective footfalls boomed through the watery silence.

Boom . . .

They were shaped like humans: with arms and legs, chests and shoulders.

Boom . . .

But it was their faceless beaked heads that made them fearsome. It gave them a pitiless, inhuman aspect: no emotion, no sympathy, no remorse.

Boom . . .

And they clearly did not need oxygen or air to operate. The three hundred feet of water pressing down on their heads had no effect on them whatsoever.

They were automatons built for one purpose and one purpose only: to kill anyone who wasn't supposed to be there.

Jack and Aloysius swam a short way back into the tunnel.

'*Jack!*' Stretch's voice came in through Jack's earpiece. '*We've penetrated Thule. We can see Mendoza, but he's stuck at a bridge, held up by some silver robots of some sort. We might be able to reach the bridge, but unless we know how to beat those silver things, we'll be dead, too.*'

Mae's voice came in next: '*Jack, we've got the same problem here at Ra! They seem to be the silver guardians mentioned in the Plato scroll: we have to get past them but we don't know how!*'

The army of bronzemen in front of Jack kept slowly advancing. He tried to think.

There has to be a way . . . he thought.

'The tablet tells us everything we need to know about getting into the cities . . .' he said aloud. 'The tablet tells us . . .'

As the bronzemen kept coming forward, one inexorable step at a time, he glanced at his image of the tablet one more time.

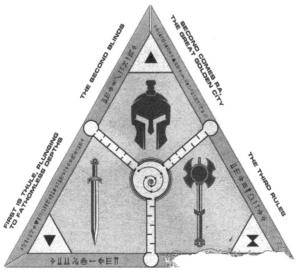

THE FIRST KILLS

Jack scanned the image desperately. 'It's got to be here. The cities . . . the weapons . . . The First Kills . . . the Second Blinds . . . the Third Rules . . .'

As Jack peered at the image on his phone, Aloysius pushed him further into the entry tunnel. 'Back up. Back up—'

Then Aloysius stopped his shoving and Jack looked up.

Four bronze automatons had emerged from coffins set into the walls of the flooded tunnel *behind* them, blocking their escape.

'*Kushma alla?*' they intoned.

'Oh, fuck,' Aloysius said.

There was nowhere to go.

They had three hundred bronzemen coming at them from in front and four coming from behind. It was like being in a slowly closing vice.

Jack and Aloysius hovered in the flooded tunnel looking this way and that, trapped.

The two leading bronzemen raised their claws, revealing their fearsome pointed tips.

At the sight of them, Aloysius's eyes went wide. 'Oh, mother of mercy.'

'There has to be a way . . .' Jack said softly. 'Think, damn it.'

The bronzemen continued to advance, their claws gleaming in the underwater haze.

Aloysius Knight swore. 'Of all the ways I thought I'd die, I never thought I'd go out like this. It's been a pleasure to know you, Captain West. See you on the other side.'

And then the lead two bronzemen raised their deadly claws, and as Aloysius Knight squeezed his eyes shut, they swung them violently at him and Jack.

'Stop!'

His eyes shut, Aloysius heard Jack's voice through his scuba helmet's speaker.

Aloysius opened his eyes . . .

. . . to see a gleaming bronze claw stopped exactly three inches from his heart. Another claw had halted right in front of Jack's chest.

And then he saw Jack, hovering beside him in the flooded tunnel, holding the Mace of Poseidon high above his head.

In that final moment, as the realisation struck him, Jack had snatched the Mace from his weight-belt, held it aloft in front of the advancing bronzemen and yelled, 'Stop!'

'What just happened?' Aloysius asked.

'*The third rules*,' Jack said simply.

'Come again?' Aloysius eyed the unmoving bronzemen warily.

They now stood like frozen statues, erect and to attention, their bladed claws now held stiffly by their sides.

Jack said, 'The tablet tells us everything we need to know. The first kills. The second blinds. *The third rules*. The Mace is the third weapon. I think the makers of the tablet neglected to include a couple of words: *the guardians*. The Sword kills the guardians. The Helmet blinds them in some way. And this Mace, well, it rules the guardians of this city. They must obey whoever holds it.'

Aloysius looked again at the crowd of bronze automatons, standing dead still in the presence of the upraised Mace.

'Well, thank fuck you figured that out when you did,' he said. 'These things speak English?'

'No, I think they just obey the Mace,' Jack said. 'I just kinda said that because I was afraid. Still, I'm not going to lower this Mace anytime soon.'

He keyed his sat-radio with his spare hand: 'Mum, Stretch. The weapons get you past the guardians. I repeat: *the weapons get you past the guardians*. The Sword kills them and the Helmet blinds them.'

THULE

After receiving Jack's call about the Sword, Pooh Bear and Stretch faced their own significant problem: getting past the three hundred bronze automatons between them and their bridge.

'It's at times like this I wish I had one of those Maghook things,' Pooh Bear said.

'In the absence of a Maghook, I have an idea,' Stretch said. 'Follow me.'

They hurried down the curving road, in amongst the buildings of the frost-covered city hanging off it.

'What are you thinking?' Pooh Bear said as he hurried to keep up.

'We take the high road and then we take the low road,' Stretch said.

His plan soon became clear.

After running a short way down the curving road, Stretch led Pooh into one of the ancient buildings overhanging the central abyss of the city.

They emerged on the flat stone roof of the structure. There Stretch leapt across onto the roof of the adjoining building—since the buildings followed the downward spiral of the road, this second roof was lower than the first.

And thus Stretch and Pooh Bear traversed their way down the city of Thule—across and down, hurdling parapets, leaping from rooftop to rooftop—paralleling the city's main descending thoroughfare and thus bypassing the army of bronze automatons filling it.

After about ten minutes of this kind of running, they came to a high crenellated battlement overlooking the bridge and here their rooftop path ended.

Now the bridge stretched out below them—a hundred metres long, with the open-sided cupola in its middle, where Mendoza and his last three Swiss troopers were stranded like trapped animals.

But the bridge had no kind of roof over which Pooh and Stretch could run to bypass the forest of bronzemen gathered on this half of it.

'Okay,' Pooh Bear said. 'That was the high road. What's the low road?'

'Down there,' Stretch said, pointing.

Pooh Bear followed his gaze. 'Oh, you've got to be kidding me.'

'It's the only way.'

'Yes, for a skinny Israeli,' Pooh said. 'Such routes are not meant for fat Arabs like me.'

Stretch smiled grimly. 'Come on, my old friend, you can do it.'

A minute later, the two of them were climbing, unseen by the mass of bronzemen, down the side of the battlement, using its uneven stone surface for finger and toeholds.

When they came level with the bridge, however, they kept going, below it, coming to the latticework of stone struts underneath the ancient bridge.

The low road.

And so, dangling from the bridge, high above the bottomless drop, moving hand over hand, hanging by only their fingertips, Pooh Bear and Stretch worked their way along the bridge, moving along its underside, underneath the many bronzemen on it, until they came to the cupola and, to the surprise of Cardinal Mendoza and his last three men, hoisted themselves up onto the bridge proper.

'What the—' Mendoza gasped.

'You should've done more homework, Cardinal,' Stretch said as he marched over to Mendoza and snatched the Sword from him. 'Now, we have to clean up your mess. Pooh, you ready?'

Significantly heavier than Stretch, Pooh Bear was still catching his breath from their hand-over-hand journey across the underside of the bridge.

He drew a pair of Arabian fighting knives from his belt.

'Ready as I'll ever be,' he puffed.

Stretch looked at the four silver statues inside the cupola. They stood motionless, for now.

Then, gripping Excalibur in both hands and with his loyal friend Pooh Bear at his side, Stretch edged into the open-sided cupola and the silver statues stepped forward.

As soon as he stepped out onto the dizzyingly high cupola, Stretch felt the sword in his hand change.

It began to vibrate ever so slightly and its grip grew warm. Stretch felt the heat radiating through its gleaming blade.

The first silverman's deadly claws slashed at him, whistling as they cut through the air.

Stretch ducked the blow and stabbed the famous sword directly at his foe's chest.

Far from bouncing off the silverman's metal body as all of Mendoza's bullets had, the hot blade plunged deep into the silver automaton and the man-shaped thing went instantly still . . . and fell.

But the other three silvermen were still in the game and they rushed forward, leading with their claws.

It was here that Pooh Bear stepped in and his two knives flashed as they parried the other silvermen's lethal blows, the steel of his blades ringing as they deflected the automatons' metal claws, keeping them away from Stretch.

This allowed Stretch to turn and kill a second silverman—slashing its head clean off—and then, while Pooh Bear distracted it, Stretch dispatched the third one with a powerful stab in the back.

But two against four was always going to be tough, and as Pooh Bear helped Stretch dispatch the third silverman, the fourth and last one slashed Stretch across his back.

'Arrgh!' Stretch yelled as he fell toward the edge of the cupola and dropped Excalibur.

The last silverman stood over him and raised its clawed hand for the killing blow . . . just as Pooh Bear came sliding across the floor between its legs, scooped up the Sword and swung it laterally, slicing at the silverman's knees.

The silver thing toppled to the floor beside Stretch. But it was still 'alive' and still trying to kill them. It slashed at Stretch, missing by inches, until Pooh Bear kicked it in the back, sending it sailing off the high bridge and disappearing into the abyss below.

And suddenly it was over.

The two friends lay inside the cupola, on the soaring stone bridge: Stretch bloody and wounded, Pooh Bear gripping Excalibur.

Cardinal Mendoza just stared at them in shock and wonder.

'Stretch,' Pooh Bear said. 'You okay?'

Stretch groaned painfully. 'I'm . . . all right. Go. You have to get that sword to the vault.'

Pooh Bear sprang to his feet.

'You!' he called to Mendoza. 'Since he saved your worthless life, help my friend! Bring him across the bridge and tend to his wound while I take this sword to the vault and empower it.'

Mendoza nodded dumbly.

Pooh Bear took off, hurrying off the bridge and down a steep ladder cut into the far wall. The ladder led to a tiny ledge where a yawning stone doorway could be seen: the entrance to the innermost vault of the secret city of Thule.

RA

'*The second blinds, the second blinds,*' Iolanthe repeated breath-lessly as she and Nobody clambered *over* the lost city of Ra.

After Jack had called and told them that the weapons overcame the guardians, Iolanthe had had a realisation.

'I know how the Helmet blinds them,' she had said. 'We have to get to that bridge.'

But to reach the bridge in the heart of Ra, they needed to out-flank the three hundred bronzemen filling Ra's single switchbacking ascending street of gold.

The way they did it was by going over it, climbing up the vines that had attached themselves to the Y-shaped uprights and then leaping across the slat-like golden roofs of each level.

It was a perilous path and one that required an athleticism that was too much for Mae. She waited at the base of the city.

As the two of them danced across the gold slats, hurdling the wide gaps, Iolanthe saw the army of bronzemen only a couple of feet below her, standing ominously to attention.

The golden slats were covered in a slippery grease of mud plus many creeping vines that had looped around the damaged roof in a thousand different ways.

As Iolanthe climbed up onto the second level, she tripped on a thick vine and toppled awkwardly through one of the gaps—to be caught by Nobody.

Beneath her dangling feet, a single bronzeman turned his eyeless beaked head neutrally up at her.

But the automaton did nothing.

They continued on, arriving at the city's third level, a short distance from the bridge where Chloe Carnarvon had stalled in her journey.

'Chloe!' Iolanthe called.

At the bridge ten metres away, Chloe spun in surprise, her eyes already wide with panic at her hopeless situation.

Seeing Chloe up close, Iolanthe now saw that her former assistant looked dirty and drained. Iolanthe didn't know that, after flying to South America from Iceland and slowly making her way to this godforsaken corner of the jungle, Chloe had been stuck in this humid deathtrap for two-and-half days, slowly losing men, ammunition, water and her mind.

Now Chloe blanched in disbelief at the unexpected sight of her old boss: shaven-headed and bruised, but alive and here.

'Iolanthe?'

'Stay there! I know how to use the—'

It was then that the bronzemen reacted.

As Iolanthe crawled across the golden slat-roof toward the bridge with Nobody behind her, a bronzeman below them suddenly punched up at Nobody's slat, hitting it with such force that the thick gold slat dislodged and abruptly, to Iolanthe's horror, Nobody dropped from view, disappearing in amongst the sea of deadly bronzemen.

Nobody landed with a thud on the moss-covered gold floor of the City of Ra amid a dozen shiny bronze legs.

Above him loomed the defenders of the city, their blank faces looking robotically down at him.

Schnick!

The nearest bronzeman's fist opened, its bladed claws bared.

'*Damn* . . .' Nobody breathed.

The bronzeman slashed. Nobody dived left—to find another bronzeman standing over him and slashing down with its claws.

He rolled right, slamming into the grime-covered golden wall.

As soon as Nobody had dropped from her sight, Iolanthe had sprung into action, dancing across the last few slats and racing to Chloe's side.

She wasn't expecting to prove her theory this way, but now she had no choice. She had to do this and she had to do it now.

'I need that!' She snatched the Helmet of Hades from Chloe's hands, ran back to the end of the golden street and called, 'Nobody!'

Peering through the first few ranks of bronzemen, she saw Nobody evading the slashing claws of the bronzemen before rolling up against the golden wall. She threw the ancient helmet to him.

'Put it on!'

★ ★ ★

The Helmet flew through the air before it bounced on the floor and rolled up against Nobody's leg.

Iolanthe's bizarre command rang in Nobody's ears.

His brain reeled. *I'm about to die! Why on Earth would I put on an old helmet?*

But somehow he told his hands to obey and, as he ducked one last swipe from the nearest bronzeman—a strike that bounced off the golden wall—he snatched up the Helmet of Hades and dropped it onto his head—

—and the attacking bronzemen paused instantly.

They pulled back, confused.

With their eyeless faces, they looked left, then right.

They're searching for me, Nobody thought. *But they can't see me.*

The second blinds them . . .

If you wear the Helmet, they can't see you.

And so, very slowly, Dave 'Nobody' Black stood and walked—walked—unharmed through the ranks of bronzemen to the golden bridge where Iolanthe stood with the still-shocked Chloe and her last few Brazilian troops.

Once he was clear of the bronzemen, Nobody took off the Helmet and gave it to Iolanthe.

'Good theory,' he said.

'Thanks. Let's see if it works again.'

And with those words, Iolanthe put on the Helmet and without so much as a pause, stepped into the cupola between the four silver guardians standing in its corners.

As she strode among them, the four silvermen didn't move. They remained silent statues.

While she was wearing the Helmet, they couldn't see her.

And then Iolanthe was through, past the deadly cupola.

After that, she climbed the stepped bridge and came to a doorway that bored into the base of the huge flat-topped mountain.

The doorway to the city's innermost vault.

Iolanthe stepped inside, disappearing into the holy sanctum of
the City of Ra.

ATLAS

Holding the Mace of Poseidon high above his head, Jack West swam—untouched, unattacked—through the ranks of bronzemen standing at the base of the colossal flooded City of Atlas.

Aloysius Knight swam with him, careful to stay close to Jack, lest he lose the protection of the Mace as well.

Slowly, they swam upward, in front of the stupendous hourglass-shaped rock formation that supported the most famous lost city on Earth.

As at the other cities, a single road ran up the flank of the rock formation. Towers, domes, obelisks and even a few small pyramids lined the road as it climbed. Four mighty vertical columns—they were the size of skyscrapers and dotted with windows—supported the upper half of the hourglass.

Up and up they swam, until they came to the bridge on the bottom half of the city: a bridge with an open-sided cupola in its middle.

Here they encountered—as the others had at their cities—four silver automatons standing like statues in the four corners of the cupola.

Jack considered swimming past the bridge, bypassing it, but he figured the rules of this game wouldn't allow that: he had to confront and overcome the silver ones.

The silver guardians did not stir as Jack and Aloysius swam through the bridge.

They were protected by the Mace.

Ever higher they swam, passing a tall tower and other ancient structures until they came to the waist of the giant hourglass, its narrowest point, where they found a sturdy square-shaped stone doorway.

And as Jack held the Mace close to it, the door slid open.

Thus, like Pooh Bear at Thule and Iolanthe at Ra, Jack and Aloysius entered the inner sanctum of the secret City of Atlas.

The inner vaults of the three secret cities were identical: each was a cube-shaped room with walls of glittering gold and a central waist-high altar cut from a slab of raw diamond.

The golden walls of each vault were covered with raised glyphs and images.

At Thule where Pooh Bear held the Sword, the walls were icy cold to touch.

At Ra, where Iolanthe wore the Helmet, due to the constant humidity, the golden walls were covered in a layer of green mould.

At Atlas, where Jack and Aloysius had brought the Mace and where everything had been flooded, the gilt walls took on a blueish hue.

The carvings on the walls swirled around Jack like images from a dream.

Many of them he had seen before.

A picture of the Great Pyramid at Giza being struck by a beam of light from the sun.

The Mystery of the Circles.

Five warriors standing behind four throned kings.

The escutcheons of the four legendary kingdoms.

There were also some he hadn't seen:

A planet and its moon.

And a drawing of five mountains with vertical shafts cut into their middles, shafts that plunged deep into the Earth.

And one other image: a reproduction of the triangular tablet that had been at the centre of *this* quest—the one that was a piece of the

Altar of the Cosmos—complete with the Thoth text at its edges and the images of the Sword, Helmet and Mace.

But there was one crucial difference.

This tablet was not shown standing *upright* as Jack had seen their triangular tablet displayed.

No. Here the triangular tablet was shown lying horizontally— flat, face up to the sky—at the bottom of a shallow oblong pool.

They swam up to the diamond altar, a sturdy chunk of cloudy, translucent, ice-like stone.

It was at the same time both elegant and rough. Its sides were uneven, coarse, while its flat surface had been planed smooth and polished to a sheen. An eerie glow pulsed gently within it.

In the exact centre of the diamond altar, embedded in it, was a pale blue gemstone, glittering and astounding, the size of a golf ball.

An identical gemstone was embedded in the altar at Thule.

A third was at Ra.

Jack swam forward, gripping the Mace. He could see what he was meant to do.

In between the three blades of the Mace was the small setting he'd seen before. It was a perfect match for the blue gemstone.

Jack held the Mace vertically over the gemstone and gently lowered it until the weapon and the gem touched.

The dimly glowing altar now came alive with light.

Radiant, blinding white light shone out from the diamond slab, lancing out into the water.

Aloysius shielded his eyes, so bright was the glare.

And with a sharp *snap*, the gemstone came free of the altar and became one with the Mace.

It shone with an ethereal light, pale blue in colour, almost like starlight.

'I think we just empowered the Mace,' Jack said.

Aloysius nodded. 'I think that's safe to say. Can we get the fuck out of here now?'

'Aye-aye to that,' Jack said. He keyed his radio. 'Pooh Bear? Iolanthe? How are you doing out there?'

In the vault at Thule, Pooh Bear had just performed a similar ritual with Excalibur.

The sword had a hollow setting at the base of its mighty grip which matched the gemstone perfectly, and soon sword and gem were one, shining brightly in the depths of the remote ice city of Thule.

'The Sword is done,' he reported.

At Ra, Iolanthe had found a small hemispherical indentation in the brow of the Helmet of Hades that matched the blue gemstone on her diamond altar.

She turned the helmet upside-down and lowered it to the altar.

The blue gemstone attached itself to the helmet and immediately shone like a star in the night sky.

'The Helmet, too,' she said into her radio.

Jack and Aloysius swam out of their vault, kicking hard with their fins, emerging from the waist of the magnificent sunken city.

Jack switched to his facemask's radio.

'Sphinx,' he said. 'We've empowered the Three Immortal Weapons. Now we must take them to the Altar of the—'

Jack cut himself off as something swooped into a hover in the water right in front of him.

It wasn't anything ancient. Far from it. It was the most modern thing of all: an unmanned submersible drone with a large metal basket hanging from its underbelly.

'*Good work, Captain,*' Sphinx's voice replied in his earpiece.

A camera on the drone stared right at him.

Jack looked up and saw the underside of Sphinx's boat high above them. He must have been up there in it, watching them.

'*Place the Mace in the drone's basket and I will order your daughter to be removed from her drowning cell,*' Sphinx's voice commanded.

Jack lay the empowered Mace in the basket. 'Okay. Now let her go.'

The little remote-controlled drone whizzed away, past the vast heights of the flooded city, returning to its master.

When it arrived at the boat, Sphinx took the Mace from the basket and marvelled at the glowing blue gem now embedded in the weapon.

'You have done as I asked, Captain,' he said into his radio-mike, 'and I consider myself a man of my word . . . but not today.'

Sphinx smiled. 'I need your daughter for the ceremony at the Altar, but I do not need you. It is time for you to die. Sorry, I forgot to mention one feature of those scuba tanks I gave you.'

And with those words, Sphinx hit a switch on his console . . .

. . . and down at the waist of the City of Atlas, the scuba tanks on Jack's and Aloysius's backs suddenly *turned off* and stopped releasing air.

Jack gasped.

Aloysius gagged.

And there, one hundred and fifty feet below the surface, hovering in front of the sunken city of Atlantis, Jack West Jr and Aloysius Knight took their last breaths.

THULE

At Thule, Pooh Bear emerged from the inner vault to find Cardinal Mendoza standing over Stretch with a pistol to his head, flanked by his last three Swiss guards.

'Give me the Sword or I finish your friend,' he snarled.

'We did what you couldn't do,' Pooh Bear said. 'We cleaned up your mess, and this is how you repay us?'

'Throw the Sword to me and stay back.'

Pooh Bear tossed the Sword toward Mendoza. It clattered against the floor.

Mendoza snatched it up. 'I serve a higher power than your gratitude. Be grateful that I don't dispatch you both now.'

And then he was gone, sweeping out of there with the Sword and his men.

The army of bronzemen that filled the single winding street of Thule now parted before him as he hurried through their midst, bowing to the Sword with the shining blue gem embedded in its hilt.

Pooh Bear dived to Stretch's side.

RA

In the jungle-covered golden city of El Dorado, Iolanthe emerged from the innermost vault of the city with the empowered Helmet in her hands, to find Chloe, flanked by her final five Brazilian troopers, waiting for her . . .

. . . with a live feed on her satellite phone of Lily in the tidal cell. The rising water was up to her shoulders.

'Give me the Helmet or the girl drowns,' Chloe said.

Iolanthe handed over the Helmet. Then Chloe and her goons fled.

ATLAS

Sphinx arrived at Lily's tidal cell in his huge motor cruiser just as the water was reaching her chin.

The crude cell was located in a small rocky inlet about two miles east of his mansion. It had been built by Barbary pirates several hundred years before as a slow and cruel method of executing traitors.

It was accessible only by boat and even then only by someone who knew it was there.

Arriving at the inlet in his cruiser, Sphinx and his butler jumped into a small Williams speedboat to retrieve Lily.

As soon as she was back on the big boat, Sphinx smiled at her. 'I was never going to let you drown. I need you. But we'll never tell your friends that.'

Then he made a phone call. 'Your Majesty,' he said coolly. 'It is done.'

'*Do you have the Mace?*' Orlando's voice said from the other end of the phone.

'And the Oracle, too,' Sphinx said.

'*Excellent. Bring them both to the Altar. My people have the other two weapons and are en route to the Rock as we speak.*'

'As you command,' Sphinx said.

'*What about West?*' Orlando asked. '*Is he dead?*'

'I killed him at Atlas,' Sphinx said, looking directly at Lily. 'After I got him to empower the Mace for you.'

'*I shall remember this, Hardin,*' Orlando said. '*You're a good man and in the new world order, you will be suitably rewarded.*'

'I am yours to command, Majesty.'

As he hung up, Lily stepped right up to him, furious.

'Where is my father?' she demanded.

'Your father died in a bar fight twenty years ago,' Sphinx said.

'You know who I mean.'

'Captain West served me well,' Sphinx said. 'But he couldn't be allowed to live. In order to save your life, he braved the city and empowered this for me.' He held up the Mace. 'And then I cut off his air.'

Lily's face fell. She felt ill.

Then the big cruiser powered up and surged across the Strait, its destination: the towering Rock of Gibraltar on the other side.

'You callous creep,' Lily said.

'Sticks and stones, girl. Sticks and stones.'

'What do you plan to do with me? You said you don't need my talent. Why don't you just kill me, too?'

Sphinx turned away from her, his gaze landing on the distant Rock.

'I can't kill you,' he said strangely. 'Not yet.'

At that moment, another man stepped up onto the bridge of the motor cruiser.

Lily recognised him instantly.

It was Jaeger Eins, the leader of the Knights of the Golden Eight, the man who, paid by Sphinx and Dion, had kidnapped her in London.

'My Knights and squires are below deck, sir, along with the back-up,' he said. 'Armed and ready.'

'We have a few hours till Orlando's people arrive at Gibraltar,' Sphinx said. 'They're flying in on supersonic military jets, refuelling in flight as they go. We'll drop you off a kilometre out from the dock. You swim the rest of the way.'

Sphinx turned to Lily. 'Come, young lady. Let's go to the Altar.'

HADES'S SECRET APARTMENT
ROME, ITALY

After deducing that the Rock of Gibraltar was the Altar of the Cosmos and sending that information to the team, Alby was sitting at his desk when Zoe called out to him from the living room.

Alby entered the living room to find her watching the TV with concern. Hades, still recovering from his ordeal at Erebus, had adjourned to his room to sleep.

A newsreader on the television was saying: '—*in what can only be described as a bizarre week, with the toppling of a building in New York; the smashing of a bridge in Venice; the unprecedented hacking of global television signals by a masked man calling on an individual named Jack West Jr; plus, of course, the terrible incident in London. After all this, one final inexplicable event has occurred: an entire group of monks has disappeared.*

'*Known as the Fraternal Order of St Paul, the monks were associated with the Gallerie dell'Accademia museum in Venice, which appeared to be connected to the incident there. It appears that the entire order has vanished, abandoning their lodgings adjoining the museum and taking all of their possessions—including several priceless works of art and sketches—without leaving so much as a trace. Neither the museum nor the Vatican would comment—*'

Alby turned to Zoe. 'The Order of the Omega is on the move.'

'But to where?' Zoe asked.

'To tackle the second trial, I imagine,' Alby said. 'The Trial of the Mountains.'

He returned to the study. Arrayed around it were the various documents and files he and Zoe had grabbed at Aragon Castle.

They'd taken documents, phones, computers; anything at the castle that might contain information relevant to their mission.

Inside one of Aragon Castle's crumbling towers, Alby had found the Knights' living quarters. They were luxuriously appointed: bedroom suites with plasma TVs, modern beds and furniture. The Knights of the Golden Eight lived in style.

In one bedroom, he had found a couple of suitcases.

A guest bedroom? he'd thought.

Seeing some files in the suitcases, Alby had just grabbed them and taken them with him to Rome.

Now he opened them.

A cover letter paperclipped to the files revealed their owner: the cover letter was from the law firm of Lehman Austen & Williams in New York, and it was addressed to Mr Dionysius DeSaxe.

Dion.

Among the documents were bank account details (amounts in the billions), property records (apartments and mansions around the world) and business records (mining and shipping shareholdings mainly).

It was, Alby realised, all of Lord Hades's earthly wealth, to be transferred to Dion upon his coronation as King of the Underworld.

There was one other thing in the sheaf.

A manila folder labelled *K.E.O.*

Alby's eyes narrowed. *King's Eyes Only.*

He opened the file.

The first few sheets contained rows of contact details: the details of the other kings and royals, plus people in government positions around the world who could be called upon to carry out a king's orders.

And then Alby saw a page titled: *THE HIGH SACRIFICIAL ALTAR OF THE COSMOS.*

'The *High Sacrificial* Altar of the Cosmos?' Alby said aloud. He hadn't heard it called that before.

He quickly read on:

> *It is imperative that those kings who are in power at the time of the First Trial cultivate their relationship with the Supreme Initiate of the Cult of Amon-Ra.*
>
> *Ensure that the Supreme Initiate is healthy—encourage him or her to have children—for when that trial is endured, it is the Supreme Initiate's singular blood that must be spilled to save all humankind.*
>
> *The notion of dying for mankind is not an easy one for anyone to comprehend. And either the Initiate will selflessly spill their own blood to that end or they will spill the blood of their offspring.*
>
> *On two of the three previous occasions when this duty was required, the Supreme Initiates of those times went willingly to their fates. On one occasion, the Supreme Initiate—the biblical figure known as Abraham—slew his son in his place.*
>
> *Of course, if you cannot cultivate a relationship with the Supreme Initiate of your time, know that their sacrifice on the Altar need not be voluntary. The continuation of the species does not require the willing participation of the sacrificial lamb.*

Alby blinked.

'The Altar of the Cosmos is a sacrificial altar,' he said to no-one.

And the person to be sacrificed on it was the Supreme Initiate of the Cult of Amon-Ra—and Abraham had been one such Initiate.

Supreme Initiate.

Alby hadn't seen or heard that term before.

He flipped to the next page, which showed a long family tree: expanding branches of parents and children travelling down through the last four thousand years.

On it were many names, most of which Alby didn't know. But popping out occasionally were some that he did: *Abraham of Ur, Nefertari of Siwa, Cassandra of Troy.*

And at the very bottom of the list was a final name that he recognised:

Milo Omari.

Alby started.

He absolutely knew that name.

Milo Omari was Lily's birth father, the previous Oracle of Siwa, also gifted with the special ability to read the Word of Thoth.

'Oh, God . . .' Alby sat up. 'This is a list of all the Oracles throughout history.'

When he had first been introduced to Jack and Lily's secret world, he had been told that the Oracle of Siwa was sometimes referred to as the 'High Priest of the Cult of Amon-Ra'.

High Priest.

Supreme Initiate.

They were one and the same.

Alby leapt out of his seat, calling, 'Zoe! Come here!'

Zoe arrived in his study just as Alby snatched up the satellite radio and yelled into its microphone: 'Jack! Pooh! Stretch! Everyone! Find Lily! Find her now! They're going to kill her! They *have* to kill her in the ritual at the Altar of the Cosmos because she's the Oracle!'

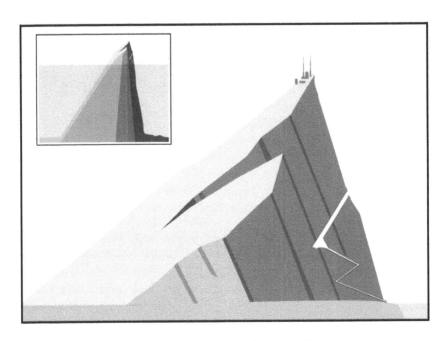

THE ROCK OF GIBRALTAR

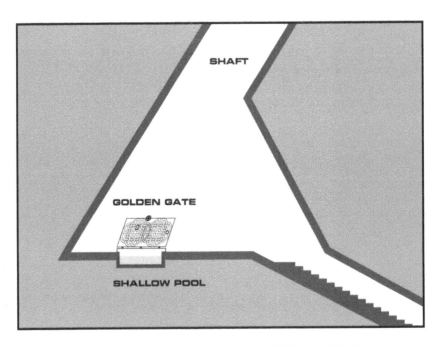

THE SACRIFICIAL ALTAR OF THE COSMOS

THE ROCK OF GIBRALTAR
GIBRALTAR, U.K. TERRITORY

THIRTY MINUTES BEFORE THE RISING OF
SAGITTARIUS A-STAR

After taking a leisurely few hours to cross the Strait—and pausing about a kilometre from the shore—Sphinx's luxury motor cruiser arrived at a military dock in the shadow of the Rock of Gibraltar.

The eastern flank of the Rock—the vertical side—leapt skyward above it, almost half a kilometre high.

The dock was flanked by members of the Royal Marines: Orlando's men.

Lily spent the whole trip staring blankly forward. The news of Jack's death had stolen any fight she had left in her. She felt worn, exhausted and profoundly alone.

Sphinx guided her through the ranks of Royal Marines and into a rough-hewn tunnel that had been dug into the base of the Rock almost eighty years previously.

This whole area of the Rock was fenced off with razor-wire and signs labelled: RESTRICTED AREA: AUTHORISED MILITARY PERSONNEL ONLY. Tourists and members of the public couldn't get near this part of the Rock of Gibraltar.

Inside the gargantuan thing, they went up several steep flights of stairs—each step etched from the limestone of the Rock—until they emerged in a high-ceilinged chamber halfway up the colossal peak.

There were three things about the chamber that struck Lily: every one of its walls was smooth and flat; there was a shallow oblong pool of water sunken into its floor; and it had a wide slanting shaft that lanced up into the ceiling like an enormous sloping chimney.

A strange-looking gold contraption lay on top of the pool: it looked like a shining golden gate, its bars twisted into an ornate pattern. It was laid flat over the pool and had hinges that allowed it to be pulled open.

Orlando was waiting for them, with the triangular tablet sitting at his feet.

With him were the other three kings: Dion DeSaxe, King of the Underworld, the American-born King of the Sea and the new Chinese-born King of the Sky.

Lily stopped short at the sight of them, shaken from her reverie. All four kings were here.

Orlando shook Sphinx's hand as he took the Mace from him.

'Hardin!' he said. 'Fine work. Simply fine work, old chum!'

Sphinx bowed low. 'A pleasure, Your Majesty.'

Orlando said, 'We are almost ready to begin. Mendoza and Chloe just landed at the airstrip and are on their way here now.'

Minutes later, Orlando's people arrived in the ceremonial chamber.

Cardinal Mendoza with the Sword from Thule.

Chloe Carnarvon with the Helmet from Ra.

Lily wondered what had happened at those two cities to create this result.

Sphinx gathered the three weapons together.

Mendoza touched a radio in his ear. 'Sagittarius A-star just crested the sun.'

Orlando stepped forward.

'Gentlemen!' he said formally. 'After the unfortunate events that occurred at the conclusion of the Great Games, I am pleased to inform you that order has been restored.

'As the man who was most wronged by that chaos, I made it my mission to be the prime agent of that restoration of order, and here we are. The three weapons have been empowered at the three cities and now I invite you all, as my fellow kings, to see me fulfil the ritual that was to be my prize as the winner of the Great Games.'

The other kings nodded.

Lily watched them, tense.

Sphinx stepped up to Orlando, holding the three weapons.

Orlando said, 'Thank you, Hardin. You're a loyal sport.'

Sphinx smiled . . .

. . . then he dropped the Helmet and the Mace and thrust the Sword deep into Orlando's chest.

The Kings of Sea and Sky gaped in horror, but only for an instant.

Behind them, Cardinal Mendoza drew a gun and shot them both in the back, dropping them.

The two Royal Marine guards at the entry stairwell unslung their guns, only to be cut down by a clatter of gunfire from the stairwell below them.

Jaeger Eins emerged with three squires, their Steyr AUG assault rifles smoking.

Lily was shocked. 'Holy shit . . .'

But the other people in the chamber weren't.

Dion DeSaxe inspected his fingernails. Chloe Carnarvon did nothing at all.

A gurgled moan made Lily spin. It was Orlando.

He wasn't dead.

As Sphinx withdrew the bloody blade of Excalibur from his chest, Orlando dropped to his knees, blood saturating his shirt.

'Chloe!' he screamed.

She barely even looked at him.

'Mendoza!'

The Catholic cardinal stared at him without pity.

Sphinx stood over Orlando and gave him a cruel smile.

'Cousin, cousin, cousin,' he said. 'It was *I* who restored order, not you. I know more about the two trials and the Omega Event than you shall ever know. When I was the presumed heir to your throne, I studied the ancient texts, learned everything I could about these pivotal times. My father even showed me the King's Eyes

Only file about this day. And then he abdicated his crown and gave it all to your father.'

As Sphinx strolled around him, Orlando glared up at Cardinal Mendoza and Chloe Carnarvon.

Sphinx said, 'Spare the cardinal and Ms Carnarvon your angry stares. They have both long been in my employ, waiting for this very moment.'

'Why?' Orlando spat at them.

'You wouldn't marry me,' Chloe said curtly. 'You happily bedded me but when I asked if we could be wed, you laughed in my face.'

'You are not prepared,' Cardinal Mendoza said simply. 'For what is required.'

'He's right,' Sphinx said. 'You were never up for the challenge of your crown, Orlando. You were never properly prepared. Just look at your clumsy attempts to open the three cities. We all would have died were it not for West and his people.

'Look also at West himself, *your* choice of champion at the Great Games. It was his actions at the Games that created this state of affairs, which means it was *your* mistake. You deserve to die this way. Bleeding out on the floor. Feel free to bleed slowly, cousin, for then you may at least live long enough to see the ritual performed.'

Sphinx turned to Lily.

'For perform it now I must.'

The intricate golden gate that lay over the rectangular pool in the centre of the ceremonial chamber was opened and Mendoza placed the triangular tablet in a matching triangular recess in the base of the shallow pool.

Then, her hands and feet bound, Lily was laid in the pool on top of it.

The water filling the ceremonial pool was about eighteen inches deep. It covered her body, lapping around her jaw and cheeks, but her eyes, nose and mouth still protruded above the surface, allowing her to breathe.

Chloe filmed it all on a video camera.

Lily went to her fate in silence, her eyes dull, her spirit broken.

Jack was dead.

Her friends were scattered around the world, their heroics at the Three Secret Cities now exploited by Sphinx and Dion and their gang of cronies.

There was nothing she could do. She was going to die here, alone and afraid.

As she lay on her back in the water, Sphinx put the Helmet of Hades on her head and placed the Mace of Poseidon in a slot on the golden gate near her feet. Their blue gems glowed eerily.

'Brave girl. This is for the world,' he said. 'It is a noble death and it will be quick.'

He closed the hinged gate on top of her.

'Open the ceiling!' he called.

Jaeger Eins spoke into a radio and in response, with a great mechanical whirring, something opened at the top of the great chimney-like shaft above the chamber.

From her captive position in the pool, Lily had a clear view straight up the sloping shaft. It must have been two hundred feet long: a dead-straight slanting shaft through which she could now see a square of the night-time sky.

Stars glistened. It was actually quite beautiful.

Somewhere up there was the centre of the universe—at the other end of a path carved by the Hydra Galaxy—facing this chamber, ready to receive the radio waves from Sagittarius A-star as they passed through Lily's sacred spilled blood and the triangular tablet.

Lily lay stoically in the pool, wearing the Helmet of Hades: the sacrificial lamb.

She found herself thinking of Jack and his smile. The special smile he reserved for her. And of the team that had raised her . . . and of Alby, ever loyal and kind, and his last words to her: 'I always loved you.'

She cried inwardly.

'Damn,' she whispered.

The section of the golden gate directly above her heart had a slit in it: a slit that matched the width of Excalibur perfectly.

Mendoza handed Sphinx the Sword, empowered by its shining blue gem.

Sphinx crossed to the pool and stood over Lily.

He carefully inserted the tip of the blade into the slot, holding it poised above Lily's heart.

The ritual was clear: plunge the Sword through the heart of the Oracle.

Lily stared skyward.

If the stars were to be the last thing she saw, she thought, then it wasn't a bad final sight.

Shortly after, with a sharp downward plunge of the Sword, Sphinx completed the ancient sacrificial rite.

Chloe filmed the entire terrible act.

Thus the first trial was overcome and liquid stone did not spread throughout the Earth's oceans like a cancer and turn the planet into a barren wasteland.

THE CITY OF ATLAS

As the sun began to sink in the sky, the flooded city of Atlantis lay still.

Nothing moved except for the odd strand of seaweed that swayed in the current.

Then . . . movement.

From the sunken wreck of the 707 aeroplane that lay up against the base of the giant hourglass-shaped city, its nose pointed upward.

Something shot out of the plane—moving fast and vertically, heading at rocket-speed for the surface—something that looked like a life raft with two men hanging from it: the two figures of Jack West Jr and Aloysius Knight.

When Sphinx had cut off their air, Jack and Aloysius had both had time for one last breath.

There was no way they could swim to the surface on that single breath of air. It was too far, a hundred and fifty feet away.

It was Jack who had pointed at the plane wreck and begun swimming for it. Aloysius didn't know what he was getting at, but without a better plan of his own, he followed.

It was lucky it was an older plane, Jack thought as he came to the Boeing 707's forward door, flung it open and swam desperately inside.

Newer planes used compressed nitrogen and carbon dioxide to inflate their escape slides, but old ones like the 707 used compressed air.

There, hovering inside the galley of the sunken Boeing aeroplane, with his final breath of air beginning to fail him, Jack pulled the plane's tightly-packed escape slide from its compartment above the door and yanked on its emergency pull-tab.

The slide immediately sprang to life, enlarging in an instant, filling with air and becoming a life raft. It expanded to fill the tiny galley.

Jack immediately wrapped his lips around its manual-inflation valve and sucked in air, glorious air.

Then he offered the valve to Aloysius and he inhaled a lungful, too.

After that, they waited for a while, taking alternate swigs from the inflated escape slide, just in case Sphinx had left men up top to finish them off if they surfaced.

Thirty minutes passed.

Jack figured that was enough time. He motioned for Aloysius to get a grip on the escape slide.

Then he pointed up.

Aloysius nodded. He knew what that meant.

Jack then shoved the escape slide/life raft out of the plane's doorway and, filled as it was with air, it shot skyward, seeking the surface.

Jack and Aloysius clung to it as it raced upward at phenomenal speed. They exhaled as they rose, a standard scuba diver's precaution, lest their lungs explode with the air expanding inside them.

Then the life raft breached the surface and Jack and Aloysius were hurled by the force of their rapid rise fully seven feet into the air above it before splashing back down.

The sand-coloured cliffs of the Moroccan coast towered above them. Sphinx's mansion crowned one cliff alongside the ancient lighthouse.

Jack spun . . . searching for Sphinx's motor cruiser, but he didn't see it anywhere. It was gone.

And then Alby's voice exploded in his ear:

'*Jack! Pooh! Stretch! Everyone! Find Lily! Find her now! They're going to kill her! They have to kill her in the ritual at the Altar of the Cosmos because she's the Oracle!*'

They found a small motorboat tied to the dock at the base of Sphinx's mansion and gunned it across the Strait of Gibraltar.

When they arrived at the Rock two hours and thirty minutes later, Aloysius pointed. 'There!'

A large number of dead bodies lay beside a restricted military dock on the eastern side of the Rock: the bodies of some Royal Marines.

Jack saw the tunnel delving into the Rock at the end of the dock and hurried inside.

'Wait! You don't know what's in there—' Aloysius called, chasing after him.

Minutes later, the two men emerged inside the sacrificial chamber.

It was empty. Well, empty of living people.

Orlando's body lay on the floor, his chest a bloody mess, his mouth agape, his furious eyes open in a sightless stare. The bullet-riddled bodies of his two Royal Marine bodyguards lay nearby.

In the centre of the space, Jack saw the rectangular ceremonial pool sunken into the floor with the golden gate on top of it.

He raced over to it, followed by Aloysius.

'Jesus . . .' Aloysius gasped, seeing what was in the pool.

'Lily . . .' Jack said softly. 'No . . .'

After the ceremony had been completed and the body had sunk fully under the surface of the water, someone must have tossed a greystone pill into the pool, for beneath the bars of the golden gate, the shallow pool was filled to the brim with a flat-topped slab of black-grey stone.

Jack saw the jawguards of the Helmet of Hades jutting ever so slightly above the surface of the solidified liquid stone at one end of the pool.

Saw the Mace sticking up from a slot in the gate at the other end.

And in the middle, right where the ceremonial victim's heart would be, was Excalibur, embedded in the stone, locked in place when it had solidified. The Sword in the Stone.

A foul layer of blood stained the golden slot through which the Sword had been plunged. Arterial blood from Lily's heart must have sprayed upward in a grisly gout when the Sword had been thrust down through the slot into her.

Jack leaned in close to the Helmet, searching for some sign of . . .

. . . and he saw them.

Several strands of long black hair curled out from the slab of black-grey stone and, being wet, they had clung to the right jaw-guard of the Helmet.

Jack's heart broke.

He knew that hair.

It was Lily's.

And there in that chamber, inside an altar the size of a mountain, watched by Aloysius Knight, Jack West Jr dropped to his knees and wept.

AIRSPACE OVER THE MEDITERRANEAN SEA

An hour later, Jack sat in the rear bomb bay of Aloysius Knight's Sukhoi Su-37, his stare blank and unseeing.

Aloysius had dragged him out of the sacrificial chamber and called Rufus. They had to get out of there. Rufus had arrived shortly after in the Sukhoi and they had zoomed away.

'Where to?' Rufus had asked.

'Anywhere,' Aloysius said.

Aloysius had then contacted all the others—Zoe and Alby; Mae, Nobody and Iolanthe; Pooh Bear, Stretch and Sky Monster—scattered as they were around the world, and told them that their mission had been achieved but at a cost: they had saved the world but only because Sphinx had carried out the ritual and executed Lily.

Over the open line, Mae gasped, '*No, that can't be . . .*'

Nobody and Iolanthe were struck silent.

Zoe had said, '*How is Jack?*'

'He's with me,' Aloysius said.

'*Is he okay?*'

'Not really, no.'

'*Those bastards. Those damned evil bastards.*'

Then Alby spoke.

'*It was a cruel bargain,*' he said, '*which Lily must have known. She dies, but in doing so, she spares the whole world a terrible fate.*

But the world doesn't feel her loss like we do. Only we . . .'—his voice cracked—*'. . . only we feel that.'*

Sombre silence followed.

Aloysius said quietly, 'Sphinx was gone. He must've moved on to the next trial with the secrets he obtained from the, er, ceremony.'

With nothing else to say, they all arranged to meet in Rome and clicked off the line.

After that, Aloysius went up front and sat in the cockpit with Rufus, occasionally turning around to check on Jack.

'How is he?' Rufus whispered.

'He's in shock. They killed his daughter.'

Then, in the back of the plane, Jack blinked out of his trance and pulled up something on his phone.

An email from a password-protected folder.

From Lily.

Girding himself, he read it:

> **Dear Dad,**
>
> It's strange to write something like this, a message from the other side. I mean, what do you write? I've thought about it a lot and this is the best I could do.
>
> Life is so peculiar. According to the world, I'm this terribly important Oracle with this extraordinary ability and you're one of the Five Greatest Warriors in all of history and yet, when I think of the two of us, I think of you calling me 'Kiddo' and of that Simpsons t-shirt I bought you saying 'World's Greatest Dad'. If only the world really knew the daggy truth about its Oracle and her warrior father!
>
> In quieter times, though, when I think of us, I often find myself recalling one event: the time when I was five or six and you took me to the ballet in Cape Town to see *The Nutcracker.* Do you remember it?

Tears welled in Jack's eyes.

'I've always remembered it,' he whispered.

It was back when we were living at the farm in Kenya with the original members of our team. I didn't know it at the time, but you were all watching me, waiting for me to reveal my ability. For me, it was just an amazing time and an incredible childhood, surrounded by loving people.

It'll sound really stupid now, but up until that day we went to the ballet together, I wasn't sure you even liked me. You can get quiet sometimes and, being a little kid, I'd taken that for indifference. But *after* that day, I knew it. You loved me. Every daughter should get that kind of unfailing love from their dad. You were the best father any girl could have. The best.

And now, here we are.

If I can only leave you with one thought, Dad, let me make it this: keep fighting. Please keep fighting.

After all, you didn't come this far just to come this far.

With all my love, your very, very, very proud daughter,

Lily

Xoxoxoxo

Jack bowed his head, staring at the floor but seeing nothing. Tears streaked down his cheeks.

The last thing he wanted to do was go on. From a gurgling baby to a playful girl on roller-sneakers to the poised and smiling college student she had become, Lily had been his world. His buddy, Nobody, often said that Jack had a special smile reserved solely for his daughter and that Jack—the famously tough and resourceful Jack West Jr—would do anything for her, anything she asked.

Nobody had been right. Everything Jack had ever done had been for Lily: taking on deadly rivals, fighting in the Great Games, saving the world. All for her, for her future.

And now she was gone. The very reason he fought.

Yet Lily, ever perceptive, had known this. And so in her final message she had written those three crucial words: *Please keep fighting*.

Now he had to keep going, if for no other reason than that his little girl had told him to.

Jack inhaled deeply and closed his eyes.

'Keep fighting . . .' he said to no-one. 'Please keep fighting.'

Then he sat up. And opened his eyes.

And there was steel in them.

'Okay, kiddo,' he whispered. 'I will.'

EPILOGUE

THE ROCK OF GIBRALTAR
GIBRALTAR, U.K. TERRITORY
4 DECEMBER, 0330 HOURS

Three days later, in the dead of night, while the rest of Gibraltar slept, three shadowy figures in scuba gear and night-vision goggles emerged from the sea on the eastern side of the Rock.

They subdued two military guards, cut through the razor-wire fence and hustled past a sign saying RESTRICTED AREA: AUTHOR-ISED MILITARY PERSONNEL ONLY. Then they slipped inside the Rock of Gibraltar, quickly ascended several stairways and entered the ceremonial chamber.

Pooh Bear, Stretch and Alby.

They found the chamber just as Jack and Aloysius had left it: dead bodies still on the floor; the fabled sword, Excalibur, lodged in the slab of liquid stone in the shallow pool; and the heartbreaking wisps of black hair protruding from one end of the slab.

They had come for the body.

Lily's body.

They'd made the clandestine journey for their friend Jack—who at that moment was in Rome with Zoe by his side, silent and stoic, but distant, grieving—to retrieve Lily so that at least she could be given a proper burial in the presence of family and friends.

The ancient chamber with its high slanting chimney-like shaft loomed above them as, covered by Stretch and Alby, Pooh Bear lifted the golden gate and bent over the slab of liquid stone and set about chipping away at it with a hammer and chisel.

He hammered gently, delicately, considerately, so as not to damage Lily's face when he eventually broke through.

Stretch and Alby kept an eye on the entrance, glancing back at Pooh every now and then. Stretch was armed.

As he worked away, Pooh revealed more strands of black hair threaded through the solidified liquid stone. He tried to hold back his tears.

Then, after a time, his chisel broke through the stone, revealing a sliver of human skin.

With great tenderness, Pooh Bear carefully brushed away the chips of stone, blowing off the finer bits, revealing a face—

—and he reared back in surprise.

'Good God,' he gasped. 'It's not—'

And then, most oddly, given the solemnity of his mission, he broke out in a wide smile.

'Stretch, Alby! Come and look at this! And call Jack. Call him now!'

THE END

AN INTERVIEW WITH MATTHEW REILLY

SPOILER WARNING!

The following interview contains **SPOILERS** from *The Three Secret Cities*. **Readers who have not yet read the novel are advised to avoid reading this interview as it does give away major plot moments in the book.**

All right, Matthew, for a moment there, we thought we'd said goodbye to Lily! After the infamous death of Libby Gant in Scarecrow *(coincidentally the novel where the Black Knight had to break the news to Scarecrow), what are your thoughts on killing off your main characters?*

To this day, I still get comments from fans about that death scene in *Scarecrow*. It impacted many of my fans really hard. But, I have to say, that was my intention.

In the first draft of *The Three Secret Cities* (*3SC*), I actually did *not* include the Epilogue with Pooh, Stretch and Alby going to the Rock of Gibraltar. So I was going to let readers hang till the next book to reveal that it isn't Lily in the sacrificial pool. But after finishing *The Six Sacred Stones* (*6SS*) with a cliffhanger, I felt that this was too harsh.

I didn't want to finish the novel on a downer. As I thought about it more, I felt it would be better to take readers to the very, very edge and then leave them with a nice bit of hope as Pooh Bear removes the chips of greystone, sees who it is, smiles and yells, 'Call Jack! Call him now!' (Remember the 'package' that the Knight brought back to Sphinx from New Zealand: Lily's brother, Alexander, was last seen in NZ living with Sky Monster's parents.)

That said, *3SC* sees quite a few nice characters die: the Twins and Sky Monster's parents get killed rather brutally. This was deliberate: I wanted these deaths to be sudden and shocking (much like Gant's). And I warn everyone: there will be worse ones to come.

(This was also why I introduced in this book the concept of the Messages from the Other Side. They soften the blow of a death, and, to my mind, even in the middle of all this action and adventure, give us some tender moments: like Lachie writing about his affection for his brother, or Lily writing to Jack. Those messages give the characters a chance to say what they truly feel. Rest assured, more messages will appear in the last two books of the series and at terrible times.)

As I've always said, no character can be safe.

We were all left on the edge of our seats when the coffin opened in the Underworld in the Epilogue of The Four Legendary Kingdoms. *Did you know what was going to emerge and the role the bird-beaked bronzemen would play in* The Three Secret Cities?

I did know, yes.

I should make it clear that when I sat down to write *The Four Legendary Kingdoms* (*4LK*), it had been eight years since *The Five Greatest Warriors* (*5GW*) had been published. Writing the Jack West novels requires a lot of historical research and I needed to take a break from that for a while. In those intervening years, I had a very enjoyable time writing a range of standalone books including *The Tournament, Troll Mountain, The Great Zoo of China* plus one Scarecrow novel, *Scarecrow and the Army of Thieves*.

And then I decided to return to Jack.

I figured if I was going to recommence the Jack West Jr series, I had to plan *all the way* to the seventh and final book. With that in mind, I wanted each book to be a fully-contained story in itself, but to also *lead into* the next novel. The coffin opening scene at the end of *4LK* was perfect for that: we had just been on a wild rampage with Jack and now something even more dangerous had been initiated! So, yes, I had to know what was coming out of that coffin.

After the surprise of bringing in Scarecrow to **The Four Legendary Kingdoms** *how did you come to the decision to bring back Aloysius Knight, who we haven't seen since* **Scarecrow,** *which was published fifteen years ago?*

I am always listening to my fans at book signings, library events and via both email and social media. One question which always pops up is: 'Will we ever see Aloysius Knight, the Black Knight, again?'

The Black Knight was very popular from the moment he appeared in *Scarecrow.* He was the anti-Schofield, the ultimate bad-ass killing machine; the good guy gone wrong. I was always keen to bring him back. I just needed the right story.

When I planned out the plot of *3SC*—with a key moment where Jack would be captured and taken to an ancient prison from which no-one had ever escaped—the moment was suddenly right there: this was an occasion when Aloysius Knight could return! I mean, who else can rescue someone from an impossible-to-escape-from prison?

(It's important to note that Zoe, Stretch and Pooh Bear try . . . and fail. It is Knight alone who succeeds, and he does so by performing an outrageously dangerous sky-dive *right into* the mile-deep elevator shaft of the mine.)

Having brought Scarecrow into the world of Jack West Jr (and thus showing that they exist in the same universe), it stood to reason

that Aloysius Knight also lives in that universe. Even more than that, it occurred to me that he might have had run-ins with groups like the Knights of the Golden Eight in his bounty-hunting travels.

Having him present when Jack believes Lily has been sacrificed was not intended to echo the moment in *Scarecrow* where he is present for Scarecrow's discovery that Gant has been murdered. I can't say I planned that. It just happened.

There is quite a contrast from the action in **The Four Legendary Kingdoms** *taking place mainly in the Underworld, and the action in* **The Three Secret Cities** *taking place simultaneously throughout the world. Was this always the plan?*

Structurally, it's actually *4LK* that is unique in the Jack West series. It is the only book in the series that (a) is set largely in a single location and (b) takes place over a very short period of time, two days.

I had wanted *4LK* to be fast, brutal and visceral. More like a taut and tense thriller than a sweeping adventure. The time was right to inject some undiluted adrenalin into the Jack West Jr world and I wanted *4LK* to race like a rocket.

With *3SC* I wanted to write something just as fast but which was more of the globe-trotting adventure readers expect of a Jack West book, one that sweeps quickly from location to location: from a metropolis like New York City to the remote Orinoco Delta in Venezuela.

Matthew, with every book, we presume you can't think of a more gruesome way to torture someone to death, and then here we have suffocation by hardening greystone! Where did the idea for greystone powder originate from?

I'm very proud of my greystone powder! I love it!

Its creation actually arose out of my need to explain how all these massive underground castles, mountain-palaces and trap systems were built. I wanted to explain that greystone could be quite easily composed into a complex shape and then set in place (it also got a brief mention in *4LK* with the hostage carriages).

I am particularly proud of the pills that form Medusa's eyes in the Tomb of Poseidon. Since I was a kid, I've always been in awe of Medusa. She is such a cool myth: a snake-haired woman whose stare turns people to stone. The tale of Medusa is also a very enduring one that's lasted for over 2,000 years.

Having adapted the Labours of Hercules in *4LK*, in *3SC* I wanted to examine and explain, in real terms, the origins of the Medusa myth. That meant coming up with something that could realistically explain the whole 'her stare turns you to stone' thing.

Creating the greystone powder was key to that. Making pills out of it and using them as the eyes of a Medusa carving was a eureka moment for me. I literally danced around my office when I came up with that, pumping my fist!

As for the suffocating deaths, well, this is just something that I fear, kind of like being buried alive. The idea of being physically trapped inside this hardening, intensely claustrophobic, totally enveloping concrete-like void scares the crap out of me. It'd be a truly *awful* way to die. I figure since it scares me, it'll scare my readers.

Having said all that, I have an even better mythological tool-of-death ready to go in the next Jack West book . . .

When deciding on your three secret cities, why choose Thule, Ra and Atlas?

Right from the moment I wrote *Seven Ancient Wonders* (*7AW*), I always wanted the key feature of the Jack West Jr series to be the strange and unexplained places dotted around our planet. Places like the Pyramids, Stonehenge and Easter Island.

This, I figured, also included *mythical* places like the Underworld (in *4LK*) and famously 'lost' cities like Ultima Thule, El Dorado and the City of Atlas (I don't really like using the word 'Atlantis', as I think it's been used too much over the years).

I particularly liked the notion of secret *cities*. When I decided on the title for this book, the idea that a city—by definition, a size-able place that once housed a lot of people—could be secret was something that I found instantly intriguing, and intrigue is always a good thing to have in a title.

Ultima Thule has always interested me because the Nazis had a thing for it. El Dorado was a myth that lured many adventurers to their deaths. And Atlas, well, it's the most famous secret city of them all.

But let me add one extra comment on this. One of the things I am keenly aware of is that readers nowadays often check Google *while they are reading* my books. They look up the myths, facts and his-torical events.

So I tried to keep the locations of places like Thule, Ra and Atlas generally in the spots where they are believed to be. The directions to Thule in *3SC*, for instance, are the actual directions found in ancient writings. It was really believed to be northwest of Britain. For El Dorado and the City of Atlas, I had a little more creative licence, since the legendary locations for both are far and wide . . . plus the happy fact that they've never been found!

And how did you come to link them to the sword, helmet and mace?

Believe it or not, but at an early stage in the planning of 3SC, I actually thought of calling the book *The Three Immortal Weapons*, since it is about the finding of the three weapons and placing them at the three cities.

In my reading about historical stuff, I've often come across famed weapons, and I liked the idea of linking three of them to some awful human sacrificial ceremony. Like the three cities, I just found each of these mythical weapons intrinsically interesting.

I then set about *adding to* their mythologies: I love the idea that Excalibur, for instance, might be a sword that has travelled over the centuries from Egypt to Rome to Britain, and that the name 'The Sword in the Stone' changed over those centuries from 'The Sword of the Rock' (names change over time, like in a long game of Chinese Whispers). The Helmet of Hades really *was* reputed to make its wearer invisible. I just asked 'to whom?' My answer: it makes the wearer invisible to the bronzemen. As for the Trident of Poseidon, I just wanted to suggest that the passage of history sometimes changes the very nature of things: just as names can change over time, so too do maces sometimes become tridents.

Which leads us to the Knights of the Golden Eight. We all know the legend of King Arthur and the Knights of the Round Table—was it fun to turn that myth on its head, and present us with the evil bounty hunters, the Knights of the Golden Eight?

As with Medusa and the weapons, with the Knights I was seeking to explain a cool legend in real terms. (When I'm doing research, I love it when I find a real-world theory for a mythical figure. For example, I'm a big fan of the theory that King Arthur was a Roman centurion who stayed in Britain.)

Back in *The Great Zoo of China* I wrote that myths and legends sanitise reality and that was my guiding principle when it came to the Knights of the Round Table.

I decided to suggest that medieval writers had *really* sanitised these Knights' reputations! I adjusted the usual notion of 'loyalty to our king' to 'loyalty *to whoever pays us*'. Having the Knights as guns-for-hire made them, at least to me, really interesting and unique; which would also explain the enduring nature of their myth.

As for their 'Round' Table: once again, I decided that constant retellings throughout history had turned an octagonal table into a round one.

(It's funny, I followed this exact line of reasoning in *The Great Zoo of China*: that whole book was about explaining a mythical creature—the dragon—in real and modern terms; giving them lightweight bone structures, strong musculature and ultra-violet eyesight; plus an explanation for how the myth of the dragon is a worldwide one.)

Any hints about what the TWO in the series will refer to?

The clues are in this book. Maybe in the pictures . . .

Is it the next book you are writing?

As I mentioned on social media earlier this year, I've actually written a new novel in my spare time: a time travel novel! (So it's not part of the Scarecrow or Jack West series.) *Really cool* time travel, with a lot of complex twists and turns. It'll be released in 2019, so my readers won't have to wait the usual two years between books.

As a kid who grew up loving excellent time-travel movies like *The Terminator* and *Back to the Future* (hello, DeLorean owner)

I've always wanted to see if I could write a cool mind-bending one . . . so I did!

Right now, I'm sitting down to plan *The Two Something Somethings* and commence writing it so it'll be released right on schedule in 2020.

How is life in LA going?

Really great. I enjoy doing meetings in Hollywood (I still get excited when I have a meeting at one of the major studios), I've made a bunch of new friends who enjoy storytelling as much as I do, and I'm quietly hopeful that an adaptation of one of my novels is on the way. This new 'golden age' of television has seen renewed interest in my books, especially the Scarecrow and Jack West series, as limited-event series. Whereas once I sold movie rights, now I get approached for TV rights, and I like that.

Los Angeles itself is a great city to live in and it really inspires my creativity. When I'm not working on a new novel, I'm doing screenplays and even a bunch of lightning-fast novellas which I hope to release over the coming years. I'm going through a creative purple patch, so I'm running with it and just enjoying it! I'll always be Australian—and I certainly still have my accent!—but it's been a very rewarding move.

As always, I just try to write something that people will enjoy. And I hope you enjoyed this book. The big finish to the series is coming!

Matthew Reilly
Los Angeles
July 2018

MORE BESTSELLING TITLES FROM MATTHEW REILLY

Contest

The New York State Library. A brooding labyrinth of towering bookcases, narrow aisles and spiralling staircases. For Doctor Stephen Swain and his daughter, Holly, it is the site of a nightmare. For one night, this historic building is to be the venue for a contest. A contest in which Swain is to compete – whether he likes it or not.

The rules are simple. Seven contestants will enter. Only one will leave. With his daughter in his arms, Swain is plunged into a terrifying fight for survival. He can choose to run, to hide or to fight – but if he wants to live, he has to win. For in this contest, unless you leave as the victor, you do not leave at all.

Temple

Deep in the jungle of Peru, the hunt for a legendary Incan idol is under way – an idol that in the present day could be used as the basis for a terrifying new weapon.

Guiding a US Army team is Professor William Race, a young linguist who must translate an ancient manuscript which contains the location of the idol.

What they find is an ominous stone temple, sealed tight. They open it – and soon discover that some doors are meant to remain unopened . . .

Ice Station

THE DISCOVERY OF A LIFETIME

At a remote ice station in Antarctica, a team of US scientists has found something buried deep within a 100-million-year-old layer of ice. Something made of *metal*.

THE LAW OF SURVIVAL

In a land without boundaries, there are no rules. Every country would kill for this prize.

A LEADER OF MEN

A team of crack United States marines is sent to the station to secure the discovery. Their leader – Lieutenant Shane Schofield, call-sign: SCARECROW. They are a tight unit, tough and fearless. They would follow their leader into hell. They just did . . .

A SCARECROW NOVEL

MATTHEW REILLY

ICE STATION

Area 7

A HIDDEN LOCATION

It is America's most secret base, a remote installation known only as Area 7.

THE VISITOR

And today it has a guest: the President of the United States. But he's going to get more than he bargained for on this trip. Because hostile forces are waiting inside . . .

HIS SAVIOUR

Among the President's helicopter crew, however, is a young marine. His name is Schofield. Call-sign: SCARECROW. Rumour has it, he's a good man in a storm. Judging by what the President has just walked into, he'd better be . . .

Scarecrow

IT IS THE GREATEST BOUNTY HUNT IN HISTORY

There are 15 targets. And they must all be dead by 12 noon, today. The price on their heads: $20 million each.

ONE HERO

Among the names on the target list, one stands out.
An enigmatic Marine named Shane Schofield, call-sign: SCARECROW.

NO LIMITS

And so Schofield is hunted by gangs of international bounty hunters, including the 'Black Knight', a ruthless hunter who seems intent on eliminating only him.

He led his men into hell in *Ice Station*. He protected the President against all odds in *Area 7*. This time it's different. Because this time SCARECROW is the target.

Scarecrow and the Army of Thieves

THE SECRET BASE

It is a former Soviet base known only as Dragon Island. It houses a weapon of terrible destructive force . . . that has just been re-activated.

A RENEGADE ARMY

The island has been seized by a brutal terrorist force calling itself the Army of Thieves, and the fate of the world hangs in the balance.

ONE SMALL TEAM

There is an equipment-testing team up in the Arctic. It does not have the weaponry or strength to attack a fortified island held by a vicious army. But it is led by a Marine captain named Schofield, call-sign: SCARECROW. And Scarecrow will lead the team in anyway, because someone has to.

Seven Ancient Wonders

AN ANCIENT SECRET

Two thousand years ago, it was hidden within the Seven Wonders of the Ancient World. Now, in the present day, it must be found again . . .

ONE HERO TO FIND IT

Captain Jack West Jr – part soldier, part scholar, all hero. The odds are stacked against him and his loyal team: nine brave companions taking on the most powerful countries on earth.

AN ADVENTURE LIKE NO OTHER

From the pyramids of Egypt to the swamps of Sudan, to the Hanging Gardens of Babylon and the boulevards of Paris: the desperate race begins.

FOR A PRIZE WITHOUT EQUAL

The greatest prize of all: the power to end the world or rule it.

AND SO THE GREAT ADVENTURE BEGINS

The Six Sacred Stones

THE END OF THE WORLD IS COMING

A mysterious ceremony at a hidden location has unlocked a catastrophic countdown to world annihilation.

ONE HERO

Now, to save the world, supersoldier Jack West Jr and his loyal team of adventurers must find and rebuild a legendary device known as 'the Machine'.

SIX FABLED STONES

The only clues to locating this Machine are held within the fabled Six Sacred Stones, which are scattered around the globe. But Jack and his team are not the only ones seeking the Stones, there are other players involved who don't want to see the world saved at all . . .

The Five Greatest Warriors

THE END OF THE WORLD HAS ARRIVED

Jack West Jr and his loyal team have been separated, their
mission is in ruins, and Jack was last seen plummeting down a
fathomless abyss.

OCEANS WILL RISE, CITIES WILL FALL

After surviving his deadly fall, Jack must now race against his
enemies to locate and set in place the remaining pieces of 'the
Machine' before the coming Armageddon.

WHO ARE THE FIVE WARRIORS?

Jack will learn of the individuals who throughout history have
been most intimately connected to his quest, but not before he
and his friends find out exactly what the end of the world looks
like . . .

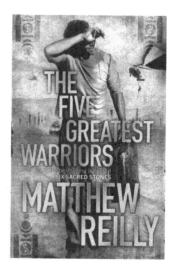

The Four Legendary Kingdoms

A RUTHLESS KIDNAPPING

Jack West Jr and his family are living happily on their remote farm . . .

. . . when Jack is brutally kidnapped and he awakes in an underground cell to find a masked attacker with a knife charging at him.

THE GREAT GAMES

Jack, it seems, has been chosen – along with a dozen other elite soldiers – to compete in a series of deadly challenges designed to fulfil an ancient ritual.

With the fate of the Earth at stake, he will have to traverse diabolical mazes, fight cruel assassins and face unimaginable horrors that will test him like he has never been tested before.

TO HELL AND BACK

In the process, he will discover the mysterious and powerful group of individuals behind it all: the four legendary kingdoms.

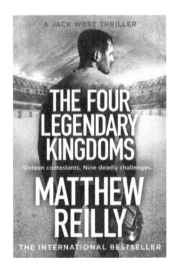

He might also discover that he is not the only hero in this place . . .

The Great Zoo of China

AN IMPOSSIBLE DISCOVERY

It is a secret the Chinese government has been keeping for forty years. They have found a species of animal no one believed even existed.

THE WORLD'S GREATEST ATTRACTION

The Chinese are ready to unveil their fabulous creatures in the greatest zoo ever constructed. VIPs and journalists, including reptile expert Dr Cassandra Jane 'CJ' Cameron, are invited to see the beasts for the first time.

ONE FALSE PROMISE

The visitors are assured by their Chinese hosts that they are perfectly safe, that nothing can go wrong.

Of course it can't . . .